Fletcher House

COTTONWOOD SUMMER

Gary Slaughter spent his early life in a small town in Michigan. After graduating from the University of Michigan, he served as an officer on naval destroyers. Over the years, he has lectured widely and written extensively on managing corporate information technology. Today, he devotes his time to creating fiction.

To Laura,

COTTONWOOD SUMMER

Enjoy!

A Novel

by

GARY SLAUGHTER

Library of Congress Control Number: 2003111961

ISBN: 0-9744206-1-1

Manufactured in the United States of America
Cover and interior design by Michael Lang and Danita Meeks
Editing and proofing by Sharon Yake
Printing and binding by Falcon Press

Published by Fletcher House
P.O. Box 50979
Nashville, TN 37205-0979

For additional copies of *Cottonwood Summer*, contact www.fletcherhouse.com.

For Joanne —

without whose unwavering encouragement

the story of Cottonwood Summer

would never have been told.

CONTENTS

COTTONWOOD SUMMER

1 THE ADVENTURES BEGIN

SPRING OF 1944 BROUGHT A SUCCESSION OF UPBEAT reports from the war. After winning decisively in North Africa, the Allies were pushing the Nazis up the boot of Italy, back to Germany where they belonged. In the Pacific, we were boldly island hopping our way toward Tokyo. And, as General Eisenhower gathered his forces in England, the long-awaited invasion of Europe was at hand.

So, when I opened the afternoon's *Riverton Daily Press*, I expected good news. But, to my bitter disappointment, the "Michigan at War" column reported two more Riverton boys killed in action. Since New Year's Day, our town's killed-in-action tally stood at a record-setting sixteen "with the heaviest fighting yet to come."

Needing a change of mood, I threw the paper aside and set off for the backyard.

The giant oak tree hugging the Reilly property line accommodated the neighborhood's best swing. Its sturdy seat, fashioned skillfully by my father from a plank of seasoned walnut, hung from heavy rope secured to a thick branch a dozen feet above the ground.

Looking forward to a good dose of therapeutic solo flying, I slammed the kitchen screen door and raced down the back steps toward my aircraft.

But I stopped, dead in my tracks!

There, sitting in <u>my</u> swing, was a strange-looking boy that I had never seen before.

He was about my size and, as I would learn later, almost exactly my age. His thick hair, matching the color of his black eyes, was butched short and his skin was heavily tanned. Immense ears framed his owl-like face.

The over-sized, olive drab army cap perched rakishly above his left eyebrow signaled a cocky demeanor. A tee shirt of alternating maroon and dirty yellow stripes was tucked carelessly into crumpled tan cotton shorts. Several passes of an adult-length, brown leather belt embossed with bucking broncos and branding irons circled his waist.

But the most dramatic element of his fashion statement was the floppy pair of canvas infantry leggings, surplus from the Great War, I guessed, which if fully laced would have extended upward, well past his knees. Two scuffed brown work shoes, in need of new soles and strings, poked out from under his doughboy specials.

The well-contrived uniform was clearly designed to intimidate. But, for good reason, I wasn't a bit threatened. Well before my matriculation to kindergarten, years earlier, I had mastered our neighborhood's rules of engagement. These were the sacred protocols used to repel unwanted interlopers like this one.

I launched my attack.

Drawing on my vast knowledge of movie tough guys, I *became* Edward G. Robinson, snarling, "Listen here, buddy! You can't use that swing, see! This is private property, see!"

Boy, was I good!

But the intruder immediately demonstrated that he was no stranger to the nuances of territorial warfare. He hopped off my swing and stepped across the border into the Reilly backyard. He now stood in a neutral country, defined as the property of any neighbor without children. Safely out of harm's way, he countered, "This isn't your property! So I can stay here all night if I want to – and you can't stop me!"

He trumped me. I didn't have a comeback.

But I didn't let him know I was stymied. Instead, I confidently claimed victory by retaking my swing seat and launching my long-overdue flight.

I ignored the would-be invader, who stood with his arms crossed, leering at me from his Reilly sanctuary. After several strenuous pumps, designed to show muscle and smooth swinging style, my adrenaline level abruptly plummeted. I felt listless and sleepy.

Suddenly, a disgusting taunt jarred me awake. "My sister can pump higher than you."

The poor sucker had broken a cardinal rule. Never interject your sister into a fight, even if she's the toughest girl in the neighborhood. It just wasn't manly.

I checkmated the ersatz soldier with a masterful coup de grace, "Your sister! Whatta you? A sissy? Why don't you go play dolls with your crummy sister?"

I failed to anticipate his violent reaction. He shot across the border and grabbed both of my ankles, just as I was beginning my ascent to the highest point of the swing's path. I pitched forward violently, out of the swing and into the air.

Ssssssshhhh! Thump!

I returned to earth a good four feet into the Reilly backyard. My landing zone was dotted with elbows of oak roots protruding from the ground. A large woody knot about the size of Joe Louis' fist knocked the wind out of me.

I saw stars and couldn't breathe.

But my adversary's fate was far worse than mine. After my involuntary ejection, the hefty swing seat continued forward and upward. Then, after pausing for an instant, the seat returned with a vengeance. My attacker was still busy gloating when the walnut missile struck – **Smack!** – like a baseball bat squarely across the forehead.

He soared backwards and landed with a *thud*. Blood poured from a nasty gash just above his eyebrows. He just sat there glassy eyed, his open mouth frozen in anguish.

Holy smokes! Maybe I killed him!

But I knew he was alive when I heard the wail. It erupted like the air raid warning from the new loudspeaker installed atop the Riverton City Hall.

"Aaaaawwwwwwwkkkkkkkkk! Aaaawooooooooooooooo!" he howled.

The bold infantryman had suddenly lost his composure. This was not the stuff that reputations were built on in neighborhoods like ours. I was momentarily embarrassed for the poor fellow.

But, as I examined my fallen foe more closely, I realized from the looks of his head wound, he was seriously injured. As I turned to dash into the house for help, our family Chevrolet pulled into the driveway.

Dad leaped from the car and ran toward the swing. The injured young stranger stood up and staggered toward our back porch. His blood-soaked tee shirt was now completely maroon. Somehow, his cap remained chaste, perched on his ear, well clear of the bloody downpour. Dad swooped him up and ran toward the car, dabbing blood with his handkerchief on the way.

Just then Mom stuck her head out the back door. Sizing up the situation, she ran toward Dad and the pathetic boy. They exchanged hurried words as Dad deposited his limp load in the passenger seat.

The shivering patient was stunned but compliant. Holding Dad's handkerchief to his forehead, he sobbed and muttered something about *swings*. I felt guilty about not feeling more compassionate.

Dad sped off toward Dr. Moran's office, which was located three miles away near Courthouse Park in New Albany, the Chippewa County seat. Simultaneously, Mom turned and started a fast-paced march across the backyard, through the garden, and toward the alley.

I fell in behind. As we settled into a moderate jog, I asked, "Where are we going?"

"To the Tucker house to tell Danny's mother what's happened!"

That was the first time I had heard Danny's name. As it turned out, the Tuckers were new to the neighborhood and lived only two short blocks away. I wondered how Mom knew the invader's name, let alone, where he lived.

The Tucker's tiny house with green asbestos siding and charcoal roof was located at the corner of New Albany Avenue and Chester Street. The huge gray-painted garage looming behind the house served as headquarters for Mr. Tucker's newly acquired auto repair business.

We arrived in the nick of time. Mrs. Tucker was about to depart for the Southside Junkyard in search of a cylinder ring for the ancient Dodge engine that lay disemboweled on her husband's workbench.

After flagging down their beat-up Dodge station wagon, Mom hurriedly introduced us. "Mrs. Tucker – I'm Marie Addison. This is my son, Jase. We live just down the alley – on Forrest Street."

Then she explained calmly, "Danny's been hurt – a nasty cut on the forehead. He needs stitches. John – my husband – just took him to Dr. Moran's office."

Mrs. Tucker nodded unemotionally and listened until Mom was finished. Then, she turned and bellowed toward the garage. Not mentioning Danny's accident, she ordered her husband to stay home and look after the two other children. Without emerging from his operating theater, a preoccupied Mr. Tucker acknowledged with a grunt.

Quickly, she leaned over the seat and untwisted the crinkled piece of bailing wire that served as a backdoor latch.

"Hop in!" she shouted.

We roared out of the Tucker driveway and swerved onto New Albany Avenue. Our bald tires screamed. We raced toward Dr. Moran's office to see if the patient had survived.

Two hours later, Danny skipped down the front steps of the doctor's office sporting five new stitches, a huge bandage across his forehead, and a fistful of wooden tongue depressors that he had extorted in exchange for a promise to knock off the whimpering.

I couldn't help smiling at my former foe. *This boy has possibilities after all!* I thought to myself.

To my amazement, Danny insisted on riding with me. Who could refuse the wounded hero? On the way home, Danny bestowed half his loot on me, four tongue depressors.

Then, following an ancient Forrest Street ritual, we slugged each other's left bicep as hard as we could. Neither of us uttered a peep in reaction to the painful punch.

As the sun set, ending that memorable June day in 1944, Danny and I swore a bond of allegiance that lasted for years, until I left Riverton to enroll at the University of Michigan.

I suppose that bond might have lasted forever but, technically, only one of us signed in blood.

EARLY THE NEXT MORNING, I was jarred awake by an ungodly noise that I had never heard before. Yet it seemed vaguely familiar.

Could it be the ear-piercing sirens of diving German Stukas preparing to drop their deadly payloads on Forrest Street? Or some poor animal caught in the cellar door? Perhaps long-dead Chippewas mounting one last war party?

Who knew? So I pulled the covers over my head, burrowed deeper into my pillow, and dismissed the disturbance as a remnant of an unremembered nightmare.

"*Jaaaaaaaaaaaaaaaase. Caaaaaaaaaaaaaaaaaaaaaaaaaan. Youuuuuuuuuuuuuuuuuuuuuuuu. Cuuuuuuuuuuuuum. Ooooooooooooout?*"

There it was again. This time, louder than before. The howl came from outside, right under my high bedroom window that overlooked our backyard and Victory garden.

"*Jaaaaaaaaaaaaaaaase. Caaaaaaaaaaaaaaaaaaaaaaaaaan. Youuuuuuuuuuuuuuuuuuuuuuuu. Cuuuuuuuuuuuuum. Ooooooooooooout?*"

Once again it came. This time in shocking full force. Screeching, rasping, and scraping up the side of the house, through my window, and down my spine where it twisted and bit me before it died.

By then, I was sitting upright in bed. As my head cleared, I began to discern words. English words. Not Chippewan.

I leaped out of bed, dragged my chair to the window, and on tiptoes pushed the chintz curtains aside. I peered down on the source of my angst. A goofy army cap and a swathe of white gauze and adhesive tape greeted my sleepy eyes. The cheerful and innocent face featured a broad grin connecting oversized ears.

Danny wore exactly the same uniform as yesterday. I wondered if he owned more than one maroon and dirty yellow striped tee shirt. Today's showed no sign of the recent carnage. Maybe Mrs. Tucker loved doing laundry as much as Mom.

In our neighborhood, boys never knocked on doors or rang doorbells. According to protocol, the visitor hid himself near the back door. Once in position, he signaled his presence by rendering his own, unique *come-out call*. Not unlike the myriad species of Michigan birds, each boy was identified by the pitch, pattern, and duration of his *come-out call*. The message never varied, "Jase, can you come out?" But it was nearly impossible to distinguish these words, unless you knew the caller.

Oddly, we employed this method of announcing ourselves even if parents, brothers, or sisters were sitting right in front of us, say, on the back porch drinking iced tea, reading the paper, or playing jacks. According to our unwritten law, they were to be ignored.

Danny's *come-out call* set a new standard as the loudest and most grating in the neighborhood. His call was in the same league as the terrifying squeaking door introducing each episode of *The Inner Sanctum* that we listened to in front of our glowing console radio each Sunday night.

As I scurried to the kitchen door, I heard my parents stir. Mom whispered, "What was that terrible noise, Jase?"

"It's my new friend, Danny," I whispered back. "Mom, can he have breakfast with me?"

Always hit 'em when they're vulnerable! I heard a mumble that I interpreted as affirmative. Then a soft wheeze told me that Danny and I would be dining alone that morning.

I opened the back door and in stepped Danny. He plopped down in my chair at the kitchen table. His eyes quickly assessed the shelves and cabinets that lined our kitchen walls.

"Does your mother fix you breakfast?"

Boy! Was he subtle!

I hurriedly assembled what I thought would be a hearty, early morning feast for two growing boys. Wheaties. Plain milk. We were out of Ovaltine. Sugar. Mom just got her June ration. White Wonder Bread. Peanut butter. Jam. Black raspberry from our patch out by the shed. Bowls and spoons. And, of course, some nutritious bread-and-butter pickles that Grandma Compton had canned. And, finally, two four-inch stacks of oatmeal cookies (without raisins) that Mom had baked especially for me.

Danny watched my every move, his face glowing with expectation. When I finished, he quickly inventoried the fare. "Do you have any mayonnaise?" he asked.

"Yep."

In a jiffy, I produced a hefty jar of Kraft's finest from the refrigerator. Danny thanked me with a big grin.

Munching away, we quietly examined the black silhouettes, side and bottom views, of enemy warplanes depicted on the back of the newest Wheaties box. Fortunately, the makers of Wheaties knew we needed all the help we could get to protect Riverton from enemy air attacks – attacks that we expected at any moment.

Having alert and informed boys looking skyward for hours each day was one of the most effective deterrents to surprise attack we could imagine. We wondered aloud if other towns near our country's northern border were fortunate enough to receive similar help from the Wheaties factory.

Recognizing the importance of this responsibility, we paused to exchange views on the relative merits of the two Nazi bombers we had just studied.

Danny offered, "I think the Dornier-17 looks – ah – nifty." (He had a way with words.)

I countered with my own intellectual deep dive, "Nah. The Heinkel-111H looks better. The Dornier-17 has a fat nose."

Bored with scholarly discourse, Danny planted his elbows firmly on the floral oilcloth covering the table. He rested his chin in the palms of his hands, screwed his comic face into a serious pose, and asked, "Whatya wanta do?"

During those wonderful Forrest Street years, I would hear Danny ask that question over ten billion times. My response as always was, "I don't know. Whatta *you* want to do?"

And then our adventure would begin.

Before giving me his answer on this first occasion, he glanced over his shoulder quickly. Then he looked me in the eye and without explanation whispered, "Do you have your own bedroom?"

I nodded, put an index finger to my lips, and motioned for Danny to follow me.

DURING THE LAST YEARS of the Depression, just before the war, my mother and father had scrimped and saved almost a thousand dollars for our first home. Without help from anyone, not even their families, they bought a lot and built a little bungalow on Forrest Street, out New Albany Avenue near Pete's Grocery-Liquor-Hardware Store.

The bungalow had five microscopic rooms. In the front, our living room curled around a wood stove that served as central heating in those days. A narrow hall led straight from the front door to a phone booth-sized bathroom equipped with a bathtub that offered only cold water. Saturday night baths featured hot water from the teakettle, recycled so the entire Addison family could share a warm bath.

In the back of the house, our cozy kitchen contained an electric refrigerator. Most of our neighbors had iceboxes. There were two miniature bedrooms next to each other on the right as you entered our front door. We stored our Christmas decorations and two ancient suitcases in a minute attic storage space reachable by ladder from the hall outside the bathroom, next to my bedroom door. That was about it.

Oh, I nearly forgot.

We also had a low-ceiling, dirt-floor cellar accessible by a steep wooden stairway that led downward between folding doors laying flat to the ground next to our back porch. In the cellar, on rough board shelves, Mom stored rows and rows of canning jars filled to the brim with various vegetables and fruit that she "put up" with her mother and sister, Grandma Compton and Aunt Maude, out at the farm.

In the cellar's coolness, we stored our supplies of potatoes, carrots, beets, onions, and other fresh vegetables harvested from our Victory garden each summer. Each variety was stored neatly in its own barrel, carton, or crate along the west wall. The cellar was one of my favorite places to spend time on those hot and muggy summer days.

DANNY AND I SLINKED through the living room, past my parents' open bedroom door where they still lay, quietly enjoying a Saturday morning sleep-in. As we crept by, I noticed Dad's loud-ticking, windup alarm clock. It was not yet seven o'clock.

When we were safely inside my tiny bedroom, I turned to Danny and said quietly, "Here it is."

His body pivoted, round and round, as he carefully scanned my room. Suddenly his black eyes widened and he pointed toward my window.

Uncle Van had sent me all of his used corporal's stripes when he was promoted to sergeant after he landed with the Army Signal Corps in North Africa. I had carefully thumbtacked these prizes, military fashion, in a straight row across the bottom of my windowsill. So, when I sat at my worktable under the window, I could look over at Mrs. Mikas' bedroom window and admire my insignia collection at the same time.

Suddenly Danny made a beeline for the worktable. He banged down in my chair, his mouth agape, babbling, "Wow! Where did you get these! What are they? I'll bet they're worth real money! Whose are they? Did whoever gave these to you kill a lot of Nazis? How long have you had them? Are they really yours? Do you have to give them back? Could I ever have one?"

Danny was obviously most impressed. I said a silent prayer of thanks to Uncle Van, who was my favorite uncle anyway, and answered Danny's questions one by one. Feeling proud and magnanimous, I made Danny's day by tenderly removing the most tattered corporal's patch from the end of the row and bestowing it on him.

Danny's eyes misted over. He was clearly moved by the gesture. Using the mirror above my dresser, he cleverly pasted the bottom end of the corporal's stripes under the adhesive tape at the top of his bandage. Then he tucked the top end under a fold in his army cap. His new rank jutted forward, centered perfectly between his ears. He looked like a fireman whose hat had been destroyed by fire, except for the badge in the front.

Danny made one final adjustment and smiled at himself in the mirror. Then he declared, "Your Uncle Van got these stripes from President Rosebelt! Now, I'm wearing 'em. How about that?"

I didn't have the heart to disabuse Danny of his fantasy, so I merely nodded.

Smiling conspiratorially, Danny winked at me and whispered, "Let's go check on the Nazi spy first, then the German soldiers and the machine guns."

He knew. My new friend knew!

AS WE BANGED OUT the kitchen door and bounded down the steps, a feeling of exhilaration filled my chest – another early morning getaway without a parent telling you when to be home!

Two fat robins *chipped* and nodded as they hunted for worms in the early sun-streaked haze hanging low over our garden. The neighborhood seemed deserted and unusually still. Even the local dogs slept silently.

Saturday morning was my favorite time to explore.

On Friday nights, Riverton's stores were open until nine. Families shopped until closing time and then headed for the town's soda fountains. We had a dozen or more back then. Evenings were capped with hamburgers, malts, and ice cream sodas. Some shoppers stowed their purchases in the car and took in the last movie at the Chippewa or Grafton.

Riverton was never an early-to-bed town on weekends. Friday and Saturday night dances at Riverton High School didn't start until nine o'clock or later when there was a home game. Then there were after-dance visits to the ice cream parlors and restaurants. Many stayed open until two in the morning.

So Saturdays were lazy mornings. Most families didn't stir until seven. This provided adventuresome boys like Danny and me with a delightful, adult-free time zone, from sunup until just after that second cup of coffee.

Ah, Saturday mornings!

Danny obviously shared my excitement and sense of freedom. His pace was brisk and his manner enthusiastic as he took the lead following the path toward the shed.

My father's shed was a one-room, clapboard out-building about the size of a single-car garage. It was nestled in the upper left-hand corner of our lot adjacent to the alley. Our Victory garden surrounded the shed to take advantage of every inch of cultivable soil. This small structure was painted white and had green roof shingles to match our house.

THE SHED WAS MY father's domain. Like many skilled laborers in our neighborhood, Dad was deferred from military service because his occupation was deemed critical to the war effort. During the workweek, he was a tool and die maker at the Burke factory, which manufactured top-secret bombsights behind high fences out New Albany Avenue, a mile past the city limits.

At home, he was his own boss. There in his shed, he spent countless evening and weekend hours repairing and electrifying sewing machines for Riverton families. For hours on end, he perched on a high stool at his workbench, equipped with a special jack for holding and turning sewing machine heads upside down with ease.

His work surface was carefully cluttered with long shuttles and round bobbins, spools of thread, broken and bent needles, leather pulley belts, strike plates, tension springs, and a dozen special tools. Behind him, against the shed's back wall, he painstakingly stored spare parts and new packs of needles in special wooden chests that contained scores of small drawers for categorization by the dozen or more sewing machine manufacturers of the time.

Dad's customers knew his odd working hours. Unfailingly, their heads would appear outside our kitchen window at mealtimes. Without hesitation, Dad would leave the table and greet them from the back porch. Then he would walk with them along the narrow dirt path interspersed with occasional stepping-stones through the strawberry and blackberry patches to his shed.

Despite long hours and family inconveniences, Dad took proprietary pride in his business and the extra benefits it provided our family. But, as a boy, the shed and the sewing machine business were merely convenient, never-ending sources of exceptionally "good junk" for Danny and me.

DANNY MARCHED TO A silent cadence. I fell in behind. As we passed the shed and rounded the corner, Danny stopped abruptly.

"Wow!"

He stared with wonder at the roof-high stack of discarded treadle sewing machine cast iron bases, wooden cabinets and head covers, and the sundry discarded parts displayed before him. He whistled his emphatic approval at the prospect of culling this rich and assorted cache.

"I'm the family garbage, ash, and scrap iron man," I announced proudly. "I dig the pits in the alley for burying our garbage and ashes. Then I empty the ashes from the living room and shed wood stoves into the coal bucket and dump them in the new pit. I cover each full pit with clean dirt, tamp it down, and replace the sod that I removed before I dug the pit.

"My other job is to use Dad's sledgehammer and axe to chop old wooden sewing machine cabinets and head covers into stove-sized pieces for winter. As a reward, I get to sell the leftover cast iron to the Southside Junkyard – at whatever price they're paying."

"Wow!" was the only response Danny could muster.

"I get lots of money – for spending and saving stamps – and my iron helps the war effort, too."

Danny's eyes almost popped out. "Can I help next time?" he implored.

"You bet!"

Pleased at the prospect of sharing my important work with an admiring protégé, I asked, "Does your dad have an axe?"

"He has a Jap sword that my uncle got at Gottacanal."

"Neat! Bring that!"

Our trek continued down the hill through ankle-high prairie grasses toward the neighborhood swamp. We startled a mother killdeer that limped ahead of us feigning injury by contorting a wing and dragging her body sideways through the grass. This act took place a few feet from where we stood.

Having solid backgrounds in Indian scouting, we knew to freeze and to search methodically for the unseen killdeer nest.

"Here it is!" Danny announced.

Sure enough, he had spotted it not more than four feet from where he stood. The slightly hollowed out patch of stone-cluttered soil contained two perfectly shaped eggs about a fourth the size of a chicken's egg. The speckled and tan spheres blended in perfectly with their pebbly surroundings.

"Better not touch 'em," I advised.

Slowly and deliberately, we stepped backwards and reset our course to give the nest a wide berth. After a few paces, we turned and observed Mrs. Killdeer transform from a helpless cripple into a scolding parent, strutting boldly and *cheeking* at us.

"We would have missed the nest altogether if she hadn't put on her act," I observed. "Wonder why she just didn't let us walk by."

"That's parents for you," Danny quipped.

As we made our way toward the swamp, Danny whistled a robust rendition of *Under the Double Eagle*. Surprised that he knew it, I joined in with gusto, scurrying to keep pace with my new leader.

When I stayed at the farm last time, *Double Eagle* had won top honors in my review of Grandma Compton's marching band record collection. I played every one of the 78-RPM records on her handsome wind-up Victrola, conveniently located (for my personal use, I was convinced) in the upstairs spare bedroom reserved for my frequent visits.

I had conducted my audition at the modest cost of just one or two tiny needle scratches. Luckily, I was dealing with marches, so the *click-*

click-clicks were usually right in time with the music. You could hardly tell the gouges were there. I'm certain Grandma concurred because she never said a word.

On our first outing, I began to appreciate just how compatible Danny and I were. For one thing, without discussing it, we agreed completely on the first rule of going anywhere – leave extremely early to allow more than ample time to explore your way to your destination.

My admiration of Danny was validated by our present heading, which was leading us away from our destination, the home of the German spy.

That's my kind of leader!

We reached the edge of the swamp, which was marked by an undulating row of yellow-green willows interspersed with cattails.

"We're lucky to have a swamp right here in our neighborhood!" Danny said.

"You bet!"

Each spring, the swollen Chippewa River sent a branch of itself southward from a breach in its bank a mile east of the Riverton City Waterworks. This branch snaked its way through the lowlands that lay at the north ends of both Chester and Forrest Streets on which Danny and I lived. After meandering for a mile or two, the branch came to its senses and headed north again, rejoining the main river just before the combined waters ducked under the Ann Arbor Street Bridge in preparation for their rapids-streaked trip through the center of town.

Whether we liked it or not, each April, the intrusive Chippewa turned our neighborhood into lakeside property. With the onset of early summer, the waters receded, stranding fish, frogs, crabs, and turtles in stagnant pools that Danny and I just had to explore. Despite pleas and warnings from our mothers, we were driven by our compulsion to investigate this intriguing phenomenon.

We would wade out from the dry safe shoreline following a minnow or crayfish. Farther and farther. We dared the murky water to eclipse our boot-tops, which it never failed to do. Before returning home, we dried our wet boots, shoes, socks, and pant cuffs on the sun-warmed sidewalk just uphill from where it disappeared into the swampy waters.

Lying on our backs with our hands behind our heads, we surveyed the white puffs of clouds, while they transformed themselves magically into objects that made up our world.

"That one's a blimp."

"Nah, it's a sunflower."

"Or a doughnut."

"Maybe a pretzel."

"Yeah, maybe."

Hypnotized by the warm sun, azure sky, and powder-puff clouds, we dreamed aloud about the future.

"Where you gonna live when you grow up?"

"Toledo."

"Where's that?"

"In Maine – I think."

"Oh, yeah."

Since the arrival of the long sunny days and warm breezes of early summer, the Chippewa had retrieved most of its excesses. Apart from plentiful potholes filled with brown icky water, mosquito larvae, half-rotted former river inhabitants, and stinky sewage-enriched muck, our swamp was perfectly passable.

About halfway through the swamp phase of our journey, Danny and I discussed the downside of having a swamp in our neighborhood as we swatted pesky mosquitoes and held our breath to avoid smelling the stench from the putrid potholes. We vowed to return, but only after the summer sun had transformed our swamp to a dry and dusty state, which invariably happened by mid-July.

We stepped out of the swamp onto Chester Street and made our way north, stomping and scraping mud from our shoes on the sidewalk, which by now had reappeared after its annual spring immersion. As if on cue, we each pulled out our shiny pocketknives and, using the largest blades, skillfully cleaned our fingernails. My nails didn't really need it, but wielding a sharp knife, even purposelessly, seemed the manly thing to do after conquering the Upper Amazon of our neighborhood.

When we came abreast of the winter sledding hill, which swept down onto Chester Street from the east, Danny veered left and picked up the pace. We trudged up the grassy hillside that crested at the Forrest Street alley. He was moving in for the kill.

"Hey, wait up!"

I closed the distance between us to enable us to communicate in a whisper as we approached our objective. Danny was clearly an expert in the art of undetected infiltration into enemy territory. He signaled for silence with an index finger to the lips. I nodded in response.

A few yards short of the alley, we hit the deck and began belly crawling toward our goal, the junction of Mr. Zeyer's garage and Wolfgang's kennel fence. Wiggling along behind Danny, I became aware of tension between my shoulder blades. And there was that nauseous feeling in the pit of my stomach, possibly related to the earlier consumption of pickles, raspberry jam, mayonnaise, and peanut butter.

As we crept closer, the form of the massive German shepherd came into view. Joining the other neighborhood canines in their routine Saturday morning job action, the Nazi guard dog and Zeyer family protector still snoozed soundly in his gigantic doghouse situated strategically in the center of the kennel.

As he snored, Wolfgang's enormous pink tongue dangled limply from the side of his mouth. With periodic half-yawns, he displayed a set of lethal choppers that sent chills down my spine.

Carefully. Cautiously. Quietly. We inched across the dirt and gravel surface of the alley. Dust tickled my nose, causing my eyes to water. I choked off a mini-sneeze by pinching my nostrils together.

Beads of sweat dotted my forehead. For the briefest instant, fear clutched at my heart. I focused on the image of John Wayne. As always, my fear immediately vanished.

The last two wiggle-and-crawl movements put us within inches of the kennel fence. Then it happened!

Wolfgang lifted his head – sort of – and opened one eye about half way. Up sprang his big brown ears. We froze.

Danny assessed the tactical situation instantly. In true commando form, he silently snatched his deadly weapon – the one hidden in his back pocket since earlier that morning – and launched it at the monster dog.

Thunk! It hit old Wolfgang right on the nose. What a shot!

At first, Wolfgang didn't move. He stared blankly at us, his adversaries. He looked bewildered and stupefied. His eyes were slightly crossed. The effect of the weapon finally struck home.

Slowly Wolfgang's head sank.

Then, with a quick flick of his huge dripping tongue, he lapped up the oatmeal cookie and swallowed it whole. He licked his slobbering chops and looked longingly in our direction. It was working!

Sensing a weakened opponent, Danny immediately launched a second missile. This time the cookie fell short, apparently lacking the aerodynamic qualities of the first. Wolfgang lifted his hulking body lazily out of his doghouse and lumbered toward us, stopping briefly to down the errant cookie.

By the time Wolfgang reached the back kennel fence, Danny was ready. He jabbed a third oatmeal weapon through the fence in the direction of Wolfgang's gaping maw. Wolfgang bent down and adroitly tongued the cookie from Danny's fingertips, swallowing it immediately.

Then the traitorous Nazi hound, displaying his finest turncoat qualities, vigorously licked Danny's fingertips for residual crumbs. Exhausting that target, Wolfgang focused his ravenous licking attack on Danny's forehead, placing Danny's temporarily appended corporal insignia in mortal danger.

Danny pulled back just in time to save his newly acquired rank. Wolfgang, indiscriminately, continued to lick the kennel fence, not seeming to notice Danny's absence. His tail wagged enthusiastically. That was our sign.

"Let's go!" Danny whispered loudly.

We flew up the kennel fence pole next to the garage using the heavy meshing as our ladder. We swung our legs over the gutter and boosted ourselves onto the roof where we instantly lay prone on the asbestos shingled surface of the Zeyer garage roof. We inched our way to the peak while Wolfgang studied our movements intently, keeping watch and happily wagging his tail.

The leafy branches from the sprawling Zeyer pear tree hung down over the garage roof providing perfect cover for our mission. When we reached the top, we gingerly spread the branches in front of us and peered over the ridge of the garage roof.

There he was!

Hans Zeyer, renowned Nazi spy, was sprawled out on a faded blue canvas and oak frame lawn chair. *Funny thing*, I thought to myself. *The neighborhood spy doesn't look particularly sinister this morning.*

In fact, old Hans looked deceptively docile, even pleasant.

He was short and chubby, a balding man of about fifty. He wore a sleeveless white undershirt and baggy brown gabardine pants with dangling red suspenders. His house slippers, worn sockless, were made of now broken-down black leather. And his battered straw sunhat, instead of covering his head, rested precariously on an enormous belly that rose and fell rhythmically with each raspy snore.

His overgrown, gray-brown handlebar moustache flapped with each expelled snort to complete the rhythm section. Last night's *Daily Press*, a pair of wire frame spectacles, and a half-drunk cup of coffee, with double cream by the looks of it, lay beside him on the grass.

It was a deceptively peaceful scene.

Danny and I asked each other with our expressions, *All that trouble for this?*

Of course, we were obligated to stay, a dictate of national security. So we squirmed quietly for a few seconds to make ourselves as comfortable as possible. The sandpaper rough coating of roof shingles held us tightly by our tee shirts, preventing us from sliding down the slanted roof onto the alley below.

We prepared for a long vigil. Who knew what evil this treasonous villain might be cooking up in that old bald head, which by now, sans sunhat, was reddening under the hot morning sun. Even the best of undercover agents have to endure the slow passage of time on stakeouts, waiting for their prey to make the wrong move. So we were patient. Very patient.

A full seven minutes dragged by.

We were fading under the influence of warm morning sun and the soothing sonata of spy snores. Our eyes lowered to half-mast. Just as slumber supplanted vigilance, we were jolted awake by an enormous sound discharged from the subject of our surveillance.

Boooooooorrrrrrrrrrrrrrrrrrrrrrrrrappppppp!

The force of that mighty gastric explosion reached upward and outward and, I swear, it caused the garage windows below us to rattle. Like yours truly, the old Hun had obviously eaten some of Mrs. Zeyer's bread-and-butter pickles for breakfast.

I made a note to myself. As soon as Germany surrenders, inform Mr. Zeyer to always take his morning pickles with generous portions of peanut butter and mayonnaise. That is, if he wants to be a real American.

My eyes met Danny's, and we could hardly hold back the laughter. Especially, when we saw poor Wolfgang making a beeline for his doghouse at the first clap of Mr. Zeyer's thunder. The fearless Nazi guard dog!

Undisturbed by the fuss he had caused, Mr. Zeyer snored on. After about two more minutes of this excitement, Danny whispered, "Let's go."

"Great!" I replied grinning.

AFTER CLEARING THE ZEYER property, we abandoned our hunched-over, military running style and resumed a more comfortable upright posture. Heading up the alley toward Dad's shed, we acted nonchalant and cool as any pair of counterspies naturally would. We quickened our pace to limber muscles stiffened by the *prolonged* stakeout atop the Zeyer garage.

While nibbling on leftovers from his cache of oatmeal weaponry, Danny kicked a small round stone that raced ahead of us like a cottontail, creating dust *poofs*, as it skipped along the alley. Seemingly pleased with his kick, he smiled to himself, re-centered his corporal insignia, and whistled a bar or two of our favorite march.

The morning sun lazily climbed upward, brightening our path. We walked silently. I pondered what new intelligence I might extract from this latest mission to add to my thickening Zeyer dossier. This was serious business. Maybe it was time to open my files to my fellow agent.

Seeming to read my mind, Danny's manner turned businesslike. He asked – no – interrogated me in a low and solemn voice, "Jase, how many times you seen the big black car?"

Geez! How did he know about that?

I was amazed, but I didn't let on. Instead, I focused on his question. I hadn't really kept track of my number of sightings. So, naturally, I stretched the truth a bit, "Five or six, I think."

"Did you always see it at the same place – at his house – I mean?" Danny pressed.

"Yep! A lot of times – I mean – a couple of times, anyway. I've seen it pick up Mr. Zeyer after he gets home from work. He comes home on the six o'clock bus."

I paused intentionally. Then I revealed my best material to Danny.

"But, last Thursday night, I got up to get a drink of water. My folks were asleep. It was real late. The moon was bright. I saw the black car again driving by – real slow. It was eerie!"

Danny stopped walking and turned to me. His eyes grew bigger.

"So I went out the back door, sneaked across the Reilly lawn, and hid behind the cottonwood tree – so no one would see me. The car stopped in front of the Zeyer house. It stood there for a long time. I could see it real clear. A four-door Packard – *with no license plates!*"

I was especially proud of this last bit of counterintelligence.

I continued solemnly, trying my best to imitate the radio announcer from *Mr. Keen, Tracer of Lost Persons*, "Finally, Mr. Zeyer got out. And I heard him speaking *German* to somebody in the car. I couldn't see who it was."

My two best gems! Danny now had information that I had never shared with anyone. I waited for his praise.

Danny weighed my words carefully, then he countered with a gem of his own, "On Thursday night, after the last show at the Grafton, Queenie – my sister – and I were the last people to leave. Queenie stopped to read a dumb movie poster. I walked on ahead. When I got to the sidewalk, I saw the big black car – it *was* a Packard – driving slowly east on Main Street."

We had independently confirmed the make of car.

Danny continued, "Mr. Zeyer was sitting in the back, next to two *really* tough looking guys in dark suits and ties. In front, on my side, there was this other tough guy holding a – a *tommy gun*. Held it down low – below the window – across his knees. Tried not to let it show. But I saw it!"

Danny seemed exceedingly proud of his detective work.

"A tommy gun! A real Thompson submachine gun?" I yelped.

Danny's stunning eyewitness evidence shed a whole new light on the case. We now knew that we were dealing with a whole sinister nest of armed and dangerous German spies. I swallowed hard and declared, "We gotta catch him."

Danny nodded grimly.

We continued in silence.

Before reaching the shed, Danny turned right, just before the Reilly combination garage and chicken coop. When we hit the sidewalk, we turned right again, heading north once more. We both knew the meaning of this course change. It would take us right in front of the Zeyer house, returning us to the scene of our earlier incursion. My breath quickened.

Danny bravely cranked up the old *Double Eagle*. We set our jaws and leaned into our walk.

The big cottonwood tree that stood right in the middle of Forrest Street's only sidewalk was our intermediate objective. The south side of the tree would provide good cover for us to reconnoiter the Zeyer spy camp situated only a half-block away. Hidden from view by the substantial girth of the venerable cottonwood, we could plot our strategy and launch our next mission.

"Let's watch from here," suggested Danny.

"Good idea," I agreed.

THE COTTONWOOD TREE WAS my old friend. It measured nearly four feet from side to side, making it impossible to pass and still stay on the sidewalk.

As Mom tells it, during the Depression, the WPA (Works Project Administration) workers began laying the sidewalk northward from New Albany Avenue. When they reached the cottonwood, they stopped. Then they gathered up all their tools, wooden sidewalk forms, gravel, and cement and started laying sidewalk, southward this time, from the north end of the street. When they reached the cottonwood tree, they stopped again.

After two attempts, the workers just couldn't bring themselves to cut down the stately old tree. That's how our neighborhood's oldest resident was spared. The WPA had a heart after all!

The residents of Forrest Street didn't mind this gigantic obstruction in the middle of their sidewalk. With reverence, on their way to and fro, they politely stepped around the honored landmark, causing permanent paths to be worn in the grass on either side of the tree.

Each summer, the cottonwood thanked us for sparing its life by shedding a magical profusion of gently floating cotton puffs. Fox squirrels cooperated by nibbling off the ends of branches and dropping them to the ground. Using sharp jackknives, we amused ourselves by slicing through these snippets at a bud joint to reveal intricate star patterns.

Because the cottonwood popped out of the sidewalk just at the crest of a long slope downward toward the river, it became a convenient point of reference, especially during my earlier years. Often, my parents would say, "You can ride your tricycle before supper. But don't go past the cottonwood tree."

In the summer, boys and girls on tricycles, bicycles, roller skates, soapbox racers, and wagons used the tree as a launching pad. Blasting off downhill, they would ride the smooth and wide sidewalk a quarter-mile or more at speeds reaching 30 miles an hour, depending on how well constructed and well oiled their vehicle was and, of course, on how daring they were.

From her front porch, our next-door neighbor, Mrs. Mikas, would shake her babushka-covered head and, in scolding Hungarian-English, cluck her disapproval of our dangerously high speeds and reckless runs, "Peeple no safe! Dum keeds gon kilt zem. Keeds gon kilt zem sefs, too. Effreebodys be ded!"

After our exhilarating runs, she would gruffly summon us to her kitchen. Without hesitation, we obeyed her in anticipation of the warm blend of aromas – baked brown sugar, onions, and paprika – that awaited us there.

When we arrived, she scolded us further, and then she hugged us. Finally, she *punished* us with stacks of warm Hungarian sugar cookies and cold milk, a blatant bribe designed to persuade us to reform. We never reformed, so this sweet ritual was repeated over and over again.

FROM THE COTTONWOOD TREE, our two-soldier patrol had an excellent view of the front and side of the Zeyer hideout. After a short strategy session, it became clear that neither of us had the faintest idea of what should be accomplished during the next phase of our campaign.

We agreed to suspend hostilities and wait for inspiration. Sitting on the sidewalk, we leaned back against the side of the cottonwood away from the Zeyer house and cogitated silently for several minutes.

Out of impatience, I offered an idea that I knew was lame before it crossed my lips, "Maybe we should just knock on his door and tell him we know. And then we could – gee – I don't know. Then maybe we could tell the police. My Dad's best friend, Sergeant Jeff – Mr. Tolna – he's a cop. And he lives almost across the street from the Zeyer house."

At least, I tried.

Danny vetoed my proposal with a snort. Then, building on the snitch component of my idea, he offered his own proposal, "Let's go over to the Shurtleif house and use the emergency phone to make a unanimous phone call to the FBI."

LIKE THE TUCKERS AND the other families in our neighborhood, we had no telephone. There was one notable exception to the no-phone rule. When the war broke out, the Riverton Central Telephone Company assigned a special emergency phone line to our neighborhood. Everyone thought of it as "our" line, our contact with the outside world. But, technically, the line belonged to the Shurtleif family who lived directly across the street from us. Mr. Shurtleif was our neighborhood air raid warden.

Whenever the air raid siren sounded from the Riverton City Hall rooftop, his job was to ensure that our neighborhood blackout was observed properly. All outside lights were to be extinguished and every window shade pulled down.

During air raid drills, Warden Shurtleif conscientiously patrolled our neighborhood checking for blackout violations. He wore his white helmet, his warden's armband, and his police whistle, dangling from his warden's lanyard. He also carried an official flashlight that he never turned on in fear of violating the very rules that he was commissioned to enforce.

He looked real spiffy in his uniform.

After making his rounds, he lifted the neighborhood telephone from its cradle and was immediately connected to a special operator down at Central. In a most serious voice, he reported, "Forrest Street Area – All Secure."

It was an awesome responsibility for an ordinary citizen like Mr. Shurtleif. But he carried out his duties flawlessly all during the war. We didn't suffer one air raid thanks to his efforts.

To be completely honest, we didn't have a *perfect* record. On one occasion, Mr. Shurtleif was unable to report "All Secure."

That night our two neighborhood bums, Gentleman Jim and Bohunk Joe, decided to light a modest bonfire down by the bus stop to roast marshmallows and sardines. Of course, the pair had been sampling a rare vintage from Pete's Grocery-Liquor-Hardware Store before their barbeque.

In his report, Mr. Shurtleif described the infraction as "a small grass fire" so his superiors wouldn't think that our neighborhood had adopted a slipshod attitude about the threat of enemy air attack.

Naturally, our two bums were very contrite the next morning. To make amends, they volunteered to join Mr. Shurtleif on his future patrols, to give him a hand should he stumble across Nazi saboteurs or the like. Mr. Shurtleif agreed to take on the two assistants because he thought they ought to pay some price for their bad judgment. Besides, he figured, he would enjoy their company.

After their fourth combined patrol, the air raid prevention careers of the marshmallow-sardine offenders were abruptly terminated. Mr. Shurtleif excused them by saying that they had sufficiently paid their debt to society. But all of us neighbors knew the real reason for their dismissal.

Convinced that a little something was needed to "keep the chill off" on those *frigid* summer evenings, the offenders carried a supply of bottled warmth. Somewhere along about the second bottle of chill-remover, his assistants broke into extremely loud singing, which very much embarrassed and annoyed Mr. Shurtleif.

Later, he told Mrs. Shurtleif it wasn't fitting to require the neighborhood to observe the blackout rules so the enemy couldn't detect us, only to have his entourage making so much noise that Nazi bombers could easily home in on Riverton even without help from blackout violators. He had a point.

In addition to Mr. Shurtleif's calls to Central, we all knew that his phone line was, theoretically, available for other neighborhood emergencies. I assumed "emergency" meant invasion of Forrest Street by German Panzers or strafing by Jap Zeros because, as far as I know, none of us neighbors ever asked to use the phone – not once – all during the war.

"WELL, WHATTYA THINK?" DANNY pressed. "We gonna make a unamimous phone call to the FBI – or not?"

My mind churned out a quick feasibility test. Like the rest of us, the Shurtleifs never locked their doors. Both Mr. and Mrs. Shurtleif worked during the day, so it would be easy to enter their kitchen without anyone knowing and use the "neighborhood" phone. Besides, if we were caught, we could explain that this was a bone fide national emergency.

Danny's plan passed the test. I expressed my approval, "I agree. Let's go!"

We hurriedly retraced our steps moving southward toward the Shurtleif house – and destiny!

Then something struck me, "I don't know how to make a *unanimous* phone call? Do you?"

Danny stopped and looked at me. From his puzzled look, it was clear that he had never used a telephone either. On the other hand, both of us had seen movie stars use the telephone on countless occasions.

With bolstered confidence, he stated simply, "You just pick up the hand thing and say, 'Operator, this is an emergency. I need to make a unanimous phone call to J. Edward Hoover at the FBI.'"

Our boy was *very* smooth! He won my vote instantly.

"Okay! Let's go."

We'd do it! Save the nation. Ah, the acclaim. All those medals!

We were within a hundred feet of the Shurtleif kitchen door when we saw them. Gads! The Shurtleifs! Both of them, just sitting there on the front porch drinking coffee and reading the paper. What'd they do, retire? Were they fired? What about the war effort? Was Mr. Shurtleif still our air raid warden?

Then it struck me. What fools we were!

"It's Saturday, Danny! We can't use the Shurtleif phone to make phone calls. They'd never let us. Besides, Edward J. Hoover will be home sitting on his front porch drinking coffee with his FBI pals."

How embarrassing! At the peak of my frustration, I reversed course and headed for our Think Tank at the foot of the cottonwood. Danny followed, looking dejected and forlorn. We flopped down and stared down the street. We were all out of ideas.

Just as we were about to call it quits, I noticed a familiar red speck in the distance. As the speck grew larger, I heard the familiar *hum* of Sherman Tolna's best wagon, the fastest on Forrest Street. Sherman was returning from his daily grocery run for his mother.

Poor Sherman had a number of things going against him. First of all, he was younger than I. Second, he was a so-called family friend, so I was often forced to play with him even though I would have much preferred the company of a dead carp. Third, there was the matter of his appearance.

In fairness to Sherman, his looks were not his fault. He looked like all the children in the Tolna family. He was covered with tight-fitting, nearly transparent skin that exposed unattractive blue blood vessels all over his spindly body. His hair was a dreadful orange color that reminded me of cooked carrots, which I didn't much care for in the first place. And his eyes were permanently red – real red – and very, very watery.

He had another very serious problem. His nose always ran, pro-fusely, down over his lips, mouth, and chin. In the winter, on his way to school, his scarf would freeze to his face. So everyday, he had to wear his scarf, like Jesse James, all through the Bible reading, the Lord's Prayer, and the Pledge of Allegiance until it thawed out.

As you can imagine, he wasn't at all popular at school. No one wanted to play crack-the-whip with him in fear of having to hold a hand coated with nose drippings. I tried not to let anyone know that the Tolnas were close family friends.

Many of the older boys in the neighborhood used poor Sherman for a punching bag. If they slugged or teased him to the point of tears, when he told his mother on them, he lacked credibility. He could bawl his eyes out all the way home but, when he arrived, his eyes and nose looked the same as they did before he left.

Because of that, I granted little Sherman a modicum of respect. Or maybe it was pity. In any case, I never punched, pinched, or squeezed him – not once. So he never had occasion to squeal on me.

I must admit that he did have one endearing quality. No matter how much I ignored him, he always came back for more. Why? Because I was the little sap's hero! He'd do almost anything for me.

As Sherman approached, his wagon rolled smoothly, not straining a bit under the load of goodies from Pete's Grocery-Liquor-Hardware Store. When he recognized me, he waved and yelled, "Hey, Jase! Whatcha doing? Can I play with you guys?"

Right!

Just what we need. Enlist this guy as our junior G-man, and Hans and his spy buddies could track us home just by following Sherman's slime trail. I was about to deflate his balloon, when an ingenious plan popped into my head. I quickly described my idea to Danny. He *whooped* his approval.

Old Sherman, my snotty little friend, you don't know it yet, but you're going to be our mole!

WHEN SHERMAN AND HIS new wagon arrived at the cottonwood, I searched his cargo of foodstuffs for contraband. I exacted my customary tariff, in this case, a hefty corner chunk from the two-pound – opps! Make that a 1.8-pound wedge of Pinconning cheddar cheese and two giant knockwursts.

I took satisfaction in my ability to remove such prizes and then cover my transgression by expertly restoring Pete's string and meat-paper wrapping to near perfect condition. Sherman, accustomed to my extortion routine, waited patiently while I stuffed the plunder into the deep side pockets of my shorts.

Danny nodded approval of my pirating skills. I could tell he was hungry, too. The pickles were wearing off.

When ambushed with his wagon of gourmet delights, Sherman gladly traded a portion of the family vittles to avoid my exaggerated threats of a painful reverse skin twist of the forearm, my diabolical Chinese Handcuff. Or a vigorous Dutch Rub on the top of his downy orange head.

But Sherman knew me well. After collecting my toll, I suffered from pangs of guilt, so I frequently granted the little frog a boon. In most cases, I would agree to play some inane kid's game with my mucous-covered victim. I attempted to do this without any of my *real* friends seeing me.

Predictably, Sherman, subtly demanding his kickback, inquired, "Whatcha doing? Can I play with you guys?"

Laying my trap, I deflected his initial parry with a surprise offer, "Sherman, this is Danny. We have a secret club. If you want to join our club, you have to promise to keep secrets."

The little toad was ecstatic. He hopped up and down, still clinging to his wagon tongue handle. The handle bounced so fiercely that I feared the Tolna groceries would be converted to sacks of soup.

"Ooooo! Yessss! I can keep all kindsa secrets. I won't tell. I won't tell. I won't tell. When! When! When! Whatta I gotta do? Yes. Yes. Yes," he sputtered.

The kid was showing symptoms of a severe case of unmet social need, so I pressed my advantage, "You have to go on a secret *undercover* mission. All by yourself. And it will be dangerous and scary. Do you still want to join?"

"Yeeeeeeeeeeeeeeeeeeees!" he screamed. The orange-haired bug was a zealot.

"You first have to take an oath of absolute secrecy before we can even tell you about the club or about your mission. Are you ready to take your oath, Sherman?" I challenged, trying to sound firm and patriotic like Paul Henried in *Watch On The Rhine*, one of Mom's favorite movies.

"Yeeeeeeeeeeeeeeeeeees!" he screeched, sounding like a freight train whistle at night.

"Okay, okay. Calm down. Put your wagon handle down and touch the cottonwood with your left hand," I instructed. "No, the other hand. Okay. Raise your right hand. No, dummy. The other one."

Danny sneered cynically, "I'm not sure this is gonna work."

I ignored Danny's comment and continued, *"I, Sherman Allen Tolna –,"* Sherman followed right along, repeating every word.

Of course, he had no idea what half my words meant. But ignorance of club law is no excuse. If he screwed up, I would personally exterminate the rat. After all, this was wartime, and sacrifices had to be made.

" – do solemnly swear to keep all club secrets – and, if I don't, you guys get to punch me so hard in the stomach that I'll throw up – and that I'll go on my secret undercover mission and obey your orders – and do it without telling another living soul about it – especially my snotty-nosed sisters who will never be members of this all-boys club – and if I should die on the mission I will not tell my mother or my father – who is a cop and would get you in deep trouble with your parents — ,"

I thought to myself, *This is going very well.* I had never composed a legal document extemporaneously before.

" – and that if I ever tell anyone about even the name of our club I will be Chinese handcuffed and Dutch rubbed until I bleed to death – and you will bury me in the swamp so deep that I can't go to school or to the grocery store with my new red wagon – "

Whew! I nearly forgot Sherm's initiation fee.

" – which I hereby deed over to the club for the exclusive use of Danny Tucker and Jase Addison – except when my Mom tells me to go to Pete's – and I'll bring the groceries to the club's headquarters – that's Jase's house – before I go home – and Danny and Jase get to pick out anything they want – and I won't squeal – so help me, God!"

Even Danny was impressed with the thoroughness of my impromptu oath.

I thought I detected an extra tear or two in Sherman's red and runny eyes as he solemnly swore, "So help you got. So help you got!

"Yeeeeeeeeeeeeeeeeeeeeeeees! Yes! Yes! Yes!"

So help *me* God! I wanted to muzzle the little creep. But the mission must go on.

"Okay! Okay! Okay, you're in. You're a member. For frogs sake! Quiet! We gotta get you ready for your first mission. Shut up! And listen! That's an order," I snapped, losing patience with the new recruit.

Maybe Danny was right! I was already wondering how to pull the skunk's membership credentials when Sherman distracted me.

"Wait! Wait!" Sherman jumped up and down raising his hand to be recognized. "What's the name of our club? What's its name?"

Oops!

The kid had a good question. Danny and I huddled on the Zeyer-side of the tree. Danny came up with the name, so he got to lay it on our first new member, "We are the Forrest Street Guards. But that's a secret name that no one is ever to know. So we'll call ourselves, FSG"

"FSG! FSG! Wow! FSG!" Sherman was bouncing again.

We needed to put this kid's energy to work for world freedom and liberty – right now. So I laid out his assignment.

First, Sherman was to deliver his groceries to his mother. I reminded him to keep his big mouth shut about FSG and his secret mission – and the pilfered cheese and knockwurst.

Second, he was to change his clothes. He had to dress in all dark clothing. Preferably black. Better yet, camouflage.

Third, he was to return to the cottonwood with his father's police whistle and his wagon. As fast as he could!

He nodded and didn't say a word. He picked up his wagon handle and motored around the cottonwood tree toward the Tolna house. Maybe I was wrong, but I thought Sherm the germ, swollen with new responsibility and pride, was standing an inch or two taller as he headed for home. Then his slimy hand reached around and gave his butt a thorough scratching through his baggy shorts. I quickly returned to reality.

While Sherman went home to prepare, Danny and I finished off the cheese and knockwurst. We had some advance planning to do, so we needed to renew our strength. We agreed on Sherman's mission objectives, our role in its execution, and, most importantly, our means of escape.

When Sherman returned, he was dressed in (Honest to God!) powder blue pajamas with built-in socks! Was the insect color-blind, too? He carried his tattered *lammy* doll slung over his shoulder. I wondered if Sherman had misunderstood the meaning of "undercover."

We expected Zorro, and we got the Easter Bunny!

Danny rolled his eyes and turned his back. His action let me know that this was *my* family friend, so I was responsible. I responded professionally by getting right down to business.

"Sherman, you know Mr. and Mrs. Zeyer, right? Your mission is to enter their house by the front door and take up position to spy on them until you complete your mission. Any questions?" I inquired, straining to be thorough and businesslike with the blinking blue bunny standing before me.

Mr. Sleepy Noddems smiled wistfully, and then interrupted my briefing by saying, "Mrs. Zeyer lets me play with her cat, Sasha. Mrs. Zeyer's nice. I like her. Mr. Zeyer's funny. He has puppets that he shows me. He makes me laugh. I like him, too."

My heart sank.

We had all the makings of a defection, even before we launched the first FSG operation. I tried to ignore my daffy little friend.

"When you get inside, find yourself a good hiding place. Someplace where you can hear what goes on. And where you can see people, like Zeyer's Nazi spy pals who come and go. Got it?"

"They have a big closet under the stairs in the living room. That's where the puppets are. I can hide there – probably," he added calmly.

He didn't seem to sense the danger of counterespionage. But what could you expect from this younger generation.

"All right! Good," I confirmed. "Danny will brief you on your objectives."

Danny picked up a short cottonwood branch that had fallen recently. Using the branch as a swagger stick, he jabbed at the imaginary list of objectives chalked on the rough cottonwood bark. He spoke with a distinct British accent, "You ahr to make a thorough sahrch of ahl rooms in the howse. Have eye made myself perfectlay cleahr?"

Without waiting for Sherman's answer, he continued, "This includes the awttic and the cellahr."

Sherman raised his hand tentatively.

"What is aht? What is aht?" Danny demanded impatiently, with an imaginary English plum properly tucked in each cheek.

"They don't have a cellar. Should I still search under the house?" Sherman asked seriously.

"No, stupid. Just search everywhere else. And, whatever you do, don't let them see you. Do you have any questions?" Danny dropped his British accent and concluded abruptly.

"Yep. What am I looking for?" Sherman inquired earnestly.

Oops! Here we go again.

Sherm had just revealed a tiny error of omission in Danny's briefing script. Danny obviously wasn't used to such a demanding audience. The pressures of war were tough on all of us.

But Danny recovered nicely, "You're looking for five items – photographs of military targets around Riverton, lists of his fellow spies, code sheets, messages from Berlin, and secret radios – probably in the attic. Got it?"

Sherm raised one skinny index finger. "Just one more question. What's a code sheet?" he wanted to know.

"It's a sheet of paper covered with letters and numbers," Danny responded impatiently.

"Letters are A, B, and C? And numbers are 1, 2, and 3, right?" Sherman inquired sheepishly.

Geez, I forgot the kid couldn't read yet.

"Sherman, just get in that house and search for anything that looks suspicious. Got it?" Danny snapped.

I could tell that Sherman was really aching to ask, "What does 'suspicious' mean?" But, being a new member, he decided not to push his luck. He nodded obediently and settled for scratching himself again.

I took over the briefing.

"Okay. Danny and I will haul you in the wagon past the hedge in front of the Zeyer house. When we get to the Zeyer front walk, you roll out of the wagon and lie flat on the sidewalk. Don't let them see you! Then we'll head up the driveway toward their garage. When we get to the backyard we'll create a diversion."

I knew Sherman didn't know what "diversion" meant, but I pushed on before he could ask.

"As soon as they come outside, we'll blow your dad's police whistle. That's your signal. You jump up and run inside. Hide in that closet. When the dust settles, start spying. We'll roll down the driveway toward the sidewalk and head downhill to make our escape. Any questions?"

Sherman shook his head slowly. He sat down in the wagon, stroked his *lammy*, wiped his nose on a scaly powder blue sleeve, and waited for further instructions. I raised my eyebrows and looked at Danny. He gave me a brave thumbs up.

The first FSG mission was a Go!

We headed down the sidewalk at a slow jog. Sherman with a goofy grin on his face bounced from side to side in the wagon. When we reached the Zeyer front walk, I whispered a curt order to Sherman, "Jump! Jump!"

In true commando style, Sherman rolled off the moving wagon, smashing down hard on the sidewalk with his elbows and knees. While we continued on toward the driveway, he gave us a glassy-eyed stare revealing his pain and shock, but we kept moving.

We wheeled into the Zeyer driveway and headed up the moderate grade toward the garage and Wolfgang's kennel. We ran low to the ground, using our best military running style. We hugged the side of the house, trying not to be seen.

As we ducked under the Zeyer kitchen window, I peeked up and saw him – the old spymaster. He was sitting at the kitchen table with a huge red napkin tied around his neck. He held a big silver spoon, upright in his right hand. Mrs. Zeyer stood beside him holding a gigantic bowl of steaming, delicious-smelling chicken soup with the corner of her apron.

She was about to set the enormous bowl down in front of Mr. Zeyer when I let out my first war cry.

"OOOOOoooooooooossssssssssssssssssseeeeeeeeeeeeeeeeeeekkkkkk kkkkkk!"

The return of the Chippewas!

Danny instantly followed suit, with the most blood-curdling variation of his visitor *come-out call* that I could imagine. I won't try to imitate it for you. Suffice it to say my hair tingled. And my ears twitched – and hurt slightly.

Wolfgang, who had previously wandered back into his doghouse for a midday snooze, responded with a deafening bellow as if in immense pain. He bolted upright hitting the top of his head against the ceiling of his house and producing a huge – *Clunk!* Then he emerged in a rage and added a flurry of bass *yowls* and *harrpps* to our diversion.

No cookies for you this trip, old Nazi canine, I thought. *But thanks for the help anyway!*

Wolfgang's head had hit the doghouse ceiling at the exact instant Mr. Zeyer's chicken soup hit the kitchen ceiling. Based on her bowl tossing ability, I concluded that Mrs. Zeyer had a pretty good pitching arm for an older woman. We could hear angry German shrieks, right after the hot chicken shower turned table-ward, drenching the old spy and his spyess.

We reversed our wagon and started our run down the driveway as the scalded couple hit the back porch! And boy! Were they hot! Their scorching German phrases followed us down the driveway.

On cue, I blew Sergeant Jeff's police whistle with great gusto – three or four long blasts. Danny and I, upright again, broke into a mad dash toward the sidewalk, followed by more angry Zeyer invectives and Wolfgang howls.

When we reached the sidewalk, I glanced back at the Zeyer front porch just in time to see Sherman's left rear bunny paw disappear inside the front door. The screen door banged shut behind him. What a graceful entry!

But our mole was in place!

At a gallop, we pointed Sherman's super speedy wagon downhill toward the swamp and river. On the run, Danny jumped in the front end and I thumped down behind him. The wagon, as if sensing we were firmly aboard, accelerated madly. We both hung on in fear for our lives, roaring northward down the treacherous slope toward freedom.

A block or so into our run, I realized I hadn't breathed since the Zeyer backyard. I took a deep breath and felt rejuvenated by our successful escape.

Suddenly, I realized something else. We were wobbling erratically, meaning only one thing. Nobody was steering.

In the front position, Danny had full access to the steering wheel, the wagon handle. So I grabbed the back of his shirt, tugged hard, and yelled, "Steer! Steer!"

No reaction. It's impossible! He didn't know what I meant. The wagon handle just dangled freely, there between his knees. By this time, we were hitting 20 miles an hour, swerving from side to side, careening down the sidewalk.

As we approached the big dip where the swamp cuts across Forrest Street, our right front wheel left the sidewalk and sliced into the embankment in front of the Borski house. We continued forward with just our left wheels on the sidewalk, miraculously, still gaining speed.

Suddenly the Borski embankment, apparently tired of the rubdown, violently pitched us left, toward the swamp on the other side of Forrest Street. As we streaked into the road, our wheels bit into the gravel spinning us left and right, then left again.

When we hit the far shoulder, Sherman's wagon and we, its frantic occupants, were launched, floating like a huge red bird, out over the swamp. I stopped breathing again!

If it had been April, our landing would have been a salutary splashdown in five or six feet of murky water. Instead, we landed, nose-down with a teeth-jarring impact – *smash crunch* – that folded the front end of Sherman's wagon like an accordion. The wagon stuck where it hit, releasing Danny and me to our fates. We tumbled head over heels for another ten feet and landed – *kersplot* – in an immense pothole for two.

We hit belly down and skidded through ooze. We stood up immediately. Our feet and ankles were mired in a good six inches of pure sewer muck. We stunk to high heaven. Not surprisingly, we shuddered, slouched over, and broke into tears of pain, anger, and humiliation.

We abandoned the crumpled red wagon without remorse. After a few minutes, we managed to struggle out of the swamp, up the bank, and onto the road. We collapsed to catch our breath. Mercifully, our injuries were limited to minor scrapes and bruises. Of course, "minor injury" didn't apply to our morale that had sunk to an all-time low owing to our current fragrance, *Eau de Outhouse.*

We sat in shock examining the fresh wagon wheel tracks that swirled and scraped across the road surface, memorializing our traumatic experience. We allowed ourselves the luxury of sobbing for a few minutes more before we attempted to collect our thoughts.

"We can't go home like this," Danny sniffed at last.

"Boy, that's for sure," I moaned.

"What'll we do? And what about Sherman's wagon," Danny muttered.

Without knowing why, I compulsively corrected Danny, reminding him of the wagon's recent transfer of title to the officers of FSG. He gave me a look normally reserved for ambulance-chasing lawyers at the scene of an accident.

We stared blankly at the swamp for several minutes without speaking. We were physically and emotionally spent. Finally, Danny lamented, "I'm really thirsty."

Thirsty? That was it!

"Bingo!" I shouted. "Our troubles are over. Follow me!"

2   BY THE GRACE OF GOD

DANNY HAD A STRANGE QUIRK. EACH TIME, HE TOOK the lead when he was supposed to be following me. To loosen the sticky mud from his shoes and leggings, he stomped across the street following the zigzagging wagon tracks, up the steep parkway and back onto the sidewalk. Decisively, he turned north toward Liberty Street. I stomped along behind confirming his route with my silence. Revolting muddy clumps littered the sidewalk behind us.

His army cap and corporal insignia were the only pieces of his apparel that weren't thoroughly filth-covered. Even his once spotless bandage was streaked with a mucky handprint from a nervous swipe just after our crash landing.

My shoes, shorts, and tee shirt were similarly soiled. But, as we clomped along, my morale began to rise, despite having to contend with the nauseating odor emanating from my swamp-soaked leader.

"Step on a crack! Break your mother's back!" The familiar words exploded over Danny's right shoulder.

Following forceful neighborhood conditioning, I immediately modified my gait to accommodate the new imperative. Left foot stomp! Miss those sidewalk seams. Right foot stomp! Miss those cracks. Repeating this awkward step, we noisily marched in unison downhill, past the swamp, and on toward the massive Victory garden planted by the Petrov family who lived on a huge double lot at the corner of Forrest and Liberty.

"Step on a crack! Break Hitler's back," Danny barked.

A change up! I quickly modified my stride to hit a seam or crack with each step. This was the toughest gait of all.

"Step on a crack! Break your father's back," Danny ordered. Another quick reversal!

Stomping and scissoring on, we cycled through all the bad guys, patri-
otically breaking the backs of Hitler, Mussolini, and, the worst rascal of all,
Tojo. Danny spat out their vile names, and I demonstrated my ardent support by banging my soles down smartly – crack after crack after crack.

As we marched, Danny had little difficulty identifying most of the
'good guys' on his list. Our mothers, fathers, grandmas, and grandpas and,
of course, Franklin Delano Roosevelt certainly deserved unbroken backs.
Danny respected all the obvious family saints. But 'sister' gave him trouble.

Owing to the domineering personality of his sister, Queenie, he
first placed her in the 'bad guy' category. Then, out of guilt, he reversed
himself. Then back again.

During our march, we alternately broke Queenie's back with her
buddies, Hitler and Tojo, and then repaired it again along with
Grandma and President Roosevelt. "Compromise is often best," Danny
declared to explain his inconsistency.

When we reached Liberty Street, we were nearly stomped out. So
Danny stopped for a breather. We had stepped on –or avoided – a good
quarter mile of cracks. Danny leaned against the street sign and smiled,
apparently satisfied with his performance as drill sergeant. I inspected
the long rows of newly sprouted carrots, beets, turnips, and radishes
that lined the Petrov garden.

Only a few small particles of mud still clung to our clothing.
However, the residual stain and odor, exacerbated by the heat of the
midday sun, remained as strong as ever. We needed a good laundering.
And, by now, we were both dying of thirst.

"Where to next?" Danny asked enthusiastically. His morale had
obviously improved, too.

I pointed west down Liberty Street in the direction of the Ann
Arbor Street Bridge and replied using my best Gabby Hayes voice,
"Over yonder."

"The waterworks!" Danny exclaimed, looking puzzled.

"Yep. The coldest drink of water in town – and it's free!"

WE WERE PROUD OF the Riverton City Waterworks. In our blue-
collar neighborhood, almost every man and many women, especially
during the war, worked at one of the town's factories, mills, or shops.
Livelihoods depended on our ability to work with our hands and our
backs. The Great Depression had ravaged our part of town.
Unemployment had been virtually total.

If it hadn't been for President Roosevelt's programs like the Civilian Conservation Corps (CCC) or the Works Project Administration (WPA), many of our neighbors would surely have "starved right to death" as Mom always put it. As a result, most neighbors ranked FDR right up there with God himself.

Our waterworks was a WPA project that brought employment back to our neighborhood. The project, not only fed our families, but also lifted the chins of our proud, but jobless, fathers and brothers.

Since its dedication in 1936, the waterworks performed a vital function for our community. Modern, powerful electric pumps drew millions of gallons from the deep wells reaching downward into the earth from the flats between the new building and the banks of the Chippewa River. The waterworks reliably extracted, processed, and pumped clear, fresh water to meet the mighty thirst of Riverton's citizens and businesses.

This magnificent brick and white marble building was one of my favorites. First, following the neighborhood practice, the waterworks was never locked. I had the free run of the place any time I wanted, night or day.

Of course, I was trained to be security conscious because of the war, so I chose not to share my discovery of lax security with anyone except Warden Shurtleif. I had strongly advised him to urge the city fathers to place a guard at the waterworks to prevent sabotage by a certain neighborhood Nazi spy. After all, I reasoned, would Mr. Shurtleif like to be responsible for German-poisoned water being pumped through water mains all over town?

No guard had been posted. So I took it upon myself to patrol regularly, especially when I was thirsty. For my convenience, a gigantic water fountain, located in the front foyer, offered the coolest, clearest, freshest water in town.

Whenever I entered the waterworks, despite my considerable effort to be absolutely quiet, the sound of my footsteps reverberated magically from the building's thirty-foot ceilings, long empty hallways, and highly polished marble floors and walls. The subdued light of the interior coupled with the symphony of soft echoes produced a mysterious mood within me.

Finally, the temperature inside was like that of an underground cavern. All year round, it remained at a constant fifty-five degrees. Entering the building from a hot and humid summer day was like walking into a giant freezer chest.

I WAS EAGER TO share my waterworks with Danny. This time, I took the lead and marched us toward the solution to all our problems. Danny followed as I climbed the long, gently pitched white marble stairs toward the front entrance, a splendid bank of six enormous brass-framed, heavy glass doors. I grasped the over-sized door handle and expertly threw open the door allowing Danny to enter. The door opened with a loud *bang* and then banged shut again as we slipped inside.

"Wowwww!" Danny exclaimed as his eyes took in the magnificent foyer.

"Let's get a drink," I suggested, delivering on my promise.

We both drank deeply from *my* water fountain. The cool, sweet-tasting water soothed every parched corner of our bruised and dehydrated bodies. We sat on the cold marble floor next to the colossal fountain to catch our breath. Then we drank again. And then, one more time.

Danny cocked his head sideways and declared, "Man, is this place nifty! What else is here?"

I led the way down the wide steps of the central staircase, which descended gracefully to the level below. As we reached the lower level, I turned to Danny. His expression told the whole story. Before us, spreading from wall to wall, lay a huge body of water. The enormous pool covered nearly an acre. Small underwater lights cast an eerie blue-green tint that illuminated every corner of the cavernous room. The water was crystal clear and absolutely placid, giving the impression of no water at all.

"Holy Ohio! Look at that! What *is* this?" Danny stammered.

During a previous solo visit, I had read the description of the pool's function on a sign near the locker room to our right. I gave Danny the benefit of my research, "When the water comes out of the ground from the big wells – out in back of the waterworks – it's pumped into this pool. Here, it rests, so chemicals and other bad stuff settle to the bottom. That way they don't stick to the sides of the water mains and pipes inside people's houses."

I continued, trying not to be too technical, "If they need to, the men who work here can put in chemicals to kill germs. But Riverton water comes from way deep in the ground. It's pure – no germs. So they don't."

Danny nodded his head slowly, obviously mesmerized.

I followed the walkway around the pool until I came to a large wooden door with an opaque glass window. The bold black and gold lettering in the center of the window read "Locker Room". I opened the door and allowed Danny to enter first.

Wide marble benches were located between two long rows of six-foot high gray metal lockers. A white three-by-five card mounted in a silver metal frame identified the owner of each locker. Danny read the names aloud as he walked down one row and back up the other, "Sam", "Bob", "Dick H", "Pete", "John S", and finally "Ivan." Our impromptu locker inspection revealed a predictable collection of coveralls, work shoes, toolboxes, rags, and water-treatment chemicals.

The far end of the locker room housed a huge shower area. We stripped off our mucky attire and threw it in a heap in the middle of the shower room floor. We turned on the hot water, full blast, and began to drown the polluted pile. Steam quickly filled the shower room. The smell of sewage was overwhelming as the hot water scoured the soiled clothing.

The drains in the shower room became clogged with our clothes – shirts, shorts, socks, underwear, belts, and even shoes – everything, except Danny's cap and insignia, which was still perched on the naked soldier's head. The water rose to a depth of nearly four inches. Then we turned off the hot water and sprinkled two containers of Borax Cleanser – *borrowed* from the locker room supply closet – over the steeping mess.

We stomp-marched another quarter mile back and forth over our laundry, mashing our clothes into the tile. Each shower soap dish contained an enormous commercial-size bar of *Lava* soap, which we used to scrub every item. Soon our hands were tired and raw from the hot water and abrasive soap. Undaunted, we rinsed our clothes thoroughly, soaped them a second time, and scrubbed them all over again.

After soaping and scrubbing to our satisfaction, we took a short break for Danny to store his headgear, temporarily, in Dick H's locker. Then we hit the showers for a long and luxurious scrub-down. Steam filled the entire locker room and everything smelled clean – like *Lava* soap. Nary a whiff of sewer scent remained.

Using the last of our strength, we squeezed all the water we could from our clothes and hung them to dry on the hot and cold water handles in the shower room. We needed a break.

As we entered the pool area from the steamy locker room, we were shocked by the tremendous difference in temperature, a good thirty degrees cooler. We sprawled naked on the icy tile of the pool deck to rest, cool down, and gaze at the bluish green water.

After several minutes of quiet relaxation, Danny spoke, "I wonder what it would be like not living in the middle."

To most people that remark wouldn't have made sense. But I knew exactly what Danny meant. He and I had been born and raised precisely at the center of the universe.

RIVERTON, MICHIGAN WAS RIGHT in the middle of everything really important. The middle of Chippewa County. The middle of the Lower Peninsula. The middle of the Midwest – which is the same as the middle of America. And we were living there in the middle of the 20th century. Right in the middle of the biggest war in history. Even bigger than The Great War!

Unlike Americans who were born out on the fringes, Rivertonians like us were extraordinarily well adjusted and stable. We were also solid citizens – patriotic, hardworking, neighborly, and frugal – all desirable traits, especially during times of war.

We reinforced these qualities by listening to family radios in living rooms all over town, reading the *Riverton Daily Press* every evening, and attending church and Sunday school on a weekly basis. Many of us, like Danny and me, expanded our horizons by anteing up the eleven-cent admission needed to see the new shows arriving twice weekly at the Chippewa and Grafton movie theaters downtown.

As you might have guessed, Rivertonians were smarter than average. Not everybody but most. We had other exceptional traits, too, but we were taught not to brag.

Ambitious, but honest, businessmen from New York founded Riverton in the early 1800's. These hardworking settlers brought solid Protestant values that formed the foundation of old Riverton's social structure.

In short order, they converted the heavy forests along the wide and winding Chippewa River into a tidy, prosperous community of sawmills and factories. Highly prized Riverton wood products – caskets, packing boxes and crates, and fine furniture – were transported to markets in far-flung corners of America over railroad tracks leading from the heart of town.

After achieving financial success, Riverton's merchants and industrialists (and their bankers and lawyers) built for themselves opulent Victorian houses in the hills above the town center. The oak and elm shaded streets of that old neighborhood still bear their names – Burke, Scott, Chambers, and Addison.

By the dawning of the new century, however, iron and steel had replaced wood as the primary raw material used to produce Riverton's industrial output. Factory owners came to rely on the special skills and labor of a new generation of workers, brawny immigrants from countries like Germany, Poland, Hungary, and Bohemia.

The new immigrants were very different from the town's original English Protestant population. These fun-loving people drank dark home brew, consumed enormous quantities of coarse sausage, turnips, and potatoes laced with onions, horseradish, and garlic, and danced noisy polkas and mazurkas on weekends.

When growing up, we didn't think twice about the nationality or religion of playmates with names like Tolna, Petrov, and Borski. Nor did we think it unusual that their parents and grandparents still spoke nostalgically, in their native tongues or broken English, about the Old Country.

The Victorian neighborhoods of the town's founders were centrally located north of the Chippewa River. The rest of the town, especially the south and east sides, consisted of factories, foundries, and railroad yards. In between these noisy, hot, and dirty industrial establishments, working class families built simple and inexpensive homes on dusty, unpaved streets overrun with crops of boys like Danny and me. This was *my* neighborhood. And I loved it!

"I WOULDN'T LIKE IT," I finally responded.

"Not living in the middle?"

"Yeah."

"Me, neither," agreed Danny.

After a few more minutes of daydreaming, I realized I was getting bored. All this water was making me wish that we had gone to the river for a swim.

Then it struck me.

We were about as clean as two boys could be. So what would be the harm in taking a little dip in Riverton's drinking water? I suggested the idea to Danny. Instead of answering me, he rolled over twice and plopped, side-first, into the drink. I followed quickly, entering the pool by way of my favorite dive, a tidy jackknife.

I demonstrated my world-class backstroke for Danny. He followed me using his best imitation of Johnny Weismuller's Australian crawl. Having reached the other side, we decided to rest.

We were hanging onto the side of the settling pool when we heard a very loud **"BAM! BAAAM!"** as one of the waterworks front doors had banged open, then banged closed.

The echoing footsteps of giant shoes tramped across the floor above us as their wearer rapidly approached the stairway leading downward to the pool area and the scene of our crime against the city.

"We're done for!" Danny whispered forlornly.

Excruciating terror gripped my chest! Danny stared at me desperately, fear pinching his eyes. A loyal drop of water, clinging to the tip of his nose, refused to fall lest it give away our position.

Scufflety clap! Scufflety clap. Scufflety clap. Down the stairs the menacing footsteps came.

An unexpected blast exploded around us. The deafening bass melody reverberated from the walls causing us both to loosen our grip on the pool edge and cover our ears.

De dee dee dum, de de de dee dee dum!

Then it dawned on me. I knew that music! It was *My Old Kentucky Home!*

We held our breath and stared at the stairway. *Scufflety clap.* A black Oxford shoe and trouser cuff came into view. *Scufflety clap.* Then we saw both trouser legs clearly. Black wool with a long stripe of black satin down the side. The cops! The United States Marines! No! A tuxedo?

"It's Gentleman Jim!" I whispered to Danny.

The relief was overwhelming.

OUR NEIGHBORHOOD CHERISHED ITS two bums. Gentleman Jim and Bohunk Joe were trusted, respected, and protected by all of us. No one mistreated them. No one spoke ill of them. No one failed to greet them when passing on the street. Children, foolish enough to whisper a taunt or utter a snicker about them in the presence of their parents, earned a good cuffing on the spot and a strong lecture at home.

No doubt about it! Our bums were the best bums in town.

My mother declared this was so because Jim and Joe filled an important community role. According to her theory, these two scruffy characters performed the "Grace of God Job" for us all.

"After the Depression, a few didn't recover when good times returned. Those who missed out serve to remind the rest of us never to take our good fortune for granted," she had explained. "So when we see Jim or Joe, we should be thankful for their gift to us. After all, we might have been one of them – had it not been for the Grace of God."

Mom always had an explanation for everything.

In short, our bums kept us humble and filled our hearts with charity that might have otherwise just dried up when prosperity struck after the Depression ended and the war began.

Judging from all the apple pie, ham sandwiches, and glasses of milk dispensed by Mom, I'd say our two bums were exceedingly effective when it came to the *charity* element of their Grace of God duties, especially when in the proximity of Mom's kitchen door.

While working outside – hoeing the garden, digging fresh garbage pits, or piling sewing machine frames behind the shed – I had often observed a warm ritual that led me to conclude that Dad and Gentleman Jim shared a special relationship, too. Frequently, Jim used our back alley as his route home from Pete's Grocery-Liquor-Hardware with a quart of "supper" under his arm.

This choice of routes was in itself a bit odd because Jim could have saved a quarter mile or so by simply walking down New Albany Avenue from Pete's to the railroad tracks just beyond Bohunk Joe's shack. These tracks led directly to Jim's hut next to the foundry.

Normally, I heard Jim before I saw him as he sauntered up the alley whistling, humming, or *dee dumming* his *Old Kentucky* theme song. If he were *dee dumming* real loudly, I knew that either he had sampled supper on the way home or he had enjoyed a particularly agreeable day without the benefit of Bacchus.

I liked it when Jim chose our alley as his route home. Seeing Jim stroll by was like watching a float in the Rose Bowl Parade. His appearance never failed to excite me.

To start off, he was a huge, once handsome, man of no more than forty. Although the rigors of outdoor living, sleeping on the ground, and his liquid diet made him appear much older. His skin was permanently coated with the dark shade of dirt common to those of his occupation. He weighed over two hundred pounds, carried on a still broad-shouldered frame of six feet three. His unruly shock of curly, gray-tipped black hair and dignified black beard were, despite Jim's chronic dissipations, always neatly trimmed.

His eyes were piercing blue. But his face was soft and sad. In public, his deportment nearly always signaled self-respect and dignity, except on those occasions when he dined out with Bohunk Joe or with an old hobo friend passing through town. In any case, everyone agreed that Gentleman Jim was the neighborhood's best-liked and certainly classiest bum.

Summer and winter, he wore the same uniform. His was the picture of formal elegance, albeit moth-eaten and worn shiny. A flowing, double-breasted, black wool overcoat extending nearly to the ground was Jim's outer layer. The next layer was an ancient oversized black tuxedo. Under that, he wrapped his huge chest in an assortment of threadbare, multicolored flannel shirts and a tattered quilted underjacket. He wore multiple layers on his feet in the form of assorted mismatched socks stuffed into his enormous black oxfords.

In cold weather, he covered his huge hands with a wide array of ratty gloves and mittens, taking care to ensure that the outer layer matched as closely as possible. On his head, he wore a crumpled, black silk top hat at a jaunty angle to the left. Around his neck, he coiled a once-white silk scarf that was at least two yards in length. In winter, the scarf was wound tightly to fend off the cold. In summer, just a couple of turns to be debonair.

None of us ever asked where he had acquired his magnificent wardrobe. All we knew, or cared about, was that Gentleman Jim was indeed a splendid sight to behold.

Each time we met, his words were the same. "Greetings! Mr. Jase Addison! How's the world treating you?" This acknowledgment always made me smile, inside and out. I truly liked Gentleman Jim. And I think he liked me, too.

The ritual that Jim and Dad shared was forever the same as well. As he sauntered by, if Jim saw that Dad was still working at his bench, he would detour and tap gently on the window. Dad would look up and smile. And, if he were at a good breaking point, he would point a finger in the air, indicating to Jim that he would be right out.

Their chats lasted ten or fifteen minutes. Then Jim would look at his non-existent wristwatch. This gesture signaled that his need for the supper under his arm had won out over his need for social interaction. On cue, Mom would emerge from the kitchen with a leftover morsel to serve as an appetizer for Jim's supper. After Jim smiled and complimented Mom on her gift, she would feign embarrassment and return to her kitchen.

Once Mom was inside, Dad would pat Jim on the arm and off he would go surrounded by a profusion of melodic variations on *My Old Kentucky Home*. How I loved that ritual!

AS GENTLEMAN JIM DESCENDED the stairs, he evidently had something on his mind besides confronting two boys who were polluting the Riverton water supply. In addition to the considerable weight of his all-weather uniform, he was carrying an enormous assortment of blankets slung over his left arm and a tattered wicker laundry basket under his right.

When he reached the pool level, the basket pitched forward, dumping its contents onto the deck. Out tumbled an unopened economy size box of *Oxydol* laundry soap, assorted socks and gloves, and a brand new scrub brush.

This little accident failed to dampen Jim's enthusiasm or his pace. He roared another *Kentucky* variation that reverberated with overpowering force from the walls of our watery cavity. Without stopping to retrieve his fallen articles, he made a beeline for the locker room, which we knew to be strewn with the drying uniforms of two young Nazi fighters.

"Gad!" I whispered to Danny when big Jim disappeared through the locker room door. "Just our luck! We take a swim in the City's water supply on the one day of the year that Gentleman Jim chooses to do his laundry."

I had just completed my sentence when we heard – nothing. Gentleman Jim had abruptly stopped singing. We strained ears in the direction of the locker room door. Still nothing. Then we heard it.

"Harrumph!" followed by "Ha! Har! Har! Haw! Haw!"

Gentleman Jim's raucous laughter filled the lower level of the waterworks. The locker room door burst open. "Where are you, you saboteurs, you?" he yelled with laughter in his voice.

"Here we are! We give up," Danny squeaked. Geez! All I could think was, "That question really didn't call for an answer!"

"Who's there?" Jim hollered, bending our way to get a better look. Silence.

"Well, I'll be!" he sputtered.

I said nothing. Danny looked like he was going to confess again so I kicked his leg – hard – underwater. He got the point and clammed up.

"Greetings! Mr. Jase Addison. How's the world treating you?" Jim inquired with his usual warm smile.

Smiling back, I confessed, "I guess you caught us. This is Danny Tucker, my new friend. I'm showing him around. He just moved here from –."

I realized I didn't know where Danny had lived before moving to our neighborhood.

Jim nodded Danny's way, and then he observed warmly, "I hadn't realized the Riverton water supply was a part of the town tour. Well, you two better get out of there before somebody else shows up."

He extended his hand toward us and added, "Come on! Help me with my laundry. Then I'll see that those clothes of yours get dried properly."

We paddled over to Jim's side of the pool where he plucked us both out of the water with an effortless sweep of his long right arm. We re-stowed his laundry supplies in the wicker basket and followed him into the locker room.

Jim noticed Danny's bandage. "Danny, why the bandage?"

Danny shrugged and offered modestly, "Swinging accident. Five stitches and eight tongue depressors. Didn't hurt."

Jim nodded understandingly while Danny retrieved his army hat and rank of office from Dick H's locker.

"Whacha boys up to this summer?" Jim inquired.

Danny answered nonchalantly for us both, "Mainly catching Nazi spies with moles and watching submachine guns and Nazi soldiers."

"Routine summer, huh?" Jim smiled at Danny.

"I suppose," Danny responded as he casually fingered his cap before reseating it on his head.

We removed our laundry from the shower room and parked it in Jim's wicker basket on the marble bench. Then we cut on the hot water and demonstrated our laundering technique for Jim, using his pile of blankets for our first load. Jim watched us with admiration. Then he joined in by peeling off the layers of his all-weather uniform. When he reached the Union suit layer he stopped. Who would have guessed that, under his elegant attire, Jim wore red, long-legged underwear?

Standing under a powerful shower, Jim soaped and scrubbed from head to toe, not bothering to remove his underwear or last layer of socks. The color of his face was magically transformed from the familiar light black to a pale tan. It occurred to me that the neighbors might not recognize him without his dirt mask.

He hummed a little *Old Kentucky*, so we joined in adding our strange harmony to his arrangement. We dumped ample doses of *Oxydol* onto the huge wad of laundry under our feet and marched back and forth to our version of the Stephen Foster standard. Foster soon gave way to Sousa as three merry launderers tromped to the beat of *Under the Double Eagle* with just a pinch of *Kentucky* for seasoning.

Once again steam filled the locker room as we tramped, scrubbed, and squeezed the stubborn foul-smelling elements of Jim's laundry down the drain. Danny and I marveled at the power of Jim's mammoth hands, kneading and wringing the laundry to a near-dry state. We repeated the laundry cycle again, then one last time, until Jim's laundry smelled as fresh as the blossoms on Mrs. Mikas' plum trees outside my bedroom window.

Finished and exhausted, we stretched out on the benches to let our laundry dry some while Jim told us about the young raccoon who shared his hillside address behind the foundry. Danny chuckled when Jim described how he had shared the last piece of Mom's best cherry pie with his new furry friend. I idly considered Jim's eligibility for membership in the FSG but dismissed the notion. How could anyone who dressed *that* flamboyantly ever work undercover?

After a few more minutes of chatter, we fell silent, lying on our backs, hands behind our heads on the cool marble bench. I lazily examined the pointy bumps of ceiling plaster and imagined them to be teeth inside a dragon's mouth. Soon, I heard deep breathing on either side of me. Both Danny and Jim had dozed off. I smiled inside and allowed myself to drift away.

"WAKE UP, BOYS!" JIM urged gently. "Put your clothes on and follow me."

He was fully dressed. But his all-weather uniform, still dripping now and then, hung heavily from his tall frame. His scarf, not at all debonair, sagged lifelessly. While he moved about the locker room gathering his laundry, basket, brush, and soap, his sodden oxfords sang a different tune. *Scufflety clap* had been replaced by *slush-a-clump*. *Slush-a-clump*.

Still dopey from our nap, we shivered into our cold, wet uniforms without complaint. Then we gathered the last of our belongings and swept the locker room thoroughly removing any sign of our being there. Danny and I each picked up one of Jim's blankets and followed him up the stairs, out the big brass door, and into the warm afternoon sun.

Burdened by heavy, damp attire, we slowly sloshed west on Liberty Street leaving wet footprints to dry on the hot sidewalk behind us. We turned onto the railroad siding that ran along the foundry's west wall and on toward Jim's "house." The loud blowers from the foundry roof made it difficult to hear, but Jim yelled that he would go ahead with the basket, soap, and scrub brush. We were to wait for him by the retaining wall.

DURING THE EARLY PART of the century, there was no railroad siding next to the foundry. Pig iron ingots, casting dies, refractory materials, and other supplies were hauled in by horse and wagon. Later, they arrived on motor trucks. Finished cast metal products left the same way.

For years, the ground where the siding now lay had been used to dispose of tons of slag and clinkers, discarded refractory, and broken castings. After the war started, when the railroad track was laid, no effort was made to remove the slagheap. It was just leveled and used as the track bed.

The bed's elevation was a good ten feet higher than the main floor of the foundry. In fact, it was almost level with the foundry's flat roof. To prevent the slagheap from sliding toward the foundry wall under the weight of a heavy train engine, a parallel retaining wall had been erected between the foundry and the tracks. Three brick support walls, stretching between the retaining wall and the foundry wall itself, created perfect catwalks to the roof where numerous huge blowers were installed to remove furnace and room heat from the foundry below. The scorching output from the robust blowers scrubbed the roof vigorously with superheated air.

While we waited, the unique foundry smell, a combination of burning coal gas, molten metal, and cooling slag, enveloped us. I remembered Mom's story about her father.

During the Depression, Grandpa Compton held a good job supervising the castings crew inside this very building. But his good fortune didn't last long. Grandpa had carelessly inspected the molten product of one of the huge furnaces without first donning his safety goggles. At that very moment, following the prescribed routine, one of the men shook down the furnace, splashing Grandpa's unprotected face with white hot metal.

Doctors struggled for months to save his vision. Unfortunately, he lost one eye and the other was severely damaged. "The medical expenses wiped out the family savings and nearly put us on welfare," Mom lamented. "But Grandpa was a good farmer, and he didn't need both eyes to succeed. So back to the farm he went!"

By the way, Mom was right again. Grandpa was indeed a very good farmer!

WHEN JIM RETURNED, WE scooped up the blankets and tiptoed across the nearest catwalk onto the foundry roof. When we reached the asphalt and pea gravel roof surface, the blistering blast of air hit us, nearly sending us over the edge. Danny snatched off his hat and corporal insignia and stuffed them deep into his shorts pocket.

Danny and I, hunched over against the wind, held hands as best we could, and inched along behind Jim who headed toward a cluster of four giant fan housings that provided a perfect spot to wedge ourselves in. Jim gave us our instructions by gesturing and nodding. His words were lost in the storm of wind and heat. We spread out the flapping blankets and sat down firmly on top of them to protect our bottoms from the hot roof.

Jim, his black curls and white scarf whipping dramatically about his face, coached us by pulling his shirttails from his trousers, untying his shoes, and otherwise exposing as many damp surfaces to the fiercely blowing heat as possible. Within minutes, I felt my face redden, my lips chap, and my nostrils crack in the intense dry heat. My shoes stiffened. I feared they too would crack when I tried to walk. Jim closed his eyes and seemed to enjoy the loud roar of our wind-whipped sauna.

My mind drifted to thoughts of Mom's laundry process and how different hers was from the waterworks and foundry method.

THE CORNER OF OUR cellar under the kitchen was covered with an appliqué of mortar and sand left over from laying the cellar wall and house foundation. This coarse, uneven ten-foot square of "floor" became Mom's laundry room. With relish, she equipped this corner with a squatty wooden bench, two huge wooden washtubs, and an ancient electric washer with an attached hand wringer. A rubber hose extending through a knothole in the sub-flooring under the kitchen sink was her water supply. Cold water only. The storm drain in the center of the cellar's dirt floor was her drain.

Every Monday, all through the year, she would lug heavy baskets stuffed with dirty laundry out the kitchen door, through the outside cellar doors, and down the steep stairs into her noisy and damp sweat shop. During her weekly laundry stint, Mom's only contact with the outside world was the squint of light entering through a pair of tiny casement windows just below ground level. Each week, she'd labor for hours using her primitive tools to process our laundry.

In winter, she hung the wash to dry on a makeshift cotton clothes-line zigzagging back and forth through large staples tacked to the floor joists overhead. The laundry took days to dry in the damp, cold cellar.

In summer, our laundry was freshened by the warm breezes that gently caressed the rows of sheets and shirts hanging from the clotheslines stretching between welded pipe frames anchored in concrete by Dad and Uncle Van just before he joined the Army and went off to the war. A breezy warm afternoon was sufficient to dry even the heaviest of articles.

Of course, once the laundry was dry, there was still the mending, sprinkling, ironing, and folding to be done. Laundry rarely consumed fewer than two full days of Mom's seven-day workweek.

THE IMAGE OF DAMP clothing waving gently in the warm sun in our backyard made me chuckle to myself. This foundry drying method might be faster, but I knew it was much harder on both our clothes and us. Now I understood why Gentleman Jim only did laundry once a year!

I glanced at Danny. His cheeks were flushed and eyes glassy as he cautiously maneuvered his army cap and insignia out of his pocket and carefully exposed them to the rigors of our first Sahara campaign.

Rommel, you old Desert Fox, you have nothing on this young Nazi hunter.

DANNY WAS THE FIRST to crack. **"Aaaawwwwwwwwwaaaaaaaak. Let's get outta here!"** he yowled.

Gentleman Jim was jolted awake by Danny's abrasive shriek that out-decibeled the roaring blowers. "Okay! Okay! Let's go," Jim mimed.

Cinching up our crinkly clothing, we arose cautiously, only to be blown violently across the roof, toward the retaining wall. We hugged Jim's flapping blankets desperately and skidded toward safety. As we tip-toed across the catwalk, our dry-baked clothing *crackled* and *snapped* with each cautious step.

When we reached the track bed, Jim took the lead. A well-worn path snaked off to the left leading us downward to his home, which was nestled against the hillside under a thick grove of swamp oaks. The hut itself jutted out from the hill like the entrance to a secret gold mine.

Danny soon let us know what he thought of it.

"Wow! This is nifty. Do you live here all the time? Where do you sleep? Isn't it cold in the winter? Can we see inside? Do you eat here, too? Where's the raccoon? How come it's so low? Who made this house?"

Jim was clearly flattered by Danny's interest, but he only chose to answer one question, "Sometimes when it's real cold, I drag my bedroll up to the foundry roof and spend the night there. Otherwise, I'm real cozy right here."

With that, Jim reached down and opened the front flap of his hut, revealing his amazing den. It resembled an oversized lower berth on a Pullman sleeping car. Because of his height, Jim couldn't stand up in his snug little home. He merely rolled in (uphill) each night and out (downhill) each morning. Because of his low ceiling, whatever business Jim conducted at home was done stretched out on the soft nest of his multilayered bed.

Despite its simplicity, the hut was an engineering marvel. After burrowing five or six feet into the hillside, Jim had laid a simple foundation of used cinder blocks. He filled the foundation with the resultant dirt to provide a level base for his bed.

Over the dirt, he spread a thick sheet of tar-covered canvas that he had carefully stripped from the roof of an abandoned Ann Arbor caboose that stood decaying at the edge of the rail yards not far away. Finally, he spread layer after layer of springy willow branches and leaves for his mattress.

Jim had framed the eight by ten foot structure with discarded timbers from scaffolding once used to wrestle huge ventilation blowers up to the foundry roof. Corrugated metal sheets from a dismantled foundry tool shack made excellent siding and roofing. From the caboose, Jim had also salvaged a compact kerosene cook stove that he installed in the back corner, under an eight-foot section of metal stove pipe that poked out of the roof and on up into the oaks. Jim had driven a dozen ten penny nails into the inside timbers to provide hooks for hanging an assortment of clothing, shoes, and burlap bags holding gifts of food, tin cans, and empty supper bottles – gone but not forgotten.

Before replacing his bedroll on the willowy mattress, Jim leaned in and extracted three bulging burlap bags from the corner next to the cook stove. The bags *clinked*, naughtily confessing their contents.

Then he shook the first blanket briskly to remove its foundry crinkle. He launched it deftly across his willow mattress. It landed perfectly, completely covering the rectangle that outlined his bed. He repeated this process with each blanket. Satisfied that his bed was properly set for his later return, he lowered the entrance door-wall and hooked the makeshift leather latch to hold it in place.

In a single motion, Jim tossed the burlap bags over one shoulder, turned to us, and asked, "You fellas want to go with me while I do my Saturday grocery shopping?"

We nodded our heads vigorously and stood up.

"On our way, we'll stop to see Bohunk Joe, okay?"

"Okay! Okay!" we replied in unison. I was sure that Danny didn't know Bohunk Joe, but I sure did.

NO ONE IN THE neighborhood knew Bohunk Joe's real name. We couldn't even agree on his nationality. His accent was strange and foreign even to those neighbors who had been born in Europe.

Some contended he was a gypsy. "Doesn't he sharpen knives, axes, and scythes better than the gypsies who visit our neighborhood in their horse-drawn store-and-house wagons each summer?" they'd say.

Others guessed he was Russian. Some said Armenian. No one really knew. And, respecting Joe's privacy to a fault, no one ever asked.

We didn't try to guess Joe's age either. We just knew that he looked old, craggy, and mean. His physiognomy didn't help.

His nose was long and hooked, bending downward toward an odd chin that protruded outward and upward to a sharp point. Drapes of wrinkled skin anchored to the bridge of his nose drooped downward over his high cheekbones. His beady black eyes peered at you from under those flaps like a weasel cornered in a pup tent. Joe only stood about five feet three and, soaking wet, couldn't have weighed more than a hundred and thirty pounds.

Part of his mystique could be attributed to his Old World fashions. He wore his dull gray stevedore's cap with puffy pleats, pulled down snugly over his bushy eyebrows. His charcoal-colored trousers were cut from coarse, prickly wool. Their high-riding waistline rose to the middle of Joe's bony chest. His pants legs – cut short, wide, and cuffless – fluttered loosely when he walked.

His black suspenders were two inches wide and very short, measuring less than a foot from his shoulders to his waistband. Under these, Joe wore a white collarless shirt of heavy, unbleached linen buttoned to the top. In cold weather, he donned a heavy, full-length woolen overcoat that was tailored like a cape and black as a winter night.

Under his flapping pants legs, you could see his dusty-colored boots were made of bulky leather with extra long shoelaces running from the tip of his toe to a point just below his knee. He wrapped the leftover laces around and around his boot tops.

Unlike Gentleman Jim, social interaction was not Bohunk Joe's forte. When he imbibed, which was a daily occurrence, he was invariably surly and argumentative. Liquor seemed to release a vicious bitterness in Joe, perhaps attributable to some unfortunate event in his life about which, naturally, none of us inquired.

Despite the pain that liquor apparently caused him, the effect was just the opposite on the neighbors. They accepted his drinking with a smile. There were two reasons for this apparent contradiction.

First, after Joe's initial drink, he completely lost his ability to communicate in English, which was barely comprehensible in the first place. So, if he did insult a neighbor, it was in a language no one could understand. People blissfully shrugged off his slurred insults. No harm. No foul.

Second, it didn't matter that Joe was foreign and mysterious. Or that he didn't handle his drinking so well. Our neighborhood was like the French Foreign Legion. You could have a secret past and act like a fool occasionally. But nobody said a thing as long as you did your job.

After all, Joe's job was that of neighborhood bum – a Grace of God position. Once Joe was assigned that role by the rest of us, there was little he could do to lose our esteem. Whether he liked it or not, Bohunk Joe had himself a lifetime appointment.

Joe differed from Gentleman Jim in one other important way. Joe was slightly more ambitious than Jim – and certainly more entrepreneurial. He worked hard for enough dimes and quarters to purchase his bottled suppers and other modest necessities at Pete's store.

He collected paper, rags, squashed tin cans, used kitchen fat, and countless other forms of sellable junk from neighborhood kitchens and garages. To us neighbors, Joe was the means to meet our patriotic duty to save, collect, and contribute our recyclables in an effort to assist our boys at the front while, at the same time, supporting Joe.

All things being equal, he made his collection rounds daily. When his two-wheel pushcart was full of sellable commodities, he would plod down New Albany Avenue to Addison Street, turn south, and head for a negotiating session – and visit – with his friend, Old Levy, who owned the Southside Junkyard.

Old Levy, a fellow European immigrant, and Joe would haggle for an hour or more, speaking a foreign language known only to the two of them. When their negotiations were completed, they would celebrate their deal with a drink.

From the beat-up metal file cabinet, next to his shabby desk, Old Levy would retrieve his bottle of peppermint schnapps and two cloudy wine glasses. The sight of the bottle would cause Joe's eyes to twinkle and his mouth to water profusely, making it impossible for him to speak clearly. After pouring each of them a dram, with deliberate ceremony, Old Levy would disburse Joe's modest proceeds from the sale.

Then the old friends would tip back their glasses and congratulate themselves secretly on winning yet another negotiating victory over the other. This familiar custom warmed Joe adequately as he trekked home, dropped off his pushcart, and headed to Pete's for his supper purchase.

Joe was also a clever trapper. Remarkably, he had staked out a short, but extremely productive, trap line along the innocuous stream that originated in the hills south of Riverton and wound northward past the canning factory and foundry until it found its way to the Chippewa River just upstream from the Ann Arbor Street Bridge.

However, when cold weather set in, he became lazy or perhaps lethargic from drink. So Joe shared the harvest in muskrat, weasel, and occasionally mink with Gentleman Jim who, when not similarly lethargic, would tend the trap line.

What a sight he was in the dead of winter, dressed formally in his trademark tuxedo and top hat, bending over that stream to pluck the furry harvest from Joe's traps. Gentleman Jim rationalized that evening attire was not inappropriate, because the entire trap line was situated well within Riverton's city limits.

"One must maintain a proper decorum when in town," he insisted.

Bohunk Joe's share of Jim's yield was all of the animal meat and one third of the cash proceeds from the sale of the pelts to Old Levy. Joe earned his share by furnishing and maintaining the steel traps and skinning the animals. Jim tended the trap line and hiked down to Southside Junkyard with pelts for Old Levy every day or two all winter. Jim didn't mind because, after enjoying a peppermint schnapps appetizer with Old Levy, he could look forward to his share of the cash paying for his supper at Pete's.

Regardless of the quantity or nature of the take, Joe added all the fresh meat to the gigantic stew pot that simmered day and night on his wood stove. People walking home from town along New Albany Avenue were greeted by enticing odors of garlic, onions, exotic spices, and wild game as they passed Joe's shack at the entrance to our neighborhood. It was a constant source of discussion and speculation.

"By the smell of it, I'd say that Joe caught a couple of mink today."

"Nah. That's definitely coon."

"Mebbe so. Mebbe so."

And so Joe's stew pot added positively to his reputation as one of two, darn good bums.

Bohunk Joe's residence was a tiny, one-room white clapboard shack that had been hastily constructed by the Ann Arbor Railroad. It had served as a temporary office and storeroom for the construction crews laying track for the sidings to the canning factory and the foundry. The location was ideal, halfway between the foundry and the canning factory right off New Albany Avenue.

Upon completion of the sidings, the shack was abandoned, so Joe moved in. He parked his pushcart along side the shack, hung his traps on hooks next to the door, and set up his foot-powered grindstone with a comfortable chair in the postage-stamp size front yard. He was in business!

Like the management of the foundry in Jim's case, the Ann Arbor Railroad found no particular reason to disturb Bohunk Joe's living arrangement. So there he stayed.

WE FOLLOWED THE FOUNDRY siding south toward New Albany Avenue. When we arrived at Bohunk Joe's shack, he was sitting in the chair beside his grinding wheel. His hat was pushed back and his beady eyes were a bit glassy. I noticed a brown paper sack on the ground beside his rickety chair. Undoubtedly he had started Saturday supper a little early.

When he saw us, he mumbled something that only Jim could discern.

Jim laughed, and then he introduced us, "Joe, you know Jase Addison. And this is Danny Tucker. Danny's family lives up on the corner of New Albany and Chester Street. They just moved in."

Joe nodded and mumbled again. This time I caught the words "shew mazzchine."

"That's right. Jase is John's boy," Jim responded, confirming Joe's garbled comment.

"E's nyshhe man," Joe declared with a rare smile.

Considering his current state of supper, I was impressed with Joe's warmness. I returned his smile and replied, "My father likes you too, Mr. Joe."

This was getting downright syrupy.

Jim rescued us, "Joe, I brought you some empty bottles and cans. Okay if I put 'em in your barrels?" Joe nodded agreeably.

While Jim emptied his contribution to the war effort into the temporary storage barrels behind the shack, Joe decided to kill a little time by taking a short nap.

When Jim returned, he asked, "Joe, could I borrow your pushcart for the grocery run? And I'll need a couple of your burlap bags as well." Joe opened one eye and responded with an approving wave of his hand.

As Jim wheeled the pushcart down the driveway toward the canning factory, Danny and I skipped along behind. With the understatement of the day, Danny observed, "Boy, sometimes Bohunk Joe's sure hard to understand!"

We crossed New Albany Avenue entering the long driveway that led to the canning factory staging yard. When we reached the yard, I looked up at the giant brick building with massive white letters that spelled out "CHIPPEWA CANNING" all the way across the factory's upper floor.

I loved this staging yard.

Soon the area's farmers would arrive in horse wagons, tractor-drawn trailers, and motor trucks loaded with a vast assortment of seasonal fruits and vegetables. The daily noise and activity of dozens of vehicles unloading thousands of bushel baskets and crates of produce was more than I could resist. All that enticing edible treasure stacked right here in this five-acre yard waiting to be processed into canned goods. This tempting bazaar began each June and lasted well into November.

In the fall, like the other boys from my neighborhood, I altered my daily route to and from Hamilton School to include the canning factory and its tempting choice of fresh pickings. The canning factory security guards didn't seem to mind our minor pilfering. In fact, they often colluded with us, tossing huge apples and peaches from the top crates that only they could reach by standing on the empty beds of produce trucks that were awaiting paperwork before returning to farms for another load.

What a blessing to live in a neighborhood that offered free samples of every fruit and vegetable imaginable, fresh from the fields.

Jim pushed on through the now-vacant yard and around the canning factory's west end until he reached the Ann Arbor railway siding. The tracks hugged the loading dock that stretched along the entire length of the building. He propelled the empty pushcart up the ramp onto the dock and rolled eastward.

Motorized conveyor belts and compact diesel tractors were used to move tons of canned produce within the building and out onto the loading dock through huge sliding doors. During the height of the season, employees worked around the clock moving the factory's output into a continuous succession of twenty-car trains.

The siding was now empty of cars, with one exception. A lone dingy freight car was parked permanently next to the far end of the loading dock. That car was obviously our destination. Jim entertained us with a jaunty variation of *My Old Kentucky Home* in time with the rhythm of rolling pushcart wheels *chirping* over expansion joints in the concrete surface of the dock.

When we reached the old freight car, I noticed an immense padlock hanging from hasps on its sliding door. The car was locked tight. Undeterred, Jim parked the pushcart in front of the padlock. He lowered the cart handle onto its rests and continued walking and whistling. At the end of the dock, he leaned over and reached behind the east wall of the building. Out came a metal ring containing a single key that had obviously been left there for him.

"Wow!" I cheered. "Can we open 'er up?"

Jim quickly unlocked the padlock and pushed the mighty door aside. Despite the age of the car, the door rolled effortlessly.

Inside we were confronted with a vast array of canned goods of various contents and sizes. There were gallon cans of tomato catsup for commercial buyers. Quart size cans of peaches for large families. Cans of pork and beans of the size we bought at Pete's. There must have been at least two hundred cases of canned goods stacked neatly inside the car.

Danny gasped and shouted, "Holy Toledo! There's enough food here to feed all the soldiers in the U.S. Army!"

Danny was prone to exaggeration, but I had to agree that we had just discovered enough canned food to keep many a family content for years. And, as I gazed at the luscious peaches depicted on labels of the first lot of cans, my stomach signaled that it must have been at least three weeks since that cheese and knockwurst had come its way. I hoped Jim would suggest that we sample this plunder – in a hurry!

As I inspected the lot, I noticed something else. Each can, regardless of size, was seriously dented in one place or another. The dented cans had failed inspection and were repacked in appropriate cardboard cartons spelling out the fruit or vegetable contained therein. Beans, pork and beans, peas, applesauce, crushed tomatoes, whole tomatoes, tomato catsup – the inventory went on and on.

Regaining my composure, I gasped at Jim, "These cans are all dented. Are they okay to eat?"

"The canning factory can't risk selling them because the contents might spoil eventually. So the company donates these cans to local charities – for immediate consumption," he explained.

Local charities like Gentleman Jim and Bohunk Joe! I thought to myself.

Jim went on, "I know a fellow who works in security here. He allows me to extract a few cans now and then for Bohunk Joe and myself. He doesn't see any harm, and we sure don't mind either. Just so people don't get the wrong idea, my pal likes me to come on Saturday. So Saturday is grocery day for Joe and me."

"Aha!" I replied.

"The only bad thing is that, if we get a hankering for pork and beans, we might have to eat up a gallon of 'em before we're finished. We can't waste any of it."

Danny and I nodded our understanding.

Jim selected a dozen or so cans that he carefully placed in the burlap bags. When he finished, he rolled the car door closed, locked the big padlock securely, and headed for the end of the dock to replace the key.

Danny and I stayed with the pushcart and watched Gentleman Jim reach around the end of the building. Just as he replaced the key, we heard a door slam loudly behind us!

"BAAAM!"

We nearly jumped out of our skin!

We turned to see an armed security guard walking toward us with an exaggerated limp. He was muscular and looked like he meant business. We froze. Then a smile spread across the guard's face. "Hey, Jim. I thought I heard you out here," he said in a friendly manner.

"Hi, Don! I was going to knock on the door to say hello before I left. How's it going?" Jim replied, like it was old home week.

Then he introduced us, "These are my partners in crime. That's Danny Tucker. His family just moved to the neighborhood. He lives over on New Albany. And do you know John Addison? This is his boy, Jase. These fellows helped me with my laundry earlier today."

"Boys, this is Mr. Paulus," Jim said, turning to us.

"Hello, boys! Yeah, I do know your Dad, Jase. I work with him out at Burkes. I work full time out there and part-time here. He's the world's best tool and die man for my money. And a terrific guy, too! According to my wife, he also works miracles with sewing machines. She thinks he's a genius."

I had never been presented with so much flattery concerning Dad. I was both proud and self-conscious. I stumbled over my words, trying to say just the right thing.

Before I could respond, Don looked up and said to Jim, "Hey, I just remembered. I set aside a case of those small cans of pork and beans for you. We got some new help in there reorganizing the retail storage area. They didn't mean to – but they knocked a couple of cases off the top of the stack this morning and dented 'em pretty bad. But they're still good. Come on in. I'll fetch 'em for you."

Don added, "Why don't you boys come too? You'll get a kick out of seeing the mountains of cans in the storage area."

"Okay! Great!" we chimed.

Don unlocked the door marked "Retail Storage #2." Danny entered first. I followed close on his heels. And Don and Jim followed behind us.

Before I was inside the door, Danny let out a whoop!

"**Nazis!!**" he yelled, turned, and ran smack into my chest.

Over Danny's waving arms and bobbing head, not more than twenty feet away, stood a dozen German soldiers, leaning against the huge storage racks of Chippewa canned goods. Just beyond them, in a folding metal chair, sat a tough-looking man with a submachine gun lying across his knees.

I gulped, turned with Danny, and ran back out the door.

3 TRADING WITH THE ENEMY

HOW EMBARRASSING!

"Geez, I'm sorry, Mr. Jim – Mr. Paulus," I moaned for the fifth time.

"Me, too. I just got scared," Danny repeated for his fifty-fifth time.

Fear is contagious. So, when Danny spooked, I spooked with him. What bothered me most was that my humiliating reaction was inconsistent with my experience and familiarity with German POWs and their armed keepers.

THE ARMY HAD ESTABLISHED a prisoner of war camp on the former Civilian Conservation Corps campgrounds just off highway M-31 about eight miles west of town. The camp had served as home to hundreds of CCC workers during the Depression. When the camp closed, its facilities were still relatively new. With a few shingles and a coat of paint, the camp was quickly converted into a prison stockade large enough to accommodate up to two thousand prisoners.

The Army called the site, "Camp Riverton." But no one in Riverton considered having a POW camp named after the town much of an honor. The year the camp opened, an alarming number of Riverton's young men returned home from North Africa and the Pacific with missing limbs or horrid burns, without their sight, or asleep in wooden caskets. This unanticipated consequence from the patriotic rush to enlist immediately following Pearl Harbor generated powerful feelings of hatred toward America's enemies – especially the Krauts and Japs – as everybody called them.

Measured against today's standards, America during the war was a hotbed of intolerance. These labels – and worse – were used without restraint by politicians of both parties, teachers, ministers, newspaper reporters, movie heroes, radio broadcasters, and the U.S. Government on propaganda posters prominently displayed on bulletin boards at the post office, in our factories, and at our schools.

Regardless of how we labeled America's enemies we knew for sure that we hated them. At that time, this emotion was a galvanizing force for good. But, in certain cases, community hatred was directed elsewhere.

Those Riverton families whose able young men did not immediately volunteer for military service, choosing instead to remain safely at home, provided another convenient "local enemy" on which to focus the revulsion and disgust of the community. "Draft dodger!" "Nazi Lover!" "Traitor!" These labels covered the situation. But the worst label of all was "Yellow Coward."

The president of the Riverton First National Bank in his role as chairman of the Chippewa County Draft Board committed an egregious sin in the eyes of our community. He intervened with the Board on behalf of his only son who worked in a meaningless job at the family bank.

The son was not so much a coward as he was a spoiled loafer. Nonetheless, he stayed at home, ostentatiously and smugly, enjoying the protection of his 4-F classification. The banker claimed his boy suffered from a rare nervous disorder. Cowardice by another name was the consensus of the town. Meanwhile the son's classmates and neighbors went off to the front line.

An infuriated community took its vengeance. During the months just before Camp Riverton opened, every last First National depositor closed his account and placed his banking business elsewhere. The bank was finished.

Adding insult to injury, the "Riverton Vigilante Committee" armed with paintbrushes and cans of yellow paint called on the banker at home late one night. In addition to the front porch and sidewalk, both the father and his "nervous" son were given a good coating of yellow, a color befitting the occasion. Fearful of further acts of vengeance, the father left town for good with his unfortunate son in tow. The banker's wife whose roots were in the community chose to renounce her husband's actions by staying behind to care for her aging mother.

This was the mood of the community when the first allotment of POWs arrived at the old CCC camp. The reception was far from friendly. Too many Gold Stars were hung in windows by mournful mothers, like Mrs. Mikas, for us to engender even a modicum of

Christian forgiveness, let alone civic hospitality, toward these unwanted Nazis in our midst.

We all wondered if we had the chance would we dare to ask them, "How many of our boys did you kill, Nazi?" "Are you at all sorry, war criminal?" "Do you think you'll go to heaven, killer of our sons?" "Don't you care about the destruction you caused?" "Why do you look so happy?" "Aren't you ashamed?"

Welcome to Riverton, Nazis!

But we were human, too. We couldn't control our curiosity – or maybe it was our morbid fascination – with the POWs. We were a paradoxical muddle of childlike inquisitiveness wrapped in simmering hatred.

When the first POW contingent arrived, the Addison family just had to see them. So Dad drove us out one Sunday afternoon. We stopped the car beside the road and stared at the thousand or so Germans a mere eighth of a mile away behind high chain link fences topped with barbed wire.

The Army engineers had clear-cut a two hundred yard swath around the perimeter of the camp to provide an open field of fire for the Army Military Police – the MPs – who manned the search lights and .50 caliber machine guns positioned atop the watch towers rising from the four corners of the compound.

We could see them clearly. The POWs stared back at us silently. It was an unsettling experience, as if we had intruded on something very private and sad, like the funeral of a family we didn't know. We didn't stay long. On the way home, none of us spoke.

After that first visit, I became obsessed with German POWs. I studied articles about them in the *Riverton Daily Press*. I listened when adults discussed the pros and cons of having Camp Riverton in our community. I watched intently when POWs traveled in the Army trucks on their way to work at local factories. I saw them working in fields near Grandpa Compton's farm. After the first year, I had seen POWs on dozens of occasions. Perhaps I hadn't been as close to them as this day at the canning factory, but I had observed them often. They fascinated me, so I learned everything I could about them.

For one thing, I knew that they all wore the same uniform – olive drab work pants, jacket, and billed cap – the uniform worn by American soldiers assigned to KP duty. There was a big difference though. Five-inch, block letters "PW" were stenciled in bold, white dye on both sides of each pant leg. And, on the front and back of their work jackets, the "PW" stood out the same way. You couldn't miss them, even at a great distance.

Ironically, I soon regretted having examined the POWs so closely because I discovered that POWs appeared quite ordinary and normal. They laughed and poked fun at each other. They were cheerful and even friendly. And it seemed that most of them were just young men, maybe even teenagers. Were these the monsters we were taught to hate by our newsreels, newspapers, and the radio? The more I learned about the POWs, the more confused I became.

However, one thing prevented me from forgetting that these men were the enemy – Nazi soldiers! Whenever I saw POWs, an Army MP guarded them with a .45 automatic on his belt and a tommy gun in the crook of his arm. Despite my increasing familiarity with our POW neighbors, this remained a serious business and these were serious times.

A few months after the arrival of the POWs, Camp Riverton officials offered the town an opportunity to use POWs for work in our factories and fields. Our community leaders were told that the Geneva Convention permitted prisoners of war to work, providing their employers did not manufacture war materials and the POWs were compensated for their work.

Surprisingly, our community leaders embraced the idea. The *Riverton Daily Press* ran enticing articles encouraging POW utilization. The camp's commanding officer, Colonel Butler, gave his sales pitch to responsive audiences at the Riverton City Council and at the Rotary and Kiwanis Clubs. The colonel even scored well at the Chippewa Grange Hall before a full house of interested, but wary, Farm Bureau members.

If anything, people of our community were pragmatic. Farm and factory workers were as scarce as hen's teeth at the height of the war. Many people worked two or more jobs during that time. So, eventually, all local businessmen and farmers concluded that, rather than leave crops unharvested in fields or production lines sitting idle on off-shifts, they would accept the alternative of inexpensive and reliable POW labor.

The Chippewa Canning Corporation employed a number of POW workers year round. But their numbers increased dramatically at fruit and vegetable harvest time.

Prisoners also worked on the nearby farms. Trucks from Camp Riverton made rounds dropping off and picking up work crews and their guards every morning and afternoon. Even Grandpa Compton had had a couple of German prisoners working for him the previous spring.

Years later, I would learn that, during World War II, the Allies captured more than three million prisoners of war. Of these, over 372,000 German POWs were held in small camps like Camp Riverton all over America, especially in those states located far from our coastlines.

But I am still convinced that none of those camps contained POWs quite like Riverton's own POWs.

DESPITE OUR BOTCHED INITIAL attempt, we were given another chance. As we entered Retail Storage #2, Danny stared sheepishly at his stiff, foundry-baked leggings. I was greatly relieved when I saw the POWs and the U.S. Army MP sergeant smiling at us. I had thought they might be angry.

The MP broke the ice by reassuring us, "That's okay, boys. These here Krauts are definitely frightening when you first see 'em up close. Yep. A real ugly bunch. But they won't bite. In fact, they're altogether, okay. Ain't that right, Otto?"

One of the POWs took a half step forward and confirmed with a grin, "Ya, dats right, Sahgen Prella." Otto looked at us, "Comb here, boyz! Da *Nazis* cahn now youse meetz!"

He came forward to welcome us.

Danny's eyes grew as big as saucers and his left leg trembled. I wasn't in much better shape. But I vowed not to embarrass myself a second time. I thought about emitting a little *Double Eagle* for courage, but I feared my gesture might be misunderstood. I ruled out *Kentucky*, too.

Don Paulus did the honors, "This is Sergeant Rick Prella and Otto Klump, the POW crew leader. Otto lived in Milwaukee for some years when he was a kid, so his English's pretty good. A lot better than my German, anyhow!"

Don, Sergeant Rick, and Otto laughed at what was obviously a standing joke among them.

Then Don introduced the three of us to Sergeant Rick and Otto, giving a bit of detail on what brought us there that afternoon, including a barb about the new members of the crew who had caused the pork and beans to be added to our shopping cart. Don then turned to Otto and nodded.

Otto repeated the introductions to his crew in German, adding dramatic inflections, wild gestures, and warm laughter. The crew responded boisterously, pointing to the two clumsy can denters, bowing to us, and smiling at each other amidst a din of rapid-fire German that was completely unintelligible to me. They certainly appeared to be a cheerful gang. Didn't they know they were supposed to be a bunch of dirty, low-down Nazi dogs?

"We were about to have supper – or maybe it's a late dinner. Anyhow, we got plenty. Why don't you join us?" Don suggested to Jim.

Jim nodded enthusiastically, turning to Danny and me for approval. We nodded, too. We were starved!

Don added, "The cafeteria isn't open on weekends, but I use the facilities to serve up Chippewa Canning's finest *can a la dent*. Let's see, this weekend's menu includes tomato soup with crackers from the cafeteria pantry, pork and beans, peas, and peaches – or is it black cherries – for dessert. Whatta ya say we head for the cafeteria?"

Don took the lead. I again noticed his awkward gait.

Jim, sensing my interest, laid his hand on our shoulders to slow us down. Once Don was well ahead of us, Jim explained, "Don picked up that limp in North Africa. His patrol stumbled on a sizeable nest of Rommel's troops. They fought all night – it got down to hand-to-hand combat. When the sun came up, Don discovered that he was the only survivor. He'd been badly wounded, and his radio'd been shot up."

Danny and I stared at each other.

Jim continued, "Friendly bedouins stumbled across him and helped him get back to the English lines. He'd been out there on the desert for nearly three days – without a drop of water. He spent several weeks in the hospital recuperating. He was lucky to have made it at all, let alone save that leg. He was awarded the Silver Star for his bravery. But you'll never get him to admit it."

"How can he stand working around all these Germans?" Danny asked.

Jim thought a minute, and then he responded, "Some people are able to let go of things. And others can't."

Jim's answer made me wonder if he were still talking about Don.

Don was right. The mountains of cartons that loomed high above us on either side of our route to the cafeteria were remarkable. "It's like walking through the Grand Canyon," I observed.

It was hard to believe that our neighborhood canning factory could produce such a quantity and variety of foodstuffs. And we had only seen a fraction of what was stored in the factory warehouse.

When we reached the cafeteria, we separated. The POWs including Otto waited in a group for us to finish serving ourselves using the soup bowls, silverware, and metal trays stacked at the head of Don's makeshift serving line.

As soon as all the Americans were seated and had begun to eat, Otto nodded and the Germans formed an orderly line. It moved slowly as each man served himself huge portions of the hot food. Then the POWs seated themselves at a row of cafeteria tables on the other side of the large dining room.

The room hummed as we hungry diners helped ourselves to serving after serving until we were stuffed. Some of us were stuck to our seats, immobilized by too much good food.

But not the Germans. They busily cleared our table, rinsed all the dishes and silverware in the immense sinks, scrubbed the cooking pots, and deposited everything in the huge dishwashing machine. Finally they mopped down the stainless steel floor erasing all evidence of our "dented contraband" banquet. While they worked, their boisterous banter continued, punctuated by loud outbursts of raucous laughter.

As we left the cafeteria for the loading dock, Sergeant Rick explained why the POWs were in such high spirits.

"Most of the prisoners at Camp Riverton were captured in North Africa or in Italy," he told us. "There are a few like Otto. He's an aviator – shot down over England. In any case they ended up as our POWs. Unless us Americans captured them or took custody of them right away, they were in for a rough time. So they wanted to be captured by Americans.

"That's cuz our Allies took a beating from German bombs and artillery shells dropping on them – killing their wives and kids. They suffered terrible – and personal. They don't like these Nazi buggers one bit. And ya can't blame 'em. No sir-ee-bob!"

Sergeant Rick paused to gather his thoughts. Then he continued, "Yep. These guys believed Hitler's propaganda about how bad we had it over here. Then they got here and saw our houses – all our cars – and our good farms and factories. That really knocked 'em for a loop. They now know that the average German family under the Nazis has never lived half as good as even the real poor families here in the U.S. of A. Yep. The families of these POWs are really catching hell right now back in Germany. Bless their little Nazi hearts."

He went on, "Yep. These POWs got it made. Nice comfortable U.S. Army cots in warm, dry cabins. Three hot meals a day – as much as they want to eat. Yep. Three hots and a flop – everyday, guaranteed. Lot better than I had it in boot camp for cripes sake. And you know what? Cuz of rationing, that POW camp store of theirs gotta lot a stuff you can't even buy downtown in Riverton. Yep. These guys are doing a whale of lot better than their buddies in the Wehrmach hightailing it out of Italy right now."

We knew he meant the German Army.

"Yep," Sergeant Rick finished. "They got it good. And they know it. But, to be honest, it sure makes my job a lot easier."

When we returned to Retail Storage #2, Sergeant Rick gave Otto and his crew a smoke break. In unison, the POWs moved out to the loading dock, leaned against the massive sliding doors, and instantly produced a variety of smoking materials and equipment including an odd assortment of pipes, small black cigars, and cigarettes, hand rolled from pipe tobacco and cigarette paper purchased at the POW camp store.

But Otto didn't smoke. Instead, he reached into his work jacket pocket and produced a precious commodity that Danny and I had seldom experienced since the war began.

Our eyes bugged out when we saw him unwrap this rarity and pop it into his mouth. We gawked longingly as Otto chewed with great concentration. Then he stopped, screwed his cheeks around, and blew a huge bubble that immediately burst – *Fllap!* – leaving pink residue from his nose to his chin. Then he repeated the process. *Flllapp!* A bigger bubble this time.

I remembered my last piece of bubble gum.

How I had regretted having to remove it from my mouth each night and stick it on the headboard of my bed. After a week, my once-pink tidbit had become disgustingly gray. Undeterred, I chomped away on that stiff chunk for another five days. One morning, I awoke and decided to have my usual morning chew. With some difficulty, I pried the hunk loose and popped it into my mouth.

As I chewed doggedly, I realized that my wad was surprisingly crunchy. I removed it from my mouth to find that I had been attempting to pulverize several sizeable paint chips. These thick chips displayed layers of white, blue, brown, and orange, all the colors of my headboard over the course of its existence.

That morning, I buried my gray blob in a humble garbage pit of its own. Since then, I had hounded Pete relentlessly, pestering him to tell me exactly when I might experience my next rendezvous with ecstasy.

Otto caught us staring at him. Without hesitation, he reached into his pocket again and proffered two tempting packages. Danny looked at me and asked, "Should we?"

I rendered my opinion immediately. "Why not?" I asserted, reaching for Otto's outstretched palm – and chewing bliss.

Our triad of bubble blowers leaned nonchalantly against the sliding door, vying with each other to produce the most dramatic pink sphere. Otto was good, obviously attributable to countless hours of recent practice. Danny and I were rusty. We *fllipped* while Otto outgunned us with *flllapp* after *fllapp*.

After chewing and popping for a while, Otto inquired innocently, "You like da booblegums, ya? Da grouchery store how much dish cost?"

I patiently explained to Otto that bubble gum was strictly rationed. That's because bubble gum contains a very hush-hush ingredient, critical in manufacturing a secret weapon that would end the war by fall.

Danny piped in. He told Otto that we had learned all this one Saturday morning when Hoover J. Edgar, the head of our FBI, had the two of us over for coffee with him and his G-men at the FBI mansion in Washington, D.C.

We embellished – just a bit. But I saw no reason to reveal Top Secret military intelligence concerning critical shortages of strategic materials to some German, even if he had just bestowed one of life's greatest pleasures on us.

War is war!

At first, our clever explanation fooled the gullible German. Otto only nodded and blew another bubble. Then he threw us a curve, "Dats probably vhy dee U.S. Army keeps all da booblegums locks up out at Camp Rivertahn. So zay cahn vatch zem all da time."

Danny and I took our turns nodding our agreement and chewing while we pondered this Nazi's inscrutable logic. But the more I thought about it, I realized Otto had just scored a point.

I was just contemplating my next verbal masterpiece, when friend Danny blurted out, "Hey, Otto, can you get more of this bubble gum for us?"

So much for subtlety!

Otto thought long and hard, scratching his chin and looking at the clouds. Finally, he countered with a need of his own, "Duz dat Pete sales der sauerkraut? Vee hass no sauerkrauts att Camp Rivertahn. Nicht gut – not good – for Chermans, no sauerkrauts."

Does Pete *sell* sauerkraut? Are you kidding? Nobody *sells* sauerkraut. I had never seen a can, jar, or bottle of sauerkraut in any store in Riverton. You didn't buy sauerkraut. You made it out of cabbages from your garden.

That was true for every family in Michigan, except the John Addisons of Forrest Street. Nobody at my house, including yours truly, could stand that soggy stinking substance. But we didn't reveal this intimate family secret to anyone, especially Aunt Maude or Grandma Compton. Unsuspectingly, each of them routinely presented us with a dozen quarts of the smelly curse every fall. Ugh!

My mother could not bring herself to say, "No thanks." Nor would she let me bury it in the alley, which I had suggested on several occasions. She wouldn't even agree to allow me to give a jar to our Nazi-loving neighbor, the dreaded Hans Zeyer.

I laughed to myself when I thought of old Hans and sauerkraut. I wondered how Grandma Compton's powerful kraut would mix with mayonnaise, peanut butter, and Mrs. Zeyer's bread-and-butter pickles.

Kaboooom!!! That's how.

I suddenly envisioned the *Riverton Daily Press* front-page headlines –

> ## OATMEAL COOKIE-LOVING GERMAN SHEPHERD DIES OF MYSTERIOUS POISON GAS
> **Neighbors Suspect Rare Riverton Earthquake At Bottom of Mystery**

I refocused on business.

Because of Mom's inexplicable guilt, our family currently possessed an inventory of about a hundred quart jars of, what now appeared to be, a very valuable trading commodity – just sitting there, gathering dust, in our cellar.

My head was spinning with the possibilities. Nonchalantly, I threw my best verbal punch at Otto's fragile chin, "How many pieces of bubble gum will you offer me for a quart of sauerkraut?"

Otto's eyes lit up. He licked his lips. And I knew –

The old kraut-loving sucker was hooked!

DANNY AND I WATCHED the twin dust tails kick up behind the pushcart wheels as Jim rolled his load of burlap-wrapped dented groceries across the empty staging yard and back to Bohunk Joe's house. When the last strains of *Kentucky* had faded in the distance, Danny announced, "I gotta get home for supper."

We headed west for Forrest Street despite the fact that it was situated about a half-mile to the east. "Let's check out the dump on the way home," Danny suggested.

My kind of guy!

Over dinner with the Nazis, for those fortunate enough to be at my table, I had conducted a spellbinding tutoring session on the finer points of effective dump browsing. Being a quick study, Danny learned that Saturday was a popular dumping day, so pickings were generally good.

We got into a rhythm, matching our stride to the spacing of the railroad ties, as we followed the canning factory siding to the main east-west right of way for the Ann Arbor and Grand Trunk railroads. At that junction, we reversed course and goose-stepped in time to a scintillating version of *I've Been Workin' on the Railroad,* making our way eastward toward our moldering objective.

In preparing to be a qualified dump lecturer, I had immersed myself in my subject. To the chagrin of my laundry-loving Mom, on occasion, my immersion was quite literal.

TECHNICALLY, THE GRAND TRUNK Railroad owned the Riverton City Dump. The hundred acres of low-lying swampland, stretching for nearly a mile along the south side of the tracks, had been virtually worthless unless you counted the annual production of a few dozen muskrat pelts and forty-two billion mosquitoes.

Then one day, the railroad offered to partner with the town by leasing this tract of land to meet the urgent need for a community dumping place. It was a marriage made in dump heaven. The forty-year lease called for Grand Trunk to build an elevated, two-lane access road along the north boundary of the swampy strip and next to the tracks. The new road ran west from Trumbull Street to a turnaround at the east end of the dump.

Dumpers entered and drove until they found the first open space, off to the right, to unload their cargoes. Out of courtesy to others, Riverton citizens carefully used all the available space at the west end before moving eastward.

The entrance end filled first, usually by the end of spring. By fall, cars and trucks had to drive nearly to the turnaround to unload garbage, trash, lawn and shrub clippings, leftover building materials, and assorted treasures for habitual dump combers like Danny and me. By late fall, the frozen ground allowed the massive railroad bulldozer to push the huge piles of compacted refuse into the swamp as far away from the access road as the hungry swamp's appetite for fill would allow. Thus the next year's dumping space was created.

I had pointed out to my eager dumpology students that the disciplined and progressive nature by which the dump filled was a blessing to us refuse aficionados. This practice allowed me to focus my search on the most recent dumpings while ignoring previously pawed piles. I filled my lecture with dazzling examples of alliteration to mesmerize my audience. And I could tell they were mesmerized by that distant, glassy look in their eyes.

Most of the school year, I walked to and from Hamilton School by way of the dump. My mother never cared much for this choice of routes. Upon my return home I seldom smelled like *Evening in Paris,* if you catch my drift. I explained that you never knew what quality junk some careless person might dispose of there. She didn't want me to miss an opportunity to strike it rich, did she?

DESPITE THE LATENESS OF the day, a dozen or more cars with trailers and pickup trucks were in the process of depositing potential prizes at our hunting grounds. Although we were well inside the dump and could have dropped down to easy walking on the access road, we chose to continue goose-stepping from tie to tie, imitating the marching style of our newly acquired Nazi trading partners.

Feeling expansive, I suggested we honor our soon-to-be kraut-stuffed associates by setting our Nazi march to music. Danny's response was positive, so I cleverly synchronized my rendition of the German *alma mater* with our gait. Danny joined me with gusto. Regrettably, we didn't know many of the lyrics, and none of the tune, but we managed to approximate the spirit of the piece.

"Dutch land goober olives! YA BOLT! Dutch land goober olives! YA BOLT! Dutch land goo -" (You get the idea.)

Repeating this masterful composition, we marched along enthusiastically and noisily until we became bored, about forty feet later. So we stopped the parade, hopped off the tracks, and made for the nuggets awaiting us in the freshly dumped garbage and trash.

Proving himself a good student, Danny found a superb sorting implement with which to manipulate the smelly stacks. He used the hook-handle end of an ancient twisted umbrella for turning and spreading discarded clutter. I selected a splintered two-by-four with three rusty spikes protruding from one end as my prospecting tool.

The area of unsorted dumpings was about the size of our Forrest Street lot. A painstaking search by an expert, accompanied by one intern, would take a mere sixty minutes, tops. So we dug in.

We labored silently, thoroughly pulling, kicking, turning, and sorting our way through revolting mounds of potential profit. I knew the boundary between old and new dumpings, so I took the western flank as our two-man patrol launched its search and rescue operation. Our work was occasionally interrupted by the discovery of an unexploded hand grenade (unbroken bottle or jar) that we skillfully lobbed at a lethal Jap machine gun nest (old cement block) wiping out every enemy soldier lying in ambush.

Danny claimed to have unearthed a number of nuggets before I raised his standards to mine. For example, I didn't relish having to wheel home a flimsy, badly bent baby carriage with no top and only one wobbly wheel. Danny protested stubbornly, claiming his father to be a master mechanic with graduate credits in restorative sciences, or something along those lines. I wouldn't budge.

Danny didn't surrender without a fight. He called my patriotism into question. Had I forgotten the war and the critical need for metals? How could we abandon our boys in the Pacific? After a rousing debate, he finally agreed that, as recycled metal, the chintzy frame would probably melt down to less than half a .30 caliber bullet casing. I cinched the argument by asserting that John Wayne's flawless marksmanship alone easily compensated for at least five thousand crummy baby buggies.

Forrest Street debating protocol dictated that when I invoked the name of John Wayne to support my side of the argument, it meant only one thing. End of debate. Jase and The Duke win! Thus, with no further argument, Danny abandoned the paltry pram and continued his search.

Predictably, your old dump maven was the first to strike gold.

There we were, four seconds left in the 1944 Rose Bowl game. The scored was tied. University of Michigan 144. Nazi State College 144. We had one last chance to win by a field goal. I, Jase Addison, would boot one of my world famous dropkicks through Nazi State's uprights. A mere seventy-five yard boot – with only a teensy gale-force wind blowing in my face. Nothing to worry about! Another world record? Sure! Why not? Ho hum.

About to launch my pigskin missile, I suddenly realized that my football rattled. I opened the cylindrical Quaker Oats container to discover four valuable marbles inside! Two tiger's eyes. A puree. And a solid blue boulder. I leaped in the air and yelled, "Bingo!"

Danny ran to my side, his eyes wild with excitement, "What is it? Oh, wow! You lucky guy! OOOOOooo! I wanta find some, too. I gotta. I gotta."

Novice dumpsters often lose their composure in the presence of dump-picking greatness.

Pocketing my find, I intensified my search to cover up my glee. I didn't want "the help" to see me gloating. Not a good example.

Within an hour, we had reached the end of our search zone. Just then, the west wind freshened, lofting the collective odor of the year's decomposing and smoldering deposits toward us. There it was, my favorite fragrance. I tried to capture its essence in my mind – a plucky smoked pig manure with subtle undertones of putrid peapod silage. Ah, ecstasy!

When we returned to the access road, we inventoried our booty.

✓ Four marbles.

✓ One pearl-handled jackknife. (Regrettably, no blades.)

✓ A valuable wad of tangled fish line with three rusty hooks and six sinkers. (Some salvage work required here.)

✓ Three mint-condition Prince Albert tobacco tins in magnificent Chinese red and black. (Perfect for burying gold in the woods.)

✓ An official business letter to Burkes from Riverton Power Company. (Still in the envelope.)

✓ A tattered colored poster imploring factory workers to work flawlessly to "Crack the Back" of our Axis foes. (The real prizewinner of the day!)

Not a bad take for boy Danny's first day on the job.

As the sun sank in the west, we headed toward Forrest Street, for real this time. I showed Danny the way. We hiked across the access road, over the tracks, along the path skirting the canning factory, and then down Milford Street, which dropped us on New Albany Avenue just west of Pete's.

As we walked by the store, we heard a familiar voice, "Hey, boys! Wait for me." Dad came up behind us carrying a small sack of groceries.

New Albany was busier than usual, so we waited for the traffic to clear. Out of habit, Danny stuck his hand in Dad's as we crossed. When we reached the other side, they continued to walk that way, hand in hand, as any father and son might. I skipped along behind carrying the dump loot.

After a half block, Dad asked, "What were you boys up to today?"

We answered simultaneously, "Oh, nothing."

If he only knew!

"GUESS WHAT NIGHT THIS is!" Mom reminded us.

"Oh, noooooo!" I groaned, demonstrating my commitment to the Boys' Anti-Cleanliness Movement.

Besides, I had only exposed myself to one short dump visit since my thorough cleansing in the public water supply. I was close to perfectly pure.

"Oh, yes!" she said, ignoring my protestations while giving me a warm hug.

"Whew! You've been playing at the dump again. Better head for that tub!"

My mom had the best nose in Chippewa County. I couldn't smell a thing.

Actually, my resistance to bathing was more ceremonial than real. In truth, I enjoyed this weekly family event.

Two giant teakettles atop the kitchen stove produced the hot water needed to perform our steamy Saturday night ritual. A teakettle of boiling hot water added to an equal measure of Riverton's finest cold water created a bath to please a king. Using two teakettles enabled us to lessen the heating time required between baths.

Despite being the family bathtub dawdler, using the bar of soap to depth charge Nazi U-Boats instead of washing behind my ears, I was always first to bathe. After I was pried from the tub, Dad came second. And Mom was last.

During my sudsy stint, Mom refilled my empty teakettle and placed it on the stove to heat for her bath. After I was wrapped in towels and whisked to my bedroom for a rubdown by Mom, Dad would inspect the condition of my bathwater. If it were too cold or badly discolored by neighborhood muck, he would pull the drain plug and start over.

If, by some miracle, my bath water was relatively unpolluted, he would add his teakettle of boiling water to mine and enjoy a more voluminous soak. When he was finished, he refilled his teakettle to allow Mom the luxury of a two-kettle bath that we Addison men knew she deserved.

For me, Saturday baths were wonderful. Who wouldn't enjoy sinking Hitler's submarine wolf packs? Or launching a surprise amphibious landing on Tokyo beach? Or dropping a two-ton bomb down the smokestack of Mussolini's presidential yacht while it lay unsuspectingly at anchor in Rome harbor?

But what I really liked about our Saturday nights was the opportunity to spend time alone, first with Mom and then with Dad, while the other bathed. This peaceful interlude with Mom, and sometimes with

Dad, invariably turned into story time initiated by brainy questions from yours truly.

After my towel rubdown, I would pull on my pajamas, hop into bed, and snuggle down into my covers. After Mom tucked me in, she would sit down on my bed. Then I would hit her with one of the intellectual blockbusters that I had been saving all week. For example, "Is eating paint chips bad for you?" Or "How come strawberries grow above ground and radishes grow below ground – and they're both red?" Or "Do fish ever sneeze?"

When Dad finished his bath, he would relieve Mom in my bedroom for a story of his own or a review of some interesting aspect of the universe as it circled around Riverton. While Mom bathed, he would answer another of my brilliant questions, designed to delay lights-out for as long as possible. Finally, my stalling tactics stopped working. And Dad would give me a last tuck. Then, on cue, I would perform my ever-inspiring rendition of "Now, I lay me down to sleep."

When Dad turned off my lights, he never failed to say, "See you in the morning, bye." And so goodnight!

Apparently, owing to some lingering unpleasant evidence of dump scavenging, Dad had chosen to reject my bath water this evening. He lowered himself into his fresh, hot bath with a deep sigh indicating that my time with Mom tonight would be deliciously prolonged.

I snuggled in and waited for her to be comfortably seated at the foot of my bed. I was about to amaze her with this Saturday night's question when she beat me to the punch.

"Jase, I want to talk to you about something that I heard this afternoon. Your father doesn't know about this, and I would just as soon keep it between you and me," she stated in her most serious voice.

Oh, oh! Now what? I thought. But I responded innocently, "Okay."

Mom nodded and continued, "Sherman Tolna was missing almost all day. His mother was hysterical. She came here to ask me to help search for him after he failed to return home for supper."

Ye gads! I had completely forgotten about the snotty bunny-mole who, when last seen, had just penetrated the Zeyer lair!

"We went door-to-door all through the neighborhood. Mrs. Reilly told us that she'd seen Sherman pulling his red wagon with you and another boy – Danny, I presume – down by the cottonwood tree earlier in the day."

"What happened? Did he come home?" I was dying of curiosity by now. Besides, I wanted to draw Mom's attention away from my incriminating association with the lost bunny boy.

"Well, yes. He did – about an hour ago – just before you came home with Dad. But it was under very strange circumstances. It seems that just after Mrs.Tolna and I called on her, Mrs. Zeyer heard a snoring noise coming from her living room closet. When she opened the door, she found Sherman dressed in his pajamas, lying sound asleep on the closet floor. He was hugging that little *lammy* doll of his and one of Mr. Zeyer's puppets from Germany."

Aha! I'll bet that puppet is full of spy stuff. Sherm the worm probably discovered it just before they gassed him, I speculated to myself. I was about to stun Mom with this gem of military intelligence when she hit me with one of her world-class gotcha questions.

"Jase, do you have any idea how Sherman happened to be in the Zeyer closet?" She looked me dead in the eye.

She's good. She's very good. She could be a licensed interrogator and work in Washington with J. Herbert Hoover at the FBI! All she needs is a short length of rubber hose to extract the real tough answers, I thought.

When the chips are down, good old Mom habitually asked a *closed* question. I had learned the hard way that at times like this she expects, and will demand, either a "Yes" or a "No" answer. She won't settle for a "Maybe" or let me launch one of my clever verbal ploys to trick her like I tricked gullible Otto on the subject of bubble gum secret ingredients.

This was all very unfair. I was presented with the horrible choice of breaking my word to my fellow FSG members – or lying to Mom. I had taken a vow of secrecy on the Zeyer undercover operation. Right? So to tell Mom the truth would be ratting on my comrades-in-arms. And that could be serious. This was wartime!

If I remained loyal to my vow and fibbed, I was still in deep trouble. Mom always knew *everything* that happened in Riverton, especially in our neighborhood. So she would find out if I lied. Besides, I had never succeeded in lying to Mom. I had tried a few times, and I ended up confessing. What is it about confession, guilt, and mothers?

There was only one solution. I didn't lie, but I didn't tell the whole truth either. Using my considerable intellect, I came up with the following brilliant defense.

"Sherman told us he liked Mr. Zeyer's puppets. Sherman put on his pajamas. He gave Danny and me his wagon. We took it for a ride," I affirmed, nodding my head with authority to indicate that I had finished my closing argument.

There! That'll hold her, I thought smugly.

Just in case, I jammed my hands under the covers, crossed my fingers, and prayed like mad for the interrogation to be over. I sure didn't want to blow Operation Mole, or worse, to be seen by my fellow Forrest Street Guards as a sniveling snitch.

Then Mom surprised me with a move that let me off the hook. She said, "Jase, I don't know where you got the idea that Mr. Zeyer is anything but a loyal American. I assure you that you are quite wrong about him. Your father would be mortified. I am sure he considers Hans a good neighbor and friend. For those reasons, I certainly hope we don't have this kind of a conversation again."

"Me neither, Mom," I vowed truthfully. But I admit I was still thinking, "What kind of conversation *was* this?"

Although I was *very* relieved to see the trial come to an end, I was still confused by Mom's certainty of Hans Zeyer's patriotism. In my heart, I knew there was plenty of damaging evidence against the old Hun. Such as, what's he doing late at night hanging around with guys who speak German, drive black Packards without license plates, and tote submachine guns?

But, wisely, I kept my skepticism to myself. I needed to buy time for Sherman's debriefing and to confer with Danny on the next step in our investigation, after telling him about the dopey behavior of FSG's under-cover bunny.

MY EYELIDS WERE BEGINNING to droop, so I was relieved to hear Dad step out of the bathtub. Mom kissed me with a hug and said, "Good night, sweetie. Sleep tight. Remember what we discussed about Mr. Zeyer. And mum's the word with Dad, okay?"

She didn't wait for my answer but headed straight for the stove to check her teakettles.

I snuggled in and waited for Dad. Before long, Dad entered, sat down on my bed, and looked at me with a solemn expression.

"Jase, I want to talk to you about something that I heard this afternoon. Your mother doesn't know about this, and I would just as soon keep it between you and me."

Oh, no. Not again! I thought. But I responded innocently, "Okay."

Dad nodded and continued, "I ran into Hans Zeyer this afternoon. He says two young boys came into his backyard about lunchtime. Whoever they were, they made a big ruckus – blowing a police whistle – shouting – jumping up and down – and so on. Before he could get a good look at them, they made their getaway out of his driveway and down the hill toward the swamp in a red wagon."

He went on, "Hans was pretty upset. Mrs. Zeyer was so frightened by the hubbub that she threw a whole bowl of chicken soup into the air. When it came down, it nearly scalded Hans. And poor Wolfgang will never be the same. He's apparently still whimpering in his doghouse."

I tried hard to generate a look that said, *I haven't the faintest idea of what you are talking about.* But after Mom's mental mauling, my Cool Look Generator had sputtered and shut down. The best I could muster was a wimpy look that probably signaled, *Where's the confession? I'll sign.*

"Jase, do you have any idea who those boys were?" he asked soberly, looking me dead in the eye.

Gads! It was one of Mom's gotcha questions. Déjà vu!

I couldn't help thinking, *He's good. He's very good. He could help Mom and J. Hooper Edgar squeeze confessions out of Fifth Columnists captured by the FBI.*

I considered giving Dad a full confession in an effort to save time. But then I thought that wouldn't be very respectful of Mom. She had invested heavily in my third-degree session just a half hour ago? How would she feel if I suddenly spilled the beans to Dad after one lousy question? I had to think of Mom's pride. Besides, weren't her last words "mums the word with Dad?" So I clammed up. And gave Dad another look of confused innocence. It seemed to work.

Then a second miracle happened. He let me off the hook, too, by saying, "Jase, I don't know where you got the idea that Mr. Zeyer could ever be a Nazi spy. Your mother would be mortified. I'm sure she considers the Zeyers good neighbors and friends. But, in any case, I don't want to have this conversation again. Okay?"

"Me, neither, Dad," I professed truthfully – again.

"And one other thing. Mum's the word about this Zeyer spy business with your mother, okay?" Dad said, looking extremely businesslike.

What could I do but agree?

Again, I was relieved to have survived my second arrest, trial, and conviction of the evening. My only residual feeling was, *What if they find out that both of them made me swear not to mention anything about what both of them already know?*

Parents are hard to figure sometimes.

I decided not to worry about it. I figured, by the time they had it sorted out, the statute of limitations would have run its course.

"Okay, son. It's time to turn off the lights. It's warm out tonight, so I'll open your window a little," Dad said, preparing to leave.

I responded with my customary "Now, I Lay Me." Then Dad turned off my light with his "See you in the morning, bye."

My room was completely dark. I stared at the black ceiling and reviewed my day. Hans the Nazi, Sherm the Worm, Gentleman Jim, Bohunk Joe, Don the Guard, Sergeant Rick, Otto the Kraut Lover, Mom, Dad, and – Danny!

What a fantastic day!

The house was still now.

As I did every night back then, I closed my eyes and listened to the sad murmur of Mrs. Mikas' soft weeping, floating out her bedroom window, through the plum trees, and into my heart.

4 PENNIES FOR HEAVEN

EARLY THE NEXT MORNING, THE SUN PEEKED INTO MY window to see if I was awake. Lazily, I lifted my head from the pillow and blinked the sleep paste from my eyes. Then I remembered.

It was Sunday!

Energized by that realization, I hopped out of bed, wrestled into my shorts and shoes, and hurried to the kitchen. Using three slices of Wonder Bread, I made myself a double-decker sandwich of peanut butter, grape jelly, and mayonnaise, in honor of Danny. I poured myself a tall glass of Riverton Dairy's finest. With my hands filled with breakfast, I opened the screen door with a rump-bump and plopped down on the porch steps to eat.

I was chewing my first bite and thinking of the day ahead when I spotted Danny coming up the alley behind Mrs. Mikas' garage. He saw me and waved. Good timing! Had he arrived ten minutes earlier, I would have been shaken awake by his deafening *come-out call*. I made a mental note not to forget to tell Danny about Sherm's closet snooze and my close call with cowardice while in the hands of my parental interrogators.

As he approached, I noticed that something had changed. He was out of uniform. His army cap, corporal insignia, and leggings were missing. The remainder of his wardrobe was unchanged except for the battered Detroit Tigers ball cap now resting on his furry head.

A new dressing neatly connecting the tips of his upturned eyebrows had replaced yesterday's broad swath of white. At a distance, his new, slimmed-down dressing could be mistaken for a bright toothy smile emanating from the top half of his face.

"Hey! Want some breakfast?" I mumbled between chews.

"Keeeerect!" Danny responded, bounding up the steps, through the screen door, and into the kitchen.

"Where are your army clothes?"

"It's Sunday. I always dress up. Wanta go to church?" Danny answered, while adding bread-and-butter pickles to a double-decker of his own.

"What church do you go to?" We had never discussed our religious preferences.

"A few! Most Sundays – three or four," Danny replied without elaborating. "You got some money for the collections."

"How much do I need?" I asked, suddenly fearing that my small cache of spending money wouldn't be enough for Danny's "few" collections.

"I got six cents," he announced smugly.

I was relieved! I wouldn't be embarrassed.

Grandma Addison had given me a treasure chest bank to celebrate my birth. She had died before I could remember her, but nonetheless I displayed her gift prominently on top of my dresser. About the size of a small brick, the bank was made from strong metal covered with richly embossed leather depicting locks, hinges, and metal straps – the hardware common to all pirate treasure chests about to be buried. But, unfortunately, the cover also displayed some less-than-macho images that I wished would just disappear. Especially the skinny-looking teddy bear and the scroll that read "BABY'S TREASURE."

The coin slot was wide enough for the occasional fifty-cent piece that came into my possession. To deposit anything larger, a door on the bottom was opened with the official-looking silver key. The bank was home to my only silver dollar, the two arrowheads that I had found in the loose gravel beside the Chippewa River, and Grandpa Compton's gift of five highly prized Indian Head pennies wrapped in ancient waxed paper.

But, mainly, the bank was a temporary repository for the few pennies, nickels, dimes, and sometimes quarters accumulated from gifts, scrap iron sales, and wages from odd jobs around the neighborhood. This was my spending money for birthday presents, penny candy at Pete's, movie tickets and popcorn, and other luxuries.

When the accumulated total exceeded my anticipated spending needs, I converted the surplus into U.S. Savings Stamps. To assist in the war effort, each morning, our teachers at Hamilton School sold these tiny stamps in denominations equal to the various coins brought to school by us frugal students. I pasted each stamp carefully into the pages of my personal Savings Stamp book. Mom and Dad let me store it in the shoebox where they kept their valuables, on the top shelf of their bedroom closet.

When all the pages of the book were full, I could convert $18.75 worth of Savings Stamps into a brand new $25.00 War Bond! I considered that one heck of a deal. Owing to my intense desire to earn the U.S. Government's free gift of $6.25 ($25.00 minus $18.75), I seldom kept over fifteen or twenty cents in spending money in my bank.

I retrieved the small silver key hidden between my box springs and bed frame and opened the bank. After Danny inspected its contents, I scooped out a nickel and one penny to match Danny's six cents. I stuffed the coins into my pocket and relocked my treasure chest. I returned the key and looked at Danny. He had a strange expression on his face.

"Don't you have a hanky?" he asked.

"Sure," I responded.

I wondered why I needed a hanky. But, compliantly, I reached into my second dresser drawer and pulled out my favorite of the two, low-mileage handkerchiefs there. This one was a mostly red and white farmer's style number that Grandpa Compton didn't realize he'd loaned me from his dresser the last time I stayed at the farm.

Danny held out his hand. I dug out my six cents and handed it over to him. He spread my hanky out on the dresser top, placed the coins in the very center, and firmly double-knotted each pair of corners to secure the bullion safely in the gob of red-white cotton.

Then Danny pulled out his own hanky wad, a blue version of my red one, and shook it at me. His coins jingled and he smiled. I jingled mine back at him. At last, we were ready to render some serious service to the Lord!

Departing by way of the kitchen door, we headed across the lawn, ducking under the low-hanging branches of the plum trees that stood in row between the Mikas house and ours. Fresh dewdrops from the long blades of grass mischievously moistened our shoes as we scuffed along. As we reached the sidewalk and turned south toward Pete's, I realized that much of the neighborhood was still sleeping.

Danny immediately took the lead and quickened the pace. He turned to me and speculated, "It's probably still early enough for us to set up the tables. If not, we can hand out those worship things."

"Can they change my nickel?" I asked, wondering whether the churches Danny had in mind were well-fleeced enough to change a big coin.

"You bet!" he confirmed with the confidence of a church big-money man.

PETE OPENED EARLY, EVEN on Sundays. He didn't want to miss those driving by who might stop to pick up a newspaper or, if they had the rationing stamps, a bit of bacon. You could never tell what people might need. Some bought fishing or hunting licenses. Others bought cigarettes, a cigar or two, or pipe tobacco. Some bought carpet tacks or flashlight batteries. Some merely stopped by after early Mass at St. Thomas Catholic Church to chitchat with Pete while he restocked his shelves.

Others like Gentleman Jim, Bohunk Joe, and their associates were known to purchase a jumbo of beer or a pint of fortified red wine as soon as Pete opened his doors. In response to concerns of neighborhood women, Pete didn't sell hard liquor until after noon on the Sabbath.

On my morning rounds, I often saw early-morning imbibers conducting wine tasting sessions and picnicking at the bus stop at the end of Forrest Street. The makeshift wooden bench, still showing signs of serious scorching from Jim and Joe's marshmallow-sardine roast, was conveniently located right across New Albany Avenue from Pete's store.

On one occasion, Jim and Joe were entertaining one of their former traveling companions who, the evening before, had accidentally tumbled off a passing Grand Trunk freight train and luckily found himself among old friends. Evidently, after a night of reminiscing, the threesome decided that a wholesome breakfast was in order. I remember their menu well: a loaf of white bread, a pound of big bologna, and a quart jar of mayonnaise.

Unfortunately, they had forgotten their silverware. So their handmade sandwiches were covered with black finger and thumb smudges as thick layers of mayonnaise were spread, quite literally, by hand.

But the sanitary aspects of the breakfast seemed to be the least of their concerns. They didn't worry much about germs. To my knowledge, Jim and Joe were never afflicted with so much as a head cold. Now, sometimes they did suffer from what appeared to be "sleeping sickness." That's when I would see them drowsily propped up against the cottonwood tree or napping beside the railroad tracks down by Bohunk Joe's shack. But, in general, they did their sipping and napping in the privacy of their cozy dwellings.

The proximity of Pete's store and the Chippewa Trails bus stop was part of the reason The Right Honorable Reverend and The Good Mrs. Squires – that's what Danny and I called them – had chosen the end of Forrest Street for the location of their Good Mission Church. There, they did a commendable job of converting and reconverting Riverton's resident bums and transient hobos to a life or, at least, a long morning of sobriety and spiritual healing.

Technically, Raymond Squires was not a real minister. He was a welder, a good one by reputation, who worked in the line maintenance gang at the Burke Factory with Dad. They had known each other since second grade. Dad had helped him in numerous ways after Raymond "got the call" to start the Good Mission Church.

Edith Squires did an exceptional job of pounding out rousing Christian hymns and gospel music on her old upright piano. More importantly, she knew how to inspire others to join her in song. Even Bohunk Joe broke into tears every time he reached his heavily accented crescendo during Edith's rollicking *"Rock of Ages."*

Keith, who was in my grade at school, was the only Squires child. We seldom saw him during our visits to the Mission because he routinely occupied himself in the kitchen doing his good works with soapy pots and pans. Other than his tendency to swear and spit excessively and to cheat some in marbles, he was an exemplary preacher's son.

The Squires had rented both halves of a dilapidated two-story duplex. The east half served as the family's living quarters and the kitchen for the Mission. The main floor of the west half housed the church "auditorium" as the Squires called it. A dormitory for about a dozen residents was located on its top floor, and a permanent collection of secondhand clothing – men's, women's, and children's – in its basement. The fire wall between the halves had been perforated with a pair of swinging doors and a long serving window from the kitchen.

Sunday morning activities started early at the Good Mission Church. Edith warmed up the griddle about six o'clock broadcasting the lovely aromas of promised pancakes and sausages throughout the duplex and into the nearby streets. This was the church's unofficial Call to Worship. By seven o'clock, the auditorium was filled with regulars from the dormitory upstairs and newcomers, many of whom, after Saturday night celebrations, had bedded down on the church's wide front porch in anticipation of an early breakfast with the Squires.

The auditorium was an improvised dining hall with a pulpit at the front. While the residents and guests ate breakfast at the hodgepodge of donated tables and chairs, Reverend Squires would preach, pontificate, and pound his pulpit. When he grew hoarse, he tapered off with responsive readings from the Worship Agenda. This single sheet of paper was typed and mimeographed – gratis, after hours – at the Burke's purchasing office by his cousin, Ethel Evans, who worked there as a bookkeeper.

Every Sunday, before the service-breakfast was allowed to begin, Reverend Squires laid down certain rules. He called them his Righteous Regulations. They were simple and practical.

"Please remove your hats when you are in the sanctity of the Mission auditorium. There's no smokin' or chewin' during the service. There's no drinkin' anywhere on Mission property – at all – at any time. All liquor bottles and trash must be removed from the front porch before we begin. Beds in the dormitory must be made and the dormitory swept clean. The tables must be arranged and set with clean dishes and silverware. The Worship Agenda must be distributed to each person in attendance. The results of your tidy work will be checked by our two Trustees who this week are – "

He never failed to gain the complete cooperation of his flock. The auditorium emptied while each hungry convert-in-training busily carried out the Reverend's wishes. Their assignments finished, they hurried back to their chairs to await their morning nourishment – both spiritual and caloric.

It was worth the wait. The Mission meals were generally hearty and abundant. While the church was by no means prosperous, it was blessed with a fine list of supporters including, evidently, the Chippewa Canning Corporation because burlap bags bulging with dented cans invariably found their way into Mrs. Squires' pantry each Saturday afternoon.

The Good Reverend concluded each Sunday sermon with a series of prayers, which he personalized by cleverly inserting the worshipper's name at the beginning of each prayer. If he didn't know a name, he would point at the man and assign him a special address so God wouldn't mistakenly shed His grace on someone other than the intended recipient.

Without fail, Reverend Squires' personal prayers began with the words, "Buddy Roe." For example, he might point at a newcomer and say, "God, Buddy Roe Bib Overalls asks Your forgiveness for his terrible sins and prays that You remove his unholy lust for demon rum and heal that ugly wine sore on his nose."

This usually brought a tear to the eye of the Buddy Roe in question and an affirming "Amen" from Edith who nodded piously from her piano stool. It was all very moving.

ON THIS PARTICULAR MORNING, Danny and I arrived in time to set the tables for Mrs. Squires and hand out the Worship Agendas.

About fifteen scruffy men, each looking like a Buddy Roe of Jim and Joe, were in attendance.

Danny and I sat at a back table, so we could easily slip into the kitchen for Keith to refill the serving dishes with hot rations for the hungry congregation. As usual, the main course was pancakes, don't-ask-what's-in-'em sausages, white oleomargarine, and syrup. Canned beets and leftover goulash from the Wednesday night Prayer Supper were the side dishes. Owing to a wartime interruption in the supply chain of affordable coffee, ersatz black tea, concocted from burnt wheat, was the featured beverage.

Mrs. Squires always served white oleomargarine. She didn't allow us to mix in the orange-yellow dye provided in the package as we did at home. She told us that this dye was "powdered vanity" planted there by the Devil himself. I was glad she explained what it really was. Before that, I had thought it was the government's way of letting us know we weren't eating real butter.

Danny and I decided to treat ourselves to a second breakfast featuring pancakes rolled around a thick bead of syrup. When the service began, we amused ourselves by pretending our pancake rolls were cigars. We stuck them in our mouths, lit them with imaginary matches, inhaled deep drags, and tapped make-believe ashes into our make-believe pants cuffs, imitating the farmers at the stockyard. After Mrs. Squires frowned at us from her piano stool, we ended our pantomime by snuffing out the cigars on the soles of our shoes and gobbling down the butts.

As Reverend Squires hit the high points of his sermon, Danny and I got in synch by nodding vigorously and tapping our toes loudly on the chair rungs in front of us. We did a good job matching our "Amens" and other responses to the thunderous rhythm from the pulpit. On one occasion, however, Mr. Squires did look at us oddly. Danny had responded with a loud "Amen" instead of "No" to the Reverend's hard-to-miss question about letting the Devil come into our daily lives.

Danny told me later that he thought forty-two correct responses to the Reverend's forty-three questions wasn't a bad score. I hadn't counted, but I definitely agreed. He then confided that he wasn't exactly sure whether "Amen" meant "Yes" or "No" in the first place. I confessed that I was a bit confused on that one myself. We agreed that the safest response would be the enthusiastic grunt used by most of the experienced Buddy Roes in attendance.

Mr. Squires followed his sermon with a most inspired series of personalized prayers. A couple of Buddy Roes sobbed noisily when they realized that, thanks to the Good Reverend, they had personally been illuminated by God's spotlight. Of course, Buddy Roe Danny and Buddy Roe Jase were recognized for their good service in setting up and tending the congregation. Danny, apparently embarrassed at being singled out before God, momentarily lost his composure and reflexively lit another cigar to calm his nerves.

When Reverend Squires finished the prayers, he produced the wooden offering plate from under his pulpit and handed it to Buddy Roe Mac, one of the week's Trustees, who sat attentively in the front row. With the hand speed of a pickpocket, Mac passed the plate to the next man who, in turn, passed it to the next. The plate zipped through the congregation like a scared bunny. When it reached Danny and me at our back table, it contained not one farthing!

Undaunted, Danny yanked out his blue hanky, untied the wad, and carefully released three copper pennies into the plate. *Plink. Plunk. Plunk.* He nodded my way, and I understood his meaning. There would be no breaking my nickel at the Good Mission Church this morning. So I pulled out my red hanky and released my only penny into the offering plate. *Plunk!*

Not wanting to risk passing our generous contributions back through *that* crowd, Danny stood up and returned the offering plate directly to the pulpit. He walked slowly with a deliberate cadence giving the impression that his march was part of the service.

Reverend Squires took the plate from Danny's hands and smiled appreciatively. Danny solemnly bowed from the waist. His Tigers cap fell to the floor in front of the pulpit. Without missing a beat, he scooped it up, bowed once more to the audience, and marched slowly back to our table. Before taking his seat, he waved his cap above his head and winked at Reverend Squires. He reminded me of our hero, FDR, on the campaign trail. What polish!

Reverend Squires' mouth was agape. Mrs. Squires couldn't contain a snorty snicker. But she quickly recovered, remembering that it was time for her part of the show.

Edith's joyful burst of Christian music spilled out of the auditorium and into our neighborhood. Her audience, reticent at first, finally lost its inhibitions and belted out, *"Jesus is our Savior and He's coming home again, so gather at the altar and confess your every sin. His love for man will penetrate the deepest, coldest heart if only you believe in Him and give His love a start.*

Jesus is our Savior and He's coming –."

After thirteen verses, I guiltily sensed a big lump of boredom *deep* in my heart – or, at least, somewhere south of my chin.

Mercifully, Danny poked me and whispered, "Let's go to see what the First Methodists are having for breakfast."

DANNY AND I HURRIED west on New Albany Avenue, passing Joe's shack and the canning factory on the way. After a five quick blocks, we crossed the street and spliced ourselves into the long line of Methodists waiting to shake hands with an elderly lady who was serving as the morning's greeter. We appeared to be the only children attending the First Methodist Church that day.

While we waited our turn, I examined the First Methodist Church thoroughly. The building was a looming, wood frame and clapboard structure painted gleaming white. It looked very pure. As did all the Methodists in line with us that sunny morning.

The Methodist congregation was definitely a cut above that of the Good Mission Church. All the men dressed in suits and ties – nary a bib overall in sight. All the women wore floral dresses, white leather high-heeled shoes, short white gloves, and soup bowl-size hats that reminded me of miniature German helmets even though I couldn't imagine Nazi storm troopers hiding their eyes behind masks of white mesh.

"Take out your collection money," Danny instructed.

Obediently, I yanked out my red hanky and waited for further orders.

Our greeter was respectfully attired in the Methodist Lady uniform-of-the-day. She too appeared very clean and pure, except for a very large brown mole on her right cheek. She also wore a perfume that reminded me of rotten muskmelons. I suspected that her sense of smell had been damaged by advanced age. She must have been well into her fifties.

Finally, it was our turn to be greeted. Without bothering to extend her hand or tell us her name was "Miss Elizabeth Bundy", as she had with everyone else, she leaned over and confronted us, using an extremely patronizing tone, "Boys, where are your parents?"

"Can you change a nickel?" Danny retorted without missing a beat.

"I beg your pardon," she spouted, springing upright and clasping her little, white-gloved hands together like a frightened chipmunk.

Danny, thinking she was hard of hearing, turned up the volume. **"CAN YOU CHANGE A NICKEL?"** he blasted using the amplitude normally reserved for my wake up call.

When she recovered, Miss Bundy swept us inside the church and stood us in the corner of the entranceway. She waved at one of the ushers and pointed out the door. He got the idea and headed outside to assume her welcoming duties.

"Now, then!" she demanded sternly, staring down at Danny. "What's this about a nickel? And please, speak softly."

Danny adjusted his volume control to a setting that obviously read, "For-Little-Old-Ladies-Who-May-Not-Be-Deaf-But-Must-Be-Stupid." He spoke *very* slowly and deliberately, "Can - you - change - a - nickel?"

His enunciation was perfect.

"Why?" Miss Bundy impatiently demanded with an upward roll of her bland gray eyes.

"So - he - can - put - two - pennies - in - the - collection - plate," Danny explained to the poor woman as he pointed at me.

"Young man, why are you talking that way? Is there something wrong with you?" she inquired, looking angrily at Danny.

Geez, this could take all day! I thought.

Finally, Danny turned to me. I had been awaiting his next instruction. "Show her the nickel," he barked with exasperation as if to say, *She obviously doesn't believe me.*

Without waiting for me to unknot my red hanky, Miss Bundy cracked. Giving in to the state of emotional bankruptcy that had overcome her, she screeched, "Yes! Yes! We have change for your nickel! Wait here! I think I have five pennies in my change purse."

Miss Bundy clucked loudly to herself as she stormed off to retrieve her pocketbook. Danny smirked slightly and put his hands on his hips. I held my nickel tightly in my hand.

An unexpected belch of deafening, and unrecognizable, organ music announced that the service was about to begin. It also announced that the summer substitute organist from Riverton High School was making her musical debut.

The usher who had relieved Miss Bundy reentered the church behind the last of the Methodists in the line. The relief greeter turned his attention to us, "Well, that's the last of 'em. Now, what can we do for you fellas? By the way, are your parents church members, boys?"

He seemed genuinely interested and rather nice, so I answered him politely, "My parents don't go to church. My mother was a member of The Church of Christ. And my father is – was – an Episcopalian."

The nice man nodded his head and turned to Danny, "How bout you, son?"

"My mother's Catholic. And my dad's a Prescopalian, too. I think," Danny responded politely.

As an afterthought, Danny inquired of the usher, "What are you serving for breakfast this morning?"

The nice man possessed a hyper-ticklish funny bone. In response to Danny's innocent menu inquiry, he guffawed so loudly that the minister stopped his opening reading from the book of Proverbs and stared out over his flock in our direction. The whole congregation followed his example by turning around in their pews and staring at us.

Apparently inspired by his earlier success with the maneuver, Danny waved at the stunned crowd and bowed deeply from the waist. This time, he caught his Tigers cap in mid-air before it hit the floor. Danny's move elicited another whoop of laughter from the nice usher standing with us. About half of the congregation joined him, issuing forth a flurry of snorts and snickers.

Suddenly, Miss Bundy banged into the church hall from a little door behind the pulpit. She screamed once and wildly waved her huge black leather purse over her head. The startled minister and congregation, pivoting in their seats, watched with wonder as she ran toward us clucking louder than ever, something about "five pennies."

Using her purse as a broom, she swept Danny, the nice usher, and me back through the church entranceway and down the stairway leading to the church basement. We stumbled down the stairs just ahead of the lethal Bundy purse-broom.

Apparently responding to a nervous need to restore order, the substitute organist began to play again, louder than before. She only knew one piece by heart. A jaunty version of *Alexander's Ragtime Band* reverberated through the rafters of the First Methodist Church. Her beat and volume reminded me of Edith Squires.

When we reached the bottom of the stairs, Miss Bundy was in a state of red-faced rage. She sputtered irrationally for several seconds in an obvious attempt to control her anger. I thought she might explode. Then she shoved five red-hot pennies into my hand and, without responding to my attempts to give her my nickel, turned her attention to our fellow felon, the nice usher.

"Mr. Carmody! Mr. Melvin Carmody! What do you mean by this – this shocking interruption of our service? Why, you – you should be ashamed of yourself! Shame! Shame! Sham – Sha – Sh – sssss –," she finally sputtered to a halt. Then, without warning, she turned on her heels and clucked her way back up the stairs toward the naughty Methodists who were belting out a last rousing chorus of *Alexander.*

For several minutes, our pal Mel tried desperately to regain his composure. His face remained rosy red while his body continued to shake with periodic waves of uncontrollable laughter. He sat down in a folding chair and put his face in his hands. He extracted a huge white hanky from his back pocket and swabbed his forehead. He tried desperately but unsuccessfully to control his mirth.

Danny and I used Mel's recuperation period to survey our surroundings. After several minutes, he settled down enough to give us, what was obviously, a well-rehearsed narrated tour of the First Methodist Church Basement. As it turned out, Mel was quite a talker.

ACCORDING TO OUR GUIDE, the basement served a number of functions. The open center area was where the Methodist Youth Fellowship, the high school group, met every Sunday night.

The sixty active MYF members were encouraged to invite guests. This made for large meetings, sometimes more attendees than could fit into the two hundred folding chairs stacked along the stairwell wall. This was especially true after the annual ice skating party. On that occasion, all the good teenagers in town returned to the church for hot cocoa and marshmallows and a spiritually provocative talk from the MYF sponsors, the young assistant minister and his wife who shepherded the group.

And, of course, there was the rather extraordinary stage, behind the heavy green curtain that covered most of the east wall. This was used for the annual Sunday School Christmas program and for the minister's meetings with his congregation. The church-sponsored Boy Scout troop used it to allow scouts to practice giving first aid to fellow troop members who pretended to be victims of Nazi air raids.

Along the west and south walls were the ten small meeting rooms. These were used primarily for Sunday School classes. Each classroom had its own bulletin board just outside its door. On a strip of yellow poster paper the name of each class was labeled in bold black letters.

There were the Shepherds, the Angels, the Disciples, the Samaritans, and so on. Each class corresponded to one or two grades in elementary, junior high, and high school. The rest of the bulletin board was used to post class member drawings of subjects covered by their curriculum for the semester.

Mel Carmody's wife Anne was the Registrar for Religious Education. "Registrar," Mel explained, "is a fancy name for the person who types the names of all the students on class rosters, orders the exact number of Sunday School workbooks for each class, and makes sure refreshments are provided for each section of Sunday School every week."

During the school year, there were two services (the early service at 9:30 and the late service at 11:15) and two corresponding Sunday Schools. The classes were often small, but this dual scheduling enabled parents to choose either service without disrupting their children's religious education. The curricula were identical, so if you signed up for the first service Sunday School and overslept, you could attend the second service Sunday School and not miss anything.

In the summer, with people off on vacations, working in their gardens, or on the golf courses, only one Sunday School section was scheduled, this during the second service. The summer curriculum was lighter, too. "Old Testament Fundamentals" gave way to "Making Musical Instruments for Children", by far, the most popular Sunday School class offered all year.

BY THIS TIME, DANNY was glassy-eyed. The dosimeter that measured his level of absorbed adult words had reached the red zone. He politely interrupted Mel by inquiring, "Where are the sheep?"

Danny surprised Mel with that one. Mel looked blankly while he put a mental bookmark in his tour script. Then he responded with, "Whatya mean?"

Danny pointed at a colorful poster outside the Shepherds meeting room showing Jesus surrounded by a flock of sheep. Mel, following Danny's point, took one look at the poster and burst into another wave of uncontrollable laughter. I guess Danny figured that Mel's laughter was preferable to his lecture.

"Hey, what's going on?"

We turned to see an attractive lady, purse slung over her shoulder, carrying three bulging grocery bags in her arms. "Mel, dear, can you give me a hand?" she requested sweetly.

Mel, still trying to catch his breath, couldn't speak. Danny, forever on the lookout for opportunities to serve, volunteered, "We'll help! We'll help!"

"Great! There are four more bags in the car – the one with the open trunk – and two boxes of Sunday School workbooks. While you boys bring those in, I'll get out the plates and cups for the cookies and punch."

Then she added, "I'm Mrs. Carmody. Who are you, boys?"

We quickly introduced ourselves and then headed for the car. In a jiffy, the refreshments and student materials were arrayed on the wooden table near the stairwell. "Mrs. C," as Danny began to call her, gave us our orders. We obediently opened the boxes and distributed the efficiently bundled and marked stacks of workbooks to each meeting room.

Mel and Mrs. C laid out the cookies and punch. When we finished our class preparation duties, we opened some folding chairs, sat down, and sampled the fare. While Danny munched on a giant oatmeal cookie, he asked Mrs. C, "Do you have a Sunday School collection?"

"Sure do. See those little boxes over on the registration table. They contain one envelope for each week of the summer session. Everyone who registers this morning will get a box," she explained, rehearsing her student orientation presentation.

Danny, half a cookie in hand, wandered over to the table. He put the cookie in his mouth temporarily and picked up two boxes. When he returned, he handed me one and mumbled through his cookie. I got his meaning. I pulled out the five Bundy pennies and deposited two of them in the first envelope. I handed Danny a third Bundy penny in repayment of his loan at the Good Mission Church.

He yanked out his money stash and added a copper of his own to his envelope. Then Danny handed both to Mrs. C without ceremony. Adding my nickel to the inventory, I explained why I owed this sum to Miss Bundy and asked Mrs. C to deliver it for me.

She turned to her husband and suggested, "You work with Miss Bundy, Mel. Perhaps you could return this nickel to her."

He held up both hands and shrugged sheepishly, "I'd rather you did it, dear. Miss Bundy and I are not on the best of terms at the moment."

She agreed then asked with a smile, "Does that mean we have two more enrollees for the summer session?"

Danny's response was a big smile. I followed suit.

After four cookies and two huge glasses of punch apiece, I figured we were on our way to our next rendezvous with religion. But Danny surprised me when he delayed our departure by inquiring, "What would two boys going into sixth grade next September be studying this coming fall?"

"Well, let's see. Sixth-graders are Angels. They'll be studying Exodus – the story of how Moses led the Hebrew people out of Egypt to the

Promised Land. You'd really enjoy that story," Mrs. C promised enthusiastically.

"Awready know it," Danny declared, licking his fingers.

"Really! Could you tell it to me?" asked Mel, half in jest.

Danny put on a very serious face, sat up straight in his chair, and adjusted his Tigers cap. Then he began his story.

"THE HEBREWS WHO CAME from Promiseland were visiting in Ejip when Hitler started World War Two. When Rommel got to Ejip on his way to North Africa, he told the King of Ejip to get rid of the Hebrews 'cause Hitler didn't like them. Rommel would have made the Hebrews put on POW uniforms and come with him, but he didn't have room on top of his Panzers 'cause he was too busy fighting American tanks in the desert – and he didn't want the Hebrews to fall off when he made sharp turns in the sand.

"So this old man named Moses, who was the General of the Hebrews, told the King of Ejip that he would take the Hebrews back home to Promiseland where they could work in the factories that made honey and milk. The King of Ejip said, okay, but the Hebrews would have to walk to Promiseland 'cause all the gasoline was needed for Rommel's tanks that were fighting Americans in the desert.

"Moses and all the Hebrews started hiking back to where they came from. When it got dark, they decided to camp next to a mountain. Before he went to sleep, Moses climbed the mountain to look back toward Ejip to see what was going on. When he got to the top, he saw that the Ejipson soldiers had borrowed some of Rommels tanks – and they were following the Hebrews. They looked real mad 'cause the Hebrews hadn't cleaned up Ejip before they left that morning.

"Moses decided to take a nap. When he woke up, all the brush on top of the mountain was on fire. The fire was started by grade schoolers who left two writing tablets under one of the burning bushes. Moses picked up the tablets and read what they had written. There was the names of Ten Commandos – you know, those British soldiers with the funny helmets, short pants, and black stuff on their faces.

"These Ten Commandos would show Moses and the Hebrews how to find their way back to Promiseland. He came back down from the mountain to tell the Hebrews, but they were too busy having a party. Moses got pretty mad and told the Hebrews he wouldn't show them what was written on the tablets. So he took off across the desert. All the

Hebrew people followed him – begging him to tell them what was on the tablets.

"When he came to the seashore, Moses prayed to God for a bridge to cross the sea. God built this underwater bridge – or something like that – and Moses and the Hebrews went across the sea to the other side. When the Ejipsons tried to follow them, God said, 'Sorry! You are on Hitler's side, so I am going to close the bridge.' So he did and all the Ejipsons were drowned, dead.

"That's why they call it the Dead Sea."

THERE WAS SILENCE IN the Sunday School room. Mrs. C just looked at Mel, her eyebrows raised. Mel stared back with his eyes wide open and his mouth clamped shut. His face was deep red. I don't think he was breathing.

Danny had done it, again! He was a Biblical scholar. No doubt about it.

Danny, unfazed by all this silent adoration, looked at me and thumbed toward the basement door. Then he said, "We gotta hurry or we'll be late for church."

After departing from the First Methodist Church, with Danny in the lead, we backtracked to the Ann Arbor railroad tracks. We veered onto the foundry siding that took us by Gentleman Jim's hillside abode.

As we trotted along Liberty Street toward the Ann Arbor Street Bridge, impatience finally got the best of me, "Hey, Danny! Where are we going now?"

"The Downtown Church-ah-Christ. And we gotta hurry, or we'll miss the start of the second service," Danny advised, picking up the pace.

"The Church of Christ? That's where my Grandma Compton goes – sometimes," I said, puffing along behind the bouncing Danny.

MY GRANDMOTHER, JANE COMPTON, was a devout Christian and a loyal member of the Church of Christ. Her faith was simple and comprehensive. She believed being a Christian was far better than not being one, so she effortlessly applied Christian principles to everything in her life. But she never proselytized or criticized anyone for not sharing her commitment. And, for reasons never discussed, only about half the family signed on. Grandpa Compton and my parents were among those missing from the ranks of the devoted.

Grandma's church had a strong presence in Riverton and in the surrounding countryside. There were two Churches of Christ within the city limits, each served by a permanent head minister. Those who attended the larger Downtown Church of Christ were generally affluent and sophisticated while members of the Westside Church of Christ were said to be "more down to earth."

The members of the two in-town congregations were adamant about which was the better church. Ironically, this same firm belief about the attributes of a "good" church frequently led members of one church, incensed over church policy or sermon content, to resign their membership and move across town to the other church. Owing to this phenomenon, a tenth of the churches' combined membership was in a perpetual state of flux.

Fortunately, the two head ministers were not in the least competitive in their attitudes or behaviors toward each other. In fact, they were the best of friends. As experienced ministers, they took this constant migration in stride and commonly briefed each other on the idiosyncrasies of the fickle families. For the most difficult cases, this briefing was unnecessary. These families changed allegiances so often that it didn't take long for both head ministers to know them well.

To serve the spiritual needs of those living on farms or small villages far from town, one-room churches had been established in the four corners of Chippewa County. Two novice ministers shared the duties of "circuit preacher" by presenting weekly services at the remote churches and ministering to their small congregations. Each preacher presented an early service at one of the four churches, bid a hasty farewell, and made a beeline to another for a late service.

The senior in-town ministers regularly swapped places with one of the circuit preachers and occasionally with each other. This helped train the junior ministers by putting them before the larger in-town congregations. It also gave the two senior ministers a change of pace and a furlough from their tougher constituents. In this way, members of the six Churches of Christ in the county were able to experience three, and sometimes all four, ministers over the course of the year.

Officially, Grandma Compton was a member of the Barrington Church of Christ located in the northeast corner of the county, about two miles from the farm. However, frequently, she would propel her Hudson Terraplane over miles of dusty country roads to attend another country church or even into Riverton to attend a town church. She claimed to enjoy the "variety and mix" of different congregations. But there was another reason for her wandering churchgoing. She had a favorite among the county's four ministers.

During the summer before Pearl Harbor, Reverend Claude Johnson and his wife Rose had lived briefly with Grandma and Grandpa Compton, just after the young couple arrived in the county. The Chippewa circuit was Claude's first preaching assignment after his graduation from divinity school in Minneapolis.

The Johnsons were unassuming, bright young people who laughed easily at Grandma Compton's wry wit and friendly teasing. They had both grown up on farms in southern Minnesota. So they were knowledgeable and skilled farm hands who gladly pitched in to earn their room and board while living in the second-floor guest room of the Compton farmhouse. Even Grandpa Compton was taken with the pair.

After a few months, the church found the Johnson couple more permanent quarters, a miniature one-bedroom cottage located on the Blake farm, just a stone's throw down the road from the Barrington church. The Johnsons reluctantly packed and left the Compton farm.

Both Grandma and Grandpa were depressed. Grandpa knew that his distaste for churchgoing meant that he would see the couple far less frequently than he wanted. Grandma, aware of the minister exchange process, knew that she would have to travel to hear her favorite young minister on a regular basis. So in the name of encouragement and support, she followed her young star from church to church like a devoted groupie. In the process, the Johnsons and the Comptons became lifelong friends.

THE DOWNTOWN CHURCH OF Christ was a tall, impressive structure of tightly laid orange-red brick. Its steel framed stained glass windows pivoted open allowing the June breeze to cool the congregation. By car, the church was three miles from the First Methodist Church. Following railroad tracks, paths along the Chippewa River, and narrow alleyways through town, Danny and I cut that distance in half. When we arrived in front of the church, we stopped to listen. The visiting Reverend Johnson had just finished the opening rituals and was thanking the congregation for its warm welcome.

A determined Danny set course for the back of the church. We entered through a small wooden door normally reserved for the church janitor, deliveries of freshly dry-cleaned choir robes from the Riverton Cleaners, and late-arriving Sunday school teachers. A long, unlighted hallway led from the door past the janitorial supply room, the choir dressing room, and into the church hall itself.

As we inched our way forward, my eyes became accustomed to the darkness. At the end of the hallway, just before it opened into the church hall behind the pulpit, I could see a dozen children, about our ages. Dressed in blue choir robes and holding folded sheets of music, they stood silently awaiting the cue for their entrance.

When we came even with the choir room door, a loud whisper stopped us cold, "Boys! Boys! Come in here. You're late."

I looked at Danny. He shrugged and dutifully turned into the choir dressing room. Naturally, I followed my leader.

The frantic whisper belonged to a diminutive woman wearing thick, dark-rimmed glasses that hung precariously from the tip of her prominent red nose. She hastily introduced herself as the assistant choir leader. "Hurry!" she ordered. "Get into one of those blue robes. Here are your music sheets."

Without hesitation, we followed the little woman's directions. Weren't we supposed to be polite and obey our elders? When we were properly attired, the little lady gave us our final instructions, "Quick! Take your place in line. When the organ music begins, follow the other children to the raised platform – right behind Mr. Johnson. Okay?"

We nodded our agreement. Before leaving the lighted room, we glanced at our music sheets to prepare for our impending performance. *Sing His Song Today.* The hymn's title sounded vaguely familiar. Maybe we had heard it at one of Edith Squires' performances. What the heck, we were ready!

The assistant choir director followed Danny and me down the hall toward the rest of the children. Just as we arrived at the staging area, the organ burst forth with a flood of harmonious tones. No summer substitute here today!

Immediately, the blue-robed children in front of us moved forward. We followed briskly. Our flowing procession stretched out in front of the adult choir and behind Reverend Johnson who turned to watch us enter. We were a splendid sight!

I went on stage first and Danny followed. The line in front of me stopped. And, as we were turning to face the congregation, I heard a shrill whisper from the hallway behind us.

"Little boy! Your hat. Please remove your hat!" came the distraught cry from the hysterical assistant choir director.

I glanced at Danny. His eyes rolled upward toward his Tigers base-ball cap, and his head shook in disbelief at the little lady's ridiculous suggestion. Being an experienced showman, he merely pretended not to hear her and continued his grand entrance.

Instead of stopping beside me, Danny strolled to center stage where he took up position behind and just to the right of Reverend Johnson. The crowd stared at Danny's hat and murmured. Danny studied his music sheet and played it cool.

The choir director, an enormous lady in a billowing royal blue robe with a white starched collar, floated majestically downward from the adult choir area behind us. When she reached our level, Madame Director glided across the stage and stopped directly in front of Danny. Leaning over, she haughtily swatted at Danny's ball cap.

Forewarned by her nasty demeanor, Danny deftly ducked to avoid her swat and stepped backwards into line with his fellow children's choir members, just beyond her reach. He held his cap tightly to his head with his right hand, the hand also holding his sheet of music, and cocked his left arm upward to fend off the anticipated foray from Missus Blue Mountain. The congregation gasped.

The mammoth choir director, her fists clenched at her sides, shud-dered with anger and frustration. Within seconds, the look of *murder* in her eyes gave way to one of profound *futility.* Danny had won. She feigned indifference and raised both hands to bring our choir to atten-tion. The organist, taking her cue, began the first verse.

The choir director waved her arms dramatically as she conducted our rendition of *Sing His Song Today.* Her precious performers, plus two interlopers, were doing a commendable job. So Danny, sensing that danger had passed, stepped forward boldly, resuming his former star's position in front of us. He opened his music sheet and tried to find his place. Once he had it, he stood up straight and let 'er rip.

" HE LOVES ME MORE THAN EVER, SO I SING HIS SONG TODAY. HE LIGHTS THE PATH TO HEAVEN, SO I'LL ALWAYS KNOW THE WAY," Danny boomed, smugly composing his own melody as he blasted away.

His explosive rendition paralyzed our blue leader. Her waving arms froze in midair. Her eyes bulged toward Danny. She mouthed angrily but silently, "Shut up!"

Danny got the message, so he just hummed along modestly and tapped his right foot softly in time with the music. His submission to the demands of Her Blueness demonstrated what I had come to believe – at heart, Danny was a team player.

Madame Blue resumed her fragile position as our leader while tiny beads of perspiration trickled downward from her wrinkled brow and collected in the fold formed by her first double chin. She was obviously a beaten woman. To shorten her painful stay in front of the congregation, she increased the pace. Her eyes darted wildly in time to the accelerated tempo of her flapping arms.

The organist and the choir responded beautifully to the change in cadence, "*HE-LOVES-ME-MORE-THAN-EVER, SO-I-SING-HIS-SONG-TODAY* (gasp). *HE-LIGHTS-THE-PATH-TO-HEAVEN, SO-I'LL-ALWAYS-KNOW-THE- WAY* (gasp)."

We were through in no time!

Our last directive from the Blue Control Tower was a sweeping wave of her massive arm that blew us toward the hallway door. As we scurried off stage to the sound of *peeps* and *chips* of approval from the congregation, Danny took up the rear.

When he reached the hallway door, Danny suddenly stopped, turned toward the congregation, and lifted the Tigers baseball cap from his head. Waving his cap proudly at his fans, he looked like the old Bambino about to enter the dugout after another grand slammer.

The crowd roared their approval and applauded noisily. Danny entered the hallway all smiles. Peeking out over his head into the joyful crowd, I saw Grandma Compton clapping enthusiastically.

Despite having to endure the annoying admonishments from the assistant choir director, Danny and I managed to change back into civvies and escape through the back door in one piece. We walked up the alley, around the church, and through the front door. We wiggled into two empty seats in the back pew and settled in for a very stimulating sermon on the influence of Protestantism on modern poetry, the subject of Reverend Johnson's thesis at theology school.

Danny's eyes glassed over. Then he dozed off. *Performers need their rest*, I told myself.

After five hours, I think, of Reverend Johnson's *very* interesting sermon, came our favorite part of the service – the offering. Danny awoke instinctively to the gentle rustle of offering envelopes, dollars, and coins dropping softly into the felt-lined collection plates. We each dug down for our two remaining pennies and waited our turn. The usher handed us the wooden dish and acknowledged Danny's onstage greatness with a friendly wink and smile.

Danny turned to me and whispered, "We only got to three churches this week. Next Sunday, let's shoot for four."

5 GRANDMA TO THE RESCUE

AFTER THE SERVICE, WE WAITED OUTSIDE FOR Grandma Compton. She had stopped to compliment Reverend Johnson on his engaging sermon and his "innovative" music program. They both chuckled when she mentioned the showmanship of the boy with the baseball cap.

As we plucked the last petals from the fading lilac blooms next to the porch steps, Danny asked, "Whose mom is this Grandma, anyway?"

I gave Danny a quick history of Mom's family.

My mother, Marie Hope Compton, came from a family of recycled immigrants. Around 1880, the Hopes and the Comptons had re-immigrated to America from Canada. As British loyalists, they had fled there just before the American Revolution, a fact seldom mentioned in Mom's family stories. But it didn't matter. They were all loyal Americans by now. Besides, the English were currently our allies.

Both families were large and close-knit. As farmers and factory workers, they seldom rooted more than a few miles away from Chippewa County. My mother's parents, Sarah and William (Bill) Compton, lived on a 100-acre farm ten miles northeast of town. There they raised four children including Mom and Aunt Maude, the girls. And Uncle Ray and Uncle Tom, the boys.

Danny nodded his understanding. My family history lesson had been just the right length. I glanced up to see Grandma Compton coming down the steps.

"How's my Jase?" she asked, giving me one of her big hugs. Then she turned to Danny and smiled, "Now, who's this?"

After the introductions, Grandma announced that she was dying for some ice cream. Just to keep her company, we agreed to join her. We all piled into the Terraplane and zoomed toward Moore's Ice Cream

Parlor. Danny, hungry after his exhausting performance, ordered a banana split. I settled for a butterscotch sundae with vanilla ice cream. Grandma had her usual, a chocolate soda with chocolate ice cream.

When we finished, Grandma said, "I'll give you boys a ride home. I have some sauerkraut in the car for your mother, Jase."

Danny's face twitched and twisted, and I shuddered involuntarily. *More sauerkraut! Just what Mom needs*, I thought to myself.

Grandma was very skilled at perceiving funny looks, especially among her closest admirers, my cousins and me. Danny and I attempted to hide our reaction to her news, but she caught us.

"Now, wait a minute here. Do you have something to tell me about my sauerkraut?" Grandma demanded.

Well, there it was. Grandma had asked a direct question, so I couldn't tell her a lie. I threw myself on the mercy of the court and confessed – for the entire Addison family.

Yep! I spilled the beans about our family's total aversion to sauerkraut – hers or anybody's – and about the huge inventory of Grandma Compton and Aunt Maude's sauerkraut jars in our cellar. Danny looked on, admiring my courage.

"Well, I'll be. How could that mother of yours grow up in my house without me knowing she hated sauerkraut? Doesn't that beat all?" chuckled Grandma, shaking her head. "And, to think, I was going to give her six more jars."

Danny, never one to miss an opportunity, inquired innocently of Grandma Compton, "Do you like to help children, Grandma *Campton?*"

He described how Otto had flaunted his pink gold in front of us innocent boys. But how we cleverly outmaneuvered the Nazi by claiming our own monopoly over Riverton's sauerkraut supply. And how we had discussed ways to persuade Mom to confess to Grandma *Campton* and Aunt Maude. And finally how her admission would release the sauerkraut hoard for the good of America's children. He really laid it on thick.

Danny gave Grandma the benefit of his thinking on where we might store the hoard and how we might transport it to its hiding place.

He ended his sales pitch with, "Whatta ya think, Grandma *Campton?*"

I knew what I thought. Danny should know the name of his prospect before beginning his sales presentation. But I kept that opinion to myself and, instead, waited for Grandma's reaction.

Shaking her head in amazement, Grandma vowed again, "Well, I'll be!"

She was obviously enthralled by the prospect of joining forces with the Forrest Street Guards against the sinister bubble gum cartel. She stared at her empty soda container for a long time, idly fingering the bent straws standing in the paper cone.

Then she snapped out of it.

"I think I've got it!" she announced. "Come on, you boys. Let's get out of here!"

While Grandma paid our check, I pulled Danny aside and whispered, "It's Grandma COMPton, not Grandma CAMPton."

Danny smirked, "I knew that. *Campton* is just how I pronounce *Compton* – some of the time."

Did I forget to mention that Danny was never wrong?

We rushed back to the Terraplane, hopped in, and roared toward Forrest Street. When we arrived, Mom was sitting on the front porch reading one of her movie magazines. She stood when we pulled into the driveway. We tumbled from the car and met her in the middle of the yard.

Grandma Compton didn't even bother to greet her. She just demanded, "Marie, you have to help me with a wartime emergency. I need all the sauerkraut that you can spare from your supply in the cellar. I only have six jars left. They're out in the car. If you have a good supply, your generosity can bring a good deal of happiness to many war-deprived children. Will you help?"

Danny and I smiled at each other in admiration of Grandma Compton's clever plea.

Mom was trapped. She nervously sputtered, "A lot of people gave us sauerkraut last year. So – so I saved yours – and Maude's – for –."

She stopped there, before she got in over her head. Then she finished by confessing, "We really don't eat sauerkraut that often. So I guess we have close to a hundred jars down there."

Grandma Compton offered a confession of her own, "Well, silly me. How I never knew you didn't like sauerkraut is beyond me. I wish you'd told me sooner."

My mother smiled awkwardly and shrugged her shoulders. Then she counseled herself, "It's time I told Maude, too."

"Okay, boys. Let's load 'er up!" barked Grandma.

As we filled the Terraplane with the heavy jars of sauerkraut from the cellar, the car sank lower and lower in the driveway. When we finished, there was barely room for Grandma to squeeze into the driver's seat. She gave Danny and me our instructions, "Hop on the back bumper and hold on for your life!"

"Gotta get this sauerkraut to those children – right away," she said loudly, for Mom's benefit.

We hopped on the back bumper. Grandma pulled out of the driveway and crawled along in low gear toward New Albany Avenue. My mother waved and stared with trepidation as we disappeared around the corner.

After a block or so, Grandma stopped the car.

"Okay, we got it. Now what?" she yelled out the window at us.

Danny suggested a plan. Grandma and I smiled and nodded our agreement. Grandma hopped into the car and ground the gears into first. We crept slowly toward Bohunk Joe's shack. Grandma pulled into his driveway and stopped the car. I hopped off the bumper and ran to the door. His pushcart was parked in its usual place.

Bohunk Joe came to the door and looked out at me. Then at Grandma, the Terraplane, and Danny sitting on the bumper. "Mr. Joe, can we please borrow your pushcart for a little while?" I asked.

Joe nodded positively and pointed to the cart. Almost as an after-thought, he offered in his broken English, "Wants schum heelp?"

Danny and I followed Joe who pushed his cart slowly behind Grandma and the sauerkraut-laden Terraplane. Our caravan proceeded cautiously across New Albany Avenue, through the canning factory's staging yard, and around the building. Grandma parked the car close to the loading dock ramp, got out, and opened the trunk.

We filled the pushcart with about half our inventory. Effortlessly, Joe pushed the first load up the ramp and onto the loading dock. We wheeled toward the shabby boxcar at the opposite end.

When we reached our destination, I retrieved the key ring, and opened the huge padlock. Joe gasped when he saw the collection of dented cans.

"Ahh!" he said. Now he knew the source of Jim's dented groceries.

Grandma was equally impressed. "My, oh my!" she exclaimed.

We unloaded the cart, stacked our jars into an empty corner of the boxcar, and returned to the Terraplane for another load. Soon, we finished.

Grandma bestowed the last jar on Bohunk Joe for his trouble. His eyes watered with gratitude and his mouth watered with hungry anticipation. He rolled away toward his shack amidst a flurry of thanks and waves.

"You don't suppose the old Bohunk is really a German do you?" Danny postulated.

We all laughed.

Grandma Compton turned to us and said, "Before we go back to your house. There's something I need to say to you."

She paused and looked at us, searching for just the right words. She finally spoke, "Sometimes it's okay not to tell the whole truth if it keeps somebody from being hurt. I know your mother thinks that way. That's why she never told me about your family's dislike of sauerkraut."

Then she added, "I'm that way, too. So I'd just as soon not have her know the whole truth about this bubble gum trading scheme – at least for now."

She looked at Danny and me with mock sternness until we nodded our agreement. Then she burst into laughter.

"Bubble gum for sauerkraut! For crying all night! What will you boys think of next?"

Danny answered her rhetorical question literally, "Now that you mention it, I do have another idea."

AS WE STOPPED IN front of our house, Grandma asked, "Jase, would you like to invite Danny to come with you to the farm today?"

"Great! Can we go now – with you, Grandma?" I asked.

Danny's huge grin revealed his opinion of my plan.

"That'd be fine. You can go home with your folks when they come out later. Why don't you pop inside and check with your mother? Oh! And tell her we'll stop by the Tuckers to be sure it's okay with them."

I darted inside and told Mom what was up. She agreed with our plan. Dad was still working on two repair jobs promised to customers for Monday. So they would join us at the farm after he finished.

"Aunt Maude's due here on the next bus, so she'll come out with us."

The mention of Aunt Maude excited me. I really liked her. Then I remembered Mom's impending sauerkraut confession. I looked into Mom's eyes for any sign of discomfort. She read my mind and patted my head. "Thank you, Jase," was all she said.

I smiled back.

When I returned to the car with the good news, Grandma cranked up the old Terraplane, and off we roared toward Danny's house.

I haven't told you yet about Grandma's driving.

NO ONE IN THE family could explain Grandma's fascination with driving. Her passion was especially extraordinary in view of her stubborn resistance to driving in the first place. Had it not been for Grandpa's foundry accident resulting in his near total blindness,

Grandma would have been very content to remain a non-driver for the rest of her life.

Grandpa had little choice but to return to farming. The Depression eliminated nearly all the factory jobs in Riverton. Besides, his disability disqualified him from that kind of work. On the farm, he could depend on his wits, his innate farming skills, and the strength of his back to scratch out a living. He was only fifty years old and in good health, so back to the farm they went.

There was just one hitch. Grandma had to do his driving for him. Oh, he could drive a team of horses (and later the farm's tractors) over the roads to the next farm. But it wasn't safe or legal for him to drive the family car. Partial blindness prevented him from obtaining a driver's license or insurance. He had to depend on Grandma for all his personal and farm business transportation needs beyond the immediate neighborhood of the farm.

Grandma reluctantly took on the frustrating process of learning how to manipulate the Terraplane's tricky manual transmission. After a grueling training period, she assumed the role of family driver.

Grandma's transformation amazed everyone. The freedom and power of driving became addictive. She accomplished Grandpa's list of farm start-up errands in record time. To practice her newly acquired skill, she invented reasons to run from the farm into Riverton. Or to the "station" (the combined gas station and general store on the main road five miles west of the farm) to buy a pound of sugar. To the Henrys, her farm neighbors, to deliver a basket of her oven-warm cookies. To the grain elevator in New Albany to check the latest wheat prices. To the stockyards to see how dairy calves were selling. And so on.

Soon, the division of labor at the farm was established. Grandpa spent his days driving Jim and Fannie or Gene and Teddy, his beloved teams of workhorses, back and forth over his fields – plowing, cultivating, and harvesting. And Grandma spent her days driving her beloved Terraplane back and forth over her county roads – delivering, purchasing, and visiting.

Friends and family compared notes on when and where around the county they had spotted the dusty green coupe with Grandma behind the wheel. They also commented, timidly at first, on the speed and recklessness of her driving. Her risky driving technique became the subject of eyewitness accounts.

"Yesterday – about ten – I saw her skid into the Sinclair station out on M-31 – near the old CCC camp. When the dust cleared, she was at least ten feet from the pump!" some cousin would report.

But Grandpa took these reports in stride. He chuckled and called her his "Barney Oldfield." The more he laughed, the less people bothered him with detailed sightings and concerns about Grandma's driving competency. Over time, he succeeded in taking these sails out of other people's wind.

Grandpa was a wise old owl, all right. But not a purebred owl. He was part chicken. After a few trips as Grandma's passenger, he began to invent reasons of his own – for staying home. Without telling Grandma, he even ordered a home barbering set from the Sears Roebuck catalog to trim his monthly trip to the barber in New Albany from Grandma's recurring errand list.

Despite the inherent dangers, I loved Grandma's speed and recklessness. To me, driving with her was more fun than the wildest ride at the Chippewa County Fair. When given the chance, I always chose to ride with Grandma over the stodgy, albeit safe and comfortable, alternative provided by Dad.

Grandma's reckless driving was the complete antithesis to the rest of her life in which she was completely reserved – except, of course, for her marvelous sense of humor and skill at practical jokes. Her fondness for placing her nasty-sounding "Whoopee Cushion" under the seat of an unsuspecting visitor was my favorite. Or was it her plastic ice cube with the "frozen" fly in it? Maybe it was her dribble glass?

Anyway, when Grandma sat behind the steering wheel of that Hudson Terraplane, no doubt about it, her personality changed dramatically.

I could tell when Grandma was overcome by the urge to drive. She scurried around the kitchen as if late for an important appointment – most likely, an appointment only recently invented. Finally, her pent-up desire would propel her out of the kitchen, through the screened porch door, and down the driveway toward the garage. Assignments for accomplishing whatever was to be done in her absence came flying over her shoulder to anyone within earshot.

Fortunately, most of my farm duties were deferrable, so I usually accompanied her. She liked that because I was such an enthusiastic fan, demonstrating my admiration with ardent "Wows!" "Oooos!" and "Greats!" as she zoomed over hills and around curves on her way to – nowhere special.

My friends couldn't understand why I was so eager to spend much of my summer vacation "stranded" out in the country. But, with Grandma as tour director, I seldom spent a full day at the farm itself.

More importantly, when on the road with Grandma, there was never a dull second.

As her frequent travel companion, I understood what drove Grandma to drive. Whenever her lust to leave struck, she was rendered powerless by a compelling fantasy. How this fantasy took form in her mind is anybody's guess. But, in my mind, there was no doubt.

Despite her abundant body and middle age, Grandma was transformed into the striking figure of a young and svelte Amelia Earhart. Her calico housedress, soiled kitchen apron, and black leather farm shoes were magically supplanted by a black, form-fitting aviatrix uniform of soft calf leather. I envisioned her sheepskin-lined, belted flight jacket, sleek trousers, snug-fitting helmet, racing gloves, and highly polished boots laced to the knee.

Marching across the driveway toward her powerful flying machine, she whipped the long white silk scarf around her neck and slid her goggles down from their perch atop her leather helmet. She methodically tightened the fit of her racing gloves, one finger at a time.

Content with the splendor of her attire, she hopped into the cockpit, revved up her engines, and ordered the wheel chocks removed. Intently, she gazed down the runway, toward Japan – and Victory.

Anyway, that's what I imagined each time Grandma launched a mission. But this is the way it actually happened.

After stowing her wicker basket, shopping bags, and voluminous leather purse wherever they would fit, she wiggled and bumped up and down until her "car pillow" was properly situated beneath her substantial bottom. Then she gripped the steering wheel resolutely, muttered to herself what I assumed was a small prayer, and started her engine with a roar.

Noisily, she ground the floor shift into first gear and popped her clutch impelling the Terraplane to leap forward. Simultaneously, she tromped the gas pedal to the floor causing her tires to spin wildly in the gravel on the way out the driveway. Once on the road, she immediately pushed the car to maximum speed, about sixty-five, where it stayed for the entire trip, no matter where her errands took her.

As she raced along, an elegant rooster tail of road dust, rising behind her, could be seen for miles across the flat farmland of Chippewa County. She zoomed through every curve without reducing speed, jostling her passenger roughly from side to side. When she reached her destination, she stood on the brake pedal with both feet and slid sideways to an abrupt stop.

THERE WAS NOTHING MORE thrilling in my young life than riding with Grandma Compton in that Terraplane. I couldn't wait to share the experience with Danny.

But, when we stopped at his house, certain complications delayed our departure. It seemed that Danny had forgotten a small commitment to his sister.

Sam and Christine Tucker had three children, all of whom had nicknames. The reputed champion swing-pumper was the oldest, a dizzying twelve years. While her name was Selma, she went by "Queenie", owing to her over-powering, imperious nature. Then there was Daniel, our "Danny", who like me was ten. Finally, the little brother, six-year-old Edward, was called "Chub."

Grandma waited in the car while Danny and I went inside to get his parents' permission. When we entered the kitchen, the family was seated at the table. They had just finished their Sunday dinner. From what I could see, the serving dishes contained an odd combination of foods, all of which had come from tin cans – peaches, Spanish rice, black cherries, and applesauce.

Mr. Tucker, wearing only his underwear, sat reading the Sunday funnies while Mrs. Tucker sewed a waist button onto his blue denim trousers. Chub was using his left index finger to paint a self-portrait on his empty dinner plate. Obviously, his preferred medium was ketchup on porcelain. Queenie, her hair in curlers, was filing her nails.

"Hi-Mom-Jase's-grandma-wants-me-to-go-with-them-to-her-farm-can-I?" Danny shot at his mother.

"Don't talk with your mouth full," Mr. Tucker responded involuntarily without looking up from his reading. He obviously hadn't noticed that Danny had missed the Tucker Sunday dinner that day.

Danny overlooked his father's transgression and repeated his question, "Hi - Mom - Jase's - grandma - wants - me - to - go - with - them - to - her - farm - can - I?"

I sensed that old Danny had committed a tactical blunder. It was the "May-Not-Be-Deaf-But-Must-Be-Stupid" cadence that he had tried unsuccessfully on Miss Bundy earlier that morning at the First Methodist Church.

His mother was about to render her opinion, not so much on his question, but on his method of delivery when Queenie took charge, **"NO! YOU MAY NOT! YOU PROMISED TO STAY WITH CHUB WHILE I GO TO THE MOVIES WITH**

DIANNE – AND MOM AND DAD GO TO NEW ALBANY."

Queenie's decibels blew me back against the screen door. My ears were ringing. I saw stars. *Voice blasting must be a Tucker family specialty!* I told myself.

At that, Danny and Queenie engaged in a heated exchange of MEGA NOISE lasting five minutes or more and getting us nowhere. I huddled in the corner with fingers in my ears and thought of the good news. I won't have to repeat the issues for Grandma. She can follow the whole argument from Terraplane in the driveway even if she has the windows rolled up.

Mrs. Tucker went back to her sewing. Mr. Tucker returned to his funnies. He pointed at *Maggie and Jiggs* and chuckled to himself. They didn't seem to notice this horrendous noise. I wondered if they were all hard of hearing.

Mercifully, Chub, pulling himself away from his art, made a suggestion that broke the tie. "I could go with Danny to the farm."

The noise subsided abruptly. Out of the mouths of babes! I felt a fondness for the little ketchup eater.

It was quickly agreed that this compromise would serve all interested parties. Queenie signaled her acceptance by resuming her filing and blowing her nail dust at us. Mrs. Tucker told us she would come to the car to meet Grandma Compton and make sure it was all right.

As we were leaving, Mr. Tucker raised his head from the funnies and inquired, "Where's everybody going?"

No one responded.

Grandma was delighted to have another boy along. "The more the merrier!" she told Mrs. T.

But, because there was no backseat, one of us would have to stretch out on the shelf in the hollow between the coupe's front seat and the back window. For fun, I had nestled in that spot before, so I volunteered. Danny and Chub shared the suicide – oops – copilot's seat next to Grandma.

Grandma ground into gear and ordered, "You boys, hang on now! Get out of the way, if you please, Mrs. Tucker!"

It was a polite but critically important warning.

When Grandma gunned the coupe, Mrs. Tucker ducked to avoid the deadly gravel stones that shot out from under the wheels. We squealed onto New Albany Avenue and fishtailed crazily. Bouncing violently, we boys giggled uncontrollably and waved at Mrs. Tucker. She waved back weakly. Then she bit down nervously on her knuckles as Grandma's green rocket disappeared from sight.

When we reached New Albany, the county seat, Chub looked for-lornly at Grandma and whimpered, "I gotta go potty."

Potty! How embarrassing for Danny! Right in front of Grandma! I thought to myself, *If he were my little brother, boy, would he be sorry for using baby talk in public!*

But the kid's faux pas didn't seem to bother Danny.

Grandma skidded into the Standard Oil station on the outskirts of town. When she returned to the car with Potty Boy, she asked us if we needed any ice cream. One wonderful thing about Grandma, she always took care of our needs in the sweets department.

According to her, this particular gas station served some of the biggest three-cent scoops in the county. I believed her assessment, because she and I had personally sampled at least twenty different pur-veyors of ice cream cones in the area.

We gladly confirmed, "Yes, indeed, we would be more than pleased to accept another delicious pre-luncheon snack before we undertake the arduous, ten-mile journey to your lovely farm, oh thank you, Grandma." Or words to that effect.

Despite his objections, young Chub only qualified for a single-dip. But the friendly gas station attendant made it an enormous one. Chub chose chocolate like Grandma. Danny had a dip of strawberry and one of chocolate. I had two whopping dips of cherry vanilla.

Grandma opened the passenger door and sat there with her legs sticking out. We boys plopped down on the curb. The attendant pushed back his Standard Oil hat, cleaned his black grimy fingernails with his bone-handled jackknife, and sucked on a toothpick while we concentrated on pleasurable slurping.

Grandma finished first. About an hour ahead of the rest of us as I recall. But she was kind enough to help each of us by smoothing our ice cream with her tongue, so it would melt down into cones more evenly. Or, at least, that's what she told us.

When we finally finished, we thanked her again and piled back into the Terraplane. After we'd settled in, Amelia started down her pre-flight checklist. She was just about to launch when our little baby talker whined to Grandma, "I gotta go potty, again."

This time Danny nearly fainted with embarrassment. I was relieved to learn that he was capable of feeling shame for "misbehaving" family members.

When we finally got on the road, Grandma informed us that she had one more stop to make. After driving another five miles, suddenly, she jammed on the brakes. We skidded across the loose gravel and jostled to a stop at the intersection of Barrington and Riverton Roads just a mile south of the farm. I knew immediately why she had stopped.

"Wild asparagus!" I yelled.

"Yes! I saw it was up yesterday when I drove by. How about gathering a big bunch for dinner?" she suggested.

Danny responded with enthusiasm, "Okay! What'll we put it in?"

Grandma fetched a tomato basket from the coupe's small trunk. Naturally, Danny led the way. We guided him down into the broad grassy valley and up to the knoll that ran along the row of wild crabapple trees. It was here that Grandma and I had harvested a sizeable batch of newly sprouted wild asparagus last June.

When we reached the spot where last year's crop had grown, I saw them, sticking their green heads above the beginnings of their wispy yellow-green foliage. Danny walked right by several luscious bunches. *Obviously, he has a picking strategy of his own*, I thought.

Suddenly, Danny turned around and asked, "What is sparagrist anyway?"

Grandma snorted a succession of hearty guffaws. She couldn't help herself. Danny really tickled her. I joined her with a snort of my own. Chub who didn't know his asparagus from his potty chair laughed like one of the guys. This caused us all to laugh so hard that tears ran down our cheeks.

Grandma collapsed on the clover-covered bank and removed the lace-trimmed hanky from her bosom where she had safety pinned it that morning. She dabbed her eyes and gave her nose a big honk. This homely sound ignited another round of uncontrollable laughter. Grandma was disabled by hilarity. She lay back and let the asparagus wisps tickle her ears.

"Oh, me! Oh, me! Oh, me!" she sputtered over and over.

After ten minutes or so, Grandma regained control. She reached around behind her and plucked two juicy, eight-inch spears of wild asparagus from the ground. She brushed off the light coating of road dust with a clean corner of her hanky. Then she beckoned to Danny and Chub. She gave them each a spear. The twin Tuckers chomped down trustingly. When the sweet wild asparagus juice reached their taste buds, their eyes popped out.

"Wow! This is good. Let's pick some more," insisted Danny. He finally got the message.

"Good idea!" agreed Grandma, squeezing a conspiratorial wink in my direction.

In no time, we had filled the tomato basket with enough asparagus for the entire Compton tribe. So we re-embarked and shoved off for the farm. When we turned onto Barrington Road, in the distance, I could see Grandpa's herd of dairy cows grazing lazily in the meadow at the edge of the woods near the top of the lane.

As we drew closer, Chub spotted the herd. "Horsies!" he shouted with excitement.

Danny, in true big brother form, *gently* corrected his little brother, "Chub, you dummy, those aren't horses. Thos'er pigs."

Grandma guffawed so hard we nearly ended up in the ditch. She slammed on the brake. We bumped to a halt just short of the driveway. Next to us, a pair of brilliant yellow and black goldfinches flushed from the lane where they had been perching on a budding thistle.

Grandma hugged the steering wheel, gasping for breath. "I declare. I declare," we heard her say between wheezes.

Danny and Chub weren't sure why Grandma was laughing so hard, but they smiled broadly. They certainly didn't want to miss any of the fun.

But I didn't laugh. It was my turn to be embarrassed.

Suddenly, I realized that the "farmification" of Danny was to be a long and difficult process.

AFTER GRANDMA RECOVERED FROM her giggle attack, she stepped on the gas and veered the Terraplane into the long, U-shaped gravel driveway. She aimed her hood ornament at the open door of the snug garage nestled between the horse barn and the granary. Just short of the garage, she hit the brakes. When the car stopped rocking, we passengers piled out to watch her make the final approach from the safety of the driveway.

Once we were out of harm's way, Grandma angled the car's wheels to the right to allow maximum space between the left side of the car and the garage wall. Then she revved the engine to a moderate howl and popped the clutch. The Terraplane leaped into its nesting place and promptly stalled with a loud *chug-a-da-plunk*. Miraculously, the car was positioned perfectly inside the garage.

Smiling with self-satisfaction, Grandma opened the car door and squeezed out through the narrow passageway. Then she retrieved our harvest of succulent asparagus from the Terraplane trunk, slammed the garage doors shut, and walked briskly along the upper curve of the driveway toward the sprawling white clapboard farmhouse with its blue-shingled roof. We three Grandma fans fell in behind.

Mick greeted us with his usual raucous chorus of *yaps, yips,* and *yelps.* He was a white fox terrier randomly splotched with red-brown and black. He and I had known each other all our lives. In fact, we were born on the very same day. Right from the start, we liked each other and spent hours playing, hunting, and playing hunting. We had bonded as only a boy and a dog can bond.

He was always thrilled to see me and demonstrated his excitement by leaping incessantly into the air. I bent down to give his ears and chin a good rub. Then I introduced Danny and Chub. Deciding they were okay, Mick smiled, as he often did, and wagged his tail. Then he turned and, by running back and forth in front of us, led our entourage to the house.

When we reached the fieldstone walk leading to the screened porch outside the kitchen, Danny wheeled around to get a better view of the farm's open yard delineated by the array of assorted outbuildings and the driveway. As his eyes traveled the perimeter of the square, he carefully appraised each of the red-painted barns, coops, and cribs.

Finally, Danny marveled, "Wow! Look at all these garages. Wonder what's in 'em?"

"Probably, old cars. Like her little green one," Chub suggested thoughtfully.

"Yep," Danny confirmed. "Probably so."

Grandma and I pretended not to hear that exchange. Instead, I changed the subject. "After we say hello to Grandpa, I'll show you around."

Just then, Grandpa came onto the side porch and opened the screen door. He was carrying yesterday's *Riverton Daily Press* in his hand. "What's all the commotion out here?" he snarled gruffly, feigning annoyance. "Can't a person read the newspaper in peace without a herd of scalawags disturbing him?"

At the sound of his voice, Danny and Chub turned toward the unfriendly noise and were greeted by Grandpa's favorite ghastly grimace. Simultaneously, they yelped, and hightailed it back down the walk away from the awful specter. Grandma, who was blocking their path, caught the pair as they collided with her considerable lower half. The whimpering brothers wrapped their arms around Grandma's bulky figure, taking refuge in the folds of her copious Sunday dress.

Grandpa was famous for his kid-scaring skills. So he put on his favorite frightening face by pulling down the lower, red-rimmed eyelid of his milky-coated blind eye with his index finger and pushing his false teeth half out of his mouth with his tongue. This usually did the trick with unsuspecting victims. Today proved no exception.

"Now, Dad! For crying out loud! Look what you've done. Put that face away. You've scared these poor boys half to death. Shame on you!" Grandma was trying hard to sound stern, but I saw her tummy quiver as she struggled to suppress yet another giggle fit.

"Come on, boys! Don't let that old goat scare you. Turn around here and see what you're dealing with," Grandma urged, peeling the tightly stuck Tuckers from the sides of her legs.

Grandpa cooperated by restoring his eye and his teeth to normal.

Grandma held a cowering boy firmly in each hand. "This is Jase's new friend, Danny Tucker. And this is Danny's brother, little Chub," she said, nodding right then left,

With a big grin on his face, Grandpa spoke amiably, "Well, you two look like pretty strong boys. Too bad it's the Day of Rest, or I'd put you to work haulin' stones outta the south field – or pitching cow manure in the barn. Are you new 'uns as good at farm work as ole Jase is, there?"

Danny, shaking off his fear, answered immodestly, "Yep! I've worked on lots of farms before."

Our young hero suffered from a unique affliction that caused countless problems during the years of our friendship. I called it "fear-based fibbing." Danny's conditioned response to any stressful situation was to tell a whopper.

"Well, let's stop all this talk about work. It's making me tired. Besides, I'm hungry! Maybe we can get ole Grandma to round us up sum'in for dinner. You boys hungry?" Grandpa inquired, winking at Grandma.

Grandma gave us each a special look that definitely warned, *Don't mention the ice cream.*

We declared enthusiastically that we were starving, too. This was not a fear-based fib. It was the other kind of fib, those that adults tell each other all the time.

Grandpa smiled broadly turning on his considerable charm. Looking right at Danny and Chub, he said, "Come on in then. Danny, I see by your cap that you're a Tigers fan. While we're waitin' for dinner, we'll tune in the Tigers game and peel us some Spanish peanuts that I been hiding from that ole Grandmaw."

Mick, who had wagged his tail patiently through the entire introduction, smiled at the sound of the word *peanuts*. He was a peanuts
lover, too. He darted in ahead of us and plunked down in his living
room basket that was strategically positioned beside Grandpa's reading
chair and in close proximity to the peanut stash. Mick only used his living room basket for short naps and peanut snacking. Once in position,
he sat upright, nervously awaiting his reward.

When we reached the living room, Grandpa snapped on the radio
and tuned in the Detroit station. The commentator was announcing
the starting lineup for the Cleveland Indians who were visiting Briggs
Stadium that day. After adjusting the volume, Grandpa sat down in his
immense red leather chair.

There were two comfortable reading chairs in the living room, both
optimally positioned to receive direct heat from the wood stove in the
center of the room. The shelves of the low stand between the chairs
were covered with his and her reading materials. Behind the chairs, a
tall floor lamp illuminated the area. Grandpa's chair was closer to the
stove than Grandma's. On cold winter nights, he could prop his toes
against the brown enamel side grate and warm his toes thoroughly.

We sat at Grandpa's feet and watched attentively while he retrieved
a round tin of peanuts from behind a pile of magazines. He poured a
handful into a small Blue Willow soup bowl kept there for this very
purpose. He positioned his black enamel floor-model ashtray with the
chrome flip top within easy reach of his chair and placed the bowl
between his knees. He was ready for action. Mick's tail wagged vigorously in anticipation.

He motioned us closer and offered us the bowl. We scooted across
the floor and, following Grandpa's lead, extracted one tiny peanut. He
then demonstrated his peanut preparation and eating ritual for the
Tucker brothers. I already knew it by heart.

First, he carefully blew the excess salt from the red skin of the
peanut. Then he rubbed the nut between his thumb and index finger
to remove the peanut's skin. He placed the discarded skin on the closed
flaps of the ashtray. He popped the naked nut into his mouth and
chewed, very slowly.

The instant the delicious peanut flavor hit his taste buds, he uttered
a satisfied, "Ahhhhhhh!" Then he deliberately depressed the lever protruding from the top of the ashtray. The chrome trap doors opened
wide and the brown-red peanut skin plunged, down the long shaft, to
the ash container in the base of the ashtray.

After Grandpa's demonstration, we four Spanish peanut execution-ers began the deliberate ritual of ending the brief lives of the con-demned peanuts before us. Three peanuts each for Grandpa and the boys. And then one for Mick. Three peanuts each for us. One for Mick. Mick was in ecstasy.

So were we.

Just as we reached the bottom of the peanut bowl, Grandma called from the kitchen, "You boys! Dinner's ready. Come wash your hands before you sit down."

Mick's ears perked up. He made a beeline for his kitchen basket, strategically situated between the kitchen table and the cooking oven, which was constantly warm. Mick used this basket for long nights' sleep and dinnertime snacking. He may have been a dog, but he was nobody's fool.

THERE WAS AN UNWRITTEN rule in our family. On Sundays, sometime during the afternoon, all four of Grandma and Grandpa Compton's children accompanied by their families were expected to "come out home" for a visit. Of course, those men serving our country in the armed services were temporarily excused, but the rest of their families were not. They were expected to be there.

Every Sunday, my cousins and I spent our visits in rambunctious play in the farm's barns, fields, creeks, and woods. Those early feelings of warm friendship and total trust that I shared with my cousins have never left me. They were my first best friends.

According to custom, the adult women served an ongoing buffet in Grandma's kitchen while they nibbled and gossiped. And the adult men assembled under the maple tree next to the house for their sessions with Grandpa. In cold weather, the men gathered around the dining room table in the front room where, for hours, they smoked and played setback, a card game similar to bridge.

Back then, the typical Michigan farm diet fell squarely in the meat-and-potatoes category. Lots of meat! First roasted, then reheated by fry-ing in pork lard. Lots of potatoes! Sometimes boiled and mashed but usually thickly sliced and fried in the grease left over after cooking the meat. Never baked.

The number of serving dishes multiplied as Mom and my aunts arrived at Grandma's house with their leftovers from the week before. Grandma would cluck her approval of every newly-arrived parcel of food then add them to her own inventory in the warming oven where they lay poised, ready to leap out onto the table.

There was no formal seating for Sunday dinner at the farm. During the afternoon, whenever hunger struck one of the men folk or children, they just wandered into the kitchen and asked, "What smells so good?" With those magic words, they were whisked into a chair by the ladies in attendance and presented with a heaping serving of warmed-up meat and potatoes.

Excellence at Grandma's kitchen table was carefully measured by how much a man or a boy could consume. Requests for second and third help-ings were highly praised. Certain gestures such as loosening your belt or unbuttoning your trousers brought appreciative smiles, knowing *clucks*, and approving pats on the back from Grandma and her crew.

AFTER GRANDPA AND WE boys stuffed ourselves with meat, pota-toes, and healthy portions of freshly cooked wild asparagus, we went our separate ways. Grandpa returned to his peanuts, newspaper, and baseball game. Danny and I thanked Grandma for dinner and escaped outside.

Our timing was perfect for two reasons. First, my cousins hadn't yet arrived. So we could explore on our own. Second, during dinner, Chub had dropped his fork. He slipped off his chair and ducked under the table to retrieve it. After a few minutes, I peeked under the table. There he was, all curled up, sound asleep on the floor. Grandma suggested we leave him there until he woke. Danny and I readily agreed. Now, we were free of our little anchor.

As we flew out the screened porch door, I asked, "Danny, where do you want to start?"

"Let's go see that big garage!"

"That's the horse barn," I corrected him, trying hard not to sound *too* morally superior.

"Right you are!" he replied as if he had known all along.

6 FARMIFICATION

I COULD ALWAYS REMEMBER GRANDPA COMPTON'S AGE because he was exactly fifty years older than I was. So, on this first weekend of June 1944, he was sixty years old. But you would have never guessed it.

He was a handsome man whose skin, in stark contrast to his shock of pure white hair, was permanently bronzed to the rich hue of cured tobacco. His one good eye was a brilliant azure. It sparkled vibrantly, especially when he laughed.

Grandpa Compton could have been a movie star. He was the quintessential man's man. I mimicked his gestures and mannerisms often, especially when I needed to impress or intimidate some neighborhood foe.

Despite his immense persona, he stood only five feet six and weighed scarcely more than a hundred and forty pounds, mostly bone and hard muscle. He appeared slight, but in fact he was exceptionally strong and agile for his age.

Grandpa was extremely self-assured, perhaps even a bit cocky. He walked with exaggerated strides and a subtle swagger. I had to trot along behind him just to keep up. And, when he wasn't atop the plow, drill, or cultivator out in his fields, I followed him everywhere.

Although a tireless walker, he also enjoyed standing. During our visits to the farm, instead of sitting on the porch, Grandpa and Dad would stand together for hours under the tall maple tree beside the driveway – talking, laughing, smoking, or just listening to the crickets. They never argued or cussed. I often joined them but I was not invited to participate. So I examined blades of grass or shined my jackknife on my sock while silently savoring their manly discourse.

When standing, Grandpa threw back his shoulders, hooked his thumbs over his belt, and tucked his fingers into his front pants pockets. By doing so, he appeared to lift himself upward to a height greater than his five and a half feet. When conversing with other men, he swayed back and forth, in time with the appealing rhythm of his speech. Distinct phrases and patterns stemming from his English heritage enriched his speech. When he laughed, which was often, he bent over backwards. When out of doors, he spat, occasionally, to underscore a point or show distain for a subject.

Despite the long hours and physical nature of his daily work, he always made time to read each issue of the *Riverton Daily Press* from front to back even though, by the time the Rural Free Delivery postman placed the paper in the mailbox, the news was a day old. He kept abreast of the latest agricultural developments by studying each month's *Farm Journal* and the bulletins and white papers distributed by the county agent at Farm Bureau meetings at the Riverton Grange Hall. And, religiously, before heading to his fields each morning, he listened to the early morning farm market reports from Chicago on the living room radio.

His lifetime of reading, listening, and thinking about a wide range of subjects during his hours alone in the fields made him an interesting and informed conversationalist. Once, when I was in high school some years after the war, I mentioned to Grandpa that I was preparing for a debate on the issue of international free trade. I asked his opinion on the topic. To my utter amazement, Grandpa promptly presented a comprehensive dissertation on this arcane subject, replete with the pros and cons of tariffs, license fees, and import quotas, all with astonishing thoroughness and clarity.

In candor, as a boy, I was most impressed by my grandfather's pure athleticism. Well into his sixties, he could perform feats of balance, strength, and agility that, even as a fair high school and college athlete, I could not perform. On more than one occasion, I witnessed him, using only his fingernails and toe tips, effortlessly scale a twelve-foot wall of slat boards to reach the top of a bin in the granary.

Anytime there were two or more grandchildren present, he could easily be coaxed to hang from his heels on the clothesline pole. Even though it was an amazing feat, after a while we became bored with seeing him just hanging there upside down like a big vampire bat among Grandma's laundry. So we would enlist the family women to persuade him to perform his breathtaking circus act. He couldn't resist the flattering requests from his daughters or wife.

In the cow barn rafters, Grandpa had constructed a pair of trapezes from fifteen-foot lengths of half-inch rope and strong pitchfork handles of beautifully polished ash. My favorite trick involved having one of us cousins climb the ladder to the east peak of the barn and grasp the handle of the trapeze hanging there. Grandpa, hanging by his knees, would swing on the west trapeze out over the haymow and back. At his precise signal, we released our trapeze, pushing it outward toward him. Expertly gauging his timing, he somersaulted niftily from one to the other. We grandchildren applauded his thrilling and perilous trapeze act.

In reality, Grandpa's act was not all that dangerous because of the soft haymow below him. Should anything go awry, he would fall a mere fifteen feet into a spongy bed of hay. Because of this low level of risk, even Grandma Compton approved of his show. Regardless, we were mesmerized by his easy ability to perform his act and would have gladly watched it every Sunday.

During most of the year, the hay wagon and other farm equipment were stored in the area between the mows in the horse barn. A trapeze fall from the rafters of this barn onto a spiky hay rake or sharp-bladed disk would not have been as pleasant as a soft landing on a bed of cow barn hay.

On one occasion, when Grandpa and I were unloading hay in the horse barn, the trip line for the hay-loading fork became entangled in its pulley carriage. The track on which the carriage ran extended along the entire roof ridge from the south peak to the north peak. The jammed carriage was stuck at a point directly above the equipment storage area.

Without hesitating, Grandpa jumped down from the wagon and scurried up to the south peak using rafters and beams for his ladder. Without the benefit of gloves, he grasped the narrow lip that ran along both sides of the metal track with his fingertips and walked himself – hand over hand – to the snarled carriage high above the floor. Then he released his right hand and used it to untangle the trip line.

During this process, he hung precariously from a narrow lip only wide enough for four fingers of his left hand to hold himself there. Had he slipped, he would have plunged thirty feet into the deadly array of farm implements below.

Once the trip line was free, he effortlessly hand-walked himself back to the peak and scurried down into the mow. Easy as pie!

Needless to say, I was amazed and eager to tell everyone about the feat I had just witnessed. But Grandpa admonished me not to reveal what I had just seen to anyone, especially Grandma Compton or Mom.

I will never forget his words, "To get the job done proper, sometimes a man has to do things that would upset the women. So, we best keep this'un to ourselves."

Until now, I have never told a soul about what I saw that day.

WHEN DANNY AND I arrived at the horse barn, I opened the wide door to reveal a startling view of the enormous backsides of Grandpa's two teams of workhorses.

Danny leaped about a foot in the air and exclaimed, "Holy Smokes! They're huge! What are their names?"

"Those two big ones are Jim and Fannie. Grandpa uses them for heavy jobs. They're really strong," I explained, pointing at the gigantic Belgians, one dapple white and the other sorrel.

"The other two – the chestnuts – are Gene and Teddy. They're younger and lighter. Grandpa uses them for smaller jobs."

"Chestnuts?"

"That's their color."

"Oh, right! Can we ride them?" Danny inquired, his eyes flashing.

"Sometimes Grandpa lets me, because I've driven them a lot. So they know who I am. Let's go inside – around in front of 'em – so we can pet 'em," I suggested, steering Danny away from the horseback riding subject.

"Great!" he yelped enthusiastically.

Danny followed me through the barn to the front of the horse stalls. Jim and Fannie cooperated by stroking our fingernails with their huge chins and necks. After about three minutes, we were tired of scratching. Gene and Teddy were less affectionate that day, but we managed to woo them by rubbing their ears, really hard.

When we finished, I showed Danny how to reward each horse with a double handful of oats from the covered barrel next to their feed trough. Danny, fearful of losing a finger, mimicked my open-palm method of horse feeding. Jim and Fannie, then Gene and Teddy, gently nibbled their snacks from our hands.

Danny looked around, then questioned me, "What else can we do here?"

"Wanta play paratrooper?"

"Yeah! Howdaya play?" he replied with his I'm-ready-for-anything look.

I led Danny back out to the area between the mows. While Danny watched eagerly, I jumped over the wall into the ground floor mow and bounded across the springy surface of the hay toward the corner of the barn. Once there, I climbed effortlessly up the side of the barn using the beams and corner supports as steps. I had made this climb dozens of times before.

When I reached the crossbeam that spanned the width of the barn, running just under the peak window, I turned around with my back against the wall. I stepped backwards onto the crossbeam and planted my feet firmly. By alternately pivoting on my heels and the balls of my feet, I slowly sidled across the narrow beam to its center. I stopped when my head was even with the window's sill. At this point, I was standing about twenty-five feet above what hay remained in the near-empty mow below.

Without hesitation, I took a deep breath and jumped. I plummeted downward.

"Geronimo!" I yelled, pulling my imaginary ripcord.

Whoosh!

I landed in the dry and welcoming bed of hay. Sunbeams piercing the barn's wall painted vivid white-yellow stripes across the cloud of dust and dried pollen that exploded around me.

Danny was astonished. His eyes were as big as saucers. He leaped up and down noisily.

"Me next! Me next! I wanta do it. Me!"

"Okay! Okay! Climb over the wall. I'll guide you up to the crossbeam."

Danny bounded to the corner and started his climb. I coached him from the mow below, "Put your foot there. No! Use your other foot. That's right. Now, grab that support. Pull yourself up onto that beam. Turn around this way. You're doing fine. Okay, move your feet like this. That's great. Okay! When you get even with the window, just jump."

Just jump, indeed!

After an exhausting forty minutes of cajoling, I finally gave up and returned to the house. When I entered the living room, Grandpa looked up from his paper. I gave him the bad news, "Grandpa, I need your help. Danny's stuck at the top of the horse barn. He won't jump, and he won't try to climb down."

"Oh, laws!" Grandpa muttered, leaping up from his chair.

When we reached the haymow, Grandpa looked up. There was Danny, stuck to the wall like a stubborn tick. Grandpa didn't waste a second. Up the corner of the barn he went. Facing the wall, he mounted the crossbeam and wiggle-stepped on his toes toward Danny.

When Grandpa arrived next to the frozen chicken, he spoke calmly, "Danny, I am going to move in front of you. I'll be facing you. When I tell you, I want you to put your hands around my waist and hold on tight. Okay?"

Danny nodded meekly. Tears of terror streamed down his cheeks.

Grandpa gracefully moved in front of Danny. When he was in position, he ordered, "Danny, put your arms around my waist – now! Hold on like crazy!"

Danny obeyed immediately. When Danny's fingers were inter-twined and his grip secure, Grandpa surprised even me. He grasped Danny's waist and leaped off the beam backwards.

As he and his frightened parachute partner fell like a rock, Grandpa yelled, "Geronimo"

Danny countered with a weak, "Geranium!" just as the combo hit the dusty hay.

Once they were safely back to earth, Grandpa sprang to his feet while I delivered a standing ovation. True to form, Danny, in response to my applause, bowed from the waist. Then, crazily, he pivoted and ran across the hay toward the route to his nemesis, the top of the barn.

Grandpa and I watched in shock as Danny nimbly climbed upward.

When he reached the dreaded crossbeam, he looked at us over his shoulder and pronounced smugly, "That was fun! I'm gonna do it again."

AFTER A COUPLE OF dozen parachute jumps, Danny and I became bored with invading Germany from the air, so we parked our C-46's in their hangars and returned our chutes to the silk locker. During our air campaign, we had heard cars pulling into the driveway, signaling the arrival of more family.

As we emerged from the barn, I saw our old Chevy and remem-bered that Aunt Maude had ridden out with Dad and Mom. Suddenly, I wondered how we would all fit in for the trip home. Uncle Van, whose corporal stripes Danny sported these days (except on the Sabbath), wouldn't be here, of course. He was doing more important things.

Uncle Van was with the U.S. Army Signal Corps. He had seen action in North Africa, Sicily, and Italy before his first home furlough last February. Everyone in the family was impressed by his rapid pro-motion and with the number of campaign ribbons that now adorned his uniform. I was totally enthralled just being around Uncle Van who, even before he enlisted in 1942, was my favorite uncle anyway.

Everyone thought his furlough hadn't lasted long enough. Nonetheless, he was back overseas now, waiting for what was coming soon. Nobody in the family spoke about it. But, I knew everyone was con-cerned because of all the news about General Eisenhower's plans for the invasion of Nazi Europe from England where Uncle Van was stationed.

Uncle Raymond, Mom's younger brother, and Aunt Betsy had brought my cousins tommy and Teddy. They were playing catch with their scuffed baseball under the tall elm tree in the middle of the circular driveway. I waved at them. They nodded slightly, not wanting to break their concentration.

We liked each other. But they sometimes behaved in strange ways if you ask me. This was not unexpected because they lived so far away – almost forty miles to the north and east of Riverton, up toward Michigan's thumb. I forgave them their idiosyncrasies, because they came from a foreign culture.

Speaking of thumbs, Michiganders customarily located their hometowns for folks by forming a mitten with the back of their left hand – fingers up, thumb right – then pointing to the right spot on the "map" with their right index finger. Of course, this method only worked for people from the Lower Peninsula.

I always supposed that those from the Upper Peninsula turned their left hand over – thumb up, fingers right – before they pointed. But I never confirmed my theory. I didn't know many people from the UP. It's a long way from the middle of everything important, unless you count being in the middle of nowhere. At least, that's how we Rivertonians felt about it.

The last branch of the family lived fairly close to Riverton, so they weren't quite as foreign. In fact, they were downright delightful.

Uncle Tom and Aunt Esther worked a small farm off M-31 west of town, out near the POW camp. They lived there with their three children, my cousins, Carol, Bobby, and Jane. Bobby was older than I, but we were close chums. We often shared Grandma's guest room and adventures at the farm during the summer.

I envied these cousins, because, among other things, each of them owned their own cow. When I delivered this nifty news to Danny, he wrinkled his nose and asked, "Who'd want a cow for a pet?"

I remembered that Danny had yet to complete his farmification program.

As usual, Aunt Esther and my cousins had come to the farm alone. Last winter, Uncle Tom, Mom's older brother, had been stricken with a fit of patriotism – or perhaps guilt – and enlisted in the Army.

He was certainly not typical of his fellow recruits, having been sworn in at the age of thirty-six. As the head of his household with three children at home, he wouldn't have been called to serve. But, he told everybody, he just had to. So the family chipped in with various forms of help to make it possible.

Uncle Tom was down in Georgia undergoing the last weeks of training to become a certified armored vehicle mechanic. The Army was lucky this time. His assignment was perfect. Everybody knew he was a whiz at fixing anything mechanical.

Much to the relief of our family, Uncle Tom was not in any immediate danger from our enemies. He had recently learned, because of his genius with engines, he would stay on the home front as an instructor. His students would then head for the real front with their units.

I didn't see Carol, Bobby, or Jane. I assumed they were in the kitchen having their first dinner of the day. Or, just as likely, hanging out in the cow barn. They were cow-crazy. But I have to admit they did have a way with Grandpa's cows. The entire herd seemed to like them, almost as much as I did.

As we reached the porch steps, Uncle Raymond, Grandpa Compton, and Dad were heading out to the maple tree for their weekly men's meeting. Dad greeted us, "Hi, boys. Have dinner yet?"

"Yep!" I replied.

"Nope!" Danny countered, as he looked longingly toward the kitchen.

Grandpa and I just looked at each other and laughed. Then Grandpa asked, "Jase, maybe you could show Danny how you do your chores when you're at the farm."

"Yes sir-ee-bob!" I responded.

Since I was four or five, I had followed Grandpa through the complex routine of morning and afternoon chores, begging him to let me help. At first, my "helping" meant *more* work for Grandpa rather than *less*. But, before long, I was capable of relieving him of a significant portion of the labor and legwork associated with the daily chores.

My assistance freed him for more important tasks. He appreciated this and took advantage of my abilities and willingness to take on even more. I loved pleasing him in this way.

Although I didn't boast about it, even to my parents, I was extremely proud of my skills, knowledge, and contribution. When Grandpa praised my work in the presence of other people, especially my parents, I walked on air for days.

But chores would have to wait. By the time I reached the kitchen, Danny was already basking in the attention of Grandma, Mom, and my three aunts. He had just committed to another huge dish of Grandma's meat, potatoes, and asparagus. The ladies beamed their approval of his healthy appetite.

"Is there any more sparagrist?" Danny inquired between bites.

"Of course there is!" Grandma confirmed, magically producing yet another serving dish of almost-fresh asparagus from the warming oven.

She smiled smugly as if she had just saved an undernourished child from starvation.

Then she turned to me. "How about another little helping of something for you, Jase?"

Her kitchen assistants all turned to me with raised eyebrows, looking extremely hopeful. I caved under the pressure and allowed, "Well. Maybe – just a little."

An hour later, Danny and I waddled out of the kitchen toward the call of chores. I re-sequenced my normal routine to give us a good long walk first.

BETWEEN THE TWO BARNS lay a spacious barnyard surrounded by a sturdy five-foot wooden fence. The barnyard was big enough to allow twenty cows or more to move about comfortably despite the presence of the semi-permanent fixtures located there, two ripening manure piles (one horse and the other cow) and the manure spreader, ready to disperse the rich contents of the two smelly collections to fields needing nourishment.

A long lane from the barnyard ran south along Barrington Road before hooking east to the ten-acre stand of woods where the herd spent their summer munching the abundant green grass under the elm, hickory, and maple trees.

By the time Danny, Mick, and I arrived where the lane turned east for the woods, I could see Bessie, the herd leader, rounding up her underlings. I pointed this out to Danny who squinted in that direction. "I don't see any cows," he reported, sweeping the horizon with his eyes.

At first I thought he was joking, but then it dawned on me. Perhaps, earlier that day, he had confused cows with pigs because he couldn't see very far. Within a few days, I was to learn that Danny was blind as a bat when it came to seeing anything at a distance – that is, until he got his new glasses.

We followed Bessie and the herd from the woods, down the lane toward the cow barn. When the cows entered the barnyard, we didn't follow them. To avoid the barnyard goop, we slipped under the lane fence and walked up the driveway. Mick left us to join the cousins who were organizing a softball game in the clover field encircled by the driveway. Chasing balls was one of Mick's favorite pastimes.

We exchanged friendly waves with the ball players before Danny and I did a pair of skin-the-cats over the cast iron pipe that led from the milk house well to the barnyard watering trough. Having made perfect dismounts, we opened the cow barn door and stepped in.

Once inside, I slid open the door to the barnyard to let the herd in. Each cow obediently slipped into its stall, stuck its head through its stanchion, and looked around for its favorite waiter – me. I was closing the last stanchion when Grandpa entered the barn carrying two shiny silver stainless steel milk pails.

"Good job, boys! I shoveled out the gutters earlier, Jase. How about feeding the herd while I start milking? When you finish, you can get on with your other chores, and I'll bed them down."

I nodded my agreement and headed for the ground grain supply, housed in a deep metal bin with a heavy, rodent-proof top. I filled the battered feed pail using the over-sized scoop. Then I dragged the heavy pail along the trough. I dropped a generous serving of the coarsely ground mixture of corn, oats, and wheat in front of each cow. Immediately, the animal began to slurp and chaw on the delicacy. By the time I had completed feeding the last cow in the row, the first one had finished her meal and, with her coarse tongue, had polished the concrete hollow in front of her to a radiant glow.

Danny followed me, enthralled by every move I made. He didn't say a word. Finally, Grandpa broke the silence.

"Danny, have you ever milked a cow before?" Grandpa inquired.

I saw the wheels turning in Danny's head. He wanted to say yes. But he sensed that, this time, more might be required of him than mere bravado. So he compromised with this pearl, "Once. I think. Maybe. Or maybe not."

Mercifully, Grandpa let him off the hook. "Come here. I'll show you how."

Danny looked my way. Panic filled his eyes. I nodded and reassured him, "It's fun."

Grandpa was seated on his three-legged wooden milking stool up under the massive belly of Bessie's second in command, Molly. This white giant was a very gentle cow and an easy milker. Danny timidly crawled up onto Grandpa's lap.

Grandpa patiently demonstrated the old thumb-finger-top-grip-squeeze-roll-down-squirt-release-start-again method of milking! The terror we had witnessed when Danny was a paratrooper-in-training returned.

"Just give it a try, Danny," Grandpa gently coaxed.

Danny nodded his head and abruptly seized Molly's nearest udder. A shudder of apprehension rippled up Molly's cowhide side. Danny squeezed with all his might. The results even startled Grandpa.

A long stream of pure white milk shot, not down into the milk pail as desired, but straight back at Danny. The prolonged squirt struck just below the bill of Danny's Tigers cap lifting it into the air. The ill-fated cap sailed upward and outward, then splashed emblem-side down in the most revolting puddle of – you don't want to know what – right in the middle of the gutter that ran behind the row of cows.

With milk dripping from his forehead and a stunned look on his face, Danny licked his lips, raised his eyebrows, and turned around to explain to a flabbergasted Grandpa.

"Yup!" he said matter-of-factly. "That happens every time I milk a cow!"

DANNY RETIRED EARLY FROM his milking career. We left Grandpa to finish milking Molly who half-closed her eyes and resumed chewing her cud. She was obviously relieved to be back in familiar hands.

Our next stop was the back shed, the oversized enclosure built over and around the kitchen door. The shed provided convenient storage for firewood and other essentials, a mudroom for Grandpa to shed his work clothes before entering Grandma's clean kitchen, and a workspace for grading and boxing the daily collection of chicken eggs.

Grandma managed the chicken and egg business. Grandpa wanted nothing to do with it. How could a heroic trapeze artist and near movie star possibly lower himself to tend chickens?

So I was offered the position as Grandma's junior partner. I performed the functions of egg distribution and sales full time and of chicken feeding and egg collection part-time, whenever I was at the farm.

Grandma was in charge of chick procurement. She also handled the other end of the cycle. When it came time each year, she was responsible for dispatching the fully-grown leghorns to "The Great Chicken Coop in the Sky" as Grandpa called it.

Among our Forrest Street neighbors, I had established a long list of standing orders for fresh farm eggs – at fifteen cents a dozen. Grandma and I split the profits fifty-fifty. Dad and Mom cooperated by making room in the car for several dozen egg cartons on every trip home.

I snatched the two wicker egg baskets from their pegs next to the egg carton shelf. One was painted green, the other yellow. We headed for the laying coop. When we entered, I noticed that all but three hens were outside. Two insiders were scratching the coop floor just for something to do. One fat hen was nestled in her box.

I pried the top off the chicken feed barrel and filled the chipped-enamel bowl with feed that Grandpa had ground at the gristmill the week before. I carried the bowl outside. Danny joined me.

The sound of the feed barrel being opened brought a flurry of clucking movement from every corner of the yard. Within seconds, the entire flock encircled me and pecked frantically at the dirt around my feet, almost as if I had already strewn their dinner on the ground.

Danny was startled when he suddenly found himself surrounded by a milling mass of gray, red, and white feather balls, uninhibitedly pushing at his legs and pecking at his toes. For fun, I tossed a small handful of feed at his feet and mimicked Tom Mix, when he fires his six-shooter at the outlaw's boots, "Dance, polecat! Dance!"

Danny clearly wasn't in a dancing mood. In fact, he was close to lapsing into panic mode again, so I hurled another huge handful in the opposite direction. The flock immediately shifted pecking venues.

Danny forced a smile and declared weakly, "That was fun!"

To change the subject and to show off a bit, I approached my favorite Plymouth Rock as she pecked furiously at her dinner. Turning to Danny, I said, "Watch this!"

I slowly placed my hands on the plump hen's back. She responded, just as I knew she would, by squatting right where she stood. I lifted the immobilized old biddy off the ground and offered the fluffy prize to Danny. "Want to hold her?" I asked. "She won't hurt you."

Danny acted as if I had just offered him a cobra. He shook his head violently. His black eyes performed an adagio dance in their sockets. I realized that I had asked too much of him. So I released my hen-friend that, without any sign of annoyance, resumed her furious pecking.

When the flock was fully engaged in their dining, I scooped up the egg baskets and motioned to Danny to follow me into the laying coop. He watched with interest as I gathered one or two warm brown eggs from every box. Finally, I lifted the feathery rump of the nesting Rhode Island Red and removed one, very warm egg from under her.

I had distributed the eggs evenly between the green and yellow baskets to give me a balanced load. I toted the baskets to the back shed and placed them carefully on the incubator table. I showed Danny how to grade eggs using the egg-sizing template. We gently placed each egg in its appropriate papier-mâché carton for the trip to Riverton.

Grandma had purchased a new supply of egg cartons that I wanted to unpack and store on the shelf. As I worked, Danny became bored, so I gave him a job to do.

"Danny, do me a favor before it gets dark. I left the chicken feed bowl out on the grass near the henhouse. Could you put it back in the chicken feed barrel – and make sure the top of the barrel is closed, tight?"

"You bet! I'm on my way!" he shouted, racing down the stairs and out the door.

As I sorted and stacked my egg cartons, I heard the final cheers and laughter signaling the end of my cousins' ball game, the chatter of the men from under the maple tree, and the buzz of the ladies finishing their cleanup tasks. I even heard Chub's voice coming from the kitchen. He must have finally awakened and crawled out from under the table.

Then I heard something terrifying! A bloodcurdling scream!

"JAAAAAAAAAAASE! HEEEEEEEEEEEEELP!"

The hysterical version of Danny's all-powerful *come-out call* startled me. I held my breath and listened again, not quite believing my ears the first time.

Absolute silence descended on the farm. The crickets stopped chirping in the orchard. Oddly, the image of cows swallowing their cuds and opening their huge brown eyes struck me.

Then it hit again!

"JAAAAAAAAAAASE! HEEEEEEEEEEEEEELP!"

I streaked from the back shed toward the bellow. My ball-playing cousins, the maple tree men, and the kitchen women joined me as I galloped toward the sound that I now realized was emanating from the small leghorn chick-breeding coop.

Grandma screamed after me, "Has he fallen! Is he hurt! What in God's name has happened to poor Danny?"

I didn't know. I didn't answer.

At the chick-breeding coop, we were greeted with a most unusual scene. There was Danny standing – no – stomping up and down on the coop's low roof. He was grasping the feed barrel top with both hands and swinging it madly, back and forth, in front of his face. I couldn't see what he was swatting at or why he was so hysterical.

Rounding the side of the coop, I was confronted by two huge red forms emerging from the evening shadows. The attackers! The gigantic Rhode Island Red rooster and his current challenger, the strapping Red yearling.

The combative birds had obviously called a truce in their ongoing battle with each other to combine forces against a common enemy, Danny!

In unison, the ominous pair of fighting fowls performed a frenzied war dance – angrily shaking their crimson combs, brandishing their menacing leg spurs, and slashing at the side of the coop. They scratched the dirt like mad bulls. Flapping and shrieking, they stretched their necks upward to taunt their helpless prey.

Danny was trapped, shuddering there, a mere three feet above the terrifying frenzy. The twin feathered demons looked as if they were about to move in for the kill. Danny looked as if he was about to faint.

"**BAAAAAAMM!!!**" The sound was deafening. Both roosters were jerked into the air and slammed into the pigpen fence.

I turned to see Grandpa Compton lowering his shotgun. The cloud of blue smoke wafted skyward and the acrid smell of gunpowder caught in my chest.

"That'll hold the sons zah –," Grandpa didn't finish.

Danny lowered the barrel top and sobbed. Grandma exhaled loudly. Dad reached up, grabbed Danny's waist, and lowered him from the roof. The farm was strangely silent again.

Dad looked Danny in the eyes and spoke softly, "The roosters are gone, son. You're all right now."

Danny blinked at Dad and said, "I wanted to be – on the roof – so – so I could see better."

"See what better, Danny?" Dad asked.

"Grandma's garden!" Danny exclaimed.

"Grandma's garden!" we all repeated. Was the boy daft?

Danny patiently explained, "I told Grandma Compton – this morning at the canning factory – that I had another good idea."

He turned toward Grandma, his wide eyes begging for confirmation. She nodded very slowly. Then her brow knitted with confused bewilderment.

As Danny continued, he looked straight at me, "So I climbed up on the little chicken garage. So I could see for myself – before I asked her – if there's room in her garden to plant a whole bunch of sauerkraut seeds."

Our jaws dropped. Nobody said a word!

DARKNESS HAD FALLEN EVEN before we started loading the car. Having farther to drive, the two non-Riverton Compton families had departed earlier.

From atop the skinny creosoted pole, the bright floodlight illuminated the driveway and yard. Swooping bats, flapping moths, and darting lesser night flyers madly circled the fixture, producing a dizzying shimmer of light below.

With hands on hips, Grandpa and Dad stared blankly into the open trunk trying to figure a way to pack all of Grandma's goodies and still have room for the spare tire and jack. Grandpa halfheartedly suggested, "I suppose we could tie the spare on the roof with binder twine."

"There's gotta be a way to get it all in," Dad insisted.

The Chevy was just the right size for our family of three. But how six of us – Aunt Maude, Mom, Dad, Danny, Chub, and me – would all manage to squeeze in was still a mystery, especially with the added challenge of finding room for ten dozen eggs in brand new cartons and the ten jars of sauerkraut that had inexplicably materialized from Grandma's cellar. And then, there was Grandma's gift to Mrs. Tucker, the butcher paper bundle containing the dressed carcass of the larger of Danny's feathered attackers.

I offered an easy solution. Danny and I could stay at the farm until next Sunday's family dinner. But Mom promptly vetoed that idea.

After several minutes of creative stuffing, all parcels and persons were finally aboard. Aunt Maude, Chub, and I were chummy-close in the backseat with half the sauerkraut. Danny sat astraddle the gearshift lever, sandwiched cozily between my folks. He was hugging the bundle containing the fallen rooster.

We waved goodbye to Grandma, Grandpa, and Mick who by this time was smiling in anticipation of his nightly peanut snack. Then we eased out of the driveway and headed into the dark, moonless night.

At first, we chatted about our interesting day. But, after a mile or so, the only sound I heard was the strain of the Chevy engine accompanied by a chorus of deep breathing.

For some time, I had looked for an opportunity to ask Dad about an event that I had observed earlier in the spring. This seemed like a good time.

Late one afternoon, I was stacking pieces of former sewing machine cabinets behind the shed when Gentleman Jim surprised me. I wasn't aware of his presence because oddly he had failed to signal his approach with a single whistle, hum, or dee dum of *Old Kentucky*.

In a hollow voice, he asked, "Hello, Jase. Is your father home?"

"Yes, sir, Mr. Jim. He's in the house. I'll go get him."

As I walked up the path toward our backdoor, I wondered what was wrong with Jim. I looked over my shoulder and saw him slumping against the shed looking sad and despondent. I noticed he had no supper bottle under his arm – an unusual state of affairs for this time of day.

In response to my call, Dad took Gentleman Jim into the shed where they talked quietly for over an hour. I sat on the back porch, flush with curiosity, waiting for them to finish. When they emerged, Dad came back to the house while Jim waited by the shed door. He didn't seem to notice me. I remember thinking how very unusual that was for Jim.

Dad walked back to the shed where he handed Jim a small number of folded bills of a denomination not known to me. Jim's eyes never left his black oxfords. He took the money from Dad and put it into his tuxedo coat pocket. As usual, Dad patted Jim on the arm, but this time Jim failed to respond. Instead, he turned and trudged down the alley in silence.

Dad watched Jim disappear into the twilight before returning to the back porch. He sat down in the chair next to me and lit his pipe. We were quiet for a while. Finally, he said, "That man has had some tough luck."

Since that night, I had wondered what Dad had meant. So I asked quietly from the backseat, "Dad, what was Gentleman Jim's tough luck? And how come he wants to be a bum?"

Although, I couldn't see Dad's face, I could tell by his voice that my concern pleased him. He spoke softly, "Jim didn't start out wanting to be a bum. It just sort of worked out that way.

"Some years ago, Jim was the history teacher at Riverton High. In those days, he was a young man with a promising future. He was loved by his students and respected by his fellow teachers.

"Jim had been an exceptional athlete. In high school and in college, he lettered in three sports – football, basketball, and baseball. He went off to the University of Michigan on an athletic scholarship. But instead of majoring in physical education – as many athletes do – he studied hard and earned his degree in American history.

"To the disappointment of many, he turned down an opportunity to play center field for the Detroit Tigers. Jim said a Michigan history major shouldn't squander his time playing baseball. He had a more important job to do – teaching high school students history and civics. So he came back to Riverton to teach and settle down. He married his high school sweetheart.

"Because of his athletic background, he was offered assistant coaching assignments in his old sports. He gladly accepted the jobs. He liked being close to those sports – and to the boys who loved them as much as he did. And he needed the few extra dollars each month that coaching paid. Remember, Jase, we're talking about the beginning of the Depression.

"In spite of their tight budget, he and his new wife were very happy. A year or so after they were married, beautiful twin girls were born.

"Then, Jase, a terrible thing happened.

"Late in January – when the twins were about two – Jim's wife and daughters were driving the family car, just north of town, on the big curve along the Chippewa River. The car spun out of control on a sheet of ice. It crashed into the big oak tree on the curve and plunged into the half-frozen river. All three of them were killed. The sheriff came to the high school and gave Jim the bad news.

"Some people suffer a dreadful loss, then get over it in time. But Jim was never the same. He was haunted by the loss of his family and terrible guilt – strangely enough. He couldn't eat or sleep. Perhaps, worst of all, he couldn't teach. The school board insisted he take a leave of absence to pull himself together. So he did. But it didn't work.

"He walked the streets of Riverton in a trance, at all hours of the night and day. Nobody knew how to help him. Adding to his bad luck, because Jim had been the last teacher hired, he was the first to be let go when the school budget was cut during the depth of the Depression.

"Eventually, he began drinking – heavily – to ease his pain, I guess. His savings soon disappeared. He sold his possessions for food and liquor. Finally, he lost his house. So he joined the hobos at their camp beside the river under the Ann Arbor Street Bridge.

"Even though the war has brought prosperity back to Riverton and to our neighborhood, it's never touched Jim. It seems beyond his reach, for some reason.

"During the last few years, he has recovered some of his spirit. But he's only part of the man he once was."

After Dad finished, I just sat and thought about Jim. Neither of us talked for a while. Then I asked, "Dad, do you think all of him will come back – someday?"

"I sure hope so, Jase. I really do."

We drove the last five miles in silence.

When we reached the Tucker house, Dad tried to wake Danny but to no avail. So he lifted my new friend from the Chevy and carried him to the front door. Danny mumbled unintelligibly and snuggled tightly against Dad's shoulder.

Mrs. Tucker, who saw us pull in, greeted them at the door. She lifted Danny from Dad's arms with ease, explaining that she was used to carrying her sleep-prone sons.

Chub was slightly more conscious than Danny. Aunt Maude propped him against the car door while she untangled her legs from the pretzel shape they had assumed on the ride in. With both Aunt Maude's hands firmly on his shoulders, Chub sleepwalked the length of the Tucker sidewalk, up the porch steps, through the front door, and into the arms of Mr. Tucker who looked a little sleepy himself.

I followed the slumbering Tuckers, carrying Grandma's butcher paper wrapped gift for Mrs. T. I quickly related the story of Danny's run-in with the roosters. His mom was so overcome with gratitude that she flung her arms around me and gave me a big smooch on the cheek. My face turned red.

Before we left, Dad warned the Tuckers, "That rooster met his end by way of Grandpa Compton's shotgun, so take care not to bite down on birdshot when you eat him."

We departed amidst a final barrage of goodbyes and thanks.

Once back onto New Albany Avenue, we began our trek toward downtown and Aunt Maude's apartment on South Addison Street. We were just about to pass Forrest Street when suddenly Dad slammed on the brakes and swerved radically to the right.

Bang! The Chevy hit the curb and vaulted onto the sidewalk before coming to rest a foot short of the Good Mission Church's front porch steps. All of us were shaken by our bouncy detour. But we were unhurt.

The cause of our near-accident was a dilapidated Ford convertible. Its brazen young driver looked back over his shoulder and honked his horn in a taunting fashion – *beep-de-de-beep-beep, beep-beep.* Then he laughed and slapped the back of his passenger, another young man with long slicked-down hair and a witless grin.

The vehicle that had just run the stop sign and squealed out of Forrest Street was familiar to our whole family. Since early spring, we had eaten its dust and listened to its raucous horn blowing as it raced up and down our street. However, this was the first time that the Ford had come close to endangering our lives.

My father exhaled loudly and stared after the convertible as it disappeared in a cloud of blue exhaust fumes to the west. His fingers still gripped the steering wheel tightly.

My mother, far from calm, declared angrily, "Those Libby girls are in real trouble now. Hanging around with those reckless no-gooders. Wait till I speak to their mother!"

"The draft board'll catch up with those rascals. Then the Army will teach 'em a thing or two," Aunt Maude declared, adding her two-cents worth.

"Well, I didn't want it to come to this, but tomorrow I've got to speak to Jeff about that pair. I know his patience is worn as thin as ours. But this has gone too far. It's time he took official action," Dad said.

"Jeff" was Sergeant Jeff Tolna of the Riverton Police Department. He was Dad's best friend, our neighbor, and Sherm Blue Bunny's father. It was Jeff's police whistle that I had used to create the diversion for "Operation Mole" just the day before.

When Dad had regained his composure, he put the Chevy in reverse and backed onto New Albany Avenue. After we were underway, he said, "Maude, sorry about this. We wanted to get you home early, so you could getta good night's sleep. You'll wanta be well rested for your moving day."

"Moving! Where are you moving to, Aunt Maude?" I cried with alarm.

My mother chuckled, "We've been saving this as a surprise, Jase. Aunt Maude is coming to live with us – until Uncle Van comes home from the war. She'll be your new roommate. Whatcha think of that?"

"Holy Cow! Neat!" I shouted, not believing my ears. "Aunt Maude! She's my favorite aunt!"

I forgot that Aunt Maude was sitting right there beside me. She squeezed me and pecked me on the cheek in response to my outburst of affection. For the second time that evening, the heat of embarrassment scorched my face.

By the time we arrived home, it was well past our normal bedtimes, especially for a Sunday night. Without my usual stalling tactics, our "Now, I Lay Me" and "See You in the Morning, Bye" rituals were completed in record time.

After Dad turned out my light, I listened to the big black crickets chirping from under Mrs. Mikas' woodpile. In the quiet darkness, I inventoried of all the exciting adventures that lay ahead:

✓ Debriefing Sherman the Vermin.
✓ Exchanging the kraut for the bubble gum.
✓ Solving the black car and tommy gun mystery.

✓ Delivering the new egg supply to my customers.
✓ Helping Sergeant Jeff arrest the Ford convertible gang.
✓ Preparing for my new roommate.
✓ Extracting hooks and sinkers from that gob of fishing line.
✓ Playing with my new best friend Danny.

As I drifted off, the familiar refrain of soft sobs entered my bedroom window. I heard my heart whisper, *Goodnight, Mrs. Mikas. Don't be sad.*

7 NEIGHBORHOOD BUSINESS

MY RETURN TRIP FROM DREAMLAND WAS PARTICULARLY arduous that Monday morning. When I opened my eyes, the sun streaks radiating across my rag rug had almost reached the wall opposite my window. At first, I feared that I was late for school. But, as my head cleared, I remembered that these were the long days of June. And summer vacation had just begun.

Instead of being jarred awake by Danny's brutal *come-out call*, this morning it was the more gentle murmur of voices from the kitchen. I slipped on my summer uniform: shorts, tee shirt, and rough work shoes for tramping, kicking, and scuffing my way through the day ahead.

It was Aunt Maude's moving day. And, was I ready!

On my way to the kitchen, I heard Dad say, "We're agreed then. You won't say anything to Louise Libby until I telephone Jeff Tolna from the plant. If he'll do his part, maybe we can end this dangerous situation without creating a neighborhood row."

Not wanting to interrupt this interesting conversation, I slipped into my chair at the table without saying a word.

"Yes, I think that's best. I'd hate to condemn the Libby girls strictly on the basis of the company they keep," Mom agreed, seeming not to be inhibited by my presence. "Even though, they oughta have better sense."

After a sip of coffee, she added, "At heart, they're good girls. Don't you think?"

"Sure, they are. Remember how they helped us when we built the shed?" Dad reminisced.

"You know who thinks the world of those two girls – and vice versa?" Mom asked.

Dad wrinkled his brow. "Who?"

"Gentleman Jim, that's who! Remember that cheating episode at the high school. If Jim hadn't intervened on their behalf with his former boss – the school principal – they wouldn't have graduated. And, without those diplomas, they wouldn't have their jobs at the canning factory either."

Dad nodded and then looked at his wristwatch.

As she cleared Dad's dishes, Mom suggested, "Why don't we talk some more tonight? Maude'll be here, too. She's got a good head for these kinda things."

Mom respected Aunt Maude's common sense. I idolized her for all her qualities.

"Your lunch pail's packed. You don't want to miss that 7:00 o'clock bus," Mom advised, hurrying Dad out the back door.

Waving from the walk, he admonished with a smile, "You be careful with my brand new Chevy – the one I'm letting you use to move Maude today."

"You be careful with my brand new bus – the one I'm letting *you* use to go to work today," she retorted.

THE WOMEN AND CHILDREN of our community "owned" the buses. The men of our community "owned" the automobiles.

The man of the house was the family's primary breadwinner. So, normally, he drove the family car to his work each day. Women and children transacted all other family business – shopping, doctor's visits, and movie matinees – utilizing the citywide bus system. Even women with important defense jobs were expected to take the bus to work.

The Chippewa Trails Bus Line operated an extensive transportation system weaving throughout Riverton and New Albany over six routes (A through F). The A Route was the most traveled route. It followed Main Street from Riverton's west city limits to the downtown bus station. Then it headed south along Addison Street to New Albany Avenue where it turned east toward New Albany. When the buses reached the county seat, they circled the block containing the Chippewa County Courthouse and then reversed course. The A Route was the longest route in the system, a sixteen-mile loop.

The Chippewa Trails buses were painted bright blue and maize, school colors for both Riverton High School and the University of Michigan. Invariably, they were squeaky clean, inside and out, and expertly maintained by the bus line's professional mechanics.

Chippewa Trails bus drivers were at all times competent, courteous, and cheerful. They wore crisp blue uniforms with maize nametags and pure white covers on their combination caps. Like the policemen they resembled, bus drivers were highly respected by the entire community.

They earned this respect in many ways. First, they drove their buses safely and at the precise speed to ensure arrival at each stop exactly on time, not a minute early and not a minute late. Moreover, they accomplished this on-time performance while providing a wide range of peripheral services.

On wintry mornings, they left their warm buses to help mothers buckle on galoshes before sending children down unshoveled sidewalks to the bus. They loaded and unloaded bags of groceries for elderly ladies who saved pennies by shopping all the way downtown instead of at their neighborhood stores. They carefully stowed oversized musical instruments, like tubas and drums, in the luggage compartment under the bus so high school students could practice at home during the week to prepare for Saturday football halftime shows.

On one occasion, I witnessed a frantic mother who stopped the bus and asked the driver, "Mr. Jenkins, have you had chicken pox?"

Mr. Jenkins confirmed that he had, when he was in third grade at Hamilton School.

The mother heaved a sigh of relief, "Good! tommy's in the last stages. He's crusted over, but they won't let him go back to school yet. Would you mind if he rode along with you today, so I can go to work?"

"That'll be just fine, Mrs. Risko," he replied without hesitation.

As he waved tommy aboard, our bus driver/nurse instructed, "tommy, you sit right here in the seat behind me. That way I can keep the other passengers away from you, and you can keep me company. When we arrive at the bus station each time, you let me know if you have to go to the bathroom. Okay?"

"Thank you, Mr. Jenkins."

"Anytime, Mrs. Risko. Now, that'll be tommy's normal fare for the day – one nickel."

The fare included unlimited transfers. So Danny and I devised a way to ride every inch of all six routes and home again – in the same day – for only five cents apiece. Of course, it took us from sunup to sundown, but sometimes we just couldn't think of anything better than an all-day bus tour of our fair city.

The Chippewa Trails buses operated from 6:00 AM until midnight every day of the week. At 5:15 AM, on one particular Monday morning, we arrived at the Forrest Street bus stop with plenty of food for our trip, a paper sack full of sandwiches – peanut butter with sweet pickle on rye. Our early arrival gave us ample time to sit on the bench and watch the delivery trucks – bread, milk, newspaper-magazine, and beer – stop and unload their wares at Pete's.

Each time Pete came out to greet a truck driver and help carry the delivery into the store, we yelled, "Morning, Pete!"

Pete waved and hollered back, "Gooda morning-ah, boyz! You-sa be gooda today! Okay?"

Like most owners of Riverton's independent grocery stores, confectionary shops, and delicatessens, Pete was Italian. And his melodious broken English was thoroughly pleasing to our young ears. Although, we shared this exchange of greetings with Pete about six times before our bus arrived, he didn't seem to mind.

When the A Route bus stopped, we hopped aboard. Our first driver was Mr. Smalley, a gray-haired man with a very pleasant disposition. Both he and his wife sang in the choir at the First Methodist Church, where Danny and I regularly contributed our presence and our pennies.

We boldly slammed our nickels into the fare box and sat down in the seat running parallel to the side of the bus, immediately across from the driver. We chose this prime location, so we could help Mr. Smalley with his bus-driving duties. Dutifully, we did our job by notifying him of each upcoming stop, warning of cars about to turn into the street ahead, lifting carriages for women with their arms full of babies and shopping bags, greeting people as they stepped onto our bus, shouting goodbyes when they departed from the back door, pulling the stop-signal cable for people laden with packages, collecting fares and depositing them – *slam* – into the fare box, and finally helping Mr. Smalley make change by doing his arithmetic – aloud – for him.

We rode the A Route bus west to the city limits, then all the way back east again to New Albany, and finally back west again to the main bus station, about twenty miles and a good two hours in all. Passenger traffic was particularly heavy that time of day, so we were extremely busy performing our driver-support duties.

We could tell that Mr. Smalley was *very* grateful for our help that morning by the way he thanked us – over and over and over – when we left his bus with our transfers in hand.

All routes passed through the main terminal. If we obtained a transfer when we disembarked there, we could change to another route. When we became bored with that one, we got another transfer and changed again. Because transfers were free, we could ride all six routes on a single nickel fare. But remembering to ask for a transfer was the key.

On that particular Monday, we lessened the burden of seven *very* appreciative bus drivers, six regulars and the substitute driver who took Mr. Smalley's place after he unexpectedly became ill when he saw us preparing to board his bus for a second time that day. And, naturally, this doesn't include the countless Rivertonians who benefited from our special personal attention.

Ah, the joy of public service!

MOM AND I SELDOM had use of the family car for the day. For my part, I took full advantage of this luxury by convincing her to drive my egg delivery route. My neighborhood clientele were impressed with my new mode of transportation. Normally it was Sherm's wagon.

Within an hour, we had delivered all ten cartons of fresh eggs. My collections, tied snugly inside my hankie, rested safely at the bottom of my side pocket. We returned home so I could deposit my share ($.75) in my bank before converting our delivery truck into a moving van.

When we arrived at Aunt Maude's apartment, she was packed and ready to go. We loaded her suitcases, hanging clothes, and cardboard boxes into the Chevy's trunk and backseat. Not a huge load, but all of her worldly possessions. Most of Uncle Van's clothing, books, and other belongings had been stored in Grandma's attic the week before.

After locking the apartment, Aunt Maude dropped her door key through the mail slot and proclaimed, "On to a new life – with fresh air!"

Aunt Maude had lived in the small, furnished apartment over Fazio's Delicatessen since Uncle Van joined the Army two years before. Fazio's was located on South Addison Street on the outskirts of the business district. From there, Aunt Maude could easily walk the few blocks to her job as a waitress behind the lunch counter at Woolworth's dime store. This worked out well because Uncle Van and she were married only a short time before he enlisted, and they hadn't yet put enough aside to buy a car.

All and all, Aunt Maude liked apartment living. "Hardly any housework," she always claimed. "I use all that extra time to make bags and bags of money."

There was some truth to this.

She worked all the extra shifts and overtime she could get. Her wages were paltry, but the tips resulting from her efficiency and bubbly personality more than compensated. She built a loyal following of customers among the shop owners, lawyers, and sales clerks who worked downtown and ate at Woolworth's each day.

The rent for her apartment was surprisingly low for good reason. There was a serious problem with living over Fazio's Delicatessen. No matter how hard she tried to avoid it, she always reeked of Italian seasonings.

Gino Fazio was fiercely competitive with the three other delicatessens in town, all owned by his Italian cousins. They vied with each other to meet Riverton's unusual demand for spicy delicatessen delights. Gino's strategy for winning was uncomplicated. He simply quadrupled the measure of oregano, basil, garlic, and onions called for in each of Grandma Fazio's recipes from the old country.

This was an exceedingly successful strategy for Gino's business. But it almost got the best of Aunt Maude.

Because this overpowering odor permeated everything she owned, including her waitress uniforms, she was forced to endure countless jokes and snide comments from family, friends, and sometimes even customers. One time, her fellow waitress, Molly O'Brien, told her that she shouldn't keep cucumbers in her apartment overnight because by morning they would turn into kosher dills.

On another occasion, she served a fresh egg salad sandwich to a regular customer who complained that Woolworth's recipe contained far too much garlic for her taste. Aunt Maude didn't have the heart to tell her that the egg salad didn't contain a speck of garlic.

But Aunt Maude took remarks about her *Aroma d'Italia,* as she called it, in stride. Still, she was very much relieved to leave its source and join me in my room where nothing smelled bad, unless you count the dead toad that I inadvertently left in my underwear drawer.

With the backseat full, I rode in the Danny position, astraddle the gearshift lever. Once we arrived, we carried Aunt Maude's things into my bedroom, but we didn't stay long. On our way to Grandma Compton's, I sat in my normal spot in the backseat next to boxes of wedding presents and Uncle Van's fly-fishing tackle, all destined for Grandma's attic.

Grandma met us at the door. Grandpa and Mick were back by the woods encouraging Jim and Fannie to tug a giant boulder out of the ground in the corner of the newly planted cornfield. Since she herself was busy baking a pie, we found our own way to the attic and stored the boxes.

Before we left, Grandma insisted that we sample the steaming pie sitting on the kitchen counter. "It's freshly picked wild strawberries. Grandpa brought them to me from the woods in his hat last evening. I couldn't resist baking a pie. The first of the season! Have another piece, Jase," she urged.

My mother warned, "There won't be any left for Dad!"

"Oh, never mind. He's too fat anyway!" Grandma rationalized, scooping about a third of the pie onto my plate.

Aunt Maude and Mom chuckled at the very notion of Grandpa being fat.

"We've gotta get back with the car," Mom explained after I had finished my gigantic second serving. "John has a sewing machine to deliver when he gets home from work. Besides, Maude and Jase have to get settled in their room."

"And we wanta hear how the Libby boyfriends like their new home down at the Riverton City Jail!" I whispered to Aunt Maude who winked at me in response.

While Grandma and I settled up for my recent egg sales, Aunt Maude and Mom said their goodbyes and headed for the Chevy. Grandma tucked her $.75 away in her change purse and then reburied it in the recesses of her huge leather pocketbook.

To celebrate the deal, Grandma slipped the last piece of wild strawberry pie, wrapped neatly in waxed paper, into the deep side pocket of my shorts. She whispered, "You'll probably be hungry before you get home."

As usual in these matters, Grandma was right. Her delectable pie was history before we reached the Riverton city limits.

Upon our return, Dad loaded the sewing machine into the car trunk. To keep him company, Mom rode with him over to New Albany where the customer lived. While they were gone, Aunt Maude and I organized our room.

We quickly agreed on where Aunt Maude would store her things. She freed up room in my chest of drawers by showing me how to fold and pile my underwear and socks, Navy style, as she called it. In the process, she discovered the source of the toad stink and volunteered to transport the dead-dry varmint, by the toe, to the alley garbage pit. Then she went to the kitchen to put away some dishware that she had brought from her apartment.

I was in my room practicing Aunt Maude's Navy sock-folding method when IT exploded in my ears.

"*Jaaaaaaaaaaaaaaaaaaase. Caaaaaaaaaaaaaaaaaaaaaaaaaaaaaan. Youuuuuuuuuuuuuuuuuuuuuuuuu. Cuuuuuuuuuuuuuum. Ooooooooooooout?*"

It was Danny's blood-curdling *come-out call*, instantaneously followed by Aunt Maude's scream and the dreadful sound of shattering glass.

I ran to the kitchen to find Aunt Maude clutching the top of her chest and breathing hard. Broken pieces of a water glass, from which she must have been drinking only seconds earlier, now lay scattered around her feet on the kitchen floor.

There was Danny, standing outside the kitchen screen door. He was dressed in his standard military uniform with two *significant* additions.

First, he sported a brand new pair of round, steel frame glasses that made his black eyes appear twice as big as before. But, most dramatically, using both hands, he waved a menacing four-foot samurai sword back and forth in front of his grinning face. He looked like a miniature, and wildly insane, General Tojo.

"Let's chop some sewing machines!" he hissed between clenched teeth.

DANNY AND I LEFT Aunt Maude wiping up the last remnants of broken glass from the linoleum floor and made our way to the pile of discarded sewing machine cabinets with our chopping tools – axe and sword. As he practiced his swing, Danny grunted repeatedly like a sumo wrestler.

Our Chevy pulled into the driveway. Mom and Dad were back from New Albany. On their way to the back door, they spotted Danny's impressive war souvenir. Mom gasped. Dad decided to intervene.

"Hey, Danny! That's a mighty fine looking sword you've got there. How'd you come by that?" he asked.

"It's a Jap sword that my uncle got at Gottacanal," Danny replied, matter-of-factly.

"Oh – at Guadalcanal – that's impressive," Dad said, repressing a chuckle.

Then, in typical Danny style, he stunned us all by adding, "After my uncle shot four thousand Jap soldiers, President Rosebelt gave it to him – for me to have."

Dad snorted! He turned his head, trying hard to swallow his chuckles.

Mom saved the day by changing the subject, "Danny! Those are wonderful-looking glasses. Are they new?"

"Yup. My mom and I got 'em at the opdishpan's office today."

"Opdishpan? Oh, the *optician's* office! Can you see better?" Mom asked, recovering quickly.

"Yup," Danny said, training his head from side to side. "I can see clear down to the Nazi's house where we –."

"Mom, can Danny stay for supper?" I deftly interrupted before Danny revealed any FSG secrets.

"I awredy ate. We had peaches and peas. But I might be able to stay. What are you havin'?" Danny asked, nonchalantly.

After Danny approved Mom's menu and *reluctantly* agreed to stay, we turned our attention to firewood. Dad convinced Danny to preserve his museum piece and use the sledgehammer instead. So we went to work behind the shed – chopping, smashing, and splitting sewing machine cabinets. We stacked cast iron treadle bases in one pile and splintered cabinet wood in the other.

While we worked, I told Danny about last evening's near-miss accident and Dad's promise to call Sergeant Tolna concerning the reckless hot-rodders. Later, I worked up my courage to ask him about his family's strange meals. Between what Danny told me and what I learned later, I was able to construct the whole story.

AFTER A TOUR IN the South Pacific, Sam Tucker came back home with a pronounced limp from a nasty piece of enemy shrapnel in his left thigh and an early discharge from the Navy. The need for further surgery, hospital recovery stints, and months of physical therapy prevented him from establishing himself in the civilian work world. Unlike his factory-working peers, he was unable to take advantage of the war-driven prosperity.

While he didn't mind taking on extra jobs or long hours, the excessive frugality required of his family really got to him. At his age, he should have been better able to provide for a family of five. To change all this, he decided to gamble on a business of his own.

Before signing the mortgage papers for the new garage, auto repair business, and house, Sam got cold feet. Screwing up his courage, he shared his secret with his father, a widower, who had owned a small grocery store in New Albany before retiring. The empathetic father encouraged Sam to set aside his fears. He wanted his son to enjoy the benefits of business ownership as he had.

Besides, Sam's father had a secret, too.

During the two years before he retired, the wily grocer had systematically increased his orders for non-perishables. His suppliers, thankful for the increased business, gladly helped him store the surplus inventory at his home, a few blocks from the store. When he closed his business, he had three hundred cases of assorted canned goods squirreled away in his basement.

At first, he was smug about his ploy. It had saved him hundreds of tax dollars. Besides, he had acquired his stash at wholesale prices. Now, he was prepared for his old age. Who knew? Maybe the country was in for another Depression. That's what often happens to the economy at the conclusion of a war.

But he soon regretted his decision for a number of reasons.

First, he was sorry about depriving the U.S. Government of several hundred dollars in income tax revenues, right at the time of the country's greatest need. He felt guilty.

Second, he saw himself as one of those horrible hoarders depicted on the posters down at the New Albany post office. He felt unpatriotic.

Third, and most embarrassing of all, he had grossly over-estimated his need for canned goods. He would never live long enough to consume half of what was stored in his basement. He felt stupid.

Sam's confession of self-doubt was the answer to his father's prayers. "Son, you go ahead and make that down payment," he urged Sam. "And I'll feed your family for the next few years. All you have to do is haul it out of my basement. Take it all, so I can live my retired years without feeling guilty."

Sam gratefully accepted. After the deal was closed and the Tuckers were snug in their new house, he set about transferring the stash. Using his beat-up Dodge station wagon, he estimated it would take thirty-six round trips from basement to basement.

From lumber he inherited with the new business, Sam built row upon row of floor-to-ceiling shelves. Then he unpacked and stored each can by category, converting the Tucker basement into a small grocery store. During the chilly early-spring months, the family saved money by burning cardboard boxes and can wrappers instead of expensive coal or firewood in their living room woodstove.

The inventory of canned fruits, vegetables, and soups of all kinds was enormous, over five thousand cans. This would surely feed his family until he was established and profitable. Free of financial fear, he turned his attention to his business.

After the family adopted their "can diet," discreet disposal of empty cans became a concern. Fortunately, meticulous recycling of tin cans had become a wartime fetish practiced by all patriotic families.

Instead of spending scarce family funds on movies, every Saturday night the Tuckers assembled in the kitchen for fun and fulfillment of their patriotic duty. They called it "Can Night."

Chub's task came first. He removed the paper wrapper from each empty can that had been stored temporarily in the coal bin at the top of the basement stairs. Because he couldn't read, he had to rely on the picture on the can. He loudly announced its former contents as he handed the bare can to Queenie.

Queenie's job, about which she never failed to complain, was to rinse out each can under the kitchen faucet before passing it to Danny or Mrs. Tucker. Using hand-held can openers, they partially cut the bottoms out of the clean can. Then they carefully pushed the tops and bottoms back inside before passing it to Sam.

Sam positioned the can in the middle of the woven straw doormat, smashed it flat with his huge work shoes, and tossed the flattened can into a burlap bag hanging on the kitchen doorknob. When a bag was full, he carried the heavy evidence to a spot next to the garage door where Bohunk Joe could easily find it when making his daily rounds.

The Can Night process worked perfectly for a month or two until Chub decided to do some work on his own, presumably for extra credit. Over the course of several days, with the motive of speeding up Can Night, Chub crept to the basement and performed his label-removing task – ahead of time.

Except for a few dozen cans located on shelves beyond his reach, Chub succeeded in unwrapping every *unopened* can in the basement. Then he rearranged the cans on the shelves according to size, not contents. He believed it looked neater. When Chub finished, the shelves in the Tucker basement were filled with nearly five thousand bare tin cans with no conceivable way to ascertain their contents.

To keep his family surprise a secret, he started with the back shelves and worked forward. Chub's endeavor wasn't discovered until the morning his work progressed to the shelf right next to the basement stairs.

When Mrs. Tucker assessed what Chub's surprise meant to the family, she nearly fainted. Chub attempted to minimize his offense by explaining that each and every wrapper was still there in the basement. Piled high in the corner behind the – well, he wasn't sure – corn, peas, pears, or, maybe, chili cans.

As you may have guessed, Chub didn't get the extra credit he sought. But Mr. Tucker did give him a few good marks on the bottom of his pants. And you would not have wanted to hear Queenie's reaction to the news.

However, the Tuckers made the best of it. They turned mealtime into an adventure with each "Mystery Can" becoming the subject of a family guessing game and an opportunity to chide Chub for the 5,000[th] time. For months after his conviction, Chub secretly maintained his innocence. But, wisely, he kept that belief to himself.

BY THE TIME SUPPER was ready, Danny and I were pretty pooped. We finished stacking the wood, stored our tools in the shed, and collected Danny's sword. Eager to tell everybody about our accomplishments, we headed for the kitchen.

As we approached the house, we heard Dad reporting on the Libby boyfriends to Mom and Aunt Maude. We picked up our pace so not to miss the news.

"Mine wasn't the first complaint the police received this morning. But, like us, nobody knew the driver's name – or even where he lived. So Jeff did some investigating, starting with a conversation with the Libby girls this morning. Then he checked with the Michigan State Police. You'll never guess what he found out."

We shook our heads and shrugged our shoulders.

"The driver's name is Harper – he's a shirttail relative of the Morris family that lives out M31 – near the POW camp. That's where they arrested him and his buddy this afternoon. But that's not all."

Dad paused for dramatic effect. We were intrigued.

"It seems that the two of them are AWOL. No! Let's see. I guess they've been absent too long for that by now. So technically they're deserters – from a Navy destroyer out of Norfolk, Virginia. And that red convertible – it's stolen! From a used car lot down by Detroit!"

We were flabbergasted. "Oh, my gosh!" we exclaimed in unison.

"The boys will spend their last hours in Riverton in the city jail. The Navy Shore Patrol – up from Detroit – collects them tomorrow afternoon. Then, they're headed for a General Court Martial. And a long stretch in Leavenworth Prison, according to Jeff."

Then Dad added, "Desertion is no laughing matter during times of war."

We all stared at each other with our mouths wide open.

"Does Louise Libby know about this?" Mom asked, out of concern for her friend.

"Jeff indicated that he'd talked with the girls after he arrested their pals and made them promise to inform her – tonight. He told me that they seemed shocked by the news. The girls insist they didn't know anything about what the boys had done. Jeff said he believed 'em."

Dad shook his head.

"Dad, will the Libby girls go to jail?" I practically shouted.

He pondered my question for a minute. Then he spoke deliberately, "I can't see any circumstance that would result in the Libby girls ever going to prison."

Boy, was Dad wrong! But none of us knew it at the time.

After supper, Aunt Maude and I walked Danny home. No one spoke until we reached the Tucker driveway. Then Danny reminded me, "Tomorrow we gotta see Sherman and get Grandma's extra sauerkrauts over to the canning factory."

I had nearly forgotten about the neighborhood Nazi and the bubble gum business. "Okay. Wanta start early?"

"I'll be at your house before breakfast. Just in case your mom forgot to go to the store, I'll bring a can of – of something," Danny promised. He waved his sword from the Tucker back porch before disappearing into the house.

I took Aunt Maude's hand as we walked home by way of the alley. The night was dark and still. A gentle warm breeze tickled the leaves of the trees and bushes along our route.

"Do you miss Uncle Van, Aunt Maude?" I asked, looking up at her face.

"Funny you should ask that right now, Jase. I was just thinking about him. Yes. I miss him very much. He's only been home once – last February – since he joined the army in 1942. That's a long time for people who love each other to be apart."

"Do you know where he is? I mean, right now?"

"Well, after his special school in New Jersey – and of course his furlough here with us – the Army Signal Corps sent him off to England. You get the news on the radio and in the paper. General Eisenhower is getting ready to send our Army across the English Channel to invade Europe. Uncle Van will go along with them whenever they go. That's for sure."

"Are you scared?"

"Yes. Ah, well, I'm not really sure. I don't want Uncle Van hurt or anything like that, but I'm awfully proud, too, Jase. Uncle Van was very courageous in Africa and in Sicily. And he's a good soldier. He knows what he's doing. So he's convinced me – mainly in all the letters he writes – that he'll be just fine. I guess I want to believe in him and not be scared."

After a pause, she added, "But I say a lot of prayers, too."

"Some soldiers didn't do so well in Sicily – I mean – especially Theo Mikas."

After mentioning Theo Mikas, I wished I hadn't. Lamely, I tried to change the subject. "Have you seen Mrs. Mikas' gold star – hanging in her window, right next to the blue star?"

"Yes, Jase. I have. It's sad. Her two sons wanted so badly to serve their new country. Now, one of them is dead and – I suppose – the other, Ivan, is about to join Uncle Van for the invasion of Europe. This is a sad time for the world, Jase. A very sad time."

I thought for a while, and then added, "Mrs. Mikas is really sad. She cries every night. I hear her from my bed. And you'll hear her tonight, too." Then I tried to add a little optimism, "But she's happy during the day. She always smiles and laughs whenever she sees me."

"Jase, you make a lot of people smile and laugh. And so does your new friend, Danny."

I really liked Aunt Maude a lot that night. It was our first night as roommates.

When we reached our part of the alley, I could see the faint light of Dad's pipe glowing from near the shed. I heard the low tones of men's voices, too. I couldn't see who was with Dad until we were just a few feet away.

One of the two dark forms turned and spoke, "Greetings, Mr. Jase Addison. How's the world treating you? Hello, Maude."

I was certain I knew what they were talking about.

FAINT STRAINS OF *Under the Double Eagle* from the direction of the Tucker house roused me from a deep sleep. Quietly, I popped out of bed and stepped into my summer uniform.

It was very early, so I resisted the urge to wake my new roommate to tell her Danny was on his way. Instead, I tiptoed out and left Aunt Maude slumbering peacefully in the twin bed across from mine in *our* tiny bedroom.

A mad symphony of bird songs greeted me as I scurried off the porch toward the alley. I intercepted Danny before he woke the neighborhood with his robust *come-out call.* He was carrying a hefty silver can that I assumed was breakfast.

When he saw me, he smiled and patted his can proudly. Licking his lips, he growled, "Hmmmm, yummy!"

When we reached our kitchen, I had mixed emotions. Optimism and skepticism.

Being an experienced can opener operator, Danny took over. He extracted his favorite tool from the small drawer next to our refrigerator. I looked on expectantly while he skillfully turned the handle. Our breakfast surprise revealed itself in no time.

"And, today's breakfast is – pickled beets! I tell you, it's pickled beets!" I announced, imitating a carnival barker. "Not exactly my favorite breakfast, Buddy Roe."

Undaunted, Danny went about his business. His recent family mealtimes had evidently hardened him to surprises. He scooped a generous serving of dark red spheres and tangy juice into our oversized cereal bowls. Then he removed a bottle of milk from our refrigerator and filled the bowls to the brim. To this he added several teaspoons of rare wartime sugar and a dash or two of cinnamon from the tin that was kept on the table for making cinnamon toast.

His preparations complete, he looked at me intently with enlarged black eyes through his new steel-rims and smiled. He raised his spoon and nodded.

Large gas bubbles broke the surface of my swirling pink concoction. I immediately thought of Dr. Frankenstein's laboratory. That didn't help! For the first time in a long while, I recited a silent prayer before picking up my spoon.

Boldly, I took the plunge. To my utter amazement, the first bite was – delicious! There was something exotic about this unusual combination of flavors.

I imagined Jap mess cooks on some island paradise serving Danny's dish to Tojo's finest in celebration of their conquests in the South Pacific. Oops! For reasons of patriotic correctness, I quickly erased that fantasy from my head. Instead, I thought of our courageous allies, the Russians, consuming bowl after bowl of their famous beet soup – "burst," I was sure they called it – celebrating their victory over the Nazis at Stalingrad. I was much more comfortable with that image.

In a way, Danny did look a little Russian. Or maybe it was Mongolian. I wasn't sure. In any case, his concoction was as tasty as any foreign dish I had ever eaten. I made a mental note to share his secret recipe with Mom and Aunt Maude.

What a way to start the day!

We stored our reddened dishes and silverware in the sink and the leftover beets in the refrigerator with the milk. Won't Mom be surprised when she sees what we've left her? Now she won't have to fix anything for Dad's breakfast.

We hurried from the kitchen. Danny had a plan. We tramped down the sidewalk to the cottonwood tree where we paused to spy on the Zeyer house for a few minutes. We hoped to catch the old Nazi loading boxes of microfilmed secrets into a German tank. No luck. The spy lair looked disarmingly peaceful this morning.

So we moved on toward our destination.

The Tolna front yard was a cluttered tot lot – tricycles, scooters, and wagons everywhere. From this vast assortment, we could easily commandeer a vehicle for our mission, a mission critical to the war effort – Operation Kraut Bubble.

The image of Sherm's new red wagon crumpled and half-buried in swamp goop popped into my head. I blinked it away. Some families have to sacrifice more than others during wartime. "Let's help the Tolnas sacrifice a little more," I rationalized aloud as I surveyed our choices.

Sure enough, there was Sherm's pre-war model parked on the front walk, ripe for the picking. We snagged it and retraced our steps to my house.

Boy, was it easy to *hock* things from the Tolnas, a policeman's family for gosh sake! And how lucky for them! We were only *borrowing* Sherm's wagon and had every intention of returning it when our mission was accomplished.

We quietly parked the wagon beside the pair of cellar doors. Holding our breath, we lifted one of the hinged flaps. It squeaked loudly. We stopped for a couple of seconds to regain our composure. Then, throwing caution to the wind, we yanked the darned thing open. Nary a squeak.

After that scare, we didn't risk turning on the overhead light. Feeling our way through the bleak and damp cellar, we located Grandma's sauerkraut on the bottom shelf where Dad had stored it.

Carefully, we loaded the wagon, two jars at a time, until we had all ten. We closed the door carefully and headed for our kraut cache at the good old Chippewa Canning Corporation. Our new conveyance squealed cheerfully as we picked up speed.

I made a mental note. Add an "Always-Oil-Your-Axles-and-Bearings" clause to squirmin' Sherman's FSG membership oath next time we have him pinned against the cottonwood. Then I remembered that we still needed to debrief the bunny boy to see if by chance he had discovered any evidence to use against the Nazi rascal and his soup-flinging frau.

As we approached Bohunk Joe's shack, an unusually pungent aroma wafted out over New Albany Avenue and into our startled noses. "Whew! Somebody must have added a skunk to Bohunk Josef's stew-pot," Danny surmised.

I nodded my agreement.

By this time of the morning, the early-arriving workers would be standing in groups on the loading dock, drinking coffee and puffing last cigarettes before entering the factory. So to avoid being observed, we circled the building clockwise to reach the old boxcar at the end of the siding. When we arrived there, we hunched down in the bushes, right under the key ring, and waited for the morning work whistle to blow.

The canning factory offices were located in the administrative wing directly behind us. From there, we could hear the secretaries and clerks, all women from the sound of it, chatting, organizing their desks, and positioning chairs in front of typewriters and adding machines, waiting for the start of the workday.

Suddenly, we heard a loud and familiar voice. Old Bubble Gum Otto, the head POW, was shouting at someone. He sounded very upset.

Curiosity got the better of us. We looked at each other, then rose cautiously and peeked over the lip of the loading dock to see Otto, his hands on his hips, scolding two young POWs who were sauntering in our direction.

They must be new. We hadn't seen them at our joint lunch-dinner last Saturday. They were very cocky, ignoring what Otto was yelling in angry German. They continued to walk away from Otto and toward us, snickered and whispered to each other. As they approached, we ducked down into the bushes again.

Suddenly, we heard an echoing set of female snickers behind us. We turned to see Anne and Barb Libby waving from the window. The two Germans hooted and hollered in response. Otto's voice drew nearer and angrier.

The girls teased, "Hey, you guys. Whatcha doing! Who's that behind you? Your papa? You're going to get in trouble with Papa!"

Then it was Otto's turn to shout at the Libby girls, "Be quietz! Go back to verk! Leave dees guyz alone. Go ons nahw. Closh da vindow und shush up."

Danny and I looked at each other. I whispered what I knew he was thinking, "The Libby girls sure got over their hot-rod boyfriends in a hurry."

As if to punctuate my sentence, the work whistle on the factory roof sounded a long and loud blast announcing 7:00 o'clock and the beginning of the first shift. Instantly, the loading dock cleared. From the office window, thirty office machines whirred like a flock of metal humming birds. The yawn and groan of the factory's waking production lines, cooking pots, and conveyor belts signaled the start of another canning day.

Under cover of the deafening noise of labor, I took advantage of the now-vacant loading dock. Standing on the wagon, I hitched myself up onto the dock, retrieved the key ring, and headed for our boxcar. By the time I had unlocked the huge sliding door, opened it slightly, and returned to the end of the dock, Danny had removed the jars from the wagon and stacked them in a row.

He popped up onto the dock. We carried our cargo, two jars at a time, into the boxcar and stored it safely with the main kraut supply. After conducting a final count of our trading stock, we relocked the boxcar door and replaced the key ring on the peg, safely out of sight.

By 7:15, we were on our way home with an empty wagon that didn't squeal this time. We attempted to perform the difficult kraut-to-bubble gum-to-pennies arithmetic in our heads in anticipation of our glorious financial future.

"Let's see – that's ah –105 jars at ten pieces of bubble gum a jar. That's ah – hmmm. That's ah – ah lot," I mumbled weakly.

I was stuck. I clearly hadn't mastered complex multiplication yet.

Then I had a bright idea. "Hey! I've got it. Let's stop at Pete's. He's a whiz at figures. Besides, he can help us decide how much to charge for each piece of bubble gum."

"Do you really want to sell it? Maybe we should just keep it for ourselves," Danny suggested.

"How many pieces can you chew in a year?" I replied, pretending to take his suggestion seriously.

"Oh, probably, two thousand," he speculated, glancing sideways for my response.

I didn't tell him what I thought of his estimate. No sense starting the day on a negative note.

We wheeled up in front of Pete's and parked Sherm's wagon. The store was busy, so we browsed while we waited. Pete spotted us out of the corner of his eye. He nodded, smiled, and gave us his usual, "Gooda morning-ah, boyz! You-sa be gooda today! Okay?"

The long line of customers, waiting to pay for their purchases, turned to view the objects of his warm attention. I waved at Pete and smiled. Danny took a long deep bow and caught his tumbling army cap with his left toe.

The customers hooted! Danny had a way with audiences.

After crinkling his eyes and twitching his nose, Pete shook his head and declared, "Dat-sa my boy, Jase. Ahnd, dat-sa Jases-sah new buddy, Dahnny Boy! Dem-sa gooda boyz."

We waved again like two visiting dignitaries. It felt good to be recognized. As we continued our browsing, I reflected on the nature of grocery shopping.

MOST HOUSEWIVES PURCHASED THE majority of their family's groceries at Graham Markets, a chain of small neighborhood "supermarkets" housed in one-story, wooden structures on corner lots located conveniently all over town.

All Grahams, as we called them, carried the exact same inventory of grocery, produce, and meat items. They were also laid out identically. Each item was located on the very same shelf in every Grahams in town. This uniformity even applied to the flagship store in the downtown business area, which sold its groceries at pennies less than the other stores in the chain for those willing to make the trip.

Stocking standardization helped customers find their favorite item when shopping away from their "home" Grahams. It also helped the cadre of clerks who rotated from store to store filling in for those on vacation or out with the flu.

The chain's owners, the Graham family, were staunch Baptists who believed that many indulgences of modern times were sinful. If you wanted liquor, tobacco products, magazines or newspapers, or even candy, you had to shop elsewhere.

And, because Mr. Graham launched his business with the opening of the downtown store, regardless of customer needs, all his stores rigidly followed the business hours of the more conventional shops owned by Riverton's tradition-bound merchants.

So as strange as it may sound, Graham Markets were never open on Wednesday afternoons. After all, it was men's day at the Riverton Country Club, the time when the town's doctors, lawyers, and merchants relaxed together on the golf course and in the clubhouse afterward.

Of course, the Grahams didn't participate in frivolous pastimes like golf, let alone imbibe cocktails, and didn't have much respect for those who did. Nonetheless, the chain remained closed on Wednesday afternoons, which the Grahams devoted to family Bible study.

The only time a Graham Market was open beyond 5:30 was Friday when all stores downtown stayed open until 9:00 o'clock. This was convenient for most customers because every employer in the region paid workers, weekly, at the close of business on Friday. Of course, Graham Markets were never open on the Sabbath or on religious holidays including Good Friday, Easter, and Christmas.

Fortunately for Riverton, the Grahams' tendency to adhere strictly to social pressures and traditional religious convention spawned a rich and colorful assortment of "alternative" markets throughout town. Most of these independents were owned and operated by recently immigrated Italian families. Generally, each specialized in a single area of non-Graham offerings and thus could properly be classified as a delicatessen, confectionary shop, bakery, or beer-wine-liquor store.

But Pete's Grocery-Liquor-Hardware Store was unique. Instead of specializing in any one non-Graham area, it covered the full spectrum. In fact, Pete's was slightly more spacious than the standard-size Grahams next door, making it the largest market in town.

Under Pete's roof, you could find almost anything you needed in the diverse areas of deli items – cold cuts, ground beef, sausages, cheeses, and so on; liquor – beer, wine, and distilled spirits; hardware; hunting and fishing equipment; tobacco – cigarettes, cigars, pipes, and chewing tobacco; candy – from penny candy to boxes of fancy chocolates; dime novels and magazines – movie, women's, outdoor, comic books (Ah! Comic books!); and toiletries and cosmetics – makeup, lipstick, and vanishing creams.

Pete's was owned and operated by Pete Giamo and his wife Tina. We called her Mrs. Pete.

The Giamos were typical independent owner-operators. For starters, they both worked day and night. I don't remember a single occasion when I entered Pete's and failed to see both Pete and Mrs. Pete working feverishly behind the counter. Their hours were horrendous for just two people. They were open from 6:30 AM until midnight, seven days a week. And they never closed for vacation or holidays. As a matter of fact, I don't even remember seeing them take time to eat.

When I think back, I can't image how the Giamos kept abreast of such a mammoth inventory or when they found time to restock shelves except in the wee hours of the morning before the store opened.

As in Pete's case, the alternative markets were often located right next door to a neighborhood Graham Market. This enabled shoppers to do a main grocery shopping at Grahams, which charged reasonable prices for staples, and then, on their way home, pop into Pete's for pipe tobacco, fishhooks, beer, magazines, pop, or candy bars.

Pete also counted on his Wednesday afternoon, evening, and Sunday hours to bring him drop-in trade from neighbors who might suddenly discover they had no milk for tomorrow morning's cereal. Or they were out of oleo. Or cigarettes. And, while they were there, why not buy a loaf of bread, even if it did cost a penny or two more than Grahams? It would save them a trip.

In addition to his non-Graham line of goods and convenient store hours, Pete had a couple of other things going for him.

First, there was Pete's warm personality. Who wanted to deal with those austere male clerks at Grahams? What a bunch of sourpusses – better suited for truant officer jobs. And Pete knew everybody in the neighborhood. He made each of us feel welcome the minute we entered his store.

While Pete was revered by neighbors of all ages, we children were his long suit. For starters, his patience was endless. Pete never said a word when we spent hours reading his extensive inventory of comic books while slurping bottles of strawberry pop. Not needing to buy the comics meant we could spend our money on his tantalizing offerings of penny candy. Some of us took five minutes selecting just one piece. Then we'd change our minds. And then, back again, to our original choice.

I once figured, if Pete had sold only penny candy, he and Mrs. Pete would have earned about seven cents an hour during the entire decade I lived on Forrest Street. But, gosh, how we loved Pete!

And Pete had a second secret weapon in the powerfully positive impact that Mrs. Pete – Tina Giamo – had on sales revenues, especially among the neighborhood men and boys.

To put it bluntly, she was a ravishing beauty. Danny and I couldn't quite decide who looked more like Rita Hayworth, Mrs. Pete or our soon-to-be sixth-grade teacher, Miss Sparks. In any case, Danny and I had deep crushes on both of these attractive women that lasted forever. Well, at least, until sixth grade.

The amazing thing is that Mrs. Pete seldom spoke because her English wasn't as good as Pete's. But, come to think of it, she didn't really have to speak. Her warm smile said it all.

Don't get me wrong. Pete was rather handsome himself, a cross between Clark Gable and Victor Mature according to Mom and Aunt Maude.

For us, the most interesting thing about Pete's was his process for checking out customers. He stood behind a wide counter, on your right as you faced him. Mrs. Pete stood on the left. You stacked the contents of your shopping basket in front of him, next to a tall stack of flat, brown paper grocery bags. The top bag in that stack was Pete's calculator.

Writing furiously with a short stub of yellow pencil, he added your grocery bill in no time flat. His crescendo came when he scribbled your total at the bottom of his column of numbers and handed the bag to Mrs. Pete.

Pete never made an error.

Once Mrs. Risko returned with her grocery bag to point out a mistake. Pete patiently re-added his column of figures as she approved his every step. When he finished with the same total as before, Mrs. Risko's face turned beet red. She ran out of the store without saying a word. Pete just smiled and waited on the next customer.

A few minutes later, she returned with a gift of apology for Pete, a huge bouquet of white irises from her garden. And, if she said, "I'm sorry, Pete" once, she must have said it a thousand times, while backing out the door.

After Mrs. Pete bagged your groceries and collected your money, she bestowed *that* smile on you and softly uttered, "Grazie." To us men and boys, the sound of that word was as glorious as *Ave Maria*.

The neighborhood men never failed to reply, "Thank you" while the neighborhood women always replied, "You're welcome." At the time, I couldn't understand why.

JUST AS DANNY AND I were becoming bored, the store suddenly cleared of customers. We scooted over next to the counter where Pete was sharpening his stubby yellow adding machine with his jackknife. We straightened the stack of paper sacks for him while he finished.

He blew the curls of wood, sawdust, and lead particles from the sharpened pencil point. After inspecting his work, he promptly returned the pencil to its place behind his right ear. Then he folded his hands against his chest and turned his full attention to us.

"Whatta can-ah Pete do for you-sa boyz?"

"Mr. Pete, this is kinda secret – a wartime emergency. We need your help. Will you do some business arithmetic for us?" I asked.

Pete's look immediately turned serious. He knitted his brow, drew his sharpened pencil, and slapped a clean bag down on the counter.

After licking his pencil lead, he nodded firmly. He was ready for business.

"Okay-ah! Mums-ah da word," he whispered, putting a finger to his lips.

We filled him in on the variables of the kraut-bubble equation. He arched over the counter. His fingers moved in a blur, scratching numbers furiously on the sack for a millisecond or two. Then he stopped abruptly. He was finished.

"Itta come-sa to $21.00 egzactally. Dat-sa at two-ah penny da peez. You-sa boyz ah rich-cha," he announced with a flourish.

Holy Cow! $21.00. I wouldn't reach that amount in my U.S. Savings Stamp book until about 1989. We *were* rich!

We thanked Pete profusely and left the store. We were euphoric with the prospect of good fortune. To celebrate, we danced a polka in Pete's driveway! Then Danny broke the mood by posing a sobering question.

"How are we going to do the swap with Otto?"

Neither of us had a clue. We stared at each other forlornly and slumped into the wagon. After about five minutes of silence, the solution came to me. Or rather, *he* came to us.

THE HOME FRONT

WE INTERCEPTED GENTLEMAN JIM AS HE STROLLED majestically toward the backdoor of the Good Mission Church for his weekly menu conference with Edith Squires. Her *Swing Low, Sweet Chariot* floated toward us through the open kitchen window.

Jim readily agreed to help facilitate the kraut-bubble exchange. Working through Sergeant Rick Prella at the canning factory, he would communicate the final count of sauerkraut jars to Otto. Then Otto and his fellow kraut-lovers could make their bubble gum purchase at the Camp Riverton PX. Assuming the bubble gum could be assembled by then, Sergeant Rick and he would set up the exchange for lunch-dinner time on Saturday.

A perfect plan!

Edith's sweet voice was now asking the neighborhood, *"Have you heard our Savior's voice a gently calling from above?"* Following her lead, we whistled our way down Forrest Street. When we arrived at our house, I asked smugly, "Wanta see my secret Nazi lookout tower?"

Danny's eyes sparkled with anticipation as I pulled Sherm's pre-war model close to the trunk of the box elder tree.

My subtle "tree ladder" was a series of alternating left and right toe-sized steps leading up the side of the tree that faced away from the side-walk. I had constructed the ladder using an assortment of sewing machine cabinet knobs and a borrowed screwdriver from Dad's workbench.

The ladder started at about eye level (for me) and ended at an ideal spot about fifteen feet above the ground. There, a platform of flat branches provided a clear view of the northeastern sky, the likely direction of approach for the Stukas and Messerschmitts I expected at any moment.

Originally, I hadn't expected to observe anything from my lookout tower except Luftwaffe attackers. But, because my roosting spot was completely concealed by thick green foliage, neighbors walking along the sidewalk below didn't know I was there. So my perch proved ideal for creative eavesdropping.

Had it not been for my hidden listening post, I might have never known that Mr. Petrov (Russian-American) "despised" Hans Zeyer (Nazi-American). Or that Mrs. Shurtleif thought Mr. Shurtleif had abused the privilege of the neighborhood telephone by calling Pete's, only two blocks away, to ask if the summer sausage was in yet. And I surely wouldn't have learned, according to Barbara Libby, that Wild Rose lipstick makes boys "ga ga." Whatever that means!

But more importantly, I was convinced that my box elder hideaway would help me trap old Hans and thus restore the trust of my parents. I just knew it!

Aunt Maude had taken time off from Woolworth's to settle into her new home. She and Mom were busy with the weekly laundry in the cellar and backyard. With Dad at work, this morning would be ideal for uninterrupted perching. So up the tree we scrambled.

When we reached the green pedestal, Danny was spellbound. His eyes grew wide as he stared at a wispy white cloud drifting our way – at eye level – or so it seemed. He shook his head in wonder.

I briefed Danny on our mission. Watch for ominous bomber and fighter plane silhouettes in the northeast skies. Listen for neighborhood counterintelligence, or good gossip if that's all that's available from the ground. And stretch out so you don't fall through the branches forming the perch floor. Any questions?

Danny assumed his duties with a seriousness that I hadn't observed in my new friend before. I was impressed. We stretched out and settled in for a long morning stakeout.

After ten minutes, Danny's military professionalism fell victim to the narcotic effect of the warm morning sun. Without warning, his head lolled sideways and came to rest on a soft bouquet of box elder leaves that provided a perfect pillow for his nap. He wheezed, ever so softly, as a small line of drool painted another stripe on the sleeve of his tee shirt.

From midmorning until just after noon, Danny and I manned our post, one of us on full alert and the other on full siesta. Regrettably, our efforts went unrewarded. No surprise air raids from the azure June skies. No spy confessions from the sidewalk below. Not a smidgen of good gossip from the usual local loose-lips.

As a matter of fact, the only neighbor who passed under our listening post was poor Mrs. Borski. I recognized the sound of her shoes shuffling slowly and sadly down the sidewalk on her way to Pete's. Soon, she would be making her way back home again.

As I woke Danny, he swatted at me and muttered an incoherent jumble of "bombers, bubble gum, and tongue depressors." I waited for his eyes to focus before urging him down the ladder. When we hit the ground, I saw Mrs. Borski plodding our way, along the sidewalk in front of Mrs. Mikas' house.

Our magical appearance from the tree above the sidewalk in front of her must have confused her. Suddenly, she veered right and set a new course, straight for our front door.

"Hurry! Grab the wagon," I whispered to Danny.

I ran to intercept her before she reached our porch steps. "Not there, Mrs. Borski. Here, let me take you home," I urged politely, cupping her frail hand in mine.

She stopped and glanced down at our hands. Then she stared at my face, vacantly, as if trying to recognize me.

"It's me, Jase Addison. You'll be okay. Let's put your groceries in the wagon," I suggested when Danny pulled up.

Mrs. Borski smiled faintly and lowered her grocery basket to our first step and released her grip. Danny caught the handle in mid-air, preventing a messy spill on our front walk.

She offered no resistance, so I guided her back toward the sidewalk. Danny set the basket down into the wagon and followed us. He spoke softly, "That's okay, Missus. We were walking your way, anyhow. Take your time, now."

So the caravan left our yard and headed north. Walking hand-in-hand, Mrs. Borski and I led the way. Danny and the grocery-laden wagon took up the rear.

As we passed, Mrs. Reilly stopped sweeping her front porch to smile warmly and wave at us. Like the rest of us in the neighborhood, Mrs. Reilly knew the Borski family story. She also knew we couldn't wave back.

WALTER AND MARTA BORSKI lived on the downhill side of the cottonwood tree, across the street from the swampy grave of Sherm's red wagon. Theirs was a sad history.

After years of hoping, they were finally blessed by the birth of their only child, Donald. They sacrificed everything for their son. But that was only fitting, they reasoned, because someday he would make them proud. Donald was to be a priest.

The day Hitler crossed the Polish border, invading the land of their birth, Donald was a seventeen-year-old senior at St. Thomas Catholic High School. When he announced his intention to postpone his seminary enrollment and to enlist in the U.S. Army following graduation, the Borskis were thrown into turmoil.

Like all Polish-Americans, they loathed the Germans whose brutality against their countrymen was an egregious wrong, nothing short of a profound sin against God himself. So, secretly, they fantasized that their son's heroism and valor would play a significant role in vanquishing the wicked Nazis and freeing their homeland.

On the other hand, Donald was their only son, the only thing they had lived for since his birth. How could they endure the pain should any harm come to their boy?

But the Borskis eventually resigned themselves to Donald's choice.

After graduation, Donald kept his word and enlisted. The Borskis hosted a lively neighborhood going-away party for him. When he boarded his bus for boot camp at the Chippewa Trails Bus Station, they cheered. Donald left for the war with his parents' best wishes founded on the comfort and certainty that God never fails to look after His good and devoted followers.

When they learned their son's unit was among the first American troops to battle the Nazis in the deserts of North Africa, they were confused and bewildered. Why would the Army send their son, a Polish boy, to fight on a continent far away from their homeland? What did they care about freedom for the Algerians? They were Poles. But, in the end, they listened to the advice of their friends and neighbors and chose not to try to second-guess God's will as carried out by the U.S. Army.

Instead, they decided to be proud. They boasted about their boy's minor promotions and accomplishments on every occasion. They told of his success at making friends among the wide assortment of young soldiers from distant parts of the country. They buttonholed fellow parishioners after Mass to show them snapshots of camp scenes that Donald had taken with the small travel camera that they had sent him.

Each night they consumed the extensive accounts of the North African campaign in the *Riverton Daily Press*. They eagerly read about the courageous efforts of American soldiers in the fight to hold Rommel's Afrika Korps at bay at Kasserine Pass in Tunisia. They were pleased to learn of the brave fighting going on there. But they were also apprehensive. They wanted to know specifically how their son and his new friends had fared in their first combat.

This news arrived when Colonel Ed Butler, Commandant of Camp Riverton, came to call on that cold evening in March 1943. Sitting in their tidy parlor, he told them that, as senior military officer in the area, it was his unpleasant duty to inform them of Donald's death in the desert. From all accounts, he assured them, Donald had died honorably.

He said he would help with details involved in returning Donald's remains to Riverton, if that's what they wished. Or he could arrange a military funeral, even at Arlington Cemetery with full military honors, if they desired. He asked them what they preferred. He inquired if there was anything more that he could do.

They didn't respond to any of his questions.

For a while, he joined them in their silence. Soon, he felt uncomfortable as if he were invading their privacy. He left the necessary papers, let himself out quietly, and returned to his office at Camp Riverton. There, he sat at his desk, staring out his window at the stark and forbidding barbed wire, wondering whether he could ever become comfortable in his role as the Army's messenger of death.

Life lost its meaning for Walter and Marta Borski.

For weeks, the couple scarcely set foot outside the house. Concerned neighbors and friends from St. Thomas brought them food and solace. Nothing seemed to help. Their priest, Father Jerome, depleted his considerable inventory of spiritual platitudes and pep talks. Whenever he used the words, "God's will", it rankled Walter and drove Marta further downward, into the black depths of her depression.

Their strong, life-long Catholic faith was severely tested. And, in the end, it simply failed the test. Walter asked Father Jerome not to come again.

After some weeks, perhaps to save his own life, Walter allowed his anger at God, the U.S. Army, and life in general to spur him to action. He returned to his job as a master bricklayer for the Riverton Public Works Department. But his jovial nature had disappeared. His personality turned from warm to cold. He was bitter in word and deed.

His friends at work attempted to console him. They made allowances for his rude behavior toward them. But, after weeks of futility, their deep reservoir of patience and sympathy for Walter finally ran dry. After all, Borski, other families have lost sons, brothers, and fathers in the war. What makes you think you're so special? For cripes sake man, get on with it!

Despite the loss of his friends there, he volunteered to work overtime and on weekends to avoid going home where the weight of Marta's depression had begun to pull him under with her. He knew she would never recover from her grief. She had left him to join Donald. He must find a way to let her go.

Soon her mental instability was confirmed. From their front bay window she removed the Gold Star left by Colonel Butler. In its place, she pasted pictures of laughing children – crudely cut from magazines and newspapers – onto the window glass. She drew child-like figures with Donald's old crayolas and hung them there for all of us to see.

During the day, when neighbors walked by the Borski house, they respectfully averted their eyes to avoid seeing her latest exhibition. If children failed to show the same respect – by stopping, gawking, or pointing – mothers and even other neighbors corrected their behavior on the spot with jolting arm-jerks and stinging pinches.

Each evening, Walter dutifully removed the latest window display, prepared a modest meal for the two of them, and tucked Marta under the covers of Donald's bed where she now preferred to sleep. Then he returned to the kitchen and finished the dishes. When his tidy work was done, he slumped into his kitchen chair to extract what comfort he could from his only luxury, a single bottle of bock beer bought at Pete's on his way home from work each day.

Finally, the ghost of the woman that had once been Marta materialized and emerged from the Borski house. She wore a hodge-podge of colors and styles. Her once-meticulous grooming gave way to the unkempt and bizarre. Her clothing was wrinkled, soiled, and lint-covered. Her hair was uncombed and her shoes untied. This was not the Marta Borski that we all knew before her son's death.

Each morning, she followed the same pattern. With her wicker shopping basket on her arm and a blank stare in her eyes, she ambled down Forrest Street. Neighbors, who happened to meet Marta on the street, greeted her as usual. But she never seemed to hear or, even, see them.

When she reached New Albany Avenue, she crossed the busy street, with scarcely a concern for traffic, and entered Pete's. There, she shopped leisurely, usually for an hour or two, filling her basket with whatever met her fancy.

She was particularly keen on items from the hardware section, packages of washers, screwdrivers, and once a pair of bolt cutters. She also shopped heavily among Pete's tobacco products. She was partial to Pete's selection of chewing tobacco and snuff. That neither Walter nor she used tobacco didn't seem to matter.

After exchanging warm smiles and goodbyes with Pete and Mrs. Pete, the only normal behavior in her day, Marta left the store with her "purchases" without checking out. Mercifully, she rarely collected perishables for her basket. Had she done so, the process by which Pete and Walter accommodated Marta's shopping visits would not have worked as well as it did. Perhaps, some shred of sanity still impelled Marta's behavior in this regard.

As it was, when Walter returned home, he invariably found Marta's shopping basket just inside the front door, on the first step of the stairs leading up to Donald's room. While Marta finished her pre-supper nap, Walter scooped up the basket and headed back to Pete's.

There, he returned each item to its proper spot on the shelf. At first, of course, he needed help from Pete who, out of respect for Walter, never left his checkout counter. Instead, he continued to wait on his other customers while he subtly coached Walter with an approving nod or slight shake of the head accompanied by a hint from a pointing finger.

After a few weeks, Walter needed no coaching. He knew Pete's inventory and shelf plan as well as Pete or Mrs. Pete.

When all Marta's items were returned, Walter selected the groceries he needed for the day including his bottle of bock beer. Of course, he paid for his selections in the normal manner. Then he returned home to prepare his wife's supper.

Every soul in our neighborhood knew of Marta's shopping habits. But no one ever talked about it. We were all grateful for Donald's contribution to the war effort and respectful of the great sacrifice made by Walter and Marta Borski. Marta's behavior, no matter how peculiar, never changed how we felt or acted toward the Borskis.

According to Mom, the Borskis' Grace-of-God example helped all of us not to become too self-absorbed with the sacrifices we were personally forced to make during the war.

AFTER DANNY AND I deposited Mrs. Borski and her grocery basket inside her front door, we crossed the street and headed toward the Tolna used toy lot to return Sherm's wagon. Suddenly, Danny stopped and, with a look I hadn't seen before, observed, "I'm glad we're still boys. The war's not much fun for grown ups."

We spotted Sherm sitting forlornly on his front porch. When he saw us, his mood suddenly changed. He sped across his yard to greet us.

"Hey, you guys! Can I play with you?" he screamed, waving one hand and wiping his nose with the other.

Danny wheezed his exasperation.

"Tell us you found some damaging evidence in the Nazi spy nest, first. Then we'll talk about playing," I said impatiently.

"I did! I did!" Sherman insisted loudly. "There were a whole bunch of books with steekas on them. And, inside, pictures of German soldiers and spies."

Danny stopped in his tracks and stared at me.

"What are you saying, Sherman? What are *steekas*?" I demanded, wondered if the blue bunny might really be on to something.

"You know those little German X's – like they put on their tanks and airplanes," he replied, drawing crosses in the air with a scaly index finger.

"Swastikas! Are you saying Hans has books with Swastikas on them?" I yelled at Sherman.

"Yeeeeeeeeeeeeeeeeeeeeeees he does! About a hundret. And I took one – for FSG!" he squealed with delight.

Danny and I were dumbfounded. Our mouths fell open. Could it be true?

"You took one of Hans Zeyer's secret German books last Saturday! And you're just telling us, now?" I sputtered, not knowing whether to be angry or elated with the snotnik's news.

"No! I just took it this morning – when I was over there playing with his puppets. It's in my room. Wanta see it?" Sherman asked, looking rather smug.

Danny stared at Sherman for a second, and then, he ordered, "You bet we *wanta*. Go get it – now!"

Sherman smiled broadly then disappeared into his house. In a jiffy, he returned with his prize.

We saw immediately that we were dealing with the *Gin-You-Wine* article. The horrifying sight of the swastika, boldly embossed on the book's spine, nearly took my breath away. My skin crawled uncontrollably. Fear griped my chest.

We examined the book closely. It was truly impressive. The heavy, red leather-bound volume resembled the Encyclopedia Britannica that nobody used in the library at Hamilton School. It contained well over four hundred pages of small type, all old style German letters. "How do they read this stuff?" I wondered aloud.

The book featured a collection of stunning photographs, each covered with thin tissue paper. The people pictured were all Nazi officials by the looks of it. There was even a group shot of Hitler, Goering, and Goebbels, the nasty triad who sat on top of the Nazi manure pile. Most of the men in the photographs were dressed in military style uniforms with swastika armbands. A few wore drab business suits. These, undoubtedly, were the German spies!

The only words that Danny and I could make out were those imprinted on the spine indicating that this was "Volume 5." By deduction, we concluded that Sherm was telling the truth. There must be a whole series of similar books in Zeyer lair.

But was this single book enough to convict old Hans and Mrs. Hans of espionage and treason? Or did we need more evidence? We discussed the desirability of a third mission by old bunny-mole.

We concluded that before we planned another operation we should ascertain the value of the evidence in hand. We had to find someone who spoke German. Someone we could trust. Being a good son, I was also mindful of my *semi-promise* to Dad and Mom about leaving Hans – the soon-to-be-proven dirty rotten krautburger – alone.

"Where can we hide this?" Danny wanted to know.

"That's easy. The same place I hide my bank key. Remember?" I winked at Danny conspiratorially.

It was unnecessary. Sherm wasn't paying attention.

We thanked Sherman with a sincerity born out of our new respect for the rat. He responded by turning redder than ever and counting his shoelaces. While Sherman savored our adulation, we tramped toward my bedroom.

With the evidence tucked in the back of my shorts under my tee shirt, walking wasn't easy. But I didn't mind. I felt a surge of optimism and impending exoneration. I belted out a booming version of *Under the Double*. Danny joined right in.

As we skipped along toward my house, I saw a welcome sight parked in the middle of Forrest Street. Danny did, too.

"Well now, folks! How'sa about an icy treat!" he intoned, sounding like a pompous radio announcer.

AT THAT TIME, MORE than half the people on Forrest Street still used wooden iceboxes for storing perishable food. Most had been purchased from the Sears Roebuck catalog in the early part of the century. An icebox consisted of an array of wooden boxes and shelves built around a central, galvanized metal-lined compartment where blocks of ice were deposited. These were the "coolant."

Over time, the ice melted. So it had to be replenished on a regular basis. In the summer months, the Riverton Ice and Coal Company delivered ice to our neighborhood twice weekly, on Tuesdays and Saturdays.

Our iceman, Mr. Stanley, drove a team of matching gray Belgians. The huge team pulled a twenty-foot wagon loaded with solidly frozen sections of ice, already scored for easy division into icebox-size chunks. This would not have been an easy load for an ordinary team of horses. Frozen or liquid, water is about as heavy as any material you can haul. But Belgians were renowned among draft horses for their ability to pull extremely heavy loads.

The ice rested on a wagon bed covered with a thick layer of sawdust that insulated the load from the hot summer temperatures. Another sawdust layer was spread over top of the ice. Finally, the whole load was covered with a thick canvas tarpaulin tied in place with half-inch rope.

During the sultry days of summer, despite efforts to keep the load cool, constant trickles of melted ice water dripped from every slat in the wagon's bottom onto the dusty street. And the Belgians left their deposits of grapefruit-sized manure balls that neighbors recovered with shovels to fertilize their rose gardens.

If Danny and I were engaged in an activity away from Forrest Street proper and suddenly craved a chunk of fresh ice, we simply inspected the street surface for telltale signs such as parallel drip lines, hoof marks, and remnants of rose nourishment to ascertain whether the ice wagon had been there yet.

To minimize delivery times and thus cut down on melting loss, an ice ordering system was used to enable the iceman to know exactly what size block you required before he left his wagon. Subscribers were provided with a card that was to be displayed in their windows on delivery day. The one-foot by one-foot card had four numbers – 10, 20, 30, and 40 – printed boldly to correspond with each side of the card. If you needed a 20-pound block, the card was turned so "20" was situated at the top of the card.

The iceman would stop in front of your house, glance at your "number" for the day, draw his trusty ice pick from its leather sheath, and quickly chisel your block from the long section of ice. Then he would re-cover the load with the tarpaulin, grasp your block with an immense pair of sharpened tongs, and hoist it to his left shoulder.

Finally, he would carry the block to your back door, enter your kitchen, and deposit your ice order directly into your icebox.

The icemen, all burly, good-natured men, were heroes to the children of Riverton. Part of their attraction related to their special garb, a shoulder to knee apron and a special shoulder pad that extended to the waist. Both were made from the finest and the thickest horsehide that money could buy. But what really set them apart was their exceptional skill with the tools of their trade, the tongs and ice pick.

Mr. Stanley, our iceman, knew there was no better way to impress his younger fans than to demonstrate his prowess with his ice pick. So after his last stop on Forrest Street, he took a minute off to carve out icy samples for everyone circling his wagon.

Danny and I were ice connoisseurs. We knew that a treat chipped from the outer surface of the block would taste horrendously salty. When there was a small number of us at the wagon, we requested a "center cut." But, when there was a flock waiting, we were content to settle for whatever we could grab as the treats literally shot at us from the tip of Mr. Stanley's pick.

DANNY AND I FINISHED our icy center cut supreme on our way home. When we arrived, Mom and Aunt Maude were in the backyard, so we quietly ducked inside through the front door and stored the Nazi tome under my mattress.

We emerged to see Dad pull into the driveway. *Gee!* I thought, *He's home early.*

He seemed to be excited about something. "Where're Aunt Maude and your mother?" he asked, slamming the car door especially hard.

Danny and I spoke simultaneously, "Backyard!"

"Come on, boys. You gotta hear this, too!" Dad called as he rounded the corner of house.

When Dad saw Mom and Aunt Maude, he shouted across the backyard, "It's come! Eisenhower's Expeditionary Force invaded France – early this morning. They call it, *D-Day.*"

Mom and Aunt Maude screamed with delight. They dropped their clothespins into the gingham bag hanging on the clothesline and ran toward Dad.

"It's all on the radio," he continued wildly. "Hundreds of thousands of Allied troops in thousands of ships. 'The biggest invasion force in history,' they say. Churchill calls it, '*The beginning of the end.*'"

Mom and Aunt Maude grinned and hugged Danny and me.

"Van's bound to be in the thick of it. Along with Ivan Mikas. The Petrov boy. Jack Risko, too," Dad reminded us, making his news relevant to Forrest Street.

I felt exhilarated. I was both happy and scared at the same time.

But that's how everybody on Forrest Street must feel about D-Day, I thought, with one possible, traitorous exception.

DURING THE WEEK FOLLOWING D-Day, people throughout Riverton spoke of nothing else. News reports informed us that the Allies – Americans, British, Canadians, and contingents from occupied countries like Poland and France – had landed in force at a place called "Normandy" on the northwest coast of France.

The *Riverton Daily Press* reported stiff Nazi resistance at the landing site. From a formidable array of steel-reinforced concrete bunkers squatting along the cliffs above the beaches, heavy artillery, mortar, and small arms fire relentlessly pounded Allied landing ships and soldiers. On the ground, the fighting was fierce. But, miraculously, the Allied forces advanced, inch-by-inch, off the death-trap beaches up onto the rolling Norman countryside.

The Germans soon knew that Normandy was indeed the primary landing site. Nazi forces, previously tricked into defending Calais, joined the battle. Reports of terrible fighting came from places with strange-sounding names like Caen, Saint-Lô, and Cherbourg.

Field Marshall Rommel, a brilliant and dangerous adversary, took command of the German forces and quickly moved his Panzer divisions into the fray. Rommel's giant Tiger Tanks outmatched our lighter Sherman Tanks. The big guns of the Tigers penetrated the Shermans as if they were made of balsa wood.

The farmland lying between the Allied forces and their objectives to the east was an extensive latticework of hedgerows. For centuries, Norman farmers had used these tall piles of fieldstones and impenetrable brush to delineate their fields and to fence in their grazing cattle and sheep.

The hedgerows outmatched the Shermans as well. Unlike the Tigers, our tanks were too underpowered to drive through them. And, when the Shermans tried to drive over them, their exposed unarmored bellies allowed German foot soldiers using Panzerfaust bazookas to destroy them with ease.

Under these horrible conditions, Allied soldiers fought the stubborn Germans for hours to gain control of a single cow pasture. With Allied timetables in shambles and forces stalled in the French countryside, the initiative shifted to the wily Rommel and the German High Command. The Germans strengthened their defenses and in no time mounted vicious counterattacks with apparent success. Casualties ran high on both sides.

BY WEEK'S END EVERYONE in Riverton was nervous and irritable. People were carping about little things and at each other. Families were desperately worried about loved ones who were surely there with their units, bogged down somewhere between the beaches of Normandy and Paris.

Naturally, all of us in the Addison household were concerned about Uncle Van. His job was at the front where he and his comrades laid telephone lines and installed switching equipment so elements of the advancing Allied army could communicate with each other.

Surprisingly, Aunt Maude was the calmest of us all. She used her battle-tested philosophy and prayers to bring her peace of mind. I decided to be like Aunt Maude. I thought only positive thoughts. Besides I had the evidence under my mattress that meant the gallows for old Hans. That was a very positive thought! And tomorrow was kraut-gum swap day – bubble gum and vast fortunes. I wondered if I could possibly get to sleep tonight?

But Danny and I still had a job to do. After D-Day, we figured that Nazi undercover activities in Riverton were likely to be stepped up as the Allies inched closer to the Rhine and ultimate victory. Driven by patriotic fervor, we spent all of our waking hours on duty at the top of the box elder. It was an exhausting schedule. This was Michigan in June when the sun hung around for sixteen hours a day.

Despite our increased vigilance, we failed to spot any Luftwaffe sneak attacks or glean any new evidence in the Zeyer case. Our overheard gossip only confirmed what we already knew, people on Forrest Street were very edgy.

On the Friday morning after D-Day, we were at our post before dawn. The eastern sky hinted that the sun would soon illuminate the soft, yellow-green wreath of box elder leaves surrounding us. Once dawn broke, we settled in for the day.

But Danny was fidgety. His patience for patriotic perch sitting was obviously waning. Finally, he asserted, "I don't like sitting up here all the time. We need another kind of camp."

I hadn't considered our observation perch a "camp." Maybe a tree house but never a camp. In any case, I humored my nest-mate by asking, "What kinda camp?"

Danny, forever the contrarian, suggested, "Let's build an underground camp."

"Underground!"

"Yeah! Someplace where we can store stuff. Like the Nazi's book. And ten thousand pieces of bubble gum. My Jap sword. And FSG dues money."

The prospect of attending future FSG meetings underground was depressing. I hoped he would forget that element of the camp idea. But Danny's notion of dues intrigued me.

"Dues! You may have something there, Buddy Roe!"

I explained to Danny that dues could deliver a number of potential benefits. For example, a modest membership fee would discourage those with only a casual interest in our cause, thus enabling us to keep FSG membership at a manageable level. But, more importantly, dues would help us to discourage riffraff from joining our exclusive club.

As I presented my treatise on *Dues: The Universal Solution to Mankind's Problems*, Danny screwed his face into that weird look of his.

Then he made a couple of points of his own.

First, he observed that membership *bloat* hadn't exactly been a problem for us. We only had three members, for goodness sake. Second, Sherman was about the only kid in the neighborhood that he personally considered to be *riffraff*, and he was already an FSG member!

"Then, why did you want dues?" I asked meekly.

"I just wanted to buy candy bars and pop with it."

"Oh! Why didn't you say so?"

Danny gave me that look again.

Suddenly, we heard voices below. Mrs. Petrov and Mrs. Mikas were exchanging their usual morning greetings.

"Gud morneick, Musses Mekas."

"Ah, Gooj morke, Mish Petrow."

ANNA PETROV, A RUSSIAN woman of about fifty, had all the characteristics of a serf from the Volga plains. Just over five feet, she weighed close to two hundred pounds. And she wasn't the least bit fat. If anything, she was muscular. She never failed to wear a babushka on her sizeable head and an apron over her tent-like housedress of bleached floral patterns. Her hands were huge and hardened from working daily in her vast vegetable garden that provided food for her family and quarters from sales of her surplus harvest to us neighbors. Her English was heavily imbued with an earthy Slavic accent that made it nearly impossible for me to understand her.

The Petrovs had raised a large family of eight children. All, but one, were married and gone. The unmarried son, Jacob, was a paratrooper serving with the 101st Airborne Division. We would learn later that he was among the first Allied soldiers to touch French soil in a daring inland drop in the early morning hours of D-Day.

Mrs. Petrov and her husband Anton hated the war and the Germans who started it. Their homeland, Russia, had paid a terrible price at the hands of the Nazi army that had killed, pillaged, and burned its way to and from the gates of Moscow only months before.

In the final tally, Russia would lead all nations in the count of those killed by the brutal Germans. Over ten million Russian citizens were to perish in the war. From the way the Petrovs felt about Germans, even those in Riverton, you would have thought that every last one of the lost Russians was a Petrov cousin.

Mrs. Mikas was Hungarian. Like Mrs. Petrov and others who came to America as young adults, her English was similarly impaired by the habitual speaking patterns of her native tongue.

Despite the shared disadvantage, the two women used English for their daily conversations and had managed – somehow – to form a close and abiding friendship over the years. But their chatting might easily have been confused with arguing. As their conversation progressed, each fought to make her point in English.

Both fell victim to the illogical behavior that afflicts many when attempting to communicate with someone of another language. When a point was not clearly understood by one, the other would raise her voice. Before long, their exchange of pleasantries sounded more like a shouting match.

Oddly, just as their conversation reached its boisterous crescendo, it ended, abruptly. With triple kisses to the cheeks and multiple pats on the elbow, they parted warmly, committing to another chat tomorrow.

AS WE LEFT OUR nest for the ground, we listened to the conversation below.

Mrs. Petrov hurriedly explained to Mrs. Mikas that today's morning chat had to be postponed. She must rush to catch the 7:00 o'clock bus to meet her daughter downtown. There her daughter would accompany her to the dentist. Mrs. Petrov didn't like dentists. Furthermore, this dentist couldn't speak Russian. And he didn't understand her English, especially with his hands in her mouth. Her daughter would act as her interpreter. And so on.

Leaning on her broom, Mrs. Mikas nodded understandingly while Mrs. Petrov took fifteen minutes to explain why their normal ten-minute chat couldn't take place that morning.

By this time, Danny and I had completed our descent. We leaned against the box elder to watch some more of their peculiar exchange. We waited for the inevitable increase in tempo and amplitude, signs of the approaching crescendo. This forever reminded me of the fireworks finale each Fourth of July at the Chippewa County Fairgrounds.

We were so mesmerized by the women's voices that we failed to hear the footsteps behind us.

"Gut morgen, boyz," said a deep voice.

Danny and I pivoted and gulped. There he was, not two feet away from us. Hans Zeyer, the neighborhood Nazi and master spy.

"Good morning, Mr. Zeyer."

"Good morning, Mr. Zeyer."

We responded reflexively out of pure, inbred politeness. He tipped his hat and passed us, heading for the bus stop. At that precise moment, the Mikas-Petrov crescendo broke. The two friends were kissing and patting their goodbyes.

When Mrs. Petrov turned to leave, there *he* was right in front of her. Instead of a kind hello, Mrs. Petrov approached Mr. Zeyer with hatred glowing in her eyes.

His eyebrows leaped in surprise at her body language. But, impelled by his own polite reflex, he stopped to allow her to go ahead of him, down the sidewalk toward the bus stop.

When she reached the sidewalk, without warning, she hauled off and bashed him with her huge black leather purse – right across the back of his head – just as he was tipping his hat and smiling.

"Schvine! Nazi Schvine" she snarled. Then she proceeded to bash him some more.

His face was contorted with agony and fear. He dropped his paper lunch bag. Last night's *Riverton Daily Press* came unstuck from under his arm and fluttered to the ground in pieces. His fedora hat rolled toward the street. His spectacles swung from one ear.

He covered his face with his arms and stood rigidly, while Mrs. Petrov continued to pummel him. "Bitte, no more! Stops dah hitz! Bitte!" he cried. "Bitte! Bitte!"

Mrs. Petrov screamed her hatred, "Peeg! Jarmin peeg. Schvine. Nazi Schvine!"

Danny and I were in shock. We couldn't believe our eyes. Like Mrs. Mikas, we watched in horror while the welts on Hans Zeyer's face reddened from the pounding he was taking at the hands of the Russian heavyweight.

"Anna! Stop!"

We wheeled around at the sound of Dad's voice. He leaped off our front porch and ran by us toward the altercation. He threw his arms around Mrs. Petrov, pinning her elbows to her sides.

"Stop! Anna! Please stop!"

She struggled momentarily. Then, at last, she did stop. She panted wildly and gritted her teeth in Hans' direction. And then, she emitted a series of thunderous, low-pitched moans that I soon realized were sobs.

Mrs. Mikas came to life and ran to comfort her friend. "Dare. Dare. Anna. Dond Hans hitz no more. Dond Hans hitz no more," she pleaded, wringing the corners of her faded apron.

Anna Petrov suddenly grew weak in Dad's arms. He released her and patted her shoulder. It was all over. She emitted another mournful sob and stumbled toward the Mikas porch.

Mrs. Mikas said, "Cums tew da kitchen. Sum hot tea you needa."

Anna followed her old friend compliantly. The pair disappeared inside.

I turned my attention to Hans who still stood motionless on the sidewalk with his hands dangling limply at his sides. He had turned white. Dad moved closer to him, grabbed his elbow, and steered him toward our front porch.

"Boys! Pick up Mr. Zeyer's things."

Numbly, Danny and I walked to the scene of the attack. I picked up the newspaper, and Danny grabbed the lunch sack. I recovered Mr. Zeyer's spectacles from the tall grass next to the sidewalk. Danny scooped up Mr. Zeyer's sizeable hat and, for some reason, stored it temporarily on his head. It covered his army cap, insignia, and huge ears, but Danny didn't seem to mind.

"Hans. Sit here in the shade a while. You've had a bad time of it. Don't worry about your bus. I'll drive you to work on my way to Burke's. Stay right there. I'll get a washrag. And some water for you," Dad insisted, very much in charge.

Hans, local member of the Master Race, sure didn't look very superior at that moment. In fact, he looked downright bedraggled and limp. He kind of reminded me of Sherm's *lammy* doll.

Suddenly, Hans noticed that Danny and I were standing there in front of him, holding his things. He said, in a half whisper, "Danke, boyz. Yew are gut boyz. Hans likes yew zere much. Danke."

"We like you, too, Mr. Zeyer," I said, responding reflexively again.

Danny didn't say a word. I thought I knew his opinion of my last comment. But he surprised me.

Suddenly, he tipped Hans' huge fedora hat and bowed from the waist.

Hans chuckled at the Dannyism even though it pained him to do so.

"Feeling better already? Good!" Dad said, returning a second too late for Danny's latest.

After a few minutes of rest, a wet washrag for his face, and a glass of water, Old Hans declared that he was "ass gut as neoh." So he collected his belongings from Danny and me and waddled shakily toward our car in the driveway.

Danny and I sat on the steps watching as Dad and Hans drove away.

"You know what I think?" Danny asked, breaking the silence.

"What?"

"I think Hans would be a nice man – if he weren't a Nazi spy."

"After we have him arrested, maybe we can visit him in jail," I suggested.

"Yeah! Before the Army hangs him," Danny added pragmatically.

9 FORTUNES OF WAR

ONLY TWO OF US WERE FLYING THAT DAY. BUT BOTH OF us were Aces, fighter pilots skilled enough to have shot down five or more enemy aircraft.

My wingman was Group Captain Peter Townsend of the Royal Air Force. All the other RAF fighter pilots were home with their families listening to the wireless. Edward R. Morrow was reporting from London on the progress of the air war over England.

Winston Churchill decided that it was okay for the other pilots to take the day off, because Edward R. was going to discuss Mr. Churchill's recent speech to Parliament. Since this speech was so important, Winnie believed all the German pilots would be home in Berlin listening to the broadcast as well.

Flying wingtip-to-wingtip in our souped up Spitfires, we patrolled the skies above the English Channel just off the White Cliffs of Dover. We hummed war songs together over our radios to keep each other company. We dove down and waggled our wings to thank the British fishermen who braved U-boat and Junker dive-bomber attacks just so we could enjoy our favorite Dover sole at the RAF Officers Club.

We were about to break for lunch when the clouds parted beneath us. Suddenly, we saw them, a tight swastika-shaped formation of 29 Messerschmitts bound for Cambridge to strafe the students whom the Germans knew would be sunbathing on the lawn between classes. These Nazis were mean.

"I say there! Have you ever seen a prettier flock of ME-109's?" Peter asked, plucky as ever. "Why don't you take the right-hand bunch? I'll handle the blighters on the left."

After adjusting our white silk scarves, we tested our .30 calibers with two short bursts that punctured the puffy white clouds dead ahead of us. At my signal, a jaunty thumbs-up out my canopy window, we peeled off and dove downward in unison at 600 miles per hour to deliver our gift of hot lead to the wicked Jerry.

We opened fire at a range of about twelve feet. We had the advantage. They hadn't seen us coming. Our blazing guns hammered rows of red-hot tattered holes in fuselage, wing, and rudder sending fifteen of the Nazi devils into smoky, downward spirals toward the churning waters below. The angry sole fishermen waited with buckets of fish-cleaning leftovers to dump on the Nazi pilots when their parachutes deposited them in water next to their boats.

"Those hobbled Huns won't much like that smelly welcome, Peter," I shouted over my radio.

"I dare say not," replied the Brit. "Serves the buggers right for missing Ed and Winnie's wireless show."

As we pulled up to prepare for our second attack, I noticed picnickers on the Cliffs of Dover waving hats and hankies and blinking car headlights to cheer us on. I waved back and smiled. A wild, approving roar erupted from the crowd.

We reached our attack altitude in no time. With the sun at our backs, we pushed the noses of our screaming Spitfires downward and surprised them again. This second pass was all it took. Once again, we had skunked the Nazi team. This time 29 to zip! Not bad for ten minutes work.

I came up on the radio to confirm our scores, "Let's see, Peter. Your total is now 459. And, if I'm not mistaken, that's 603 for me. Right?"

"Rightee-oh, Colonel Jase. Taken all around, it's been a jolly good day. Jolly good, indeed. But have you considered the pesky problem we've made for the ground crew lads? As 'tis, our aeroplanes are completely covered with stenciled swastikas. Where will they possibly put 29 more?"

"Let's go to lunch at the diner in downtown London. We can tackle this tough problem over a couple of drinks. I'm craving a frosty strawberry soda. How about you?"

"Tally ho! Roger dodger!" he replied gleefully in British pilot lingo.

Peter banked his Spitfire and hightailed it toward our usual post-victory landing spot in Trafalgar Square, right next to Admiral Nelson's statue. We used to land in Piccadilly Circus but we agreed that it was too dangerous with all those double-decker buses circled around us. If there was anything that Peter and I believed in, it was "Safety First."

I followed at a leisurely pace allowing me to cool my machine guns and straighten my scarf.

Our landing approach took us in low over Buckingham Palace where we saw King George, Mr. Churchill, Premier Stalin, and President Roosevelt standing on the roof. They were holding big signs that read, "Way to Go, Jase! Way to Go, Peter!" We responded with a nonchalant wing wobble and continued our descent over Kensington Park straight to our rendezvous with strawberry sodas.

Air raid sirens and tugboat horns from the Thames whooped their congratulatory welcome as we landed. The sirens continued as we hopped down from our wings and shook hands in front of the throngs of applauding Londoners. They continued as we entered the London Diner. They spelled out my name in Morse code – J-A-S-E.

Now, they were screaming out my name in plain English!

"J a a a a a a a a a a a a a a a s e . C a a a a a a a a a a a a a a a a a a a a a a a a n . Youuuuuuuuuuuuuuuuuuuuuuuu. Cuuuuuuuuuuuuuum. Ooooooooooooout?"

I FELT A HAND on my shoulder. I turned. Was it Eleanor Roosevelt, again? No! It was Aunt Maude.

"Jase. Jase. Wake up!" she whispered loudly. "Danny's outside calling for you. I've never heard such a racket. Go on out and ask him to please be quiet. It's Saturday – and it's real early. It's still dark outside."

As Aunt Maude pulled the covers over her head, I tumbled out of bed and scurried to the kitchen door. There he was, in his full dress uniform complete with sword. I could see in the dim light that he was holding a brown bag full of – something.

"Come on in! But be quiet. Everybody's asleep," I whispered, waving him to the kitchen table. "I'll get dressed."

When I returned to the kitchen, breakfast was ready. Danny's main course was some kind of gray meat sandwich with mayonnaise and pickles. I chomped down without hesitation. It tasted good but somewhat strange to me.

"What is this?" I asked.

"Cold venison meat loaf – from last night's supper. My dad shot it."

"I thought so."

My stomach quivered slightly. I had never been keen on venison. My aversion may have stemmed from the fact that most deer meat came from deer. And I really liked deer, as animals, not sandwiches.

But venison was common fare for most families around Riverton. This was especially true during the war when rationing curtailed the supply of beef and pork. To compensate, many of our neighbors chose horse-meat as their alternative source of animal protein. Mercifully, we could count on Grandma Compton for *real* meat – beef, pork, and chicken.

When Aunt Maude and my parents joined us at the breakfast table, Danny launched a *very* long lecture on the relative merits of wildlife sandwiches. After several hours, or so it seemed, Dad politely interrupted and rose from the table, explaining that he had some important sewing machine repair jobs waiting for him in the shed. Taking advantage of the opportunity, I suggested that Danny and I re-commandeer Sherm's wagon and head for our appointment with Jim and the POWs. Mom and Aunt Maude looked relieved.

"WHATYA GOIN' TO BUY with all the bubble gum money?" Danny asked as we jogged along.

"I guess I'll save mine. Or, maybe, buy a wagon."

"I might buy a pet turtle. Or a rattlesnake."

"A rattlesnake!"

"Maybe we can buy some pop and candy bars for our secret observation post, too."

"That's a better idea," I confirmed. "I don't think rattlesnakes care much for heights."

We chattered nervously all the way to the loading dock. When we arrived, we paused to survey the scene.

About halfway down the dock, Jim was engaged in conversation with Otto. Don Paulus was sitting in a folding chair concentrating on polishing his badge. Sergeant Rick Prella was leaning against the wall smoking a cigar. His tommy gun was cradled in both arms. He looked bored, but he brightened when saw us.

As we drew closer, we were amazed to discover that the conversation between Jim and Otto was – in German! Jim greeted us with his customary warmth and explained, "Otto was giving me a lesson. I haven't spoken much German since my college days. We had to take a couple of years of a foreign language to graduate."

That was the first time I had heard Jim speak of his days at the University of Michigan.

Otto smiled and reported on Jim's progress, "Jims, da Chermin speeks preeta gut. Ya, preeta gut. Otto teech him sum pronoucings, dats ahl."

Danny looked at me, and I knew what he was thinking – Jim and Hans' Nazi book.

Otto turned to Danny and inquired, "Zo vats dat vagon for? Too hawl avay da loads of booblegum?"

"Yep! Where is all *da booblegum*?" Danny replied, with a smirk.

Otto, Jim, and Sergeant Rick broke into laughter. Don Paulus looked up wondering what joke he had missed.

"Zo vair's da sauerkraut, too?" Otto retorted.

At that point, Jim took charge of the exchange, "Otto, why don't you go fetch your bubble gum. I'll help the boys round up their sauerkraut. We can meet back here for a final count. Then, if everybody's happy, we can load the sauerkraut into Sergeant Rick's truck for the trip back to Camp Riverton. Okay?"

Otto nodded his head.

Don Paulus added, "When the deal's done, we can all have dinner in the cafeteria to celebrate. How 'bout that?"

We all agreed.

We followed Jim to the end of the dock. He reached around the building and snatched the key ring from its usual place. He unlocked the sliding boxcar door and rolled it open. Once inside, we turned toward the corner where our 105 jars of smelly delight were stored.

We stopped. The corner was empty! Not a single jar of kraut in the whole boxcar.

"We been robbed!" groaned Danny.

DANNY AND I WERE in shock.

How could we tell Mom – or Grandma Compton and Aunt Maude – about the missing sauerkraut? Who were the crooks? Why did they do it to us? And what about our fortune?

While Jim, Sergeant Rick, Otto, and Don Paulus huddled to discuss the situation, Danny and I sat in Sherm's wagon, staring longingly at the twenty-one red and yellow striped cartons of bubble gum stacked on a canning factory dolly in front of us.

Jim spoke first, "I'm most concerned about Jase and Danny. They're such trusting boys. Having grown up in Riverton, they've never experienced anything like this before. I feel responsible because they relied on me to find safe storage for their sauerkraut. Now look what's happened."

Don added, "I'm not surprised that somebody got into the boxcar. Heck, lots of people knew about the key. It was no big secret. I kept the door locked mainly to discourage passing hobos from sleeping in there – or eatin' those dented cans."

"Right!" shouted Danny, inexplicably.

"Technically, removing the jars from the boxcar is a crime," Don continued. "And, by rights, I could involve the Riverton Police. But, because only the sauerkraut was stolen, I gotta feeling that this crime is somethin' other than common larceny."

"Good point," agreed Jim.

"Well, if this turns out to involve the prisoners, it'll give the POW community work program a big black eye," said Sergeant Rick. "Colonel Butler ain't going to like that one bit. And another thing. I ain't no lawyer, but if military law applies in this case, the penalties for the POWs ull be bloody severe. To be honest, I wouldn't want Otto or his crew to get into hot water. Mosta them guys is pretty good Joes."

Sergeant Rick went on to explain that he had personally vouched for our deal with the Quartermaster Sergeant who ran the camp exchange. A lot was riding on being able to locate the sauerkraut so it could be delivered to the POWs at the camp. Many of them had given up store chits they earned working in the community to buy the cartons of bubble gum in anticipation of the exchange. Without the sauerkraut, he would have to return the bubble gum to the PX and the chits to the POWs.

"I'd hate to take that gum back. I know how much it means to the boys. But my neck's on the line – and so is Otto's," he added.

Otto was the last to speak. As the others shared their impressions, I had watched his face turn redder and redder. By the time he spoke, he was downright angry. Smacking his hand with a fist, he sputtered, "Dis es ah bad ting. Doze boyz ist gut boyz. Ahnd vee madz ah deel. Otto ist d'ashamed."

He stared at us and spoke, slowly and deliberately, "But Otto tinks he noze vat hoppen ear. Otto tinks he noze who da dirty ratz ist."

With that, he turned and stormed across the loading dock and through the door to the can storage area. Like the rest of us, Sergeant Rick was surprised, but he followed Otto into the building anyway.

We looked at each other, but none of us moved.

After five minutes of mutual fidgeting, Don initiated an exchange of small talk that lasted another ten minutes or so. At that point, it became clear to me that Otto and Sergeant Rick weren't coming back, at least, not right away.

I nudged Danny and suggested, "Let's go home – and tell Mom and Aunt Maude."

Danny nodded and stood up.

Jim explained to Don, "I better go along – so I can fill in Jase's folks on what's happened."

Don offered, "Why don't I find out what's going on and come over to the Addisons after my shift ends at 4:00 o'clock?"

"I hate to leave with an empty wagon," Danny moaned.

But that's exactly what we did.

WHEN JIM, DANNY, AND I arrived, Mom and Aunt Maude were making chicken sandwiches from the remains of one of Grandma's recent gifts. Mom had also made a huge bowl of one of my favorite dishes, potato salad turned deep pink by the addition of canned beets.

Wonder where she got those beets? I asked myself.

Aunt Maude announced, "There's plenty to eat for everybody. Iced tea for the adults. Cool milk for you boys."

The idea of lunch cheered me up.

"Do you have any peanut butter? I like chicken and peanut butter." Danny explained.

Aunt Maude gave Mom a funny look as she reached into the cupboard for the peanut butter jar. Mom shut her eyes and pursed her lips, but she didn't laugh. Danny, however, smiled broadly.

Dad took a break from his sewing machines and joined us. After serving ourselves, we men folk adjourned to the back porch. Dad and Jim took the chairs. Danny and I sat on the steps balancing our plates on our knees and gripping our glasses tightly between our feet.

When we finished eating, Dad asked innocently, "How'd the gum-for-kraut swap go this morning, boys?"

My cheer faded. I didn't respond.

Driven by his conditioned response to stress, Danny fibbed.

"It went fine. Got twenty-one cartons of bubble gum. We just left them at the canning factory – so we could come home for lunch before we started selling them," he explained, with a straight face.

Jim and I looked at each other in amazement. Then, ignoring Danny's fabrication, Jim broke the news. He described to Dad how we all had banked on the kraut being safe in the boxcar and how he felt responsible because he had arranged for its storage. He expressed his concern for us boys – and for Grandma Compton, Aunt Maude, and Mom.

However, Jim ended on a hopeful note, "I think Otto may be on to something. He was extremely upset. And he claimed to have a good idea of who was responsible. I'm sure Otto and Sergeant Rick will get to the bottom of it."

Danny and I nodded our heads in agreement.

Dad didn't speak at first. Then he asked, "How'd you leave it with Don Paulus?"

"He promised to stop by here and update us after his shift ends at 4:00 o'clock."

"Good. I've never met Otto or Sergeant Rick, but Don's a good man. So why don't we hold off on saying anything to the ladies until he gets here?" Dad suggested. "Maybe he'll have some good news by then."

We men all agreed.

When Danny and I entered to deposit the dirty dishes in the sink, Aunt Maude and Mom were seated at the kitchen table. Mom was admiring a new housedress pattern that Aunt Maude had bought for her at Woolworth's. They hardly noticed us.

On our way back outside, we paused at the backdoor while Jim described his recent attempt to play Dutch uncle to the Libby sisters, "For the sake of their reputations, I strongly advised them to stop associating with roughnecks like those Navy deserters. But I'm not sure I got through to them."

"Maybe they've just got to go through this – roughneck stage – on their way to growing up," Dad offered between puffs from his pipe. "But you did right to warn them. It coulda sunk in. Yah never know."

"The war does funny things to people," Jim added. "But, at heart, they're good girls. I just hope they can stay out of serious trouble – until they learn to use good judgment."

At that point, Danny turned to me and said, "Let's go for a walk down by the cottonwood tree."

I WAS GLAD DANNY suggested a walk. It sure beat just hanging around waiting for news from the canning factory. When we finally returned to the house, I could see that Jim and Dad were still sitting on the back porch sipping yet another glass of iced tea and assessing the state of the world.

Grandma Compton's car was parked in front. She was just leaving when she saw us. "Hey, boys!" she bubbled and waved. "Jase, I just spoke to your folks about borrowing you for a few days this coming week. Grandpa could use your help with the drilling."

"Hoorah! When?" I shouted.

Drilling was one of my favorite farm helper jobs.

"You can bring your things when you come out tomorrow for Sunday dinner. Danny can come, too. If it's okay with the Tuckers."

Danny looked at me as if he had just discovered gold. "Yes! Okay! Yeeessss! Let's go ask my mom right now," he insisted frantically as he pivoted and dashed toward home.

"Okay, Grandma. We'll ask Mrs. Tucker. See ya tomorrow!" I shouted over my shoulder as I waved goodbye and raced after Danny.

Grandma waved back. Then she hopped in her Terraplane and gunned it.

When we arrived at the Tucker garage, Sam Tucker was on his hands and knees sorting through a collection of spark plugs strewn over a sizeable area of floor covered with newspaper. Danny recognized his opportunity and struck fast. "Jase's-grandma-wants-me-to-go-to-her-farm-tomorrow-for-a-few-days-okay?" he blurted out.

His dad, still gazing at all those plugs, responded with a resolute, "Hmmm."

"Thanks, Dad!" Danny replied, confirming the parental permission and pulling me toward the garage door.

Mr. Tucker wished us luck with another firm, "Hmmm."

"Goodbye, Mr. Tucker," I said out of politeness.

There was no response.

WHEN WE GREW UP in Riverton during the war, there weren't many ways to get into trouble or to expose ourselves to danger. At least, that's how we saw it. So, most of the time, Danny and I didn't bother to ask for specific permission to pursue our adventures.

But we were considerate and sensitive. We knew that parents needed to feel important. So, once in a while, we asked permission for something, just to help them out.

On many occasions when obtaining permission was a must, we sought subtle ways to bypass our parents. Why chance a "No" from a parent when your chances of obtaining a "Yes" from almost any other adult were so much greater?

Grandmas and favorite aunts were always good for a quick okay. Even nice neighbor ladies, like Mrs. Mikas, would do in a pinch. But we had to be careful to avoid being charged with "intentional bypassing," especially when the adult in question was a bit rusty on normal rules and regulations for boys.

For example, one hot September day, Danny and I got permission from Bohunk Joe to miss school for the purpose of learning his secret techniques for carp fishing in the Chippewa River. Who wouldn't have jumped at this once-in-a-lifetime opportunity for learning? Surely, Joe's "old country" method of baiting hooks with dough balls made from wheat flour, cotton batting, and beer was more important than mere arithmetic or spelling. And, as Joe's full cooking pot proved that evening, we had completely mastered our carp-fishing lesson.

So what was the problem?

It's simple. While Joe's Yes-answer was a piece of cake to obtain, we had bypassed parents, teachers, and, of course, the truant officer. After we arrived home that evening, it became clear to Danny and me that those bypassed were heavily Pro-School – and Anti-Carp.

After considering their point of view for a second or two, we decided to agree. As I mentioned earlier, from time to time, it's important for boys to help parents feel important.

WITH PERMISSION FOR DANNY'S stay at the farm in hand, we walked back toward Forrest Street along New Albany Avenue. When we reached Pete's store, Pete poked his head out the door.

"Boysa! Coma here. Petesa gotta dah idea!" he hollered.

Pete had given our imminent windfall of bubble gum a lot of thought. He told us how frustrating it had been not being able to replenish his inventory from his suppliers. Seeing the disappointment on the faces of neighborhood children day after day was almost more than he could bear.

Pete then asked how we planned to sell our bubble gum. We admitted that we hadn't given it much thought.

"What did you have in mind, Mr. Pete?"

"Howsa about Petesa buysa all you bubbledagum for $21?"

"All right!" I replied, without thinking twice.

"You gotta deal!" Danny concurred.

"But wait a minute! Mr. Pete, how much will you charge per piece?" I inquired.

"Two centsa piece. Joosta lika you boyz. No profits. Joosta for da kids"

"Then you *really* got a deal."

"Whensa she coma den, da bubbledagum?"

Oopsy!

Pete had posed a tough question. We hadn't mentioned the small snafu involving the missing sauerkraut. So we told Pete that we weren't quite sure. But, as soon as it arrived, he'd have his bubble gum.

After shaking Pete's hand like real businessmen, we crossed New Albany and headed for my house. Danny was silent. I knew what he was thinking. *What if we never see the kraut or the gum again? What would we tell Pete? Or Mom? Grandma? Aunt Maude?*

Suddenly, our thoughts were interrupted by the long, loud blast of a truck horn!

We turned and saw the huge Army truck, bouncing up Forrest Street. The canning factory POWs were standing in the open cargo bed. They shouted at Danny and me and pointed at Otto who was balanced precariously on the truck's forward rack, flapping his arms like a gooney bird. In each hand, he held – a jar of sauerkraut!

"Holleeey Cow!" yelled Danny.

I was speechless.

The truck skidded to a stop under our box elder tree. Sergeant Rick and Don Paulus hopped down from the cab. They wore huge smiles. Aunt Maude and Mom came out the front door, and Jim and Dad joined us from the back porch.

Otto gruffly ordered two of his men off the truck. The other POWs jostled them and shoved them to the ground. The pair brushed them-selves off and held out their arms while those on the truck loaded them down with carton after carton of delicious and valuable bubble gum!

I looked at Jim. His eyes glistened. I thought he might break into tears. I turned away before I joined him. Danny's mouth stood open. He swept his army hat from his head and stuffed it into his mouth.

As the first load came up the sidewalk, I recognized the two POWs. They were the defiant pair who had given Otto a bad time and hooted in response to the Libby sisters' jibes from the office window.

The two misbehavers looked worse for wear. Their uniforms were disheveled and torn in places. Buttons were missing. Red scuffmarks covered their hands and faces. One sported an eye that was nearly swollen shut. A small cut on the other's upper lip still bled a little.

Pointing at the two suspects, Otto announced in a booming voice, "Dats dem! Da dirty ratz dat tooks da sauerkraut. Look atz dem, boyz. Dem ist badh!! Bot, wit ah teeny bit of convincings dem tells uz vhere vas hid das sauerkraut."

Otto tucked his thumbs behind an imaginary vest and concluded, "Ahd, Otto keepz his promizz to you boyz."

A little bit of convincing! I'll bet, I chuckled to myself.

Otto then turned to Aunt Maude and Mom. He clicked his heels and formally introduced himself as "Herr Kaptain Otto Klump of der Cherman Luftwaffe."

What flowed from Otto next can only be described as a profusion of flowery flattery and ardent appreciation – from every humble and grateful POW in Camp Riverton – for the immense generosity and kindness of these two wonderful – and, incidentally, beautiful women – and for an even more wonderful *Grandmamma* – for providing the poor, deprived POWs with over a hundred delicious and nutritious jars of their national dish – that he knew would be the best they ever tasted. And all of this will never be forgotten. Never! Ever!

I thought Otto might swoon. Instead, suddenly, he stopped and bowed deeply from the waist. None of us moved or said a thing. None of us, that is, except Danny who returned Otto's bow with one of his own. This time no one laughed. We were all too stunned.

When the twenty-one cartons of bubble gum had been stacked on our front porch, Otto ordered his two "badh boyz" back onto the truck. As they rejoined their fellow POWs, the villains were punched and jostled by their colleagues, perhaps for our benefit. Nonetheless, I was pleased to see these two lugs roughed up some more. After all, they had nearly ruined our day. No, our whole lives! And for what reason?

As the POW truck chugged up Forrest Street, Otto and his men waved their thanks again and again. When they had disappeared from sight, we turned our attention to the bubble gum.

"I'll get the wagon!" chirped Danny. He seemed eager to experience the payday awaiting us at Pete's.

Don Paulus had not joined the others on the truck but lingered to brief Jim and Dad on what had transpired that afternoon at the canning factory.

"I appreciate your staying, Don. I'll give you a lift home after we finish."

"No thanks, John. I normally take the bus to work on weekends – so the wife can have the car for grocery shopping and such. She works at Michigan Electric Motor – on the assembly line – during the week. Did you know that MEM was hiring again? Anyway, itta be no trouble catching the bus after we're through. I enjoy riding the bus to be honest."

For a decorated war hero, Don seemed a bit nervous or perhaps self-conscious. Nonetheless, I wanted to hear what he had to say, so I asked permission to stay and listen. Danny asked, too.

"It might be more comfortable if we reconvened on the back porch after everybody has a cold drink – iced tea, water, or milk," Mom suggested.

"Will the bubble gum be safe here?" Danny inquired warily.

We all nodded.

As Dad helped Mom and Aunt Maude with the drinks, he briefed them for the first time on what he knew about the stolen kraut. Mom and Aunt Maude were aghast. They were angry that anyone would do that to us boys. Don Paulus readily agreed from his seat in one of the back porch chairs.

After a deep swallow of iced tea, Don began his report. He told us in detail all that he had learned, starting with a history of the POWs at Camp Riverton. We all listened intently while he spoke.

"MOST POWS AT THE camp are older fellows like Otto – he's around forty. These older POWs aren't ardent Hitler lovers – or even members of the Nazi party for that matter. For the most part, they're just patriotic Germans who joined the Army to defend their Homeland – at least – that's what they say.

"These older soldiers were already adults when the Nazis came to power in 1933. So they know something of what Germany was like, before Hitler and his henchmen rewrote history – convincing those who were younger that Hitler was God and all Germans were invincible Supermen.

"The older ones don't tend to be as idealistic – or fervent – about the righteousness of Germany's cause, either. And, I know for a fact, they're real glad to be here at Camp Riverton – instead of fighting in the hedgerows of Normandy or on the plains of Russia, right now.

"Erik Baden and Klaus Reitter – Otto's two dirty rats – are truly a different breed. First, they're a generation younger than most of the other POWs. Their first exposure to Nazism was as members of the Hitler Youth – an evil Nazi version of the Boy Scouts.

"Like many Germans their ages, they're loyal Nazi party members – and zealots. Unlike the older POWs – Otto and the others – they *say* they resent their comfortable surroundings here. They consider helping Americans, in any way, to be treasonous behavior. That's what they say, but – in the case of these two bad boys – that's not how they act. Typical Fascists. Do as I say, not as I do.

"A good proportion of the younger Germans – like Baden and Reitter – were captured around Monte Cassino during the Italian campaign earlier this year. So they're relatively recent arrivals to Camp Riverton. These two are members of the elite Schutzstaffel – the SS. They have to take a personal oath to Hitler. That makes them particularly nasty – real troublemakers.

"Wisely the U.S. Army dispersed these bad actors throughout the POW camp system – to prevent any one camp from having more than a handful of them. These are the only two SS troopers at Camp Riverton. They were both made part of Otto's work group – so his older men could keep them in line.

"In other POW camps, the true Nazis refuse to work for the Americans – even in non-military jobs like the canning factory. But these two didn't refuse. They compromised their so-called principles for two reasons, I'm told.

"First, they enjoy spending what they earn. The canning factory pays the Army 52 cents an hour for their time. And the POWs receive their cut – 80 cents a day – in the form of chits that they can spend at the camp exchange for personal articles like stationery, reading materials, cigarettes, and – oh, yeah – bubble gum.

"Second, they both seem to be very interested in the young female workers at the canning factory. They can't hang around young women when they're standing on their political principles locked up out at Camp Riverton. So they volunteer to work.

"Some principles, huh? Some Supermen!

"Otto is a commissioned officer in the Luftwaffe – the German Air Force – these two juvenile delinquents are enlisted men. But, because Otto isn't an SS officer –or a member of the Nazi party – they don't respect, obey, or even cooperate with him. So Otto suspected these two right from the start. He figured they'd do almost anything to discredit or embarrass him. I guess he was right.

"At first, Baden and Reitter denied having any knowledge of the missing sauerkraut. And they presented a pretty good case. How could they have had time to remove 105 jars from the boxcar and hide them somewhere? Doesn't Otto constantly watch them like a hawk? What were they going to do with the sauerkraut? They certainly couldn't have smuggled it back to Camp Riverton riding in an open truck – having only their pants pockets for a hiding place. They couldn't have eaten all of that sauerkraut at the canning factory. And how could they have sold it? Otto would have found out. Wouldn't he?

"Still, Otto wasn't convinced. He was sure they were guilty. But he needed evidence – or something – to pry the truth out of these rascals.

"Otto announced that he needed to confer with Sergeant Rick and me in the security office. During his absence, his men took matters into their own hands. They held a 'court martial' and Baden and Reitter were found 'Guilty.' Not your typical American trial, I'd say. But, nonetheless, the two 'guilty parties' served the first portion of their 'sentence,' which – from what I can gather – amounted to a good old fashioned thrashing at the hands of the 'jury.'

"Then the sentence was suspended, and the rats were given the choice of serving the rest of their sentence or remembering where they might have misplaced the sauerkraut. Miraculously, they regained their memories. When Otto returned, the dirty rats were singing like dirty canaries.

"All 105 jars were found – in perfect condition – stacked in a locked, office supply closet over in the administrative area – the east wing of the building. Now, how those 105 jars got there is a mystery. Obviously, someone had to help them hide the jars there, because only a few supervisors have keys to that closet. In order to open it myself, I had to dig out the administration department master key that's kept in the security office safe.

"Sergeant Rick and Otto will continue to interrogate the pair, and it's my job to see if I can find out who at the canning factory might have helped these skunks. To be honest, I can't imagine anybody from Riverton being mean – or stupid – enough to be involved with these low-down sauerkraut thieves."

Jim and Dad looked at each other. Mom and Aunt Maude looked at each other. Danny and I looked at each other.

Danny broke the silence, "I think we might know somebody that stupid."

10 BACK TO THE FARM

THAT NIGHT AS I LAY IN BED, I REVIEWED ALL THAT HAD happened that day. First, we were shocked by the discovery of the missing sauerkraut. Then the kraut criminals were nabbed, amid strong suspicions about the identity of their co-conspirators. The bubble gum fortune was saved. And, thanks to Pete, our $21.00 profit – two ten-dollar bills and two half-dollars – was nestled safely in my bank. And I'd almost forgotten Grandma's exciting news about Danny joining me to help Grandpa at the farm tomorrow!

Hans' Nazi book under my mattress poked my back reminding me of old Hans speaking German in the middle of the night to strangers with tommy guns in black limousines with no license plates. We had to get Jim to help us with that book! I was positive that the outcome of the war depended on it.

My mind was racing.

According to the revised Saturday night bath ritual, Aunt Maude had taken her bath first. Now, she was curled up in bed, drowsily reading the latest *Saturday Evening Post*. She had already yawned three times. I kept count.

"Aunt Maude," I asked. "Did you get a letter from Uncle Van, today?"

"Yes! Yes, I did. From England – just before the Normandy invasion. He was excited to be a part of General Eisenhower's grand operation – they call it *Operation Overlord*. He hoped you were happy having me as your new roommate, too."

"I am, Aunt Maude. I really am!"

"Jaaaaaaaaaaaaaaaaaaaaaase. Caaaaaaaaaaaaaaaaaaaaaan. Youuuuuuuuuuuuuuuuuuuuuuuuuuu. Cuuuuuuuuuuuuuuum. Ooooooooooooooout?"

I pried open my sleep-filled eyes. A glance at Aunt Maude's clock told me it was 5:30 AM. And it was Sunday morning.

"This is ridiculous!" I said under my breath.

In my mind, I prepared a sermon on courtesy for you-know-who. When I reached the back door, my irritation gave way to amusement. Danny was sporting a new outfit. His army garb had been replaced by a striking cowboy, or was it sailor, motif?

His Sergeant York leggings and rough leather shoes were gone. Instead, he wore a gaudy pair of shiny, red and white plastic-leather boots. The bib of his neckerchief (a blue-white farmer's hankie) was draped casually over his left shoulder, Hollywood cowboy style. I recognized the hankie as last Sunday's penny wrapper, so I assumed church was off the agenda this morning.

On his head, he wore a dainty white straw hat with a turned-up brim and a bright chartreuse hatband, its forked ends dangling to one side. Had it not been for the missing white netting, I would have sworn it was the exact model worn by the Methodist women we had encountered the Sunday before.

I couldn't tell if he was trying to look like Shirley Temple or a Portuguese fisherman. But I guessed that my pal had snitched his new "cowboy" hat from his mother's closet. I also concluded that his mother's closet had no mirror.

His right thumb was hooked, swagger style, over a thick cowboy belt that sagged a good two inches below his navel. A long sprig of green alfalfa grass drooped from his lips. I could see through his steel frames that his black eyes were deliberately set at half-mast. In his left hand, he was toting a small, battered suitcase of scruffy brown leather.

"Howdy!" young Shirley Cowpoke drawled, banging his bag to rest on the porch chair. "I'm ready to go."

"It's not even six o'clock in the morning. We don't go out to Grandma's until afternoon."

"Oh!" he whimpered, revealing his acute disappointment. "Whatta ya wanta do, until then?"

I was stumped for a minute. Finally, I suggested, "Let's count our bubble gum money!"

"Okay! Great!"

We quietly entered my bedroom, scooped the bank from my dresser, retrieved the key, and returned to the kitchen table. After counting our bubble gum fortune about thirty-five times, boredom set in. And it still wasn't six o'clock.

"Wanta look for four-leaf clovers?" I proposed hopefully.

"Nah. I can't bend over too good with my new boots. And my cowboy hat falls off easy," he explained, well aware of his limitations.

"Wanta help me dig a new garbage pit?"

"Nah. I don't want to get dirty."

I wondered how he expected to perform as a farm helper. Then I remembered his first visit to the farm. Based on his milking proficiency with Molly and his animal husbandry expertise with a certain pair of now-deceased red roosters, how could his attire possibly make him less capable?

"Wanta go for breakfast at the Good Mission Church?" I suggested as a last resort.

"Good idea! I'm hungry. Hey! Maybe we can help set up!"

BUDDY ROE BIB OVERALLS was reclining on the Mission front porch. He appeared still groggy from the previous night's liquid supper. When he heard us climb the wooden steps, he opened one red eye at a time.

As the unofficial morning greeter, he smiled shakily and welcomed us, "Good morning, little boy. Hello, little *girl*. What's your name?"

At that, Ole Bibs broke into wheezy laughter. Danny wasn't amused. "Let's go inside – and have a cigar!" he ordered.

Our arrival brought a smile to the face of Edith Squires who sat demurely on her piano stool. She pretended not to notice Danny's new wardrobe.

Without being asked, we organized the tables and served breakfast to an unusually small congregation. Evidently, the recent wave of warm weather had prompted many of the Mission's winter residents to migrate to their summer quarters, the popular hobo campsite under the Ann Arbor Street Bridge. But no one seemed to mind the intimacy of our small turnout.

We finished our serving job and sat down to enjoy the service and, naturally, our hearty breakfast. The main course was lima beans and peaches with a healthy side order of Edith's delicious pancakes. While mashing the two main ingredients together into a green-orange mush, Danny claimed it was one of his favorite combinations. In light of his recent experience with surprise tin can meals, I believed him.

Edith's repertoire was zippy and bright, her voice strong and clear. Her breathtaking rendition of *Onward Christian Soldiers* was in keeping with the theme of the sermon. As Danny beat time noisily on his chair, Edith smiled approvingly.

From his homemade pulpit, Reverend Squires spoke passionately of the exploits of our valiant boys at Normandy. He lauded their courage as they struggled through heavy fighting and hedgerows. Soberly, he predicted that many more Gold Stars would adorn Riverton windows as casualties from this great battle were tallied.

Gripped with patriotic fervor, he implored us, his congregation, to search deeply into our hearts. The search was conducted quickly because there were so few of us – Bibs, Danny, and me, plus the two older gentlemen who by then had lapsed into after-breakfast snoozes.

Undeterred, the Good Reverend really let 'er rip. Did we hear the call? The call to service for God and country! Will we answer the call? Right here and now! By confessing our sins, changing our wicked ways, and enlisting in the United States Army!

"Who will pledge?" he shouted, demanding a show of hands.

His only taker came from the back row. It was the cigar-chomping cowgirl wearing the funny hat.

Our donation was exactly the same as the other members of the congregation that morning, a skillful thump on the bottom of the collection plate designed to conceal our pennilessness.

Then we set off for the First Methodist Church.

WHEN WE ENTERED THE church, the minister was reading the Bible lesson. He paused momentarily. His friendly smile prompted his curious congregation to turn and look our way.

Danny removed his straw hat and waved it over his head like Hopalong Cassidy. A gush of chuckles rose from the parishioners. After swallowing a snigger, the minister brought his flock back to order and took up where he had left off in the scriptures.

I'll say this for buckaroo boy, he sure knew how to work a room.

I was good at remembering words and passages from Bible stories because our teachers at Hamilton School read them to us, at great length, every morning. But I didn't recognize this morning's reading, which according to the minister concerned sin and redemption. I knew what "sin" *was*. Who didn't? But the meaning of "redemption" had me stumped. I asked Danny if he knew. He confidently assured me it had something to do with dental hygiene.

Instead of taking a seat, we stood in the back of the church. After three long minutes, we were bored, so Danny elbowed me and nodded toward the door. Just as we turned to leave, we saw *her* sweeping down on us like a red-tailed hawk.

Miss Elizabeth Bundy snatched our collars, stood us up straight, and marched us toward the front door. Was this any way to treat potential new members? Customer relations not being foremost in her mind, she hissed, "Out of the nave now! To the narthex!"

What was she saying? Nave? Narthex? I assumed she had forgotten her false teeth?

"Take that off your head! And put it back – this instant!"

Since she was concentrating her rage on Danny, I felt relieved. But what was she talking about?

Seemingly unperturbed, Danny pivoted, swept the dainty straw hat from his head and hung it gently on one of the coat hooks that lined the entrance hall. He turned to Miss Bundy and raised his eyebrows. His expression clearly communicated, *There! Is there anything else I can do for you?*

Miss Bundy answered him by angrily thrusting her open palm forward until it thumped Danny's chest. She hissed again, "Give it to me! Now!"

Shrugging his shoulders, he reached into his back pocket. Out came a white wad that he promptly deposited in Miss Bundy's bony little hand, which by now was trembling with anger. When he released his grip, the wad expanded, puffing up to reveal its true nature.

White netting!

So the old cowhand hadn't rustled his new hat from his mother's closet after all.

I had no idea how Danny managed to *borrow* Miss Bundy's favorite Sunday bonnet. And I didn't ask. But my respect for his resourcefulness had just taken an upward turn.

After leaving the First Methodists, we detoured to his house where he ducked inside to change back into his standard army garb. When he joined me again in the driveway, I validated his decision, "That looks a lot better."

"Really!"

"Yep."

"Then let's go drill the farm!" he shouted, holding an invisible hand drill in one hand and turning its crank with the other.

Obviously, Danny needed a little more tutoring before he took his *Farm Implement Familiarity Test.*

As we approached our house, we saw Dad carrying something to the car. It was a jar of sauerkraut! He turned when he saw us, looking guilty and embarrassed. We had caught him in the act!

"Mom found this one – behind the jam on the kitchen shelf," he confessed. "We thought it would be a good idea to take it to the farm – for the other Comptons."

I shrugged my shoulders and smiled as if to say, *That's okay, Dad. Don't worry about it. We had plenty of jars for trading.*

From behind me, however, I heard Danny's scolding voice, "That'll be ten bubble gums, if you please, Mr. Addison!"

"NOW, THAT LOOKS MUCH better. Doesn't it, Dad?" Grandma asked.

Grandpa lowered his newspaper and stared at Danny standing next to the living room wood stove. "Yep! Now you can take him to your women's meeting over at the Barrington church," he quipped. "Nobody'll suspect a thing."

"Dad! You hush up. He'll sleep a lot better, now he's dressed properly. And we don't care how he looks. Do we, Jase?" Grandma declared, giving me one of her back-me-on-this-or-else looks.

"Oh, yeah. I wore that one – once," I admitted. "It's nice."

That was the best I could come up with.

Danny had blundered when he forgot to include pajamas in his little brown suitcase. He learned the hard way that Grandma didn't tolerate boys sleeping under her roof with anything less than appropriate nightclothes. I had learned that lesson myself several summers before.

When Grandma got wind of Danny's packing omission, she immediately provided the new farmhand with one of her favorite nightgowns, white cotton with delicately embroidered borders of intertwined violets. "We're always prepared for a sleeping emergency," she informed Danny as she handed him the unwanted sleepwear and patted him on the head.

To say the least, Danny was not thrilled. As he saw it, this was no sleeping emergency. He declared it a "Sleeping Disaster"! He pleaded with Grandma to sleep in his army uniform, in case he was needed to repel Nazi storm troopers who might descend on the farm in the middle of the night.

Nice try! I thought to myself, trying to visualize Hans Zeyer and his SS buddies, Lugers drawn, sneaking up the dark driveway from the horse barn.

Grandma's reaction had been downright unsympathetic and maybe even a bit unpatriotic, "Oh, piffle! Go on with you. Get dressed now, and then let's have a look at you."

After some initial embarrassment, Danny's angst melted away.

A snack consisting of a few dozen Spanish peanuts with Grandpa, smiling Mick, and me really helped. Soon, Danny was comfortable in his third uniform of the day.

We all settled in for another horrifying episode of *Inner Sanctum*, "Death at Midnight", starring Raymond Foster. With the radio show's eerie theme song in the background, the echo chamber voice of the announcer even ensnared Grandma. She usually retreated to her kitchen when Grandpa and I tuned in our favorite Sunday night mystery show. She complained that *Inner Sanctum* gave her the heebie-jeebies.

About five minutes into the hour-long program, Danny announced that tonight's killer was Mr. Green who turned out to be an undercover G-man. After the show, Danny explained that he had purposely announced the wrong killer, just to throw the rest of us off track.

On that predictable note, we called it a night.

THE NIGHTLY RITUAL AT the farm included a subject that I was taught not to discuss in public. Nonetheless, I must tell you, having no inside plumbing presented a challenge for someone from town, especially in the dead of winter.

Technically, there was *some* inside plumbing. A cold-water tap at the kitchen sink brought icy water from the deep well next to the back shed. But that was it. No hot water. No bathtub. And, above all, no toilet!

Each evening right before bed, Grandma changed into her night-clothes and headed for the kitchen. There she sliced a lemon in two and carefully squeezed the juice into a teacup. Then she added a double dollop of hot water from the teakettle that constantly simmered on the kitchen stove.

Once the concoction had cooled, she tipped the warm lemon water into her mouth and exercised her cheeks vigorously. Squishing noisily, she gave her teeth a good rinse. Then, after a little gargle, she promptly swallowed the whole mouthful.

"Ahhh! Lemon juice. It's good for the constitution," she guaranteed.

Invariably, Grandpa asked, "How is it for the Declaration of Independence?"

Giving Grandpa a patronizing smile, she removed her false teeth and placed them in the same teacup. Then she covered her pink and white removable smile with water from the tap and set the cup on the shelf above the sink. Next, she snapped on the yard light, grabbed her flashlight, and headed for the "Hers" outhouse.

That was our cue. The men of the house, Grandpa, Jase, and smiling Mick, followed her out the backdoor. Once outside, we turned left toward the regal spy apple tree that grew tall above the back porch that served as Grandma's laundry area. Once beyond the tree, we stopped and proceeded to "water" the tall grass that lined the boundary of the orchard.

Upon our return, Grandpa removed his false teeth and scrubbed them thoroughly under the water tap using the small, curved wooden brush that hung from a brass cup-holder next to the sink. Then he placed his teeth inside his own cup, topped it off with water and parked it next to Grandma's on the shelf where both sets of smiles napped together until the next morning.

As always, he yawned and wished me a final good night. Then he drifted off to change into his nightshirt and tumble into his bed with the rock-hard horsehair mattress. Then Grandma wished me a good night. But only after she ensured that all bedrooms were equipped with a clean porcelain chamber pot for our use during the night.

On his first visit to the farm, Danny wanted to know why Grandma and Grandpa had two outhouses. His question made me laugh.

The "His" outhouse was actually closer to the backdoor than "Hers." That's because His was dug and built first, just west of the leghorn chick-breeding coop and up against the hog yard fence. Hers, the newer and nicer of the two, was dug and built last, just east of the same coop.

During my grandparents' early years on the farm, there was only His, an ample "two-seater" that was fine in every respect. But Grandma got a bee in her bonnet about the need for a new *privy*, her fancy name for *outhouse*.

For three summers, Grandpa resisted her pestering for a new and improved model. Finally, in a moment of weakness, he caved in. Yes, she would have her new privy – whether it was needed or not.

When the new outhouse was finally erected, Grandpa confirmed his conviction that Hers was unnecessary by continuing to use His. Despite Grandma's insistence, he steadfastly refused to tear His down and fill it in. And, in protest, he refused to set foot in Hers.

For years, the outhouse-privy stalemate continued, putting the entire Compton family in a quandary. Which do we use? If we use His,

Grandma will think we're siding with Grandpa. If we use Hers, how will Grandpa feel?

Because I spent more time at the farm than the others, I knew from overheard conversations that Grandma and Grandpa were well aware of our dilemma. In fact, they secretly agreed that tearing down His would result in "the family not having anything to talk about."

Regardless of the choice we made, one of them would feign mild irritation. Then, after everyone departed, each would describe how guilty we had acted when they caught us using the "wrong" one. Over the years, Grandma and Grandpa shared a good many chuckles at our expense before going to bed on Sunday nights.

DANNY AND I SHARED the spindly, metal-framed double bed in my favorite room, the upstairs Victrola room. After placing the clean chamber pot under our bed, we snuggled into the puffy down quilts and reviewed the day's events.

Danny assessed each branch of the Compton family whose members had spent another Sunday playing with cousins, exchanging family gossip, analyzing the war, and consuming Grandma's smorgasbord.

"I liked Uncle Tom's family best. I mean – not better than your Dad and Mom, of course. Or Aunt Maude. Or Grandma and Grandpa," Danny sputtered, frantically backpedaling. "And, Uncle Raymond's family's real nice, too.

"And, I really liked riding out to the farm in your car, too," he offered as an afterthought, attempting to change the subject altogether.

Even though there was plenty of room for Danny in the backseat with Aunt Maude and me, again he insisted on straddling the gearshift lever. So he sat in the front seat between Mom and Dad.

Army boy gripped the lever tightly with both hands during the entire trip. So, each time Dad needed to shift, Danny was able to *help* him. From his centerline perspective, he was also able to announce each upcoming turn and warn Dad whenever a car got closer than a mile or two. Danny accomplished these vital tasks using his new glasses to read aloud each and every word on each and every billboard, building, and mailbox, all the way out to the farm.

"Does your family have homemade ice cream every Sunday?" Danny inquired, while he dreamily hugged his fluffy pillow.

"Good question," I replied.

As best I could remember, Grandma only went to the trouble of setting up the ice cream churn on the Fourth of July and for the annual Barrington Church of Christ ice cream social that she hosted each year after the strawberry harvest. Today was definitely an exception.

I guessed that today's homemade ice cream, creamy rich and laced with extra sweet canned peaches, was in honor of Danny who had flattered Grandma the first time they met. Danny had told her that she was the "best grandmother in the world" because she knew how important it was for boys, like him, to have ice cream as often as possible in view of the terrible deprivations brought on by the war, and so on. And so on.

Danny had never seen an ice cream churn before. Fascinated, he quickly volunteered for the first turn at the churn handle, a favorite task for all of us cousins. After assuming the job, he stubbornly refused to relinquish his position despite complaints from my cousins and gentle urgings from Grandma.

He stood in the shade of the maple tree whistling *Under the Double Eagle* and churning away for nearly two hours while the rest of us played softball, annie-eye-over the corncrib, and hide-and-seek. He had found his niche and, by golly, he wasn't giving it up.

Hide-and-seek gave me the opportunity to study Danny for a long time without his knowledge. From my hiding place under Grandma's hydrangea bush, I concluded that Danny was the most unusual boy I knew. Since I could remember, I had longed for a true best friend. Now, for better or worse, I had one.

GRANDPA AND GRANDMA WERE up well before first light. Grandpa always enjoyed his first cup of Grandma's coffee at the kitchen table before he commenced his morning chores.

Sounds from the kitchen woke Danny first. He hopped out of bed and immediately removed Grandma's nightgown. When I opened my eyes, he was back in his army uniform, sitting on the side of our bed. He looked quite relieved at being dressed normally again. Normal for Danny, that is. I couldn't blame him.

"Aren't you hungry?" he inquired eagerly.

"Yep! Why don't you go on down while I get dressed," I urged my friend who, inexplicably, seemed a bit shy that morning.

But he took my advice and disappeared down the stairs. I smiled to myself when I heard Grandma and Grandpa's warm greetings from the kitchen below. I also heard Danny fall for Grandpa's morning standard,

"Up before breakfast, eh?"

"Yep!" Danny replied.

I dressed in my farm clothes, tumbled downstairs, and entered the kitchen. Danny looked up from the table and beat Grandpa to the punch, "Up before breakfast, eh?"

Grandpa smiled and turned back to finish the calculations he was making on a pad of paper on the kitchen table. "I'll bet you're figuring how much seed and fertilizer we'll need," I speculated innocently, showing off a bit for Danny.

Grandpa smiled. "How'd you know that?"

Of course, he knew how I knew. For the last three summers, each time before we drilled, I had seen him go through this calculation. But Grandpa went along with my little show for Danny's benefit.

When I sat down, Grandma turned from her stove and gave me a funny look, "Jase, if you're as hungry as Danny, you'll probably want the same breakfast."

Again, she gave me that funny look. I got the hint. "What's Danny having, Grandma?"

"Well, let's see. First, he's havin' coffee with lots of milk and sugar – brown sugar is what he prefers. Then he wants some hickory-smoked bacon and eggs. Then he says he'll have a bowl of oatmeal with fresh cream – that's what I'm havin'. Next, there's Grapenuts – steamed with hot water first – with milk and brown sugar. That's what Grandpa is thinking about. Then he wants some fresh bread toast – four slices, he says – with strawberry, blackberry, *and* blueberry jam. Next, he wants some prunes. And, finally, he'd like to finish up with some molasses cookies. Just a few, he tells me."

Grandma had spelled out Danny's order with the skill of a truck stop waitress.

I reacted without thinking. "Holy Cow! Danny, what are you doing? We came out here to help Grandpa, not to eat breakfast all day long!"

I felt a little guilty about my accusation, but evidently, my message got through. Danny stared at me, weighing my words carefully. Then, much to my surprise, he nodded his head in agreement.

Turning to Grandma, he said, "Cancel that blueberry jam order, please."

11 DRILLING DAY

"FEED YOUR ANIMALS BEFORE YOU FEED YOURSELF," Grandpa said, scooting his chair back from the table.

"I'm with you, Grandpa," I replied.

Looking up from heaps of bacon and eggs, Danny gazed at us, trying to decipher the meaning of Grandpa's maxim. Abruptly, he dismissed us with a wave of his fork, "I don't have any animals – so, I'll stay here. Okay, Grandma?"

Grandma smiled, "Okay, Danny. Eat up! I need your help while the boys are off chorin'."

Danny smiled at the prospect.

Following our routine, Grandpa milked the cows while I fed the animals – horses, pigs, chickens, cats, cows, and, naturally, Mick. As Grandpa carried his last brimming pail into the milk house, I let the herd out into the barnyard freeing them to graze their way to the woods.

Pouring the final drops of milk into the cream separator, Grandpa declared us deserving of a hearty breakfast. Our chores had consumed the better part of an hour.

When we entered the kitchen, the warm air was filled with mouth-watering scents. I noticed that Danny was working on his fifth course. Or was it his sixth? Anyway, he was eating a huge bowl of steaming Grapenuts.

Grandma glanced up from the hot stove, wiped her forehead with her apron corner, and winked at us. "Well, sit yourselves down, while I pour you some coffee," she instructed. "Danny's still working on his breakfast, so you can join him."

I never told my parents that Grandma served me coffee for breakfast. Her theories relating to children's nutrition ran contrary to accepted standards of the day. She was particularly unyielding on the subject of coffee.

"In all my days, I never saw coffee – or anythin' else – stunt the growth of any young farm hand," she maintained.

I was glad. I liked Grandma's strong coffee, especially when it was diluted with raw cow's milk and thickened with sugar.

That morning, I chose a bowl of hot oatmeal with brown sugar and fresh cream. Grandpa stuck with his hot Grapenuts. Grandma encouraged us to try some of her new cinnamon and raisin bread. We both ate two, oven-toasted slices with butter. Danny bragged that earlier he had consumed six. I didn't doubt his claim.

When Grandpa left the table to refill his coffee cup, he whispered something to Grandma. While I couldn't hear the whole comment, I did pick up the words, "Danny" and "tapeworm." Grandma snickered and smacked him on the back pocket with her spatula.

Danny was too absorbed with buttering his Grapenuts to notice.

"Weather looks good. So, with luck, we should finish the whole twenty acres today," Grandpa reported.

I interpreted his code.

We'd make it if I tended the markers and replenished the drill hoppers with seed and fertilizer without Grandpa having to stop the drill and if Grandma brought noon dinner to the field. Providing we used both teams to keep them fresh. And providing he had calculated right, and we didn't run out of seed or fertilizer. And providing we didn't experience an equipment breakdown. And, of course, the weather had to stay good. Indeed, we just might be done by dusk.

Given the best of circumstances, I knew we were in for a long, hard, dusty day. Grandma would help with the evening chores as was her custom on long workdays for Grandpa and me. Who knows? Maybe Danny could help, too.

Grandpa had completed fitting – plowing, disking, and dragging – the field where we would be working. Earlier in the year, he and I had removed the new boulders that cropped up each spring and deposited them at the nearest hedgerow. The field was ready for sowing. Today, it was Michigan beans.

First, Grandpa harnessed the lighter team, Gene and Teddy, and drove them to the huge watering trough next to the cow barn. The cast iron pipe bringing ice-cold water from the deep well below the milk house replenished the trough. As a boy, I liked drinking from that pipe because the combination of minerals from the pipe and water created a delightful tart flavor.

Knowing they would soon be working, the horses drank deeply. When they'd had their fill, they shook their heads and snorted to let Grandpa know they were ready. They loved work and were impatient to begin.

He led them back to the horse barn and hitched them to the wagon parked in the grass outside the wide sliding doors. He pulled the team and wagon alongside the granary. After tying the reins to the top of the high front rack, he climbed down, opened the sliding wooden door, and stepped off the wagon onto the granary floor that was level with the wagon bed. This height offered protection against moisture and vermin and made for easy loading.

"Go on up, Jase," he ordered, motioning for me to assume the driver's position.

I climbed up the front rack until I could comfortably hang my arms over the top. I was standing on a cross-rail about eight feet above the wagon bed. I untied the reins and grasped them firmly using my finger-over-finger grip.

"Whoa, Gene. Whoa, Teddy." I said quietly, informing the spunky chestnuts that I was now their driver.

To me, driving horses was an enjoyable, but serious, business. Because I was good at it, Grandpa often asked me to perform this duty. Everyone in the family said I had a real knack for it. To me, driving horses was easy, like steering a bicycle, except you used reins instead of handlebars. Later in life, I would consign conning a five hundred-foot, four thousand-ton naval ship to same category.

My attitude toward horses undoubtedly contributed to my success. I never doubted for a moment that the horses knew more about accomplishing work with horses than I did. Other drivers needed to be in charge. Not me. I believed my job was to communicate what was needed and then let Fannie or Teddy, the team leaders, take it from there. Incidentally, each leader was the lady of the family, a fact frequently mentioned by Grandma when she thought Grandpa could use a little course correction.

Don't get me wrong. From all outward appearances, I was an in-charge teamster. I knew all the commands. And believe me I was impressive. "Gee" meant turn right. "Haw" meant turn left. I suppose, everybody knows the meaning of "Gittiyup" and "Whoa." Grandpa's horses also responded to a dozen other commands including "Back Up", "Slow Down", "Pull Hard", and "Stop That." Of course, they responded best to "Attaboy." Who didn't?

As I steadied the horses, Grandpa dragged the heavy seed bags from the granary out onto the wagon. Earlier, he had calculated exactly how many bushels per acre we would need to ensure full coverage. The bags, doubled-tied with binder twine, were stacked upright against the rack below me.

Next, he wrestled the required number of bags containing war-scarce chemical fertilizer onto the wagon. The fertilizer was stacked behind the precious seed bags to keep them from tumbling over and spilling.

Because we were sowing beans, he loaded several tin cans of nitrogen-fixing bacteria culture. We stuck these down between the seed bags along with the jug of water provided by Grandma. Finally, using binder twine, Grandpa tied a can opener for the culture cans onto the wagon rack.

"When you drive to the field, keep an eagle eye on these bags. Don't let 'em spill over."

"Okay, Grandpa."

"Why don't you wait here in the shade while I hitch up the other team?"

After harnessing Jim and Fannie, Grandpa led them to the water trough where they topped off their tanks. He returned to the horse barn and opened the wide sliding doors to the implement storage area. Then, he backed Jim and Fannie through the doors and hitched them to the massive seed drill. Grasping the reins, he hopped up to the driver's seat mounted on the counter-balance arm behind the drill. Slowly he drove out of the horse barn, down the driveway, and past the granary where I stood waiting with the wagon. The disengaged gears and wheels of the drill *clicked* and *tinkled* melodiously as it rolled along.

I gently urged Gene and Teddy to drop in behind. The two rigs moved slowly across the yard toward the soon-to-be bean field next to the woods where languorous cows would spend the day lazily chewing their cuds and watching us work. As Grandpa picked up speed, I dropped back to avoid the giant dust clouds kicked up by his team and the drill. I sampled the familiar taste of airborne dirt for the first time that day. I would have to get used to it.

As we passed the house, Danny was standing on the steps outside the screened porch. When he spotted me driving my team from my perch high above the wagon, he grinned and waved madly.

We soon arrived at the field. Grandpa motioned for me to go ahead. My destination was the grassy hedgerow under the huge oak. Once there, the giant tree would shade my wagon and its valuable cargo.

"Gee, Teddy. Gee over, Gene," I advised, pulling lightly on the right pair of reins.

The team responded smartly by veering slightly to starboard. This modest course change put my wagon wheels on a path that gradually intersected the furrow defining the margin between the field and the hedgerow. I drew back slightly on the reins slowing the team and allowing the wagon to roll easily, one wheel at a time, down into the furrow then up onto the higher elevation of the hedgerow. I stopped the team where I knew the wagon would be shaded for most of the day. My load was now conveniently positioned for the work ahead.

Grandpa pulled his team into the shade and jumped down. "You're a natural-born horseman, Jase! Yes, you are!"

That's all it took. Fueled by Grandpa's single compliment, I could have worked until dawn the next day. I immediately thought, *I wish Danny had heard that.*

Grandpa brought me back to earth.

"Let's load the drill hoppers first. We'll put half-full bags of seeds and fertilizer on the drill bumper so you can reload the hoppers once we're underway. Then you can take Gene and Teddy back to the barn. While you're gone, I'll make a couple of passes around the perimeter to form the head rows. I won't need to use the markers. But I'll need you for settin' em after that, so hurry on back."

"Okay. I will, Grandpa."

"After you water the team down again, just let 'em graze in the pasture by the horse barn. But leave 'em harnessed. Just snap their traces and reins on their quarter straps – you know. It's gonna be a hot one today, so we'll spell Jim and Fannie afore long."

After filling the seed hoppers with beans, we wet them thoroughly using Grandma's water jug. Then we opened a can of black bacteria culture and sprinkled the contents over the wet beans. This insured that the beans, as legumes, produced the vital root nodules, which replenished plant-edible nitrogen in the soil needed for the next crop – corn, wheat, or oats – in the rotation. We mixed the ingredients thoroughly until our arms were sooty to the elbow. The last step was to fill the fertilizer hopper with the white powder from the heavy paper fertilizer sacks.

When we finished, I unhooked Gene and Teddy from the wagon and walked them back to the cow barn trough where they consumed another enormous drink of water. Then, as Grandpa had taught me, I arranged their traces and reins allowing them to graze without entanglement.

They looked disappointed at being discharged so early. Their eyes pleaded, *Please! Let us work, too.* Then they noticed the juicy crop of rye grass at their feet, and their sadness disappeared.

On my way back to the field, I noticed Grandma's Terraplane was missing from the garage. There was no sign of Danny either. "Probably had an attack of ice cream deficiency," I speculated aloud.

AS MORNING GAVE WAY to midday, I sensed a slight faintness brought on by hot sun, lack of water, and the many hours since breakfast. I scolded myself for mimicking Grandpa's extraordinary practice of abstaining from drinking water between breakfast and dinner when he worked in the fields. From the start, Grandpa had pushed the team relentlessly. We had only stopped twice to reload seed and fertilizer bags and cans of bacteria culture.

For nearly five hours, I had grappled with these heavy bags to top off the hoppers and had mixed the beans and bacteria culture thoroughly while balancing precariously on top of the moving drill. As Grandpa turned us around at the end of each run, I had raised then lowered the unwieldy marker poles to cut a new path in the soil for the horses to follow as they hauled the heavy drill back and forth across the field.

A blinding cloud of dust swirled upward as the ingenious machinery below me sliced deep trenches, drilled in seed beans at preset intervals, added a proper dose of fertilizer, and neatly recovered the trenches to form a swath of exact rows stretching out behind us. The choking dust when mixed with saliva and sweat formed mudpacks around my mouth, eyes, and ears. My buttoned shirt collar and farm-hanky bandana provided only minimal protection. Grandpa, seated behind and above me in the driver's seat, fared no better.

I had just reset the markers for our next pass when I saw Grandma and Danny crossing the field toward us. Danny was pulling the wooden milk wagon, loaded with "dinner", the farm term for the sumptuous noon meal. They waved at us enthusiastically. I admit that I was glad to see them. Their arrival signaled a welcomed break from the heat, dust, and deafening noise.

With an extended arm, Grandpa directed the dinner wagon to the supply wagon that I had parked under the oak tree. Danny adjusted course and aimed his wagon's tongue at the oak oasis.

At the end of the pass, Grandpa reined in Jim and Fannie. He jumped down from his seat and pulled the metal clutch handle forward to disengage the drill.

Ching! The handle snapped and pitched forward dangerously, just missing his chest.

Grandpa responded with the one-word expletive that he reserved for distressing occurrences. I appreciated his frustration. We stared at the broken assembly. The yoke holding the clutch handle had broken cleanly into two halves causing the handle to dangle uselessly under the drill. There was no way to operate the clutch without leverage from the long handle.

We were out of commission.

After a few seconds of shaking his head, Grandpa rationalized calmly, "It's not the end of the world. I'll just run this over to Old Nate. He can weld the yoke so it's good as new."

Grandpa pulled the pliers from his side overalls pocket, where he always kept them, and removed the nut, bolt, and cotter pin that coupled the yoke – or should I say two halves of the yoke – to the clutch and to the clutch handle. He wrapped the hardware in his hankie, tied them in a tight knot, and stored them in the fertilizer hopper with the clutch handle, so they wouldn't be lost.

He fished a length of binder twine from his back pocket supply and lashed the two halves of the yoke to the hammer loop sewn onto the right leg of his overalls. Then he stuffed the bound halves deep into his large front pocket.

"I don't want to lose these guys," he explained.

Grandpa unhitched Jim and Fannie, leaving the inoperative drill where it stood. We followed the horses as they plodded toward the oak tree. When we were within shouting distance, Danny yelled, "Boy! Have we got a surprise for you guys!"

Just what we need! I said to myself.

"What's the trouble, Dad?" Grandma asked as Grandpa hitched Jim and Fannie to the wagon.

"Broken clutch yoke. But I'm fairly sure Old Nate can weld it and have us back in operation in no time. I better get it over to him before I take time to eat, though."

"Oh, Dad! And you and Jase were makin' such good progress. Don't worry about dinner. It's a cold meal anyway. Want me to drive you over?"

"No, I can get there just as fast by horse and wagon from here."

"Take some cool tea before you leave. You been in that hot sun since breakfast."

Grandma had carefully arranged her enticing field dinner in the shade of the giant oak tree. She fetched the iced tea jug and poured two tall glasses for Grandpa and me. I spit a couple of times to clear the dust-mud from my mouth and emptied the glass in two long swallows.

The throbbing pain behind the bridge of my nose told me I should have followed Grandpa's example. He drank more slowly, smiling at Grandma and shaking his head, "Boy, this really hits the spot, Ma."

He finished his tea and hopped on the wagon. "It's a simple job. Shouldn't be gone more than an hour."

At that, Grandpa roused the team and pointed them in the direction of Old Nate's barn that loomed in the distance. As an afterthought, Grandma shouted, "Ask Old Nate to join us for dinner? There's plenty!"

Grandpa nodded and applied the reins to the Belgians' rumps, urging them into a lumbering amble, their fastest speed.

AS I SAT DOWN in the grass, Danny's eyes widened with excitement. He was about to speak but Grandma beat him to the punch.

"Danny, can you save your surprise until after dinner – when Grandpa gets back from Old Nate's?"

Danny grimaced. Then he looked dejected, a victim of surprise interruptus.

"Let's have us a snooze while we wait for Grandpa," Grandma suggested, sinking into the tall grass under the oak.

Danny recovered quickly and agreed. We hunkered our backsides against the massive tree trunk and watched the honeybees going about their grocery shopping among red clover blossoms encircling us.

Before long, all three of us were sound asleep.

"GEE, FANNIE. ATTAGIRL. WHOA, Fannie!"

Grandpa's commands, the pounding hooves, and wagon rumble jarred me awake. In the distance, I saw the team and wagon come to a dusty stop right in front of the drill. Grandpa jumped down and gave Fannie a "thank you" slap on the rump. Fannie stomped her right foot and snorted in response.

Grandma yawned and stretched, then rose to ready our picnic dinner.

I trotted across the field toward Grandpa. Danny, blinking away his sleep, soon caught up with me. When we reached Grandpa, he proudly showed us the perfectly welded and completely restored clutch yoke. He insisted we caress the tidy bead of the weld line with our fingertips.

"Fine work! Expertly laid weld every time!" he proclaimed.

We hummed our approval. Old Nate, by any measure, was only a fair farmer but he more than made up for it with welding skill.

Grandpa extracted the clutch handle and hankie-wrapped hardware from the fertilizer hopper and reassembled the clutch components. After tapping the cotter pin into place, he returned the hankie and the pliers to their appropriate pockets and tested the handle. Up! Down! Up!

"Good as new! No, sir! Better than new!" Grandpa declared enthusiastically. "Hop up on the wagon, boys! We're late for dinner."

We hopped aboard and held on for dear life.

"Dad, what happened to Old Nate?" Grandma asked when we arrived.

Nate Craddock was an elderly, bachelor farmer who lived by himself on the adjoining farm. According to Grandma, his was a desolate life, so she assumed complete responsibility for his welfare. And she did so with great fervor.

"Said he'd be along soon," Grandpa chuckled. "Probably wanted to take a bath before he saw you."

Grandma constantly fretted about Old Nate's senility-induced idiosyncrasies, especially his progressive lack of concern with personal cleanliness and the state of his attire. Grandma was permitted to disparage Old Nate in this way, but no one else had better. Grandpa knew this but, every now and then, he pulled her chain anyway.

"Now, Dad. He's an old man. Just gotten a bit slack since he come down with the Arthur Ritus," she scolded. "That's all."

Grandpa backed off. He certainly didn't want to fuss with Grandma *before* she served his dinner! So he spoke admiringly about Old Nate, "You'da never thought he was an old man if you'd seen him weld that yoke together. Man's a genius with a welding rod and torch. Honest to Betsy! And he still refuses to take my dollar for it!"

"Well, he's just a good neighbor, Dad. And he knows we'll always look out for him."

At that moment, Old Nate's dark form materialized at the opening in the hedgerow that led from the Craddock farm to the bean field. Slowly, he floated our way, like a solitary vulture drifting low over the field. His form rigid from arthritis. His feet his only moving parts. I shivered involuntarily as he drew near.

"Now, Danny. Old Nate's a bit scary for boys first meetin' him. But he's got a heart of gold," Grandma explained, rising to greet her neighbor.

Grandma was wise to forewarn Danny. Old Nate was one, frightening old man! Even so, Grandma and Grandpa admired him. I had heard them sing his praises on numerous occasions. But, when you saw him for the first time, you forgot anything good you'd heard about him. You just reacted to what you saw.

I glanced at Danny. His face was twisted with fear. His eyes bugged out and his mouth opened wide.

OLD NATE'S MOST DISTINCTIVE physical characteristic was his color.

He was by far the "blackest" man I had ever laid eyes on. Not that his skin color was naturally black. In fact, his true skin color was surprisingly pale. I learned that the day he rolled up his shirtsleeve to show me the faded blue-purple image of a ferocious wolverine that had been tattooed on his forearm some fifty years before.

However, everything he wore, including his visible skin, was solid black. More accurately, his outer layer was the color of grease, acetylene soot, and plain dirt, the byproducts of the hours he spent in his garage puttering with his machinery and operating his welding equipment.

According to Grandma, Old Nate was once a model of good hygiene, a state to which she valiantly strived to restore him. But, as pain from his arthritis progressed, he gradually lost interest in soap and water. It had been years since he last washed either his body or his clothing.

Beneath the dirt and grime, thanks in part to Grandma's efforts, his clothing was similar to that of Grandpa and the other farmers in the area. He wore denim bib overalls, blue chambray shirt, billed cap of stiff gray cotton, heavy cotton socks, and white long-legged underwear. So he knew how to be presentable. But he just chose not to. Instead he wore his clothes until they became so filthy and rotten that they were about to fall off his body. Then he changed them, when he got around to it, perhaps once a year or so.

At least, that's how Old Nate operated before Grandma got involved. Soon after they met, shortly after the Comptons moved to the farm, she became obsessed with "encouraging" Old Nate to change clothes more often. This power struggle, in all its forms, lasted for more than fifteen years. It became a major preoccupation for Grandma, Old Nate's self-appointed caretaker, and a source of amusement for the rest of us.

During the early years, Old Nate made the mistake of asking Grandma to buy his clothing for him. But only when she happened to be shopping for Grandpa, he had insisted. This was Grandma's license to meddle.

The issue boiled down to this. When Grandma bought Old Nate a set of new clothing, she expected him to wear it. Immediately! Old Nate, on the other hand, had his own timetable. Sometimes he preferred to keep his new clothing in reserve for a month or two before he expended the effort to change into it.

His procrastination nearly drove Grandma crazy. So she stepped up the pressure.

At first, she delivered his new attire and told him that she wouldn't leave until he changed clothes and gave her his current blackened uniform for proper disposal. This worked for a while. But Old Nate soon discovered that he could counter this tactic by merely ignoring Grandma's threat.

When she demanded he change or be stuck with her looming presence in his grimy living room for the rest of the day, he acted as if he didn't mind and devised strategies for outlasting her. He slumped into his broken-down black leather chair and pretended to nap. Or he left her in the house while he rearranged his workbench out in the garage. Or he turned on his radio and listened to the afternoon soap operas. That ploy really got to her. Grandma hated soap operas.

To counter her adversary's success, Grandma conceived a new line of attack, the old "carrot and stick" approach.

Her carrot came in the form of baked goodies from her oven. Grandma knew from experience that Old Nate had a weakness for homemade cookies, especially old-fashioned molasses. Most of the time, she could coerce him into a new set of clothing in exchange for her delicious bribes.

And, when he became stubborn, she pulled out her stick.

"I'll just call the county nurse. She'll come out and stick a hypodermic needle in your rump and put you to sleep," she threatened. "Then the nurse and I will strip you bare, scrub you with soap and hot water, and dress you in your new clothes – whether you like it or not."

His choice was clear. Would he prefer, the carrot (cookie) or the stick (in the rump)?

Now, I can't really say that I took Grandma's threat all that seriously, but I wasn't the one Grandma was trying to coerce. Old Nate didn't want to chance it, so he gave in every time.

Grandma chalked up a success when the black moldy pile of Old Nate's clothing came flying out his back kitchen door. After using his coal shovel to deposit her prize in Old Nate's outhouse, she returned home, claiming credit for yet another victory.

During the years of Grandma's war on Old Nate's filthy attire, she demonstrated extraordinary perseverance. But, despite Grandma's success at dressing Old Nate in a new outfit at least three times a year, she never once succeeded in forcing him to bathe.

In addition to his blackness, Old Nate possessed other off-putting physical characteristics. First, he was nearly bent over double by debilitating arthritis. According to Grandpa, this old man, peering up at you from under a horrible hump on his back, had once stood well over six feet. And he was once reputed to have had great strength. He even won a ten-dollar prize by out-wrestling a black bear at the Saginaw County Fair back about 1901 or so.

His extremely long and sharp nose and his eerie blue eyes, peering at you through the fallen shock of wispy white hair, contributed to his frightening appearance.

Worst of all, Old Nate had no teeth. So, when he spoke, his words slithered out of his mouth and *hissed* when they hit the air.

Grandma told me that Old Nate once had a perfect set of teeth – white, straight, and strong. But, during the siege that bent his body, perhaps owing to bad eating habits hence poor nutrition, all his teeth had fallen out. However, he saw his toothlessness as a minor inconvenience, except when he spoke and failed to be understood or when he grappled with a tough piece of meat that refused to be subdued by vigorous gumming.

Grandma once told Old Nate that he needed a set of false teeth. She humbled herself by removing her own to show him how easy they were to manage. His reaction was predictable.

Why on earth did she think he needed false teeth? Didn't he have a hunting knife to reduce the big pieces of food to a manageable size? Had he ever claimed to miss "hith" natural teeth? False teeth! Just an unnecessary extravagance! Did she think he was made of money?

In this case, Old Nate won that particular battle. But, Grandma won the war by changing her "carrots" to ginger snaps.

Although it wasn't very Christian of her, she gloated (just a little) each time she watched Old Nate gumming away at those leather-tough cookies. But he never once complained. And she never again mentioned false teeth, either.

WHEN OLD NATE TOOK his place under the oak, I was eager to see how Danny and Old Nate might interact. I was soon to know.

All through dinner, Danny stared at Old Nate as if he were a two-headed man in a circus sideshow. Old Nate didn't seem to notice. He was too busy using his hunting knife and pink gums to attack Grandma's dinner. The ravenous old man loaded his plate with cold fried chicken, chilled mashed potatoes with congealed yellow-orange butter, and stacks of fresh whole wheat bread.

Grandma treated "field dinners" as opportunities for culling out leftovers. On this occasion, one of her side dishes was an unappetizing bowl of shriveled, once-green peas. Old Nate was the only one among us who expressed interest in this dubious offering. He balanced the bowl on his knee. Then, using his hunting knife, he skillfully scooped out a dozen hardened peas, rolled them back and forth on the flat side of the blade, and with a flick of his wrist tossed them smartly into his mouth.

Danny was astonished. He stopped eating to stare as Old Nate flashed blade after blade of peas into his churning mouth. Danny's wide-eyed fascination had reached the impolite point, so Grandma intervened. When Old Nate turned to chat with Grandpa about the finer points of welding, she frowned and shook her head at Danny. He frowned right back and gave her a look that said, *What can I do about it? He's the weird one, you know.*

As if sensing what was needed, Old Nate turned to Danny and spoke, "Whathh shhure name young fella?"

"Ah – I. Huh?" Danny sputtered, apparently caught off guard by Old Nate's sudden attention.

"Yer name. Whaa thhhey call ya?" Nate repeated as he snatched another drumstick from the fried chicken dish.

Danny seemed unsure of his answer, but finally he blurted, "I'm-Jase's-friend-Danny-Tucker. We-got-$21.00-from-the-bubble gum-that-we-traded-for-Grandma's-sauerkraut. And-we-know-that-Hans-Zeyer-is-a-Nazi-spy-because-when-Sherman-snuck-into-his-house-and-found-a-"

Old Nate lowered his drumstick and stared at my flustered friend. Now, Danny was the two-headed man in the sideshow.

He's gone berserk! I thought, wanting to punch Danny in the left bicep to shut him up.

But Danny recovered nicely, "Grandma and I have a surprise."

"Whaaa?" Old Nate asked as he bit down on the drumstick, whipped his razor-sharp knife to his mouth, and sliced off a chunk.

"We're going to Granville to see the outdoor movies tonight!" Danny announced smugly.

Old Nate didn't seem to comprehend Danny's words. He stared at Danny absently for a second or two.

Then he turned back to Grandpa and continued his welding tutorial, "When ya weld cathht iron –"

"What's that you say? Oh – cast iron. Yep. Go on, Nate."

"When ya weld cathht iron, you gotta have high-nickel content welding rodthh. If ya don't, know what happenthh?"

Without missing a beat, Danny recited the answer to Old Nate's rhetorical question, "You get hot spots in your bead – it'll break down on yah."

"Right!" declared Old Nate, smiling toothlessly at the young welding prodigy in our midst.

An astounded Grandma spoke for us all, "Well, I'll be dipped in sugar!"

LATER THAT AFTERNOON, WE returned to the horse barn to swap teams. Jim and Fannie needed a rest, and Gene and Teddy needed to show their stuff.

"What time will you finish tonight, Dad?" Grandma asked.

"Oh, I'd say by about seven – or maybe seven-thirty – depending."

"Well, don't worry about the evenin' chores. Danny and I will see to 'em."

I had my doubts about that, but I didn't say a word.

"And we'll have hot baths waiting for you," Grandma promised.

Fantasies of hot baths with exotic perfumes from fresh bars of *Lava* and *Lifebuoy* filled my imagination. Danny wrinkled his nose and said, "Baths? Where's the bathtub?"

Grandma patiently described her process for preparing outdoor farm baths to Danny, "We use the cast-iron, pig-scalding kettle."

Danny smirked at the mention of *cast-iron*. Missing the significance, Grandma continued.

The huge black pot rested on a heavy grill supported on three sides by specially constructed stone walls, rising about three feet above the ground. The open end of the stone foundation allowed for building and replenishing the wood fire that heated the mammoth vessel. Because of the amount of water to be boiled, it was necessary to start the fire hours in advance of the bath.

Danny had a question or two.

"Yes, we do use the kettle to scald real pigs – during butchering season every fall," she assured him.

"Yes, the pigs are dead before they're scalded," she swore.

"Why? Because scalding makes it easier to shave the pigs."

"No, we don't save the pig hair for wigs."

"Yes, that's right, scalding does make it more sanitary to make pork roast, chops, ham, and bacon out of pigs."

"Yes, I'm positive that bacon comes from pigs."

"No, bacon doesn't come from whales," she vowed, despite what he had heard at school.

"Yes, I like bacon, lettuce, and tomato sandwiches, too."

"Yes, I think pigs are quite fat."

"Yes, pigs do resemble hipper-pot-a-mouses."

Sometimes I believed Danny was a real challenge to one's patience. But Grandma didn't seem to mind. She just called him a "caution", whatever that means.

As Grandpa and I finished our preparations for returning to the field, Danny carried several armloads of firewood from the woodpile inside the back shed to the kettle grill. He dumped his load on the ground next to Grandma. She carefully stacked the wood under the kettle and around the sheaf of kindling that she had lashed together with binder twine.

Satisfied with her stacking, she soaked the wood with kerosene from the can stored on the gasoline and oil barrel rack under the pear tree by the driveway. Danny helped her wrestle the huge kettle forward on the grill, so it was positioned squarely over the wood stack.

Then she ordered Danny to stand back, about fifteen feet from the grill. Danny retreated obediently, stuck his fingers in his ears, and stared at Grandma expectantly. She took a kitchen match from her apron pocket, scratched its head on the field stone foundation, stood way back, and tossed the flaming match into the kerosene-soaked wood.

As the flames and black smoke billowed skyward, she instructed Danny to fetch the four pails from the milk house while she primed the pump that stood over the well next to the back shed. When Danny returned, Grandma pumped the handle until each of two pails was about half full. Just right for Danny, she calculated.

Grandma filled the remaining pails while Danny scurried down the path toward the wood fire, his load sloshing as he ran. He climbed the steps to the platform next to the pig-scalding kettle, set one pail down, and poured the water from the other into the empty kettle. When the water hit bottom, it hissed and sizzled. Startled, he jumped back. But, after recovering for a second, he boldly dumped the second pail into the steaming kettle.

Grandma and Danny repeated this process until the kettle was half full. That way it wouldn't be too heavy for Grandpa and me to use the wooden kettle yoke to push it back, away from the fire.

"Jase and Grandpa can add cold water to bring the temperature of the boiling water down. So it's just right for a bath," she explained to Danny.

He nodded like a good student.

Grandma moved her laundry bench from the back porch to a spot next to the kettle grill. From the house, she brought a pile of fresh towels and washcloths and placed it on the end of the bench nearest the steps to the platform. She unwrapped two fresh bars of soap. First, the gritty *Lava* for the tough dirt. Second, the orange-pink *Lifebuoy* for the finishing touch. Finally, she arranged the soap and Grandpa's brush and comb tidily on the bench next to the towels.

Danny and Grandma stood back and admired their work. Danny turned to Grandma and said, "I'm feeling a little grimy myself. Would it be okay with you if I have a little bath, too?"

"After helping me with the chores, you're bound to need one."

She had that right.

WE FINISHED RIGHT ON schedule. When we returned to the house, Grandma proudly announced that she and her "new hand" had completed the chores. Then she rolled her eyes. Danny smiled smugly.

After storing the drill in the horse barn and bedding down the horses, Grandpa, Danny, and I took turns enjoying our baths, while Grandma prepared a late supper. It was a hot meal this time, just as she had promised. There was plenty of time before dark and the start of the Granville movie, so we slowly scrubbed the dust from our ears, nostrils, and hair. The bath was luxurious!

Danny and I wrapped ourselves in our bath towels, dumped our dirty clothes on the laundry porch, as Grandma had instructed, and headed for the Victrola room to dress. Once there, Danny and I reviewed Grandma's collection of fine marches on 78-RPM records.

I selected Danny's favorite and placed it on the turntable. I wound the crank fully and carefully lowered the heavy needle arm to the spinning record. The sound of *Under the Double Eagle* filled the house.

From that point on, throughout the entire evening, Danny whistled his favorite march.

But, at supper, Grandma had to ask him to desist. That was after he sprayed her with mashed potatoes when he hit his crescendo for the thirtieth time. When peaceful silence finally descended on the supper table, I decided that *Under* was quickly becoming my personal *un-favorite* march.

After supper, we squeezed into the Terraplane and flew out of the driveway on our way to Granville. You would have thought we'd be exhausted after a day of hard drilling, but I could tell that Grandpa was just as excited as I was to spend a night on the town.

"What's in Granville – besides the outdoor movie?" Danny inquired during a lull in his whistling.

The short answer to Danny's question was "not much." But it wasn't for lack of trying.

THE VILLAGE OF GRANVILLE was located on a scenic stretch of the Chippewa River just ten miles north of Riverton. Both Riverton and Granville were founded at about the same time, back around 1830.

In the early days, there was intense competition between the two towns. They vied with each other to be the center of commerce for the region. The mayors of the two villages established a standing wager, a smoked ham to the mayor whose town had the greater population on each New Year's Day.

After a couple of decades of watching the prize ham head south to Riverton each year, interest in the competition sputtered and finally died out altogether. Clearly, Riverton had emerged as the preferred place to live, work, and shop.

Granville's population came close to hitting a hundred back in 1850 or so. But, suddenly, growth stopped and the population leveled out at about 85 souls, which was still the population of Granville on that Monday night in June of 1944. This figure included the dozen young men who had joined up after Pearl Harbor and listed Granville as their "Home of Record."

Riverton's victory in the population race didn't mean that Granville was completely lacking in qualities. On the contrary, there was much to recommend it. For example, just after the First War, the town elders had acquired a pleasant section of forest along the east bank of the Chippewa River for use as a township park.

Located about two miles east of Granville, the park extended north from the main road for more than three miles. There, people from all over the county picnicked, played ball, and celebrated family reunions in its spacious pavilion. Fishing was exceptionally good in the stretch of river within the park's boundaries. And Boy Scout troops from all over the region pitched their tents in the remote campgrounds located at the far north end.

Of course, there was also the Granville Church of Christ, a quaint white wooden structure with a splendid steeple. This was by far the most picturesque of the four, one-room churches on the Riverton circuit. Grandma Compton liked to attend services there, especially when Reverend Johnson was preaching.

However, Grandma was drawn to the Granville church for another reason. Over the years, a number of Hopes, her father's family, had been members there. Now, most of them resided peacefully in the cemetery, a rolling parcel of sparse woods and prairie adjacent to the church parking lot. Grandma felt an obligation to visit there every so often, just to whisper a greeting to her great aunts and uncles.

No description of Granville would be complete without including the small, one-room schoolhouse where children from families in town and from the surrounding farms educated each other, with a little help from their pretty young teacher. For their efforts, the Granville School Board conferred its standard diploma proclaiming that each of them had successfully mastered eight grades and were therefore fully prepared to take on the world. And many did just that, while others trekked down to Riverton to attend high school.

The town had a small, but prosperous, commercial element as well. Its most prominent business was the Granville Co-op, a cooperative grain elevator that purchased the harvests from local farmers. From Granville, boxcar loads of grain, beans, and corn were shipped to far-distant food processors over the tracks of the Michigan Central Railway. This rail system connected Riverton and Granville to the cargo holds of the super-long Great Lakes freighters docked in Bay City. Area residents also used the Granville Depot to ship business and personal parcels by Railway Express and to shuttle down to the Grand Trunk Railroad Station in Riverton where they could connect to cities all over the continent.

Granville also had an impressive, albeit small, array of retail businesses that lined its main street. Like other rural communities in the region, these merchants attempted to meet every need of those living in town and on nearby farms. These establishments included a bank, farm implement dealer (where the town parked its only fire truck), gas station, grocery store, ice cream parlor, clothing store offering the latest fashions, a hardware store, and a post office that was really a part of the hardware store.

The frugal Dutchmen who owned many of the farms around Granville prided themselves on arranging their lives so they never had to drive that extra ten miles down to Riverton and back. They sold their cash crops to the Granville Co-op. They put their money in Granville's bank. And what few goods, not produced at home, that they needed for their farms and families they purchased right there, in Granville.

Most of these Dutch farmers were so contemptuous of the Big City (Riverton) that they refused to purchase automobiles. This forced them and their large families to stay near home and conduct their business in Granville. They covered the distance to the village in austere, horse-drawn buggies, competing with the Amish for slots along the hitching rails.

The town's merchants depended heavily on customer loyalty. Unlike their counterparts down in Riverton, they wisely modified their business hours to fit the lifestyle of the average farmer. From the beginning of May until the end of September, Granville businesses were open until nine o'clock every Monday, Wednesday, and Thursday evening.

On Monday night, traditionally the slowest of the three, merchants blocked off the main street and showed a free movie to entice customers into town. And it worked.

Because it was late before it was dark enough to start the movie, nearly ten o'clock on those Mondays in June, merchants looked for ways to encourage potential customers to arrive early and shop. They enlisted the support of local, would-be entertainers to don clown costumes, juggle balls, or engage folks in modest games of chance.

The Granville mayor, The Honorable George Simmons, was famous for raising hundreds of dollars for the Boy Scout troop that met at the Granville Church of Christ. He was skilled at separating players from their nickels and dimes with his "walnut-shell-and-hidden-pea" game. This good-natured scam brought farmers to town early in hopes of beating the clever mayor at his game. Of course, the farmers' wives took advantage of this opportunity to shop for a new church hat or needed birthday present.

Mayor Simmons had never lost. And the local farmers never stopped trying to break his perfect record. The resultant proceeds continued to enrich the Boy Scouts. And Hizzonor continued to enjoy the public limelight on which all politicians thrive, even in towns as small as Granville.

The weekly movie was shown using the town's old movie projector mounted on a farm wagon parked in the middle of the main street. Soon after sunset, the town's four streetlights were extinguished. The movie image shimmied as breezes lapped at the huge cream-colored tarpaulin hanging from a rope strung between the flagpole atop the hardware store and the bank's chimney across the street. A single tinny speaker, built into the case of the projector, served as the audio system for the outdoor theater.

The antique projector was certainly the appropriate device to show what movies fell within the town's meager film budget. Most shows were talkies, but not always. Sound or silent, you could bet on seeing a western, usually Grade B or below, starring the likes of Hoot Gibson, Tom Mix, the Durango Kid, Hopalong Cassidy, Johnny Mack Brown, Buck Jones, Bob Steele, Tex Ritter, Red Ryder, or – if we were really lucky – Lash LaRue.

In addition to westerns, the town's film procurer had fondness for Boris Karloff. So, more often than I would have preferred, we endured the horrifying exploits of old Boris, mostly in the silent format! But we didn't mind. We were at the movies! And they were free!

As the sun slowly set, people drifted toward the street to claim their favorite viewing spot. Folding wooden chairs, blankets, empty beer cases, and milk stools filled the street. While we were forever hopeful, the movie seldom started smoothly. The ancient projector had a voracious appetite for brittle celluloid, the very stuff from which Granville's cinematic delights were made.

At the first sign of projector trouble, Mayor Simmons would hop up on the wagon to lend his moral support and technical advice to the town's most qualified projectionist, the teenage soda jerk on loan from the Granville Ice Cream Parlor. Despite the normal initial hiccups, the movie invariably started, sometimes even near the beginning! The first intelligible flicker invariably prompted an immense cheer from the crowd and a clasped-hands-over-the-head victory gesture from the friendly mayor.

Then an awesome silence fell over the town as the mesmerized audience became totally engrossed in the movie. This silence was broken by frequent roars of approval when Lash, or one of our other heroes, proved their hero-hood by releasing the lovely heroine (and all of her heavy mascara) from her bonds seconds before she was about to perish under the wheels of an onrushing train. The plots of these old westerns seldom varied. But we loved them nonetheless.

The night's entertainment climaxed with an animated cartoon, usually in black and white and, more often than not, starring Felix the Cat. When the cartoon ended, the crowd again roared its approval with cheers and applause. This was Mayor Simmons' cue to restore the street lights, which helped contented movie-goers find their way to treats at one of Granville's establishments and afterward to their cars or buggies.

There was nothing more splendid than a summer Monday night in Granville!

BY THE TIME WE arrived, our anticipation was nearly unbearable. While Grandma and Grandpa parked the Terraplane behind the bank, Danny and I scouted out the sights on the main street that, by then, was filled with shoppers and saunterers. The fading sunlight promised it would soon be dark enough to start the movie.

"Excuse me, sir. What movie is showing tonight?" I inquired of the chubby man dressed in a red, white, and blue clown suit.

He lifted his big red nose in order to speak more clearly, but it didn't seem to help much. He wheezed and whistled, "Gene Autry, I think. Somethin' about guns and tumble weeds, I heard somebody say."

"Great!" yelled Danny. That was all he needed to know.

"Why don't I spread out our blanket on the porch over in front of the hardware store? That way we'll have our place. Besides, I want to see what the hardware store has in the way of new flashlights," Grandma explained.

"Okay, we'll see you over there in a little while," Grandpa replied.

"Dad, you stay away from the mayor. We can't afford more Boy Scout tents," Grandma chuckled.

After Grandma had disappeared into the crowd, much to my delight, Grandpa turned to us and suggested, "Let's go see how the mayor's luck is holdin' out!"

As usual, the mayor had set up his shell game in front of the Granville Farmers Bank. A dozen men and boys had stopped to watch his sleight of hand show. The mayor was seated in a comfortable-looking office chair. In front of him, three walnut half shells were arranged in a straight line across the surface of a small wooden table. He was chiding one of his regular customers.

"Got another nickel for the troop, Henk?" he teased.

Henk Armansfoort, a stubborn, red-faced Dutchman, was determined to beat the mayor at his silly game. And he'd been determined since the summer before last and forty-five dollars worth of nickels ago.

"Ya. Letz go agin," Henk barked, arching his gigantic frame over the small table for a better view.

The mayor lifted the right hand shell to reveal a shiny green dried pea. He replaced the shell and set his hands in motion, rapidly rotating the three shells over the shell-worn surface of the tabletop. Suddenly, he stopped, folded his arms, and nodded at Henk.

"Da middle shell. Ya. Dats vere itz zat," Henk stated firmly.

"Nope!" Danny loudly informed everyone in attendance.

"Vhatz dat?" Henk demanded angrily, looking as if he might bop poor Danny for having the audacity to contradict him.

"It's not in the middle one. It's under the end one. That one, right there!" Danny assured old Henk, pointing confidently at his choice.

"Nah! Itz da middle von! Lift eet up, Meyor!"

Danny shrugged at Henk then turned and smiled conspiratorially at Grandpa and me.

"You should have listened to the boy, Henk," the mayor advised.

He lifted the empty middle shell to show that there was no pea under Henk's choice. Then the mayor lifted Danny's choice, revealing the elusive pea.

"Boel mest!" Henk roared as his face darkened to deep purple, frightening degrees beyond its normal crimson.

He glared at the mayor, then at Danny. With a huff, Henk slammed his nickel into the mayor's upturned hat and stormed away mumbling incomprehensible Dutch oaths.

"Who's next?" the mayor inquired, soliciting the crowd.

"I'll give it a whirl – but with one condition. I get to use the boy as my spotter. Okay with you, Bill?"

The familiar voice from behind us had addressed his question to Grandpa.

"And one more thing. All my winnings go to the Church of Christ camp fund."

Immediately, I turned to see the smiling face of Reverend Johnson, the former boarder at the Compton farm and Grandma's favorite circuit preacher. Danny and I hadn't seen him since his inspiring sermon on Protestantism and poetry.

"Grandpa, it's Reverend Johnson!" Danny announced enthusiastically. "Is it all right for me to win some money for Reverend Johnson's camp fund?"

At that, the small group of onlookers chuckled and looked at each other. Danny grinned and tipped his hat.

"It's okay with me if it's okay with Mayor Simmons," Grandpa confirmed.

"Let's see the color of your money, Reverend," the mayor demanded, smiling self-confidently.

After losing twenty-five straight dimes to Eagle Eye Danny, the mayor was no longer smiling. But Danny was in his element.

Reverend Johnson, who had put up the first dime, contented himself with collecting Danny's winnings. As word spread about the whipping the mayor was taking at the hands of an unknown boy, an excited crowd gathered to watch. That didn't help the mayor's morale.

Thanks to Danny's pea-spotting proficiency, the mayor's three-year winning streak had come to a surprising – and embarrassing – end. He was beginning to sweat, especially when he was forced to open his wallet to extract a dollar of his own, not Boy Scout, money. The crowd sensed his distress.

"Can you break a dollar, Reverend?" he inquired sheepishly.

"Sure can, Mayor!" exclaimed the Reverend who was happily watching his camp fund swell.

"Better yet – it's getting dark. We have to start the movie soon. Why don't we raise the stakes and have one last go at it? What do you say, Reverend?"

"What kind of stakes are we talking about, Mayor?"

"Well, I got this fiver in my wallet. You got – what –two-and-a-half dollar's worth of my dimes in your hat? How 'bout your dimes against my fiver? That's double or nothin'. Whatya say, Reverend?"

"Just a minute. I'll confer with my partner."

Reverend Johnson gave Danny a questioning look. Danny glanced at the mayor, then at Grandpa, and then at Reverend Johnson. Finally, he turned to me and winked.

"Let 'er rip, Mayor!" he shouted fearlessly.

The crowd roared its approval.

The mayor was possessed. His hands whirled over the tabletop. After a final dizzying flourish, he suddenly folded his arms and nodded at Danny.

Danny stared at the mayor for about two minutes. The crowd was hushed. Finally, the mayor demanded, "Pick a shell, son!"

Danny continued to ignore him. Then he made his move.

The crowd gasped, when Danny leaned over the table, reached into the mayor's vest pocket, and plucked out the green pea.

"I guess we win, Reverend!" Danny declared smugly.

12 MOM JOINS UP

"WHERE *IS* THAT BOY? I'VE GOT TO MEET HIM. JANE? Jase? Yoo-hoo! Yooooo-hoo!"

Danny and I were in the back shed sorting eggs. We hadn't heard her drive up. But we sure heard her now!

"Yoo-hoo! Where is everybody? I'll just stay for a little bite, then I've got to get on over to the Henrys' for a one o'clock. Whatcha got good? I'll check your piano, too. It's been hot. Whatya hear from Van?"

On entering the kitchen, we were greeted by her expansive backside. She was bent over with her head inside Grandma's refrigerator. Making herself right at home, our visitor was constructing a heaping pile of last night's cold leftovers on one of Grandma's oversized dinner plates. Oblivious to our presence, she turned her attention to the collection of hot leftovers storied in the warming oven above Grandma's kitchen stove.

She noticed Danny and me just as Grandma entered from the laundry porch.

"Jase! There you are!" she exclaimed. "And there you are, Jane!"

Turning to Danny, she bubbled, "Is this the hero of Granville? Danny, isn't it? It's all over the county. Tell me all about it!"

Pleased to hear of Danny's celebrity, I jumped right in, "Aunt Mary! This is my friend, Danny Tucker."

Danny raised his left hand and wiggled his fingers at her.

Wiping her hands on her apron, Grandma spoke warmly, "Did you find enough for your lunch? Sit down at the table, Mary. I'll make you some tea."

"Oh! No thanks, Jane. I can't stay but a minute. I'll just finish my little snack and be on my way."

Her little snack would have easily fed a war-torn family in China for at least a week and ten days. Like all of Grandma's sisters, I knew Aunt Mary had a big appetite. And I'd never seen her eat sitting down.

"Danny, come here. Tell me *all* about your win over that pompous Mayor Simmons. How'd you do it? Gimma the scoop!"

Danny opened his mouth to speak. But he stopped in mid-word when Aunt Mary licked her thumb and pointed her fork toward the front sitting room.

"I want to check Grandma Jane's piano. Tell me in there."

We all adjourned to the seldom-used room where Grandma's upright Baldwin occupied a place of prominence. Aunt Mary thumped down on the piano bench, placed her overloaded plate on the piano top, and straightened her smock.

With one hand, she deftly forked morsel after morsel from the plate into her mouth. With the other, she nimbly ran the scales, up and down the keyboard, with an expertise honed by thirty-five years of drilling those notes into the heads – and hands – of hundreds of budding pianists.

"Now, go ahead! Tell me what happened, Danny!"

Ignoring the cascade of loud piano notes and the rapid fork-movements of Aunt Mary's express luncheon, Danny forged ahead. He related the Granville events in elaborate detail and, naturally, without a trace of modesty.

Nearing the climax of his soliloquy, Danny described the poor mayor's demeanor after being caught with the pea in pocket. To place the mayor's transgression in its proper moral context, he presented a brief dissertation on the relative virtues of church camps and Boy Scouts. And, naturally, he ended with his customary bow.

Aunt Mary was so amused that she was barely able to finish those two last bites and that final Do-Re-Mi on Grandma's piano.

"Wonderful! What a story! Oh, thank you, Danny! Thank you so much!" she squealed, mussing his hair fondly with her fingers.

"Piano's in fine tune, Jane. The heat hasn't affected it one iota. You need to keep practicing. Get these boys interested. I'll take them on when they're ready. No word from Van yet – I assume. I'm late. Gotta run. Thanks for the snack. Be good, boys. Bye, Jane! Say hello to Bill," she added.

She rushed through the kitchen, out the screened porch door and into her Ford. Clump, clump, clump! Bam! Bang! Roar! Zoom! Poof! She disappeared into a cloud of dust! According to the kitchen clock, her visit had lasted exactly eleven minutes.

As we watched the dust settle back down onto the driveway, Danny asked, "Who *was* that?"

Grandma chuckled, "That was my *little* sister, Mary. She's a terrific piano teacher. Lives in Riverton. But has students all over the county. She stops in for a quick bite, maybe once or twice a week. Never know when she'll show up."

"She's nice!" Danny affirmed.

"Thank you, Danny. She's a pearl," Grandma agreed, hugging his shoulder. "You boys need some dinner. Then I'll run you home."

We'd finished drilling the beans. The chicken coop was cleaned – ugh! The garden was weeded. The rose trellis out by the pump was painted white. The woodpile was restacked to make room for the fall replenishment. The lawn was mowed. The mousetraps in the granary were baited. The cats were all fed.

Danny had even taken a horse-driving lesson that ended abruptly when he declared a preference for driving automobiles! Gene and Teddy were relieved at his choice of conveyances. Once again, Grandpa and I were amused and mystified by Danny's eccentricities. I realized I was beginning not to notice them.

Four fun-filled days had come to an end.

Danny turned in his borrowed nightgown proclaiming that he preferred it to his own pajamas. Obviously, he was mad! But Grandma was delighted!

After a last hearty dinner with Grandpa and Grandma, we loaded our bags into the Terraplane. In the driveway, we scrubbed Mick's head goodbye. As always, he stopped smiling and went into a funk. His despondency took its usual form. He sprawled out in the dusty driveway and covered his eyes with his paws. Grandpa nudged Mick gently with the toe of his work shoe to remind him that he was being impolite.

We bid Grandpa and his pouting pooch goodbye and blasted off in our Terraplane rocket ship. As we flew along, Grandma informed us that she had a stop to make on our way home. The more stops, the merrier was my attitude.

Grandma skidded to a halt in the parking lot of the Riverton Livestock Yard. "I need to check the berries," she explained.

DANNY AND I WERE extremely fortunate to live within a mile of the "stockyard." That's what everybody around Riverton called it. Livestock auctions were held there on Thursdays, all year round.

The stockyard owners provided all the necessary services and facilities to support the process of bringing sellers of livestock (farmers and breeders) together with buyers of livestock (those same farmers and breeders plus the local meat packers). The owners provided a professional auctioneer, the indoor auction ring surrounded by banks of comfortable seats, holding pens, loading docks and runways, boarding barns, and a fine lunch counter or "café" as it was called. Profits came mainly from boarding fees for animals temporarily housed at the stockyards and brokerage fees charged to owners of animals sold at auction. To the delight of the area's frugal farmers, the café broke even.

When Grandpa Compton took me to my first auction, I was positively enthralled with the unique array of sights, sounds, and smells. The loudspeaker blasted the incomprehensible, and yet seductive, singsong voice of the lanky auctioneer who wore fancy blue jeans, a powder blue country-western sports coat with sequins, and an impressive white Stetson hat. Before each sale, the agitated cattle, horses, sheep, and pigs bellowed their protests before bursting from their holding pens into the auction ring. Finally, a sharp *crack* of the auctioneer's gavel declared the conclusion of each sale.

The front row of seats directly across the ring from the auctioneer was occupied by a colorful collection of professional buyers resembling a long line of owls. Each winked an eye, twitched a nose, or lifted an eyebrow to signal his latest bid to the sharp-eyed auctioneer.

From the busy café scrunched into the rafters above the brightly lighted ring, smells of ham and eggs, hamburg sandwiches, hot dogs, garlic pickles, and steaming hot coffee wafted downward, out over the buyers, sellers, and enraptured sightseers like me. It was a mouth-watering experience.

The auction was the heart of the stockyard business and Grandpa Compton's main area of interest. But, after a few visits, for me, the allure was gone. Perhaps, because I hadn't raised a cow from calf-hood. I wasn't a buyer or a seller of pigs. My profits for the year didn't depend on the whims of market prices for cutters or pork bellies.

Unlike Grandpa and his fellow farmers, radio reports describing how the government's latest rationing rules or mass mutton purchases by the Army Quartermaster Corps would affect the economic lives of farmers in the upcoming year hardly affected me at all. At least that's how I saw it. But, as a devoted grandson, I didn't want Grandpa to know I was bored.

Years before, Grandma had become bored with all this business, too. So she joined the throng of women from surrounding farms and from Riverton neighborhoods as they pored over the produce displayed by vendors on improvised counters and shelves outside, in the parking lot between the auction building and New Albany Avenue. Every Thursday, throughout the spring, summer, and fall, these vendors sold an incredible volume of locally grown fruits and vegetables of every imaginable variety.

Not all women who shopped there were actually in the market for carrots, cantaloupes, or cherries. Like Grandma, they were interested in gathering information on new varieties for home gardens or purchasing extra quantities of fruits or vegetables needed for winter.

Women at the stockyard were as concerned about prices of produce being sold from trucks, wagons, and buggies in the parking lot as their husbands were about the prices brought by livestock in the auction ring. Some of the women used these prices to calculate whether they could exist on their gardening skills if they were ever widowed or if another Depression forced farms into foreclosure as in the '30s.

Of course, being women like Grandma, they also came to the produce vendor area to catch up on local gossip with friends, neighbors, and relatives. Thursdays at the stockyard also provided them with an ideal opportunity to express their sympathy to those who had lost husbands, brothers, and sons to the war.

In the midst of this swarm of womanhood and assorted vendors, Danny and I found our place. At first, we volunteered our time. Danny was particularly skillful at maneuvering us into positions of responsibility and, ultimately, of high esteem among the vendors and their friendly lady customers.

But we didn't win acclaim instantly. We paid our dues every Thursday, especially that first summer.

We constructed display shelves from boards and cement blocks. We hauled lugs of strawberries from the back of panel trucks and passenger cars. We stacked muskmelons in attractive pyramids under the shade trees that lined the parking lot. We made cardboard signs listing offerings and prices for vendors who didn't write so well. We restocked shelves. We sacked purchases and carried bags of produce to customer car trunks, allowing the vendor to stay with his merchandise and convert shoppers into buyers with his banter.

After a while, many vendors trusted us enough to act as their cashiers. We collected dollars and made change. We stood in for vendors who needed a break for coffee at the café or a haircut for a Friday funeral.

On one occasion, our favorite apple vendor was stricken with an unusually debilitating case of bourbon poisoning and implored us to man his booth, while he snoozed in the cab of his truck. We did so, loyally, from early morning to late afternoon. After our stint, we dutifully turned over the day's proceeds – every penny – to the grateful vendor. He gave us a ride home and told our parents, over and over, what wonderful sons they had raised, while he off-loaded three bushels of his best Yellow Delicious at each of our doorsteps.

At the stockyards, we learned that loyalty had its rewards.

In time, our vendor friends gladly paid for our lunch at the stockyard café, "Here's a quarter for you, Danny boy – and a quarter for you, Jase, my friend. Buy yourselves a hamburg – or hot dog. Get some chocolate milk. But make it snappy, though. I need you back here – real soon. Okay?"

But we never accepted tips from customers. When we were offered a gratuity, we touched the bills of our caps and explained, "No thank you, ma'am. You keep that money. Let's just say we carried your fruit today for – The Boys Overseas."

I have no idea how we came up with that line, but it certainly was effective. In fact, some ladies reacted with such excessive emotion – tears, sobs, weeping, and swooning into the trunks of their cars – that we learned to refrain from delivering the full version when dealing with them. Instead, when these emotional women offered us tips, we would simply smile and say, "Thank you, ma'am. But you know our policy."

That really knocked their socks off!

As our reputation grew, the more astute vendors sought us out. When we arrived early on Thursday morning, they hollered, "Hey, boys! How about giving me a hand today? Got some nice ripe peaches for your mothers. Café lunch special is meat loaf. I'm buyin'."

Once they realized that securing our services meant increasing their day's profits, they offered attractive incentives. Rewards for our commitment to work usually came in the form of crates of unsold, and sometimes overly ripe, produce from their stock at day's end. And, because we lived close to the stockyard, they promised to cart us home along with our booty after we helped them close up shop.

They openly competed with each other for our services, "Hey! Don't work for that cheapskate. Remember the lunch I bought you boys last week. Two desserts! Look! I got you a bag of peanuts today. Hey!"

Of course, among the twenty vendors who regularly sold their produce at the stockyard, we had three favorites. But that doesn't mean we chose to work only for them. After all, how many bushels of over-ripe tomatoes can one family consume in a summer?

Danny and I always worked as a team. Early on, we decided that, when we worked together, it was fun. But, when we worked alone, it was just plain work. So, naturally, we chose fun.

Some vendors tried to convince us to work separately, "Come on," they'd say. "Gino's stock is down. He doesn't need both of you! Whatta ya say? Please? Give me a hand today. I brought plenty of strawberry pop – the kind you like, Jase."

Whenever this came up, we used a modified version of our no-tip line, "We never split up out of respect for – The Boys Overseas."

Unbelievably, that line worked every time, too.

AFTER GRANDMA FINISHED HER important stockyard business, comparing berry prices and chatting with forty ladies, we headed for Forrest Street. When we arrived home, there was a khaki-colored Army car parked in front of our house.

"Oh, dear God! Please, say it isn't so," Grandma prayed aloud.

When Grandma, Danny, and I raced into the kitchen, we saw Mom putting a match to the gas burner under a fresh pot of coffee. Aunt Maude was arranging oatmeal cookies on a dinner plate from Mom's good china set. They both looked up, surprised.

"Is it Van? Tell me!" Grandma implored, looking at Aunt Maude fearfully.

At first, Aunt Maude was mystified by Grandma's question. Then it hit her. Her expression softened. She reached across the kitchen table and took Grandma's hand.

"Oh! No, Ma. It's nothing like that," Aunt Maude assured her. "Colonel Butler – from Camp Riverton – he's here to talk with John. Some sewing machine business, that's all."

"Thank God!" Grandma cried, grasping at her collar. "I thought –"

"Sure you would, Ma," she agreed. "When you saw an Army car what else could you think? Even I –"

She didn't finish. She just patted Grandma's hand.

"Thank God for me, too," Danny announced, expressing my sentiments exactly.

Aunt Maude smiled at Danny and me. Then she offered us an oatmeal cookie. Danny took three. I settled for two.

When the excitement subsided, Danny and I lugged our suitcases into the house and plopped them down on my bed. The *clink* of Danny's samurai sword reminded me of my last stiff neck and the unfinished business with Hans still hidden under my mattress. Danny told me that he needed to carry his suitcase home, but only after he had sampled a few more of Aunt Maude's cookies.

We sat on the bed and speculated about the purpose of the colonel's conversation with Dad. Then we heard them talking as they walked up the path toward us from the shed. We listened intently. When they reached the back porch, Dad gave Mom some stunning news.

"Marie, we've got a surprise for you. The colonel tells me that America desperately needs your services. How would you like to work for the United States Army – out at Camp Riverton among the prisoners?"

"What's this?" Mom asked in amazement.

The back porch was soon crowded with the curious – Grandma, Aunt Maude and, naturally, Danny and me.

Colonel Butler smiled, "Perhaps I should explain."

"Why don't I fix us all a cup of coffee first? And we have some oat-meal cookies to go with it," Aunt Maude suggested.

"Great!" yelled Danny.

Danny helped himself to two more oatmeal cookies from the replenished plate. I took a rain check. We all settled in on the back porch to hear Colonel Butler's explanation.

The colonel told us that his public relations campaign to sell local businesses and farmers on the benefits of employing German prisoners of war had been very successful. With the coming of the planting sea-son, demand for POW labor had nearly outstripped the supply of able-bodied prisoners. During the workweek, the camp was virtually empty as prisoners and their armed guards traveled to jobs at factories, busi-nesses, and farms throughout the county.

"With so many of our own boys overseas, the German POWs are a godsend. This is good for Chippewa County, good for the war effort, and good for America," he proclaimed, obviously reciting a line from his boilerplate speech to local farm groups, chambers of commerce, and veterans organizations.

We nodded our agreement.

"Selfishly," Colonel Butler admitted, "the prisoner work program is also a good thing for me and my Military Police. It makes our jobs a heck of a lot easier."

"How's that?" Dad asked.

"A fully employed prison population is a happy prison population. Since we launched the community work program, the number of dis-ciplinary problems has almost dropped to zero. In fact, POW morale is so high that dozens have submitted letters requesting to stay on – in America – after the war ends. They never had it so good."

"That's for sure!" said Dad.

"Except for a few bad apples – that I need to discuss with you later – my POWs are a very manageable lot. And I'm convinced that this is a direct result of the program."

Then the colonel turned serious.

"However, there's a dark cloud on the horizon threatening to rain on the current sunny disposition of my prisoners. And I think Mrs. Addison is just the right person to help me drive that cloud away."

We couldn't imagine what he meant, but we were really intrigued. He continued.

"The Army – being the Army – has only seen fit to issue each prisoner two sets of work uniforms. You've seen them – those with 'PW' stenciled on the fronts and backs. But much of their new work is fairly rough – clearing brush, buzzing firewood, and working around dirty machinery – both on farms and in factories."

Having seen POWs working these jobs, we knew what he meant. We nodded our understanding.

"Germans take a fanatical pride in their appearance. So they're highly upset about the wear and tear on their uniforms."

"Can't you order new uniforms?" Aunt Maude asked.

"I've tried. But, unfortunately, my requests for supplementary allocations have been consistently denied. Uniforms are scarce commodities. There's rationing of ready-made clothing – and of wool and cotton fabric. Besides, my superiors have informed me – in no uncertain terms – that providing fighting uniforms for the swelling ranks of the Allied army far out-weighs the need for work uniforms for mere prisoners of war."

"That's terrible!" Grandma exclaimed.

"Don't get me wrong. I understand the reasons for the denials, but it sure doesn't make my job any easier."

The colonel took another sip of coffee before going on.

"In recent weeks, the problem has become more acute. By military law, POWs are required to wear their prison uniforms at all times – especially when they leave the camp. However, the farmwomen in the community have taken pity on the POWs and have been encouraging them to break this regulation."

"I've heard about this," Grandma said, knitting her brow.

"When POWs arrive for work, some of these women insist that they change into their husbands' spare overalls. While the prisoners work in the fields, these women patch and mend the uniforms with their sewing machines – or, by hand, with needle and thread. At the end of the day, the prisoners return to camp dressed in refurbished attire.

"Lately, the condition of the work uniforms worn by prisoners lucky enough to draw farm assignments has greatly improved, while the uniforms of those unfortunate POWs assigned to non-farm businesses and factories have further deteriorated."

"Well, I'll be!" Mom declared.

"To top it off, just last week, Sergeant Prella – over at the canning factory – got wind of a Black Market business in uniform repairs. One of his canning factory POWs paid an enterprising POW farm worker five day's worth of camp exchange chits merely to swap uniforms for the day. The POW guaranteed that the farmer's wife would insist on mending his friend's tattered uniform. And he was right – and four dollars richer."

"Sounds like the situation *is* getting out of hand," observed Aunt Maude.

"Yes. But I think we've come up with a solution. I reviewed Army regulations and discovered that prisoners are authorized to wear 'special protective clothing' when involved in work that might damage their uniforms – or their bodies. The reg doesn't specify how much of their uniforms have to be worn under the protective clothing. Army skivvies and a tee shirt are enough as far as I'm concerned. And we can get plenty of them."

"I bet I know where you're heading!" said Mom.

"As long as the protective clothing is marked with the 'PW,' signifying 'Prisoner of War', and providing this lettering meets certain minimum dimensions, then the protective clothing – coveralls, we're thinking – are bona fide Army Reg."

"You're going to make these POW coveralls!" Mom speculated, correctly. "Where will you get the material?"

"That's the most interesting part of the colonel's story," Dad interjected with a smile.

"When I challenged my Quartermaster Sergeant, Red Johnson, to find a way to procure enough material to manufacture adequate quantities of POW coveralls, the old Wizard of the Warehouse responded with two words, 'pup tents!'"

"Pup tents!" Danny yelled. "Just as I thought."

We all looked at him before the colonel continued.

"While requisitions for additional POW work uniforms – or woolen or cotton fabric – are routinely denied, pup tents are an entirely different matter. Red really knows how to get pup tents! In fact, he already has a good supply – stored in the camp supply building.

"When we established Camp Riverton last year, Red noted that the camp's authorized initial inventory of equipment and materiel included twenty pup tents. So he ordered the twenty. When his shipment arrived – in two large trucks – he discovered the mistake of the Quartermaster crew at HQ. They had shipped him *twenty gross.*

"His counterpart, the Quartermaster Sergeant at HQ, isn't thrilled about accepting responsibility for his clerk's *tiny* ordering error. He steadfastly refuses to authorize return of the excess – amounting to exactly 2,860 tents."

"2,860 pup tents!" Danny repeated.

"Yep! Pup tents are made out of a light – but strong – canvas fabric. At first, they're a little stiff from the waterproofing treatment. But I know – from personal experience in the field – that it only takes a few rains to dissolve that waterproofing. The camp laundry can turn these tents into soft, pliable material in no time. And the color is right – Army khaki – with regulation 'PWs' made from appliqués of this canvas bleached white. At least that's how we figure we can do it."

"Pup tents into uniforms. Have you ever!" Grandma said, shaking her head.

"We estimate we got enough tents on hand to outfit each prisoner with two pairs of coveralls! Sergeant Prella has seven volunteers from his work group alone who would willingly be trained as seamstresses – I mean tailors – to cut the patterns, bleach the material, and sew them together.

"I'm acting in response to a strong recommendation from Otto Klump who insists Mr. and Mrs. Addison can solve the Army's problem. Otto maintains that Mr. Addison is the best sewing machine man in Michigan – if not, in all of America. And that you, Mrs. Addison, are an equally competent teacher of sewing machine and tailoring skills."

How Otto had come to hold such high opinions of my parents was anybody's guess. But, as far as I was concerned, Otto had it just right. Of course, I was a bit biased.

"I think Mr. Addison and I have agreed on terms for purchasing six sewing machines. But installing a sewing machine center at Camp Riverton won't amount to a hill of beans without your involvement, Mrs. Addison."

Mom was speechless. We all were!

"I have to caution you, however – the Army can't pay you as much as you could make down at Michigan Electric Motors. But the working conditions will be good. I had thought it might be best to deliver the instruction after seven o'clock on weekday evenings."

"It sounds – I just can't believe –," Mom stammered. "When do you need my decision, Colonel Butler?"

"If you want to think about my offer over the weekend, I'll understand. After all, it means you'll be out of the house a number of evenings each week for some period of time. Could be some hardship on the family.

"But, if you want to move forward – as I hope you will – I would appreciate your putting together ideas for how to proceed. I can stop by on Monday afternoon to get your answer and to discuss the curriculum, schedule for starting the training, and so on. I would also like to take you out to the camp, so you can see where I think the sewing machines should be set up and where the training can be done."

"That sounds like a good idea," Mom agreed.

"As a matter of fact, I'd like your opinion on all of this before I decide on the final location. Why hadn't I thought of that before?"

Mom was clearly flattered by the colonel's offer.

"Colonel Butler, your offer is most appealing. But I'm sure you understand that I have to discuss this with my family before I can give you my decision."

"Marie, now that I'm living with you, I can fix supper – and do other things – so you can get away to help the Army. You've been wanting to do something to assist the war effort. This sounds like a perfect opportunity," said Aunt Maude.

"I agree fully," Dad added.

Mom told Colonel Butler that she looked forward to giving him her decision Monday afternoon. She conceded that she couldn't imagine why she wouldn't say yes.

Danny looked at me. The wheels were turning behind his eyes. I knew what he was thinking. Wouldn't it be terrific having Mom as an FSG spy inside the prison walls of Camp Riverton?

Colonel Butler seemed very pleased with Mom's positive reaction to his proposal. But he didn't leave right away as I expected. Instead, he paused to peruse our garden and to take a long drink from his coffee cup. Then he turned to Danny and me. "I've got some unfinished business to discuss with you two boys as well."

Danny dropped his oatmeal cookie. I looked Colonel Butler straight in eye and asked, "What would that be, sir?"

"Otto Klump and Sergeant Prella briefed me on the episode regarding the sauerkraut theft over at the canning factory. It's not surprising that Baden and Reitter were at the bottom of it. According to their Nazi thinking, stealing your sauerkraut was *honorable* behavior. It's their duty to do anything to hurt the enemy. And, sadly, their definition of *enemy* includes you boys. But their fanatical thinking can't justify what they did, and I personally do not condone or excuse their behavior."

Who wouldn't want to be an enemy of the Nazis? I thought to myself.

We watched Colonel Butler intently. He stood taller and assumed an official air.

"No, it just wasn't right! Yours was a fair business deal – and a good deal for all of us. I can't tell you how much homemade sauerkraut has improved the disposition of my prisoners. So I am profoundly sorry that this sordid twist of events occurred. Therefore, on behalf of the United States Army, I would like to apologize to each of you for any inconvenience – or hurt – that this affair might have caused you."

Danny gave me a look that I interpreted as, *Wow! An Official U.S. Army apology!*

I answered first, "Thank you, Colonel Butler. We're okay with how it turned out, sir. We know those two are rotten eggs. But we finally got the bubble gum. And we've already sold it to Pete's store. Now, everyone in the neighborhood can buy it at the same price we paid for it. So everything turned out just fine."

"That goes for me, too," Danny chimed in.

"Good! Delighted you boys feel that way."

He appeared relieved, and then tense again, "Now, I want to share something with you that's a military secret. I wouldn't want anybody but us here to know about this. Will you agree to keep it a secret?"

Who did he think he was dealing with anyway? Could we keep a secret? "Oh, yes," we vowed. "We swear on the bark of the cottonwood tree." (This last part was lost on him, I'm sure.)

Undaunted, the colonel continued, "We're not going to take any disciplinary action against these two scoundrels – at least, not yet. Instead, we're going to let them rejoin Otto's work gang at the canning factory."

This news surprised us.

"We've met with their security people – including Don Paulus whom you know. They're eager to discover who stole the administration department key, unlocked the supply closet, and helped those rascals hide the jars of sauerkraut in there. We all agreed that it would improve our chances for getting these answers if Baden and Reitter were back at their jobs where we can observe their behavior. Does that make sense?"

I nodded my head in agreement with his strategy. Danny agreed. I wondered if we should share our theory on the identity of the insiders, but I let it go and simply concurred with his approach.

"Good! I didn't want you to see them reinstated at the canning factory, unless you were aware of our thinking – aware of the trap that we've set for them," the colonel concluded.

Then he turned to Mom again. "Not to put pressure on you, Mrs. Addison, but would you be available to take that tour of the camp tomorrow afternoon? It might help you make a better decision over the weekend."

"That sounds like a good idea," Mom agreed.

After shaking hands all around, we followed Colonel Butler to his car. He got in, waved, and stepped on the gas. After going only a few feet, he braked to a sudden stop and stuck his head out the window.

"Almost forgot, Mrs. Addison. There's an additional advantage to accepting this teaching position. If you can coordinate your schedule with another one of our instructors, we'll gladly provide you both with transportation to and from the camp each evening."

"That sounds wonderful. Who's the other instructor?" Mom inquired.

"I'm sure you know him. He lives just down the block. His name is Hans Zeyer."

Kaboom!

The name exploded in our ears. Danny and I saw red! We nearly fainted.

Our neighborhood's only dirty stinking rotten Nazi spy was also – a United States Army instructor? What could Hans Zeyer possibly teach his Nazi brethren? Jail-breaking skills?

The very idea of my dear, sweet mother sharing cozy rides with a Kraut devil who is plotting the violent overthrow of the United States of America – right from Forrest Street – was almost too much to bear.

Danny spoke for us both, "This is a dee-saster!"

13 BAD NEWS DAY

EARLY NEXT MORNING, DANNY AND I MET IN OUR kitchen to discuss the Hans Zeyer situation. Before getting down to business, we sampled oatmeal cookies from Mom's cookie jar. Thanks to Danny, our sample size was fourteen.

Sipping the last drops from the newly opened quart of milk, we agreed to devote the entire day to strategic planning. But where would we hold our session?

Danny suggested the boxcar, the scene of the kraut crime. After cogitating on that option for a while, it finally dawned on us. For our session to be private, the car door would have to be closed. Planning in pitch darkness didn't appeal to either of us.

So the boxcar was ruled out.

Next, we considered our box elder lookout post. Today promised to be bright and sunny. But how could we hold top secret discussions when anyone could sneak up under the tree and listen in? The box elder leaves were too thick to detect infiltration from below. Besides, having to combat the recent infestation of box elder bugs made it hard to concentrate.

So the box elder was ruled out.

"I've got it!" Danny declared with a devilish grin. "How about the First Methodist Church?"

"No good. This isn't Sunday. Itta be locked."

"Doesn't matter," he stated matter-of-factly.

I believed him.

We tiptoed into my bedroom, careful not to wake Aunt Maude, and removed Hans' Nazi book from under my mattress. I grabbed my bank key, removed the entire bubble gum profit ($21.00), and stuffed it into my pocket. Regardless of what plan of action might result from our planning session, we were ready!

DANNY'S POINT OF ENTRY was a basement window hidden behind a large spirea bush that hugged the back of the church. While I watched, he deftly wiggled through the window and dropped with a *thud* to the floor below.

"Close the window, then meet me at the front door. I'll let you in," Danny instructed.

"Aren't you going to lock this window?"

"Nah. I leave it open so I can get in whenever I need to."

"Okay," I said, wondering why his answer sounded logical to me.

As I approached the front of the church, the door suddenly opened. "Can't come in unless you gotta donation for me," Danny said with a grin on his face.

"I'm saving my money. If Sergeant Tolna catches us here, we'll need it for our bail."

"What's a *bale?*"

"I'd rather not talk about it."

Danny shrugged and led the way to the basement. We pulled chairs up to the same table at which we'd once shared punch and cookies with Mel and Mrs. C. Our first order of business was to inventory the unresolved issues.

"Okay," Danny began. "If Hans is a U.S. Army instructor, why is he riding around in the middle of the night in big black Packards – with *no* license plates. And with guys who carry tommy guns and speak German?"

"And how come he has books like this all over his house?" Danny demanded, waving the Nazi book under my nose.

"And who's going to tell Colonel Butler it was probably those Libby sisters who helped the two Nazis steal our sauerkraut?"

At that moment, I didn't consider the Libby sisters an urgent issue, but I didn't want to stop Danny when he was on a roll.

"Okay! Okay! What else?" I prodded.

Instead of continuing, Danny suddenly went silent. He put his chin on his hands and stared at me. After a few minutes, he declared, "We gotta take this book to Gentleman Jim."

"Okay. Let's go."

Nodding his head, Danny declared, "This was a good planning session!"

After wrapping the book carefully inside the pillowcase that I had requisitioned from our linen closet, I followed Danny through the church front door, which locked when it slammed behind us. We set off for Jim's bungalow next to the foundry.

At Bohunk Joe's shack, we turned onto the foundry siding. We saw a faint wisp of smoke rising from Jim's hideaway. "Good! He's up. He's probably cooking breakfast," I speculated optimistically to Danny.

"I wonder if he has anything good to eat," Danny pondered. "Aren't you hungry?"

I didn't answer. But I wondered if Grandpa's tapeworm theory might have some merit.

A faint refrain of *My Old Kentucky Home* whistled toward us. Our whistles joined the chorus to signal our arrival. No use surprising him.

Jim smiled as we tumbled down the bank behind his hillside house. Raising his teacup, he gave us his usual, "Greetings! Mr. Jase Addison. Mr. Daniel Tucker. How's the world treating you?"

Gentleman Jim looked amazingly alert for so early in the morning. *Must have had a small supper last night*, I thought to myself. *Or maybe he thinks it's Sunday, and he wants to be at his best for breakfast at the Good Mission Church.*

"Sit down, boys. Can't offer you much – except sardines and crackers. I was just having some for breakfast. Got plenty of onions, mustard, and pepper to go with them, too."

Even though Jim was offering one of Dad's favorite snacks, I hadn't yet developed a taste for sardines. They were too fish-oily for me. And the idea of crunching down on those little bones sent a shiver up my spine. So I passed.

Without blinking an eye, Danny announced, "I'm starving! I'll have some, please."

"Whatcha got under your arm there, Jase?" Jim inquired between bites.

"That's why we're here," I replied, fighting back an immense feeling of embarrassment, guilt, or something. "What do you think this is?"

After wiping his oily fingertips on his tuxedo trousers, Jim pulled Hans' book out of the pillowcase. His eyes widened when he realized what I had given him. He leafed through the pages very slowly. He stopped every so often, knitted his brow, and moved his lips, absorbing the German text. It seemed an eternity before he finally looked up and spoke to me.

"Where did you get this book?" he probed, staring at me with his penetrating blue eyes.

"It belongs to Mr. Zeyer," I answered, purposely leaving out some important details.

"Why do you boys have it?"

Oops! Confession time!

Now, Jim had been square with me for as long as I had known him, which was my entire life. So I told him the whole truth of the matter including how I had seen Hans being dropped off late at night by a dark, suspicious vehicle and how Queenie and Danny had seen Hans in the same vehicle with a tommy gun-toting passenger. Finally, I described our surveillance of old Hans and our elaborate scheme for inserting Sherm, our mole, into the Nazi spy nest. He stifled chuckles when I described Danny's oatmeal missiles and Sherm's commando outfit.

But he turned serious when I told him about our loud police-whistle diversion, the scalding spilled soup, and the wagon crash in the swamp. I related how this had all happened mere minutes before he caught us that day, washing our clothes at the waterworks.

Jim nodded and looked at the Nazi book again. "But you didn't tell me how you came to have this book."

"Oh, I almost forgot," I continued. "That was the result of Sherm's independent operation."

I told Jim how Squirmin' Sherman had crawled back into the spy nest on his own and cleverly plucked the evidence from under the noses of the Nazis there.

"Now, I see. But why did you bring it to me?"

I reminded Jim that we had heard him speaking German with Otto at the canning factory. Then I told him about Colonel Butler's visit yesterday. About my Mom's new job. And about the dumbfounding revelation that old Hans was a United States Army Instructor of some sort.

"This whole situation has gotten too confusing. We need your help in figuring it all out. What should we do, Mr. Jim?" I pleaded in earnest.

"Yeah, what shoo – should we do?" Danny echoed, spraying cracker crumbs all over Jim's tuxedo.

Jim brushed off his coat sleeve, tipped his top hat forward, put his hands behind his head, leaned back, and closed his eyes. Danny and I stared at him. *Why would he take a nap at a time like this?* I wondered.

After a long while, Jim opened one eye, "You boys never make it simple, do you?"

Gentleman Jim agreed that this was a confusing problem. But he told us that he was certain of one thing, we had to discuss this whole matter with my parents. And the sooner the better! And, of course, Sherm's parents and the Tuckers would have to be told as well.

Danny and I resigned ourselves to our fate and agreed to talk with Dad and Mom that very evening after Dad returned from work and

Mom from Camp Riverton. Jim assured us that he knew it would be difficult for us, so he promised to come by the house later to lend his moral support.

Then he bestowed his second piece of bad news.

"My German's a little rusty, but I can't imagine why anybody would be suspicious of a book describing in agonizing detail the history of the German postal system. And how the National Socialists – the Nazis – went about making dramatic improvements in the efficiency of home mail delivery after Hitler's rise to power. From what I can make of it, this book is a piece of Nazi propaganda designed to instill a sense of pride in German postal workers and convince the world that Nazis are better than the rest of us."

"What!" I exclaimed.

"Geez!" wheezed Danny.

Our valuable spy evidence had turned out to be a pep talk for demoralized German mailmen. How embarrassing! Danny looked at me and wrinkled his nose in disgust. I was with him all the way.

Jim had yet another piece of unpleasant reality for us. Somehow, we boys – Danny, Sherm, and Jase – must return the book to Hans and apologize for our misdeeds. He hoped Hans would accept our apology and leave it at that. But he emphasized that Hans was perfectly within his rights to insist that additional measures be taken. I didn't like the sound of that.

"Maybe I should hold the book until I come by later," Jim suggested.

A thousand things tumbled around inside my head.

Apology! Serious matter! How could we have gone so wrong? What about the midnight rides in the secret spy sedan? And the tommy guns? Doesn't that evidence count for anything?

But we agreed. Jim should keep the book until we could find the best way to return it to Hans.

On our way home, I could feel the tension building in my neck and shoulders, "We need to relax!"

Danny had the perfect solution, "Let's take a bus ride!"

"FAMILY OF THREE – AT a nickel apiece. That's fifteen cents total. How will you be paying, madam? Very well. Fifteen cents from a quarter. That'll be a dime in change, driver. No! A dime. That's right. Now, you got it, sir."

Danny could be *so* helpful!

"Sorry for the delay, madam. Watch your step, now. Please move to the rear of the bus. Careful now, children, mind your mother. Oh, thank you, madam! Only too happy to be of assistance."

And he was *so* courteous!

We spent most of the day touring Riverton and New Albany along the A Route with Mr. Smalley, our favorite bus driver. The five hours of helping Mr. Smalley calculate correct change, navigate streets, and avoid collisions had really raised our spirits. But, for some reason, it didn't do much for Mr. Smalley.

By the time we pulled the bell cord signaling our desire to end the fun, Mr. Smalley didn't look so well. Danny thought that our chauffeur might be coming down with something. When we stepped off the bus at Forrest Street, we promised our driver that we'd be back for another tour in a few days, after he felt better.

No, sir! He didn't look well at all.

WE ARRIVED HOME A little tired, so we headed for our box elder observation post. We stretched out in the warm sun and counted the white puffy animals as they raced across the blue sky. After a few minutes tallying clouds, despite the box elder bugs, we were fast asleep.

The sound of tires crunching gravel signaled Dad's return from work. We woke and slid down the tree just in time to see Colonel Butler's car heading our way from New Albany Avenue. Mom was back from her orientation visit to Camp Riverton.

Colonel Butler shook Dad's hand and nodded to us boys. Mom waited for us to finish our greetings before bubbling, "Oh, John, I can't tell you how impressed I am with the facilities the colonel has set aside for my sewing classes. I really want to do it – if it's okay with you and Jase."

"Of course, it's all right," Dad assured her. "It sounds too good to be true if you ask me."

I added my endorsement, "Yeah, Mom. It'll be keen."

Colonel Butler asked hopefully, "Can I count on you then?"

"Yes – definitely!" Mom declared with a grin.

"Great! You can start anytime – even tonight if you want."

Danny chimed in, "Could you make Jase and me some of those POW coveralls, Mrs. Addison?"

Geez, Danny, I thought. *I know we're in big trouble, but I don't think we'll serve our sentence at Camp Riverton.*

Mom looked at Danny quizzically. "Why do you want POW coveralls, Danny?"

"To wear to school," he replied, without blinking an eye.

Evidently, Mom couldn't think of an appropriate response, so she changed the subject, "Colonel Butler was telling me about the nature of Hans Zeyer's teaching assignment out at the camp. It's absolutely incredible. He promised to fill you in, too – in return for a glass of iced tea."

Upon hearing Hans' name Danny's expression turned to one of concern. At the moment, "Hans Zeyer" was not my favorite subject either. Nonetheless, we joined the others in the cool shade of the back porch.

"I can't tell you everything about the program that Hans is a part of, because much of it's still classified. But I can tell you enough to convince you that America is lucky to have a citizen like Hans," Colonel Butler predicted.

Here is what he told us, coupled with what I have learned since, about Hans' "program."

THE HARD-WON SUCCESSES OF the Allies in North Africa, Sicily, and Italy brought with them a number of challenging problems. Among the most difficult was how to manage the hundreds of thousands of captured German and Italian soldiers, airmen, and sailors who were entitled to the privileges and benefits accorded to prisoners of war by the Geneva Convention.

Dealing with the sheer numbers of POWs was an enormous headache. In America, we provided facilities and personnel to accommodate over 370,000 German prisoners. This doesn't include thousands of Italians, Japanese, and other members of the Axis forces who were also turned over to us.

The German prisoners were particularly difficult to manage.

Since the early 1930s, when Hitler and his National Socialists came to power, young Germans had been brainwashed by a pervasive, insidious, but extremely effective propaganda machine. The Nazi's mass brainwashing of the German citizenry is acknowledged as the most successful in history. Even highly educated, open-minded German citizens were systematically converted into arrogant, racist, and belligerent Nazi zealots by the sinister bombardment of propaganda.

And Nazism's hold over German soldiers did not end when they became prisoners of war. Captured Nazi leaders forced their fellow POWs to resist all attempts by their American captors to lessen the power and influence of Nazism in our prison camps. At first Nazism thrived among the POWs, making it nearly impossible for the U.S. Army Military Police to manage the network of camps under their command.

Something had to be done. So the War Department established a top-secret organization called the Prisoner of War Special Projects Division (SPD). Under the aegis of SPD, educators and political scientists, all experts in the nuances of Nazi Germany, were assembled in Washington to design and launch an elaborate plan for reeducating and reprogramming German POWs.

The plan had two main objectives.

The first was to change the attitude of the average German prisoner toward American democracy and thereby lessen the influence of Nazism in the camps. Success here would make the Army's prisoner management job a lot easier.

The second was to create a cadre of democratic thinkers among the POWs who would assume positions of leadership in the new German government after the war ended. Success here would influence Germany's transition from a culture highly susceptible to totalitarianism to a culture highly resistant to any form of government other than democracy.

In its wisdom, the Pentagon chose a palatable name for its plan to reeducate and reprogram Nazi-brainwashed POWs. It was known as the "Intellectual Diversion Program" or IDP.

Most German POWs had never been exposed to American or British literature or arts. Under IDP, prisoners were provided with German-language versions of the works of authors such as John Steinbeck, Robert Louis Stevenson, and Mark Twain. American magazines and newspapers were distributed in POW camps. American and British movies, dubbed in German when possible, were shown regularly.

Community work programs were begun to enable POWs to labor side by side with ordinary Americans and to visit farms and other places of business – the products of the power of American capitalism and democracy.

Classes were offered in American history and political science. Then, more practical subjects were added to the curriculum including vocational specialties such as auto repair, electricity, and horticulture.

POWs were given the opportunity to earn academic degrees by enrolling in courses taught at the camps by faculty members from nearby universities and colleges. This aspect of IDP was extremely popular among the Germans who placed a high value on academic achievement.

Under the terms of an agreement negotiated by the International Red Cross in Switzerland, German prisoners of war in America could take college courses taught by American professors and receive credits granted by German universities. And, similarly, American prisoners of war in Germany took courses taught by German professors for credits granted by American colleges.

Many German POWs earned their degrees in subjects that would make them influential when they returned to Germany after the war ended. The most popular courses were those leading to a degree in education. Attesting to the success of the IDP, an unusually high proportion of former POWs ultimately filled positions of importance in Germany's post-war government in Bonn.

The same was true in the case of at least one American POW who earned his undergraduate degree from the University of Maryland while a prisoner of the Germans. When he was discharged, he earned an additional degree in law and went on to become the Attorney General of the United States. His name was Nicholas Katzenbach.

AT THIS POINT IN his briefing, the colonel paused for a long drink that nearly emptied his glass. Not one to miss an opportunity to be hospitable, Mom asked, "Who would like more iced tea?"

As our glasses were topped off, Dad observed, "This is incredible all right. I assume that you're going to tell us about Hans' role in all of this."

"Absolutely! That's the most interesting part," the colonel said. "First, let me tell you a little about Hans' background."

He took another sip of tea and then continued.

"Hans Zeyer graduated with a degree in civil engineering from a prestigious German university right after the First World War. He worked for the City of Berlin during Germany's first and – unfortunately – short-lived experiment with democracy known as the Weimar Republic. That government fell under the weight of a collapsing German economy and the resultant threat of mass civil war. Finally, after a series of autocratic leaders, Hitler and his Nazis came to power in 1933. When that happened, Hans Zeyer and his young wife left Berlin to seek their fortune in America.

"Hans is a very unusual German. He is staunch advocate of democracy. Political science is his passion. As a young man, he read extensively on this subject. He became convinced that representative democracy as practiced here in the United States is the best form of government on the planet. But that's not all.

"Because he is also a highly educated civil engineer, he's greatly respected by his German POW students. They address him by his formal academic title, Herr Doktor Zeyer.

"In Hans' classroom, German students are exposed to subjects never allowed in Nazi-run schools. His political science class – conducted under the auspices of Michigan State College – is the most popular course offering at Camp Riverton. Hans is successful because he never insists that his students accept his high opinion of America. He just presents the facts and lets them draw their own conclusions.

"Even though he's the dedicated deputy director of Riverton Public Works and an outstanding political science teacher at Camp Riverton, Hans is a simple man at heart. He doesn't seek public acclaim. As you know, he and his wife lead a rather quiet life here on Forrest Street."

Danny gave me another funny look that I interpreted as, *That's what you think, Colonel Butler!*

I tried not to let Danny distract me. I refocused my attention on the colonel's words. I needed to hear the next part.

"The Zeyers fully sympathize with neighborhood families whose children are now fighting the armies of their former Homeland. If the Zeyers had had children, there is no question that they would be wearing American uniforms. The Zeyers took their oaths as new American citizens on the same day Hitler invaded Poland to launch the Second World War.

"But Hans fights the Nazis in his own way. Hans and the other IDP professors have managed to convert thousands of Germans into openminded, democracy advocates who now see America in a new light. These converts have overthrown their Nazi leaders in POW camps all across the country. Today, they enthusiastically sign up to work in our fields and factories. And many have asked to stay in America after the war. We owe a huge debt of gratitude to Hans Zeyer and others like him."

We were fascinated by what Colonel Butler had told us, especially the part about old Hans. But what about our other evidence? The black sedan. Tommy guns. And speaking German in the middle of the night?

When he finished, Colonel Butler turned to Mom, "If you want to start this evening, I can have the car pick you up and drop you back. Hans teaches tonight, so we'll be coming by for him."

"That sounds perfect. I'll be ready," Mom replied, nodding her head.

"Generally, we pick up Hans – and other instructors around town – in our second car. You can't miss it. A big, black government-issue Packard. Looks like a hearse. We use it for dropping off MPs who relieve each other – on the second and third shifts – at the factories in the area. They carry tommy guns so don't be alarmed. Also, the driver will be Sergeant Gunter who likes to practice his German with Hans. You may not get a word in edgewise."

Danny and I were in shock!

"There goes the evidence!" Danny whimpered.

Fortunately, nobody heard him but me. But how right he was! How could we have made such a mistake? We had old Hans all wrong. Jim was right. We owed Herr Doktor Hans a major apology. And we needed to return his stolen book – right away – regardless of the consequences!

As Colonel Butler's car turned onto New Albany Avenue, the A Route bus stopped in front of Pete's. The door opened and out stepped Hans who was just returning from work. He crossed New Albany and walked toward us.

When Dad saw Hans, he said, "I think I just might like to wish Hans a good evening. What about the rest of you?"

Danny sputtered, "I – I – need to be getting home."

What?

As I turned to give Danny Deserter a piece of my mind, I saw Gentleman Jim coming up the sidewalk, just this side of the cottonwood tree. Under his arm, he carried our evidence, still wrapped in Mom's pillowcase.

Hans approaching from the south! Jim approaching from the north! Dad and Mom waiting for them on the sidewalk. We were trapped!

It seemed to take forever for Jim and Hans to arrive at the same spot under the box elder tree in front of our house.

"Good evening, Hans! Good evening, Jim!" Dad said cheerfully for all of us.

"Hello – everyone," Jim replied tentatively and then, he turned to Hans. "Mr. Zeyer, I believe this belongs to you."

Hans took the parcel and removed the evidence from the pillowcase. He opened the book and then looked very puzzled.

"One of my textbookz – from da POW camp. But dis copy isn't mine no more. I give dis copy to little Shermanz." Hans declared, handing the book back to Jim.

Danny slapped his forehead. I knew how he felt.

Hans elaborated.

He had ordered a number of these particular Nazi propaganda books from a special Pentagon book supplier in Washington. He wanted his POW students to see for themselves how the Nazis had lied to the German people. He had dozens of copies of this book at his house.

One of his students had discovered that this particular copy was missing twenty pages from the middle of the book. Hans marked this copy with a bold "X" on the inside cover, so he wouldn't distribute it in his class by mistake.

He showed us the "X."

He said that he had used this copy in class to demonstrate that even Nazi Supermen could make printing errors. Hans chuckled at his own "choke" as he called it.

That gave me the idea for what I would do to Sherman the next time I saw him.

When Little Sherman came by to play with Hans' puppets, as he usually did several times a week, he saw the book. Sherman was fascinated. Probably because of the swastika on the spine, Hans speculated. Then Hans laughed, recalling how Sherman had difficulty pronouncing *swastika*.

Sherman asked to borrow the book. He wanted to show it to Jase and Danny. Hans assured Sherman that he could borrow it, but wouldn't he rather *have* it as his own? Sherman was ecstatic. He hugged the book to his chest. Hans feared he might faint from excitement. Hans wiped Sherman's nose and sent him on his way with the defective textbook as a cherished gift.

Hans would never consider taking the book back. What would Little Sherman think? And what was Jim doing with Sherman's book in the first place?

Jim looked at Danny and me and shrugged his shoulders.

Mom and Dad looked at Jim.

Danny looked at me and hissed, "The little worm lied to us!"

I AWOKE LATE THE next morning. Stumbling into the kitchen, half asleep and still in my pajamas, I was surprised to find Aunt Maude, Mom, and Dad hunched over a special morning edition of the *Riverton Daily Press* spread out on the kitchen table.

They looked up at me when I entered the room. There was fear in their eyes. A glimpse at the paper told me why. A three-inch banner headline leaped out from the front page.

London Terror Stricken

HITLER LAUNCHES SECRET WEAPON
Jet-Propelled Buzz Bombs Fall on City;
Hundreds Killed as Panic Reigns

No one spoke. They just looked at me, eager to learn of my reaction. My cheeks burned. I felt confused.

Finally, I asked, "Does this mean we're not going to win the war?"

My mother chewed a fingernail. Aunt Maude stirred her cold coffee. And Dad continued to stare at the paper. No one answered.

FOLLOWING D-DAY, IN A desperate effort to turn the tide, Hitler ordered his forces in northern France to launch a lethal barrage of his dreaded secret weapon, the V-1 rocket.

The "V" stood for "Vergeltungswaffen" that meant "Weapon of Reprisal." Hitler chose the civilian population of London and other cities along the southern coast of England as the V-1's first victims.

The V-1 pilotless airplane was powered by a pulse-jet engine and carried a single bomb containing nearly a ton of deadly explosives. After launching from its catapult, the ominous rocket attained an altitude of three thousand feet and a speed in excess of 350 miles per hour. Fortunately, the range of the V-1 was relatively short, a few hundred miles at best, and its guidance system was primitive, making specific targeting nearly impossible.

The V-1 was dubbed the "Buzz Bomb" because of the loud buzzing sound emanating from its jet engine. Once the Buzz Bomb reached its target area, the engine shut down, and the distinctive buzzing suddenly ceased. People on the ground held their breath during a brief period of horrifying silence that preceded the impending explosion.

Unlike the Luftwaffe's conventional bombers and fighter aircraft, the V-1 could be launched in any weather and at any time of the day. During the eighty days following the first attack, the Germans pounded London and the surrounding area with as many as a hundred V-1 bombs a day.

By summer's end, Allied forces would push the enemy away from the coast of France and beyond the relatively short range of the V-1. Mercifully, attacks on English cities then became impossible.

Despite its short duration, the V-1 campaign proved to be extremely successful. Nearly sixty percent of the 8,500 rockets launched by the Nazis found targets. Luckily, British interceptor aircraft, barrage balloons, and anti-aircraft fire brought down the rest.

In all, the V-1 accounted for 17,000 casualties including 6,000 killed, massive destruction to buildings in London and environs, and months of unnerving, around-the-clock horror for the British people. In addition, over 2,000 Allied airmen lost their lives in raids attempting to destroy the V-1 manufacturing facilities near Norhausen. Using slave labor – Jews, Poles, Gypsies, and other Nazi-labeled "subhumans" – from nearby concentration camps, the Norhausen facility still managed to produce 29,000 V-1 rockets during the war.

The end of the V-1 rocket attacks was not the end of the bad news for the citizens of London. In September of 1944, Hitler launched his next and even more effective Weapon of Reprisal.

The V-2 was a 2,000-pound, high-explosive bomb propelled by a sophisticated liquid fuel rocket. The V-2 reached an altitude of fifty miles and then plummeted downward toward its target at a speed of four thousand miles per hour, making this Nazi missile impossible to intercept. During the last days of the war, over one thousand V-2 rockets rained destruction on the city of London.

OUR SOLEMN BREAKFAST ENDED when Danny appeared at the backdoor. He tapped lightly, opened the screen, and entered the kitchen.

What happened to his signature come-out call? I wondered. He quietly sat down at the table and stared at the newspaper.

He looked at each of our somber faces before speaking, "Secret Weapons make me hungry. What's to eat?"

On that uplifting note, the adults rose from the table and hurried to catch up with their daily responsibilities.

Mom headed for the cellar to complete one more load of laundry before beginning the weekly ironing. From the kitchen, I heard her greet the new, fat toad that I had spotted under the cellar steps only yesterday.

Dad dropped Aunt Maude at the bus stop where she caught the westbound bus to Woolworth's. Then Dad turned east toward his job at Burke's.

I made a bet with myself. Tonight, I was convinced, would bring opinions from Dad's fellow workers and Aunt Maude's customers about the V-1's possible effect on the war. We would likely hear reaction to the news of Hans' contribution to the war effort. And congratulations on Mom's new teaching job at Camp Riverton. These last two topics were far too interesting not to be a major part of the morning news delivered by Dad and Aunt Maude to their captive audiences at work.

When Danny and I finished our breakfast, my friend closed his eyes, rubbed his tummy, and asked, "What are we going to do about these Buzz Bombs?"

The answer was obvious!

After I donned my summer uniform, Danny and I manned our posts at the "V-1 Spotter Center" in the crown of the box elder. We strained our ears listening for the telltale buzz of this nasty new weapon. The sound coming closest to a V-1 buzz was the sustained burp from Bohunk Joe as he and his pushcart rolled under our tree.

Then we heard a car pull onto our street. It came to a stop right under us. The door slammed and quick footsteps hurried up the sidewalk toward our front door. We froze and listened, dying of curiosity.

Whoever it was knocked several times and then called out, "Mrs. Addison. Are you home? Mrs. Addison! Are you there?"

Danny and I recognized the voice just as Mom came around the side of the house from her clothesline in the backyard. "Hello, Colonel Butler. What brings you here this morning? I wasn't expecting to see you until tonight."

"I'm here on some very unpleasant business. Unfortunately, I need to deliver some bad news – the worst kind of news – to someone you know. And I was wondering if you might come with me. This case will be a tough one to do alone."

"I don't know if I –. What am I saying? Of course, I will. Come inside, please – while I clean up some. And I guess you'd better deliver the news to me first."

We heard the door open and close behind them as they entered the house. Their voices were barely audible. Then we heard Mom's wail, "Oh, God! No! Oh, dear God, no!"

I was struck by a deep concern for Mom. Then, suddenly, fear gripped my chest. "It's Uncle Van!" I screamed.

I couldn't move. My eyes glazed over with tears. Danny looked at me sorrowfully with tears welling in his eyes, too.

"What should we – ," Danny stopped abruptly, when our front door squeaked open.

"Thank you again, Marie. I know this won't be easy for you. Please wait a minute. I need to get some paperwork from my car."

The car door slammed. And Mom and Colonel Butler walked away from us in the direction of Pete's. We heard their footsteps turn up the front sidewalk of the house next door. There was a knock on the door followed by the sound of halting footsteps across the screened-in porch.

Then we heard Mom's voice, "Hello, Mrs. Mikas! May we come in?"

There was a pause – only for a second or two – followed by an excruciating cry.

"Gahd, gahd noooooo! Nodt my Ivan! Nodt Ivan – dead, too. Ooooooh! Gahd no!" Mrs. Mikas shrieked.

Danny and I were stunned. "Not Ivan, too," I moaned. "First Theo. Now Ivan. It's not fair!"

Still stunned, Danny and I descended from our tree perch and sat on our porch to wait for Mom and Colonel Butler. We were in for a long wait. But it didn't matter because time stood still. We sat in silence, not knowing what to say to each other.

I thought of Mrs. Mikas' soft sobbing in the middle of the night and wondered if it would ever end.

After what seemed like an eternity, Dad pulled into the driveway. He waved as he got out of the car. Neither of us had the energy to wave back. He paused momentarily to look at the army car. Then he walked quickly toward the porch.

"Jase! What's happened?"

"I think it's about Ivan Mikas. Mom and Colonel Butler are over there now. They've been gone for a long – quite a long time," I replied, fighting back my tears.

"Mrs. Mikas – she cried – real loud," Danny whispered to Dad. "She – she must be awful upset – and sad."

"Ivan, too. Oh, no! This damnable war! Who'll be next?" Dad demanded angrily.

He sat down beside us and stared at the sidewalk. The three of us were still sitting silently when Aunt Maude arrived home from work. After hearing the ghastly news, she announced, "I'm going over there."

After depositing her purse on our porch, she walked across the lawn, up the steps, and into the house. Aunt Maude had been there for a good half hour when we heard the Mikas' screen door open and close. Mom walked across the lawn toward us. She looked drained.

As she approached, we stood up to greet her. She didn't say a word but she gave each of us a long hug – Dad, me, then Danny.

Finally, she said softly, "She'll be okay – I hope. But it wasn't easy. Colonel Butler – he – nobody could have done a better job under the circumstances. I don't know how he does it – death after death."

We stared at her trying to let her words sink in.

"I'm glad he asked for my help, though," she continued. "I think I made it a bit easier for him – if that's possible."

Mom looked at us for a response but we were speechless. Nodding, she acknowledged our silent validation of her role in Colonel Butler's dreadful mission.

"This might not sound important in view of what's happened here this afternoon, but I need to change my clothes and get ready for my first class tonight," she explained, almost apologetically.

Dad recovered enough to say, "No. No. Your class is real important, Marie. They're depending on you to be there. Life has to go on – even during wartime."

Apparently fearing that he had sounded trite, Dad quickly changed the subject, "What can we do to help?"

"Well, thanks. When the Colonel arrived, I was in the middle of taking the wash off the line. Jase, you could finish that job for me. Just put what's left on the line in the basket out there on the lawn. Then set it in our bedroom. Okay?"

I nodded and stood up. Danny joined me.

"John, you could you give me a ride out to the camp. Colonel Butler didn't think his visit would take this long. He was going to take me out when he finished. But he'll be there for some time, I'm afraid."

"Of course! I'm ready to go when you are. Will you need a ride home?"

"No, I can arrange a ride back with the MPs. But another thing! I didn't have time to put anything together for supper. Maybe you boys could eat at the diner tonight. And don't worry about Maude. She and I can have a bite when I get back – later."

That was the first bit of good news that I'd heard all day. "Dad, can Danny come with us to the diner?"

"Sure! Danny, go home and ask your mother. Then get on back here on the double! Okay?"

Danny was running before Dad had finished, "Okay! Ohhhhhkaaaayyyyy!" he hollered over his shoulder as he sped around the corner of our house heading for home.

THE CHOP SUEY DINER was an unusual restaurant for a small Midwest town. In the tradition of its New Jersey and Maryland counterparts, Riverton's only diner had once been an old railroad dining car.

No one could remember why it was parked on the deserted siding next to the Chippewa Lumber Yard just off South Addison Street. But the diner's close proximity to Riverton's in-city factories was ideal. So when the diner's current owners approached the lumberyard's manager and explained what they had in mind, he approved their plans to convert the dining car into a diner. That was back in the mid-1930s.

This decision was beneficial for all concerned. First, it was the only eating establishment in Chippewa County that never closed. Second, it served exceeding generous portions of plain-cooked meals at very affordable prices to its largely blue-collar clientele. Third, its coffee was the best in town, bar none.

The diner was particularly busy just before and after the start of the three workday shifts. Between six and eight in the morning, four and six in the afternoon, and eleven at night and one in the morning, you were lucky to find any of the Chop Suey Diner's forty booth and counter seats free.

Part of the attraction for me was riffling through the diner's remarkable menu and salivating over the wide range of choices. Hot roast beef sandwiches deluxe. Steak and eggs with fried potatoes. Pork chop sandwiches. Hamburger and French fries. Chipped beef gravy over toast. City chicken dinner. Swiss steak with mashed potatoes and gravy. Pies. Cakes. Egg custard. Ice cream – three flavors. And, I almost forgot. Chop suey!

I could never figure why the diner had such an extensive menu when, by my observation, the two house specialties – hot roast beef sandwich and steak and eggs – accounted for at least ninety percent of the meals served. But who was I to question the menu selections of those who managed such a successful enterprise?

The citizens of Riverton thought "Chop Suey Diner" was a perfect name, because it was owned and operated by the town's only oriental family. No one cared that the diner's Chinese name didn't square with the fact that the oriental family in question, the Nakayama family, happened to be Japanese.

Now you would think the only Japanese family in a small Midwest town during the war would have earned the contempt of Rivertonians, especially immediately following the sneak attack on Pearl Harbor. But, this hardworking family of four – father, mother, and two teenage daughters – never suffered from prejudice or abuse. On the contrary, the blue-collar workers of Riverton held this particular Japanese family in high esteem.

I know I'm repeating myself, but this is important!

Looking back on the those days, I wonder how this admirable family really felt about the newspaper headlines, post office posters, and general conversation that branded Japanese as Japs, Nips, Yellow Rats, or worse. If stereotyping and hate-filled labeling ever bothered them, they never showed it. Regardless of how they felt, the Nakayamas' enormous dignity prevented them from saying a word. On the other hand, when could they have possibly had time to read a newspaper or listen to the radio?

My favorite waitress was the younger daughter Nikki. She was extremely patient with us boys and always gave us over-sized portions of the desserts included in the price of any entrée. Her sister Mitsu was nice enough, but she tended to pay special attention to the adult males who dined there. Looking back on it, Mitsu probably earned more tips than Nikki. Most boys weren't big tippers back in those days. But it didn't really matter to the Nakayama sisters. They dutifully turned over every penny of their tip money to their mother, anyway.

Aneko, the mother, spoke better English than her husband, Dai. She positioned herself behind the cash register and watched the diner's operation like a hawk. A coffee cup never reached half empty before her shrill command in Japanese corrected this serious breakdown in service. The daughters jumped at her command and quickly refilled the cup, always with a big smile.

Each time you presented your check to Mrs. Nakayama at the cash register, she asked if your meal was satisfactory. Then she made a great show of re-adding the check to verify her daughters' arithmetic, which never failed to be perfect.

When she handed over your change, expertly apportioned for optimal tipping, she inquired about your health and that of each member of your family. Next, she wished you a Happy – whatever holiday was next.

Her final gesture was to offer a small after-dinner mint from the silver bowl she kept beside her cash register. Classy!

Mr. Nakayama was a peerless short order cook as well as competent chef. He ran the kitchen as if he were playing ping-pong with a dozen opponents at the same time. He sprinted tirelessly from the stainless steel refrigerator behind him, to the huge sizzling grill, then to the dish rack, and finally to the service counter. Only to repeat this trek over and over again, hundreds of times each day. To my knowledge, he never failed to prepare each order exactly right. And he never slowed down.

Amazingly, the four Nakayamas cooked and served hundreds of scrumptious meals daily, while still finding time to keep the diner sparkling clean, 24 hours a day, seven days a week. And, to top it off, they were pleasant and exceptionally courteous.

I have no idea when, or if, the Nakayamas ever slept. I don't even know where they lived. Or what they did with the profits from their successful business. Some claimed they brought family members to this country from Japan after the war. Others say they bought a huge artichoke farm near Salinas in California. But no one knew for sure.

When I returned to Riverton, after being away for some years, I discovered that the Chop Suey Diner and all the Nakayamas had vanished. And nobody could tell me what happened to them.

Terribly saddened by this news, I realized I still had a crush on Nikki.

THAT NIGHT, DANNY AND I went oriental.

We both ordered Mr. Nakayama's special chop suey served to us by Nikki, the world's best waitress. Dad ordered his favorite, hot roast beef sandwich deluxe with enormous scoops of creamy mashed potatoes and peas and carrots, all covered with thick, brown beefy gravy.

Predictably, our meals were delicious and the servings were huge. But, for some reason, I didn't feel much like eating. Surprisingly, Danny and Dad felt the same way. We picked at our dinners. We even declined dessert. I'll repeat that for emphasis. We *all* declined dessert!

On our way home, we agreed that this had been a terrible day. Just too much bad news! But Dad observed optimistically, "Well, there is one good thing about this day. It'll soon be over."

When we turned onto Forrest Street, we saw the Army car still parked in front of our house. Mom and Colonel Butler were standing in the front yard beside the porch. They appeared to be waiting for us.

"Good! Mom's back from class!" I cheered, when we hopped out of the car.

As we approached the porch, Mom turned to Dad. "John, I'm afraid there's more bad news."

Then she looked at Colonel Butler who said soberly, "Baden and Reitter – our two sauerkraut thieves – failed to show up this afternoon for the truck that brings the POWs back to camp from the canning factory. Apparently, they've escaped."

"I don't believe it!" Dad exclaimed.

"Well, wait till you hear this part," Mom added. "The Libby girls – Anne and Barb – are missing, too. And so is Louise Libby's car."

We were stunned.

Colonel Butler summarized the situation, "We obtained conclusive evidence that the two girls helped Baden and Reitter with the theft. Their fingerprints – on file at the canning factory – matched those found on the sauerkraut jars hidden in that supply closet. We got word this morning – from our Criminal Investigation Division down at Fort Custer. The girls were summoned to meet with the CID folks at the canning factory Security Office this afternoon. But they never showed up."

He paused before going on.

"Yes, sir. Everything just magically disappeared – the Libby girls, Baden and Reitter, and the Libby family car."

"What's going to happen now?" asked Dad.

"Well, for starters, the Chippewa County Sheriff, the Michigan State Police, and the FBI have all been called in on the case. By now, the two men – and the two women – are the subjects of a massive statewide manhunt. Wanted posters. Roadblocks. APB's – that's All Points Bulletin. The whole works!"

"Holy Smokes! Do these girls have any idea of what they've gotten themselves into?" Dad asked.

"From what I've learned about them, I'd say they haven't the faintest idea of how serious this is. At this point, our two SS rascals have most likely found a way to arm themselves. Law enforcement officers involved in the manhunt have been instructed to shoot first – and ask questions later."

"Shoot first and ask questions later!" I repeated, echoing the colonel's words.

"That may not be the worst of it. This is wartime. If the girls did help the prisoners escape, the FBI guys are determined to see the girls charged with *treason*, no less!"

"My, gosh. Are you saying they could go to prison for this?" Mom asked, in disbelief.

"If they're lucky!" retorted the colonel.

"Lucky!" Dad exclaimed.

Colonel Butler played his trump card, "Wartime treason is punishable by death."

No one spoke. We considered the gravity of the colonel's last statement. It was so hard to believe. We were talking about the *Libby* girls! They live just down the street from us! Our neighbors!

Finally, Danny broke the silence. He looked at the colonel and inquired seriously, "How will they do it?"

Not understanding Danny, the colonel asked, "Whatcha mean?"

"Firing squad or hanging?" Danny inquired dryly.

Mom glared at Danny. We all joined her.

Impervious to censure, Danny shrugged his shoulders. "Just wondering, is all."

14 THE PRIZE FISH

NEWS OF THE POW ESCAPE SPREAD LIKE WILDFIRE throughout Riverton, across the state, and around the country. Radio stations in Detroit, Flint, and Chicago broadcast hourly updates as the search for the escapees widened.

By the next morning, dozens of reporters from newspapers as far away as New York City had invaded our town. They came by car, bus, and train. Hotel Riverton was filled to overflowing. Even our two shabby boarding houses were solidly booked for the first time in history.

The presence of this unexpected army of reporters affected us all. There were no available seats at the Chop Suey Diner for workers just ending their shifts. Riverton Cab's entire fleet consisting of two, pre-war taxis logged a record-setting number of trips, hauling news-hungry reporters to every corner of town. City buses were packed with fast-talking strangers reeking of coffee, bourbon, and tobacco, their pockets stuffed with pencils, pads of paper, and racing forms. Aunt Maude's tips increased dramatically as the inexpensive eats at Woolworth's attracted news hounds, eager to pad their expense accounts.

Riverton Central operators worked overtime to cover the increased volume of long-distance calls between reporters and their newspapers that resulted in stories with revolting headlines like this one:

> **NAZI-LOVING GIRLS MASTERMIND
> BREAKOUT FOR POW PALS**

Or this one:

> **SMALL TOWN TOOTSIES TURN LOOSE
> HITLER'S BAD BOYS**

And even this one:

> ## HUNS AND HONEYS HOTFOOT IT
> ## OUT OF HOMETOWN HOOSEGOW

The voracious reporters focused their frenzied attack on the easygoing Chippewa County Sheriff, Ray Connors, whose duty it was to apprehend the escapees. Surrendering to unrelenting pressure from the press, the timid sheriff agreed to regular morning and afternoon press briefings in the Riverton High School auditorium, the county's largest public meeting place.

Interrupted from his normally quiet summer routine, the high school janitor grudgingly dragged three tables from the cafeteria and arranged them in a row across the front of the stage. Those being interviewed sat in chairs behind the tables and looked down on the throng of fidgety reporters jammed together in the first several rows of the center section.

Sheriff Connors opened his initial briefing by reading a short statement outlining what was then known about the escape, which wasn't much. Then he introduced those individuals he believed would be of most interest to the reporters: Colonel Butler, Don Paulus, poor Mrs. Libby, and finally Riverton's mayor and the chief of police, who technically weren't involved in the case, but insisted on sharing the limelight with the accommodating sheriff.

After enduring two tedious hours of futile questioning of the clueless interviewees, Sheriff Connors concluded the briefing. Without a word of thanks, the throng of reporters rose as a body and rushed out of the auditorium, leaving their subjects staring down on empty seats.

The boorish reporters elbowed their way up the stairs to the typing classroom where they fought each other for use of the twenty upright Underwoods. After a brief burst of frantic pecking, with stories in hand, they rushed to the Grand Trunk Railway Station to browbeat Riverton's only telegraph operator into filing their copy ahead of the competition.

By the end of the first day, the reporters were starved for new news. They burrowed deeper and deeper into the community for any information that could be construed as relevant. They interviewed employees who had worked with the POWs and the girls at the canning factory. They interrogated Pete and Mrs. Pete who had sold groceries to the Libby family. They questioned the girls' teachers. On a tip from

Buddy Roe Bib Overalls, they grilled Bohunk Joe, who knew zilch about the case, but graciously offered to sharpen their knives for them. Dressed in their best aprons, neighborhood ladies reluctantly agreed to impromptu cross-examinations as they swept dust and offensive reporters off their front steps.

Naturally, the pushy journalists unearthed details about the Libby girls that were not flattering, like the high school cheating incident when Gentleman Jim had stood up for them. They learned about the girls' attraction to ruffians and no-gooders, including the AWOL sailors who had run us off the road. Somehow, they even got wind of the sauerkraut theft at the canning factory and the girls' involvement in the heist.

When reporters knocked on our door and insisted on interviewing Danny and me, Dad put his foot down. He told them that we boys would *not* be available for comment for the next several days because, "We'd be gone fishin'!"

WE ASSEMBLED AT THE Tolna house well before sunrise. As Sergeant Jeff loaded the last of the fishing tackle into the trunk of his police car, Danny asked Dad sleepily, "Mr. Addison, what time is it?"

"Oh, about seven minutes past night."

"Why go fishing so early in the morning?"

"It's when the Big Ones bite best," Dad explained.

"Bite what?"

"The bait!"

"Oh, yeah!"

As Dad slipped into the front seat with Sergeant Jeff, Danny turned to me and whispered, "What's bait? And what's a Big One?"

"You'll see!" I promised.

About once a quarter, Sergeant Jeff and Dad went fishing for the Big Ones – northern pike and largemouth bass. Dad customarily took off from work on a day that Sergeant Jeff was on call. That way they could use his police car instead of tying up either the Tolna or the Addison family car. By choosing a weekday, they avoided the crowds of fishermen who occupied all the good fishing spots along the Chippewa River on Saturdays and Sundays.

In the case of an emergency, they never fished more than ten miles from town to allow Sergeant Jeff to be within radio range of calls from the police dispatcher. In all their years of fishing, Sergeant Jeff never received such a call.

This was the first time I had been privileged to accompany them on one of their fishing trips. But it wasn't for lack of trying. The summer before, when Grandma, Aunt Maude, and Mom planned to spend the day at the farm putting up dill pickles, I nearly convinced Dad to let me come. I argued that canning pickles was not sufficiently macho for an impressionable young man like me, especially compared to going after the Big Ones. He didn't disagree, but I spent the day picking cucumbers anyway.

Our first stop was Homer Lyle's bait shop.

As Sergeant Jeff came to a stop in front of Homer's house, I nudged Danny, "Let's go see Homer's bait!"

Dad went up the back porch steps and knocked softly on the kitchen door. Mrs. Lyle opened the door and smiled, "Hello, boys. Beautiful morning. Thanks for stopping by. Homer'll be right with you."

We could hear the *thump-thump-thump* as Homer made his way to the door. When he came into view, Danny's eyes opened wide to get a better look in the early morning grayness.

Homer was an elderly man who was horribly twisted by an old affliction that no one ever talked about. He walked awkwardly with the assistance of wooden crutches, thickly padded with rags carefully wrapped around the handgrips and underarm rests. He wore worn gray work trousers with black suspenders and a sleeveless undershirt. On chilly mornings, like this one, he wrestled on a brown wool cardigan, his bony elbows protruding from ragged pear-shaped holes.

We followed Homer as he hip-hopped down the porch steps and along the dirt path leading to the small, unpainted wood shack about thirty feet from his back door. Between grunts of painful exertion, he hummed confidently under his breath to let us know that he didn't need our sympathy.

Upon reaching his bait shop, Homer pried open the plywood flap that served as a door, and hopped inside. We waited for him to prop his crutches in the corner and seat himself awkwardly on his four-legged stool. Scooting across the warped wood-slat floor, he positioned himself within easy reach of the bubbling water tanks, mysterious wire-mesh cages, and wooden boxes that housed his current inventory of assorted live bait.

When he was situated, he turned to Dad and asked, "Who's the new lad, John?"

"This is Danny Tucker – lives around the corner from us. His dad bought the garage business there on the north side of New Albany Avenue."

"Oh, yeah," Homer said as he inspected Danny closely. "So, Danny! Y'er a fisherman are ya?"

"Yep. But I only go for the Big Ones," Danny replied matter-of-factly.

Homer was impressed. Dad looked at me and grinned. Sergeant Jeff blinked his eyes, bit his tongue, and tried hard not to laugh.

Homer turned back to Dad and initiated the ritual that I knew would determine where and how we would be fishing that day, "What kin I do for you, John?"

"Well, Homer – like Danny said – we wanta go for the Big Ones on the Chippewa. Whatya recommend?"

"I'd recommend hellgrammites for bass. They're hitting 'em right above the dam down at Chippewa Town."

"Hey, that sounds good."

"Yeah. But I ain't got no hellgrammites. All out."

"Oh, that's too bad. What else ya recommend?"

"The pike's been hitting chubs upstream ah the New Albany mill. You know that wide spot you get to from the east side ah the river?"

"Yeah. Sure do? Big pike in there. Sounds good."

"Don't have no chubs, neither."

"Oh, that's a shame. What else ya recommend, then?"

"I'd say rock bass with crickets – down back ah the waterworks – but you wanted tah fish for Big Ones, dint cha?"

"Yeah, but if that's all the bait you got, I guess we'd have a lotta fun with rock bass. Not bad eatin' either. Sure! We could go for them today."

"Ain't got no crickets neither – not in season yet."

At this point, Danny gave me a funny look and whispered, "What does he *got*?"

I ignored him.

"Well, I guess we're skunked," Dad declared with exasperation, following the rules of Homer's ritual.

"Nope, you're not. Largemouth 'er hittin' night crawlers – up just this side ah the campgrounds in Granville Park. Show 'em a lotta worm. Use two hooks on one leader. Or, if you got any them new crawler harnesses, they'd do good," Homer instructed with a sly grin on his face.

"Don't suppose you'd have any night crawlers?"

"Got plenty. Why didn't you ask right off?" Homer chided as he flipped open the top of the nearest crawler box.

Without responding to Homer, Dad smiled softly and winked at Danny and me.

"How about your usual order plus a dozen or two more ta cover the boys?" Homer suggested.

"That'd be good, Homer."

"Eight dozen then. That's four bits."

"Only four bits? You don't wanta charge me that little. Now, do ya, Homer?"

"These is the last ah my crawlers – lot smaller than the first in the batch. Not that these ain't lively enough. But they's on the smallish side. About like biggish angle worms."

Homer filled a tomato juice can with maple leaves from the crawler box. Then he gently transferred each fat wiggling crawler from the box to the can. Ignoring Homer's protests, Dad paid him a full dollar instead of the fifty cents that Homer had insisted on.

As we turned to leave, in uncharacteristic candor, Homer lamented, "Don't know if I kin go on much longer, John."

We all stopped and stared at Homer, while he mounted his crutches, hopped through the doorway, and paused to close the bait shack door behind him. Once again, he turned to Dad with a forlorn look on his face.

"My bait supplier – you know, the Jansen boy – been with me ten years, almost. He just signed up with the Marines to go in after graduatin' high school – in jest ah coupla weeks. I'm down ta about nothin' no more. Don't know if I kin go on much longer without some boy ta help me stock back up – and keep me there."

I looked at Danny. Danny looked at me, nodded his head slightly, and grinned conspiratorially. I got his meaning.

He didn't know 'bait' from 'bananas' a minute ago, now he wants to go into the business! I grumbled to myself.

That's what I thought. But this is what I said, "Maybe Danny and I could help you, Mr. Homer. We could come over and talk about it – tomorrow, if you like – when we're not going fishing."

Dad looked at me proudly. Then he assured Homer, "If Jase says he can help, he can help. If that's okay with you, Homer."

"*Okay* with me? Ha! Who'd you think I had in mind all along, John?"

Homer's face broke into a crinkled smile as he winked at Danny and me.

GOLDEN GLIMMERS OF IMPENDING daylight danced in the eastern sky as we slowly made our way along the dusty, riverside road toward the north end of the park. I pressed my forehead against the car window and stared into the dark, heavily wooded landscape where ghostly forms of idle picnic tables and swing sets patiently awaited the arrival of families with children. The *chinks* of still-hidden cardinals emanated from the shadowy pines.

"Let's park just this side of the campgrounds – below the rapids where we caught that big lunker last year. Remember that, John?" Sergeant Jeff asked, breaking the silence.

"Sure do. That's a good spot, Jeff. About the only place you can turn around – unless you drive all the way up to the turnaround – at the far end of the campgrounds."

"That's right. I wouldn't wanta have ta call a tow truck ta haul my patrol car out of the ditch."

We parked and unloaded the fishing tackle, bait can, and picnic lunch that Aunt Maude had packed the night before. By the time Dad finished showing Danny how to bait his hook, Sergeant Jeff and I had our lines in the swirling, foamy water just below the rapids, the spot where Homer had predicted good luck.

Danny summarized his opinion of hook baiting with one word, "Yug!"

My line floated lazily downstream, toward the old log that was jammed against the rocks on our side of the river. I was about to reel in and recast when – SMACK!

"Holy Smokes!" yelled Danny.

Gritting my teeth, I yanked my rod backward and upward to set the hook. The huge black bass broke the surface and shook his head vigorously, attempting to dislodge my hook.

I had never seen a fish dance like that before. My steel rod bent radically in response to the hefty fish's valiant efforts to escape.

At first, I lost ground. My reel screamed and yards of line payed out as the monster fish, dashing upstream, easily overcame my drag setting. When he reached the rapids, he paused. I took the advantage. With great difficulty, I twisted my reel handle slowly to retrieve my line an inch at a time. The muscles in my forearms ached with fatigue, but I held on stubbornly.

The birds in the trees above us, sensing the drama of the moment, stopped chirping and watched the fight. Danny clicked his tongue and *oowed* every now and then, providing the only sound effects.

"Keep your rod tip up, Jase," Dad gently coached. "That's it. Let him do all the work – 'til he's tired out. Then you can reel him in, easy as pie."

After what seemed like a two-hour battle, my prize fish suddenly surrendered. I reeled the monster to the river's edge. Dad steadied my line, reached down, and hooked his thumb in the fish's mouth. Then he lifted my catch from the water and held it high for all to see. The fish was absolutely gigantic!

"Dad, is he a record-setter?" I panted.

"Well, he's certainly above average for a largemouth – if I don't say so, myself. But I'd guess you're a few pounds shy of a record," Dad speculated. "This uh'll probably run about five pounds. Whatta you think, Jeff?"

"Oh yeah! He's five pounds – easy. Good fish, Jase!" Sergeant Jeff agreed, patting me on the back.

"Can you eat a – a bigmouth?" Danny inquired.

"Largemouth!" I corrected. "Sure. They're as good eatin' as any pan fish."

Danny gave me that look. I knew he wanted to ask, *"What's a pan fish?"* But I didn't give him an opportunity.

Even though I could barely lift my catch, I was bound and determined to be the one to remove the hook. When I finished, Dad slipped my prize onto the stringer and lowered the fish into the water next to the bank. At first, the exhausted fish heeled over but eventually righted itself and began to tug gently against the stringer line that Dad had secured by jamming its pointed metal end-piece into the grassy bank.

"Why don't you take a breather while the rest of us try to find his relatives, Jase?" Dad suggested.

Without further urging, I collapsed on the bank of wispy green grass that still glistened with morning dew. All around me, circles of white mushrooms stood at attention, acclaiming my triumph. I closed my eyes and tried to relax, but I couldn't subdue the raging pride I felt in my chest.

Dad smiled at me. Then he cast his bait well upstream from the log and let it drift down toward the spot where my lunker had been lurking. Sergeant Jeff put his bait in the water as well.

Danny chose to take a fishing time out. Instead, he examined my largemouth, resting in the cool shallows of the Chippewa. He leaned over the bank and cautiously lowered his finger into the water just in front of the big fish's nose. Instantly, the terrified fish recoiled with a splashy lunge that nearly jerked the stringer out of the ground.

Danny leaped back, stumbling over his own feet. His backside smacked down hard against the bank. Immediately, his face clouded over with surprise, fear, or embarrassment, I wasn't sure which. But none of us could help ourselves. We all started laughing. And, finally, so did Danny.

The first catch of the day sharpened our determination to land a real record-setter. We cast our bait back into the roiling waters and waited patiently. Then we cast again and waited. And cast again. And waited. Again and again.

Sergeant Jeff and Dad stood silently, staring intently down their lines into the silvery water. They seemed to be hypnotized. I had seen this phenomenon before, but I honestly didn't understand how it happened. My guess was it occurred after you had fished for a few years and then grew up.

After two hours, two gigantic peanut butter and jelly sandwiches, and two dozen fruitlessly expended night crawlers, both Danny and I were just plain bored.

As the heat of mid-morning descended upon us, we devised ways to stay awake. We dragged our baited hooks in front of my prize fish to tempt him to strike again. We scratched our initials in the mud. We lay back on the grass and examined the intricate lattice of oak branches overhead. We pulled out our jackknives and played mumblety-peg, including the dangerous off-the-tip-of-your-nose variation. Still we were bored.

Finally, I asked, "Dad, can Danny and I go exploring?"

"Huh? Oh, sure! Why don't you hike up into the campgrounds? Maybe you can find some Indian arrowheads along the bank. Used to be a lot of them there. When you get back, we'll sample that leftover chicken and you can count all the fish we'll have caught by then."

While Dad finished chuckling, Danny and I reeled in our lines and stored our casting rods in the open trunk of the police car. Excused from our fishing duties, we marched northward to where the road ran between two huge boulders that jutted out from the dense woods to form a natural entrance gate to the campgrounds. Along the way, we kicked at stones and discussed the profit potential of the wholesale bait business.

Upon entering the campgrounds, the narrow dirt road curved gently to the right, paralleling the course of the river. This curve afforded privacy to the dozen numbered campsites nestled among the tall oaks along the river's edge. We couldn't see more than a couple hundred feet of the road ahead.

As we proceeded northward, we stopped to inspect the picnic tables, stone fireplaces, woodpiles, and trash barrels at each campsite. The soles of busy camper shoes had worn holes in the grass carpeting surrounding the tables and fireplaces. The campsites were surprisingly clean and free from debris.

At the Campsite #11, I pointed out a rusty casting rod, propped against a tree next to the riverbank. "Whosit belong to?" Danny asked.

"Somebody left it there – by mistake – I guess. Nobody's touched it, though. Everybody figured the owner would return someday and claim it. Dad told me it's been here for about ten years now."

"I wonder if it still works."

"I doubt it."

"Maybe we should put up some reward signs around town."

"Reward for doing what?"

Before Danny could contrive one of his clever answers, we rounded the bend and stopped dead in our tracks. We couldn't believe our eyes! There in the turnaround at the end of the road stood Mrs. Libby's blue Plymouth sedan with all four doors wide open.

Without uttering a word, we ducked down and moved off the road into the woods, to our right, away from the river. When we were safely out of sight, Danny whispered nervously, "Do you see anybody? Where are they?"

Before I could answer, we heard giggles, guffaws, and splashes coming from the river. A tall thicket of blackberry bushes between the river and our hiding spot prevented us from seeing who was having all the fun.

"That's got to be them!" I whispered loudly to Danny. "Let's sneak through the woods until we get to the turnaround – over there beyond the car. From there, we should be able to see perfectly."

"Right!" Danny whispered back.

With Danny in the lead, we quietly crouch-walked through the damp woods. When we reached our destination, even though the partying splashers were only fifty yards away, we still couldn't see them. The car was blocking our view.

I grabbed Danny's arm and whispered, "Stay here. I'll crawl under the car and take a look."

Danny nodded and whispered back, "Don't forget!"

"Don't forget what?"

"Shoot first and ask questions later!"

Geez! I had almost forgotten that we were dealing with armed desperados. I shook my head at my partner's untimely attempt at humor, lowered my body to the road, and crawled carefully toward the sound of raucous laughter and water play.

When I reached the other side of the car, I lifted my head and cautiously peered toward the river. There they were! The Huns and their

Honeys! Those Nazi-Loving Girls! Those Small-Town Tootsies, playing splashy-water with their POW Pals.

At first, my cheeks burned with anger and disgust. Then my stomach knotted with fear. However, I had accomplished my objective, a confirmed sighting of the two escaped Nazis and the Libby sisters.

But now, it was time for reinforcements. We had to get back to Sergeant Jeff and Dad. They would know what to do. I reversed course and crawled back toward Danny, the woods, and safety. I cleared the edge of the car and stood up expecting to find Danny where I'd left him.

But he was nowhere in sight! Panic!

"Danny! Danny! Where are you?" I whispered frantically.

I scanned the woods to the south, half-expecting to spot him high-tailing it toward the protection of Dad and Sergeant Jeff.

"Here I am!"

I nearly jumped out of my skin. The voice had come from inside the car behind me. Reflexively, I turned around and saw Danny sprawled out on the front seat.

"What are you doing in there?"

"Just looking around."

"Geez! You scared me to death. Let's get out of here," I ordered as I hunched down and began crouch-running back into the woods.

As we rounded the curve in the road, Campground #12 disappeared from sight behind us. So we un-crouched and veered out of the woods, up onto the gravel road. Once there, we ran as fast as we could back to our fishing spot.

Sergeant Jeff and Dad snapped out of their spells when they heard our noisy, high-speed approach. They stared at us with concern. We stopped and pointed toward the campgrounds.

Catching my breath, I stammered, "It's them. The Libby girls – and the two escaped POWs!"

Between gasps, Danny added, "They got – Mrs. Libby's car, too!"

"Lord! Did they see you?" Sergeant Jeff asked excitedly, instinctively reaching for his pistol that today was in the glove compartment of the patrol car, instead of at his side.

"No! They were too busy playing in the water. They look like they're on vacation – or something," I sputtered indignantly.

"John, we gotta get some help out here. These guys could be armed – and they're certainly dangerous. This isn't even in our jurisdiction. This is Sheriff Connors' territory. But we're here. So we gotta do something before these rats escape again."

"Boys! Are they armed? Did you see any guns of any kind?"

We shook our heads no.

"Where exactly are they?"

We told him Campsite #12, the last one in the campgrounds, next to the turnaround where the Libby car was parked.

Sergeant Jeff was quiet for a few seconds. Then he announced his plan.

"Okay, here's what we're going to do."

First, Sergeant Jeff would radio the Riverton Police dispatcher and explain the situation. Then he would ask to be patched through to the sheriff's office, so he could request reinforcements. Once reinforcements were on the way, he would pull his police car up to the campgrounds entrance and park it between the boulders, thus preventing the POWs from escaping by car.

After that, he would sneak up through the woods and keep his eyes on the fugitives until reinforcements arrived. At that point, he was certain, the sheriff would deploy his deputies to surround the foursome before closing in for the arrest.

"How does that sound to you guys?"

We approved.

Sergeant Jeff headed for his car radio to launch his plan. All went well with the dispatcher. Every deputy the sheriff could muster, a squadron of MPs from Camp Riverton, and as many officers as the Riverton Police could spare would soon be on their way.

Apparently, the sheriff had made it very clear that he wasn't planning to contact the Michigan State Police or the FBI. "They're too busy manning roadblocks down at the state line," the sheriff had insisted. "Besides, these are local girls – and local POWs, for that matter – so, I want to make this arrest with local officers of the law."

Sergeant Jeff suggested we leave our fishing equipment where it was and ride with him in the police car to the campground entrance where he would establish the roadblock. We all piled into the car. That's when Sergeant Jeff's well-laid plan disintegrated.

"Drat! I can't believe it. We musta left the door open. Maybe the overhead light was on. Or, you don't suppose, it was that little trunk light, do ya? Doesn't matter. This battery's dead as a doornail. We can't use the car for a roadblock. At least, the radio has its own battery. We can still communicate," Sergeant Jeff rationalized, trying to extract some good news from the bad.

"They could escape by car at any time now!" Dad declared apprehensively. "How long – ya think – before the sheriff arrives?"

"Guess another twenty – thirty minutes. I told them not to use their sirens. And not to use the radio either. I don't want our Nazi buddies to hear 'em coming."

"That makes sense!"

"Well, shoot! I guess I'd better radio in and tell them about my dead battery. Boy! This is embarrassing!"

Sergeant Jeff lifted the hand mike and broke the bad news to the dispatcher.

When he finished, Dad had an idea of his own. "Jeff, somehow, we gotta stop 'em from getting away in that car before the sheriff gets here!"

"I was just thinkin' the same thing," Sergeant Jeff agreed. "Bad enough having a dead battery. But if I don't do something – and they escape again! I gotta prevent them from using that car to get away. If they try, maybe I can get the drop on them – even without reinforcements. But I'll need help from you guys."

He explained what he had in mind.

"It's a little risky, Jeff. But, if we stay down and out of sight, I think it'll be safe enough," Dad concluded. "You agree, boys?"

Casting aside all caution, we nodded our heads. Sergeant Jeff and adrenalin were in charge of our destinies. Sergeant Jeff nodded resolutely and retrieved his pistol from the car.

According to plan, we crept through the woods and took our places. Sergeant Jeff's spot was just off the turnaround, immediately behind the car. That way, he could jump out and get the drop on the POWs if they attempted to drive away. The rest of us assumed positions on either side of Sergeant Jeff. We had the car completely surrounded from our hiding places behind the thick bushes that ringed the turnaround.

We watched the two couples sprawled on blankets on the soft grass next to the picnic table. They ate from tin cans warmed in the fireplace and drank wine from a bottle, identical to the other bottles strewn around their campsite. Time passed very slowly.

Then it happened!

In the far distance, we heard the faint whine of a police siren heading our way. Obviously, somebody hadn't gotten the word on the need for a silent approach. We weren't the only ones who heard the siren!

Baden and Reitter jumped to their feet, speaking rapidly in German. They slipped on their shoes and ran for the car. The girls gathered their towels around themselves and ran after the two men, pleading not to be left behind. The Nazis ignored them.

When the POWs reached the car, Sergeant Jeff stepped out of the bushes with his pistol drawn.

"Hands up! Put 'em behind your head! Step back away from that car!" he ordered, sounding utterly determined.

Whether they understood English or not, the startled POWs did exactly as Sergeant Jeff demanded. When he found himself in complete control, Sergeant Jeff further reinforced his position by shouting at his "backups."

"Keep 'em covered, boys! You got that, John?"

A deep voice came from the bushes to Sergeant Jeff's right, "Check! Sergeant Tolna!"

"Officer Daniel?"

A not-so-deep but gruff-sounding voice came from the bushes to Sergeant Jeff's left, "Check! Sergeant Tolna! I got 'em in my sights! Just let 'em try something!"

Geez! I thought. *Not now, Danny!*

"Officer Jason?" Sergeant Tolna barked.

My voice added its authority, such as it was, from the bushes, "Check. Mister – ah – Sergeant Tolna!"

The Germans were clearly impressed. Everything was going well until the girls appeared on the scene.

Anne Libby shouted at Sergeant Jeff, "How dare you spoil our fun! Haven't you ever been young – and in love? What's the harm?"

She moved closer to Sergeant Jeff.

"Stand back, Anne! Stand away from those prisoners!" he ordered, waving his police revolver to make the point.

His words must have given her sister an idea. Barb lapsed into a hysterical fit and threw herself at Baden. Then she turned to face Sergeant Jeff, putting her back against Baden's chest. Dramatically, she extended her arms to protect her dear POW.

Baden evidently didn't feel very protected. He took matters into his own hands. He brutally seized Barb and, using her as a shield, stepped backward toward the open car door.

Once in position, he pushed her away and jumped behind the steering wheel. At that instant, both girls converged on Sergeant Jeff, wrapped their arms around his chest and pinned his revolver arm to his side. Helplessly, he watched Reitter dive for the backseat and slam the door.

We expected an immediate roar of the car engine. But nothing happened. Baden just sat there, motionless, behind the steering wheel.

Finally, Sergeant Jeff freed himself from the tangle of sobbing Libby girls and leveled his gun on the POWs in the car.

"Get out of there!" he roared.

Baden slumped over the steering wheel. Then he slowly opened the car door and stepped outside with Reitter. Both raised their hands submissively. This time, they looked totally defeated.

Sergeant Jeff's timing was perfect.

At that very moment, the caravan of sheriff vehicles, police cars, and Army MP jeeps roared through the campgrounds entrance gate. Within seconds, a small army of law enforcement officials encircled Mrs. Libby's Plymouth.

We decided it was safe to come out of the woods.

Sheriff Connors patted Sergeant Jeff on the back. "Nice job, Jeff. Well done! Who are these other fellows? Your deputies?"

Naturally, Danny took another deep, sweeping bow.

LATER THAT AFTERNOON, MORE than just reporters crowded the high school auditorium for Sheriff Connors' press briefing. News of how Sergeant Tolna, with help from John Addison and the two boys, had apprehended four dangerous fugitives spread like wildfire. Evidently, everybody in Riverton decided to attend the briefing to hear the fantastic story first hand.

The auditorium was filled to capacity. People crowded outside the bank of doors, hoping to catch a glimpse of the local heroes. Those close enough to hear relayed the questions and answers over their shoulders so their neighbors behind them heard the news almost as soon as they did.

Sergeant Tolna, dressed in his best uniform, Dad, Danny, and I joined Sheriff Connors on stage. We were his only interviewees for the afternoon briefing. Mrs. Tolna, Mr. and Mrs. Tucker, Mom, and Aunt Maude were given front row seats. Excited reporters, city dignitaries, and a few lucky Riverton citizens filled the rest of the auditorium.

What an assemblage!

After the sheriff's brief statement, the reporters peppered each of us with about four hundred thousand questions. Yes, we'd gone fishing. Caught only one fish. A five-pound largemouth bass. Still on a stringer out in Granville Park, we supposed. Yes, we changed our voices to fool the POWs. Sure, we could demonstrate, "Check! Sergeant Tolna!" It went on and on. And on.

After three hours, Sheriff Connors pointed at a haughty newsman in the front row and spoke those long-awaited words, "This will be the last question, ladies and gentlemen."

The newsman, recognizing the significance of being last to ask a question, made the best of it.

"I'm still perplexed by one aspect of your story. It just doesn't make sense to me. When the POWs jumped into the car –."

He paused for dramatic effect. Then he continued, "Why did they just sit there instead of starting that engine and making their getaway? Do any of you know what stopped them?"

The arrogant reporter *demanded* an answer to his question by pointing at each of us seated on the stage, "What is your answer, sir? No idea. Hmmm. And you, sir? No idea. Hmmm."

Danny was the last interviewee to be polled. When the intimidating finger pointed at him, Danny reached into his pocket and pulled out the answer. He held it high for the astonished crowd to see.

"Maybe *this* had something to do with it!"

It was Mrs. Libby's ignition key!

15 NIGHT CRAWLERS

BADEN AND REITTER WERE STALKING ME FROM BEHIND the blackberry bushes next to Sergeant Jeff's police car. Out of the corner of my eye, I saw that each of them was armed with a tommy gun, a Luger automatic, a dozen German-style hand grenades, and a silver samurai sword. They were wearing their full-dress SS uniforms with shiny black knee boots and striking red, black, and white swastika armbands.

But I didn't allow their presence to distract me from my primary mission, landing the 250-pound largemouth that I had hooked in the swift current of the Chippewa. The behemoth was nearly whipped. Two more days – three at the most – of strenuous struggle, and I'd land that husky record-setter.

A scratchy voice from Sergeant Jeff's car radio behind me caught my attention. Holding my rod in one hand, I sidled to the car and snatched up the microphone. The dispatcher repeated his call.

"*J a a a a a a a a a a a a a a a s e . C a a a a a a a a a a a a a a a a a a a a a a a a a n . Youuuuuuuuuuuuuuuuuuuuuuu. Cuuuuuuuuuuuuum. Ooooooooooooout?*"

I shook the sleep from my head, tumbled out of bed, and slipped into my clothes. Then I headed for the kitchen to greet my fellow "Hero of Granville Park" as Aunt Maude had dubbed us last night.

Drowsily, I gazed out the screen door. It was Danny all right. Dressed in his standard weekday uniform, he was carrying a – what? Was it a butterfly net?

Upon closer inspection, I realized he was holding a former mop handle. A heavy wire loop was fastened to the handle's end with badly bent staples, evidently the result of inept hammering. Netting of fine white cheesecloth, fashioned from what was once a window sheer, had been attached to the loop by twisted bobby pins. Queenie's best, I surmised.

"Let's catch us some crawlers!" Danny proposed, smiling too cheerfully for this early in the day.

I didn't have the heart to tell my comrade how night crawlers were really caught.

After a simple breakfast of rye bread sandwiches – prunes, pickles, and black walnut meats with mayonnaise, mustard, and paprika – we headed for Homer Lyle's bait shop.

We were extremely excited about the prospects of becoming bait moguls. Danny's new crawler net bobbed up and down in time with our enthusiastic chorus of *Under the Double*. As we followed the familiar route past the swamp, waterworks, and foundry, we arrived in no time.

In response to our knock, Mrs. Lyle answered the door. She stared quizzically at Danny's net. Then she said, "Hello, boys. Homer's expecting you. He'll be here in a minute. Oh, I have somethin' for you."

She gave us each two warm butter cookies. "To keep away the hungrys," she explained with a wink.

We spent our waiting time constructively, munching and inventorying important things. We tallied 36 clothespins clipped to Mrs. Lyle's clothesline and 18 bright blue morning glory blossoms decorating the lattice next to the porch. Seven black-brown starlings picked at seeds and grubs in the small patch of fescue centered in the Lyle backyard. Twelve old license plates were neatly nailed to the wall just inside the open garage door. One of them came from Pennsylvania!

We were just counting the silver-headed roofing nails that held the tar paper in place over the forsaken bait shack window when we were interrupted by Homer's *clump-clump-clump*. As he pushed the screen door open with his crutch, he greeted us with a crooked smile.

"Howdy, boys! See you're up before breakfast."

Danny gave me a knowing look. I winked back.

"Good morning, Mr. Homer," we both replied.

Homer puffed down the steps and hummed his way to the bait shack. "Let's talk out here. That way, I kin show you things."

After Homer assumed his normal position on his stool, he announced, "Before we get down ta bait business, I gotta know how yer fishin' went yesterday."

I described exactly what had happened. Not wanting to sound boastful, I carefully omitted the part about the POWs and the Libby sisters.

"We used casting rods with night crawlers strung on two hooks – on one leader. We fished near that old log just downstream from the rapids on the upper end of Granville Park. Four of us only had one strike all morning – my first cast – I caught a five-pound largemouth. He looked real healthy – no grubs burrowing into his back, like some fish you see toward the end of summer."

"How'd the crawlers hold up in them rapids there?"

"They were firm and rubbery. So they stayed on the hook a good long time. We kept them in the shade – in your can with the maple leaves. We wet them down a little every hour or so. That kept them fresh and wiggly."

This pleased him.

"Keep in mind – if crawlers ever gets woozy on ya, just add some coffee grounds. Perks 'em right up."

We nodded our understanding.

Then Homer reflected on his words. "Ha! Coffee *perks* 'em up! That's a good one!"

As Homer finished chuckling, I realized that I had reported every nuance of our fishing experience. Now, I understood why Homer's fishing recommendations were so timely and reliable.

Later, I would learn that some of his regular customers didn't care to take time for Homer's lengthy interrogation after their fishing trips. But he never let these too-busy people know that he was disappointed. Instead, he simply removed them from the list of those who benefited from his valuable tips.

Danny summed it up beautifully, "You scratch my hand, and I wash yours!"

When I had finished my report and answered each question to his complete satisfaction, Homer was content to move on. Getting down to business, he reached into his back trouser pocket and removed a carefully folded piece of white lined paper.

"I made a sumry, so's you know what I need – and how much you make if you supply me with it – givin' today's prices ah course."

He handed the paper to me. Fascinated, I unfolded it quickly. I leaned toward Danny, so he could read it, too. Homer's summary was written in the same shaky, old-fashioned style that characterized Grandma Compton's handwriting. Like Grandma, he used a sharp-pointed pen and black ink.

The summary spanned four columns with these headings:

1. Bait   2. Unit   3. Price (6/44)   4. Supplier Share

In the "Bait" column, Homer had listed the various baits comprising his "ideal" inventory:

- **Night Crawlers - Large**
- **Night Crawlers - Small**
- **Fishing Worms**
- **Crickets**
- **Hellgrammites**
- **Crabs (Crawfish)**
- **Suckers**
- **Chubs**
- **Shiners**
- **Corn Borers**
- **Mice (Live)**

The third and fourth columns were by far the most interesting to Danny and me. The amounts shown there indicated that Homer was proposing an equal partnership. For example, his current price for a dozen "Night Crawlers - Small " was "12 cents" and his "Supplier Share" was exactly half that amount, "6 cents."

Danny and I nodded our agreement and sealed the deal by enthusiastically shaking Homer's gnarled hand. We were elated! Homer was ecstatic! We were his new bait suppliers.

But his jubilant mood quickly changed to a more serious one, befitting the importance of the training that he was about to present. We sat on the floor slats with our backs against the wall and prepared ourselves to receive Homer's wisdom.

His first lecture was on night crawlers.

"Most himportin' step in ketchin' crawlers is lawn waterin'. Soon after sunset, fresh-watered lawns yields dozuns of long, fat, healthy crawlers. Yah use a good flashlight and creep up on 'em – real quiet. You'll ah see 'em all stretched out – ta almost their full linth. Jest the tips ah their tails stuck down their hole, for ah quick escape if yah ain't fasta nuff.

"Good crawler hunters uses ah light touch when snatchin' up crawlers. That's the only way not ta hurt 'em. Your grab's got ta be quick and firm enough ta git 'em. But light enough ta not sqwash 'em."

Homer's first lecture lasted a good hour, covering every aspect of catching, storing, and feeding night crawlers. I could have used a bit of a break between lectures, but Homer began our second lecture without pausing. The subject was an overview of the other baits in his desired inventory.

"You need ta learn the trade of huntin' and gatherin' all different kindsa bait. The Jansen boy – who's helped me goin' on ten years almost – has promised ta work with ya afore he goes off with the Marines. He'll show ya everthin.' The best spots in town ta kitch suckers and chubs – and ta net shiners. The location of all the stony shoals in the Chippewa – and the exact times during the year – that produces the big takes of crabs and hellgrammites. He knows it all."

After another hour, Homer's second lecture finally came to a close. We thanked Homer profusely for sharing his experience. We were now fully prepared to assume our role as his bait suppliers.

As Homer was closing the bait shack door, Danny candidly admitted that he had heard of "hellgrammite" before but had always believed it to be one of those traditionalist religious sects, something close in philosophy to the Mennonites.

Homer responded with a loud snort.

Although I tried not to, I guffawed like Grandma Compton.

Waggling his crawler net, Danny graced us with his impish grin.

ON OUR WAY HOME, Danny and I compared the attributes of the bait business with those of the sauerkraut-bubble gum game. After our recent POW adventures, we agreed that we preferred dealing with worms of the *crawler* variety to those of the *SS* variety.

As we walked up Forrest Street, I saw Aunt Maude heading our way from the bus stop. At the same time, Mom emerged from the house with her broom and began sweeping the porch.

When Aunt Maude came within shouting distance of the house, she yelled, "Guess who's out of jail?"

"Who?" Mom asked.

"Sheriff Connors released the Libby girls this morning. Just heard it from the bus driver," Aunt Maude announced. "Reporters had a field day interviewing the girls on the front steps of the county jail. And apparently the girls put on quite a show."

"You gotta be kidding! I thought they were on their way to prison – or even worse," Mom said, shaking her head in disbelief. "Wonder if Louise knows."

We stood there contemplating this latest twist in the Libby case when Sergeant Jeff's black police cruiser rounded the corner, crawled down Forrest Street, and stopped under our box elder. He greeted us as he opened the car trunk, "Hi, Maude. Marie. Boys! I figured you might want your fishing tackle."

Danny and I walked out to meet him.

"Just got my car back. Needed a new battery. Rods and tackle box for you, boys. And your picnic basket, Maude. Nary a leftover, thank you. Jase, I have some bad news for you," he said, handing me the empty stringer.

"Oh, no! Where's my bass?"

"I'm afraid it was stolen – and eaten. But we know who did it, if that's any consolation. They left their footprints in the mud."

"Who?"

"An otter family. I'd say a mother and two young ones from their tracks. So your prize fish went for a good cause."

"Aw, nuts! I wanted Mom and Aunt Maude to see it."

Sergeant Jeff patted my shoulder and smiled, "Next time!"

Then he turned to Mom and Aunt Maude, "Heard the news?"

"Maude just told us. How on earth did Sheriff Connors justify letting them go – after all that treason talk?"

"The sheriff never wanted to charge them in the first place. You know how softhearted he is. He told reporters that the girls may have been dumb, but they weren't criminals – let alone traitors."

"I agree with the *dumb* part," Aunt Maude said.

"The sheriff said that the girls aren't Nazi sympathizers. Just did it on a lark. He said he couldn't hold them in jail for an act of juvenile delinquency. They aren't even twenty-one years old, yet."

"Did he talk to any – any higher authority – before releasing them?"

"Yeah, he did. Apparently, he called somebody he knows – a federal prosecutor – down in Detroit. Got the guy to agree with his position. So, this morning, he just let 'em go."

We shook our heads in amazement. *What next?* I asked myself.

"When I first heard about this mess, I felt real sorry for the Libby girls – and even more so for Louise Libby. But, after learning how they acted out in Granville Park – to be honest, I've stopped feeling sorry for them," Mom admitted.

We all nodded our agreement.

"As a matter of fact, I'm still a bit peeved!" Mom continued, encouraged by our support. "They endangered your lives out there.

That includes John and the boys! The least they deserve is a – good spanking or something. But sounds like the sheriff's let 'em off the hook, altogether. He's a good man, but sometimes he's too lenient."

"Well, we may not have heard the last of it," Sergeant Jeff said with a twinkle in his eye.

"Is there something you haven't told us?" Aunt Maude wanted to know.

"This isn't for publication, but my chief talked to one of the FBI guys. Apparently, they're really miffed. For starters, the Sheriff didn't call the FBI to join him in the arrest. And, if you recall, they were the ones who talked about treason charges in the first place. I'd say the girls aren't out of the woods, yet. They could still be rearrested by the FBI – and charged with a serious crime."

"Holy Double Crow!" Danny spouted.

"You can say that again!" Mom agreed. "This is nerve-racking!"

"I'll keep you informed," Sergeant Jeff promised as he drove off.

On our way into the house, Mom inquired, "By the way, Maude, what are you doing home so early?"

"The store manager let me off – my reward for double duty during the reporter siege. But I don't know what to do with myself!" Aunt Maude confessed. "Maybe I'll take in a movie."

"Oh, no you don't! I've got a job for you. You're going help me do something with the four chickens Ma dropped off this morning."

"Four chickens! Where'd she get four chickens? Are they some of her layers? The leghorns aren't ready for plucking yet."

"She told me she traded for them – with Mrs. Henry."

"Lord, isn't she something? I wonder what she gave Mrs. Henry in return. Has anybody seen Pa lately? How many chickens is an old farmer with one blind eye worth nowadays?"

We all snickered at that one.

"I was thinking, maybe we can roast one for supper and boil the others for soup. Whatcha think?"

"Boy, that'll be a lot of chicken soup. What're we going to do with all of it?"

"I could use two quarts of chicken soup – for a special purpose. Would that be all right, Mom? Aunt Maude?" I asked.

Aunt Maude glanced at Mom and furrowed her brow. But then, they both nodded yes.

"Thanks. And Mom, can Danny and I water the lawn?"

Being unfamiliar with the nuances of night crawler hunting, Mom looked a bit surprised before saying, "Sure! It could use some watering."

WE CONNECTED THE HOSE to the spigot under my bedroom window. Then we attached the brand new lawn sprinkler that Aunt Maude had bought for Mom at Woolworth's. Its colorful porcelain head was shaped like an open pond lily.

When we turned on the hose, the fine spray from a dozen small holes in the delicate lily petals fell broadly across the backyard grass. Danny and I sat on the porch steps and watched as the bright midday sun painted miniature rainbows on the clouds of mist drifting over the garden.

Out of the blue, Danny declared, "Boy! I'm really hot!"

Suddenly, he tore off shoes and socks and raced toward the sprinkler. With a powerful leap, he attempted to fly through the spray. But he had misjudged his launch point by a yard or so. Instead of jumping over the sprinkler, he landed on one bare foot, smack in the center of the porcelain lily's array of razor-sharp petals.

Danny's momentum carried him beyond the hazardous sprinkler. He landed on his backside in the grass at the edge of the garden. Looking stunned, he just sat there holding his left ankle and moaning strangely. Blood gushed from an S-shaped gash on the bottom of his foot. It was ghastly!

"Mom! Mom! Come quick! Danny's really hurt!" I screamed.

Mom took one look out the screen door. Then she shouted to Aunt Maude, "Bring lots of towels! Hurry!"

Mom quickly brought Danny's bleeding under control by tightly wrapping towels around the injured foot. Then she laid down her plan, "Danny needs stitches. We have to get him to Dr. Moran's – right away. Jase! Run as fast as you can to the Tucker house. Tell them what's happened. Get Mrs. Tucker to bring her car here – and hurry!"

I sped down the alley and crossed Chester Street. Before arriving at the Tucker house, I saw that their station wagon was nowhere in sight. Nonetheless, I pounded and pounded on the back door. When no one answered, I ran to Mr. Tucker's garage and pushed the side door open. The garage was empty.

I returned home at top speed. "Nobody's home! Their car's gone!" I yelled, running through the garden.

"Okay. We'll use my backup plan, then. Maude! It's almost time for the two o'clock New Albany bus. Run to the corner and flag him down. Then wait for us. Don't let that bus leave without Danny!"

"I don't like doctor's offices," Danny muttered, his first intelligible words since his tragic leap.

We gave his comment what it deserved, benign neglect. He didn't seem to mind.

"Jase! Zip down to the Tolnas and borrow Sherm's wagon. Go!"

I shot by the cottonwood and down the street to the Tolna yard. I grabbed Sherm's pre-war model and retraced my steps in record time.

Mom and I lifted Danny into the wagon. Mom grabbed the wagon tongue and gave me some additional orders, "Go inside and make sure the chicken soup is on the lowest burner setting. Then turn off the hose. After that, meet us at the bus stop."

After completing my assignments, I ran to the stop. The bus had just arrived. Mom and Aunt Maude conferred hurriedly with Mr. Smalley. He nodded and lifted Danny out of the wagon.

He deposited Danny on the seat next to Aunt Maude who caringly put her arm around the shivering boy. Mom and I took our seats. Mr. Smalley left the bus one more time to deposit Sherm's wagon in the luggage compartment.

A corner of the towel fell from Danny's foot. I could see that he had lost a lot of blood. His face was pale and moist with perspiration. He caught me staring at him. Instead of saying anything, he just stuck out his tongue at me. I laughed, and he laughed back.

He'd be okay!

Dr. Moran's office was located in the former dining room, parlor, and maid's quarters of his family's huge Victorian house. It was situated on a large wooded lot about two blocks from the bus stop. We thanked Mr. Smalley, bid him farewell, and quickly hauled Danny to the Moran office-house.

When we arrived, Mom and Aunt Maude went inside leaving Danny and me on the front walk. Seconds later, Dr. Moran bounded down the porch steps toward us.

"Back for more tongue depressors, eh?" he quipped, gently lifting Danny from the wagon. "I know your game, young man."

Danny didn't laugh. He looked frightened and frail. Mom followed Danny and the doctor through the front door, across the reception area, and into the inner examining room. The nurse hovered nearby. Aunt Maude and I trailed along behind. We stayed long enough to hear the doctor's initial assessment of Danny's wound. But the room was small and crowded, so we decided to wait outside.

Aunt Maude and I sat silently in white wicker chairs on the wide wrap-around front porch. We watched a pair of reddish-brown fox squirrels chase one another up and down the massive elm trees that canopied the Moran property. A clap of thunder and a gust of wind announced a heavy rainstorm that burst from the dark clouds above the elms. The squirrels scattered and the temperature immediately dropped a good twenty degrees. We stared at the stream of water gushing from the downspouts out onto the front lawn.

After the storm had settled into a steady downpour, I asked Aunt Maude, "Do you think Danny will be able to walk okay?"

"Remember, Doctor Moran said that it was a bad cut, but a lucky one. It didn't damage any of Danny's tendons – or bones – or anything."

"Oh, yeah. I forgot."

Aunt Maude smiled at me, and then she declared, "I know what I'm going to do when I get home."

"What?"

"I'm going to take a hammer to that horrible lawn sprinkler. The edges of those lily petals are as sharp as razor blades! Then I'm going to tell Mr. Powell – at the Woolworth store – to take those deadly weapons off the shelf. And another thing. I'm paying for this doctor's visit. No argument about it."

I knew she was right. There would be no argument about it. Not when Aunt Maude made up her mind.

Just then, Dad's car pulled alongside the curb.

"How'd you know we were here?" Aunt Maude asked as he came up the steps.

"I stopped at Pete's before going home. He told me the whole story. He watched all the action from his store window."

"Doesn't anything happen in the neighborhood without everybody knowing about it?"

"Nope!" Dad said. "Thank goodness."

Danny babbled incessantly all the way home. Keeping time with Dad's windshield wipers, he never missed a beat.

Back. When he grew up he would be a doctor.

Forth. Doctors were good guys.

Back. Doctors had pretty nurses.

Forth. He liked wearing Dr. Moran's stress-a-scope.

Back. Does every doctor have a little rubber hammer?

Forth. He would have two rubber hammers when he became a doctor.

Back. He had nineteen more stitches now.

Forth. Would he get a prize for having accumulated two dozen?

Back. Who wants a tongue depressor?

On the subject of tongues, I began to wish that Dr. Moran had put a stitch or two in Danny's.

Dad had pinned a note on the Tucker backdoor to let them know what had happened to Danny. When we pulled into the Tucker driveway, the note was gone. Just as Dad was poised to knock, Mrs. Tucker threw open the door. She looked terrified.

"He's fine. He's fine. He's out in the car."

"Thank God!" she declared with relief.

"Dr. Moran says he'll need to stay off his left foot for a few days and keep the dressing dry – until the stitches come out – in ten days."

Mrs. Tucker nodded her head, absorbing Dad's words.

"We're sure sorry. Our new sprinkler had razor-sharp edges. My sister-in-law – Maude – gave us the sprinkler. Maude feels responsible, so she paid for the doctor's visit."

"That wasn't necessary. Boys will be boys, for crying out loud! Is she in the car? I'll go talk to her."

"Well, you're welcome to try. But once Maude makes up her mind – "

Dad was right. Mrs. Tucker couldn't convince Aunt Maude to change her mind.

A light rain was still falling, so Dad covered Danny's wounded foot with his hat before carrying him inside. I followed along pulling Sherm's wagon. We left it with Mrs. Tucker in case she wanted to haul Danny somewhere before he was back on his feet.

Just as we were saying goodbye, Mr. Tucker pulled into the driveway with his station wagon fully loaded with used tires. Dad briefed Mr. Tucker while I returned to the house to promise Danny I would come by to see him in the morning.

Then we headed for home.

AFTER A LONG FAMILY conversation about the Libby girls, Mom and Aunt Maude went back to their chicken project. Dad and I adjourned to the back porch. The rain had finally stopped. The breeze was soft and balmy. We were in for a lovely evening.

"With all that's gone on, I forgot to ask. How'd your discussions with Homer go?"

I told Dad all about our visit with Homer.

"That sounds good. Yes, sir. A real business opportunity. I'm proud of you, son."

I leaned back in my porch chair and enjoyed the warmth in my chest created by Dad's words.

As an afterthought, Dad reflected, "You might say that Danny's injury was caused – at least, indirectly – by night crawlers. Sad thing is – after this nice rain – you wouldn't have needed to water after all."

"Yeah. And, now, I've lost my crawler hunting partner – even before his first night on the job."

"Well, I wouldn't mind filling in for him. Haven't gathered crawlers for a long time. I need some practice!"

"Great! Thanks, Dad."

"Hey in there! That soup sure smells good!" Dad hollered into the kitchen through the window.

"Good timing. Lookie here!" Mom held up a quart of marvelous saffron-colored soup for us to admire.

"Could I please have my two quarts now?" I asked.

"They're here waiting for you. It's darn good soup, if I don't say so myself," Aunt Maude bragged.

I wrapped the two, still-hot jars in Mom's red checked dishtowels and nestled them in Aunt Maude's picnic basket. Then I carefully carried the basket down the back steps and headed for the cottonwood tree. Over my shoulder, I heard Aunt Maude say to Dad, "Now, where do you suppose he's going with that soup?"

I knocked and waited. I was very nervous. It seemed to take forever for someone to answer the door. Finally, I heard footsteps.

When she opened the door, I smiled and said, "I owe you an apology, Mrs. Zeyer."

"LOSE SOMETHING OUT THERE?"

"Very funny!"

Mom chuckled. Then she posed a serious question, "Really, how're you guys doing?"

"Marie, you wouldn't believe the number of night crawlers in this yard. But it's been, what? Three – or maybe four – years since I hunted them last. They've really multiplied since then."

"How many you got so far?"

"I got about two-thirds of a coffee can. How 'bout you, Jase?"

"About half a can."

"Do you know that it's almost eleven o'clock?"

Neither Dad nor I answered. We were too preoccupied with our search for crawlers.

"I'll help if you want," Mom volunteered.

"Swell. There's a flashlight in the nightstand on my side of the bed. I think the battery's good. Oh! You'll need a container. And will you turn off that porch light, too? It's easier to see with just a flashlight. Besides, I don't want to get in trouble with Mr. Shurtleif for not observing the blackout."

"There's no air-raid drill tonight, Dad."

"I know. Just kidding."

Mom disappeared into the house. A minute later, she joined us in the backyard. The three of us were hunched over looking for prey when Aunt Maude came out on the porch.

"You guys lose something out there?"

"Very funny," Mom responded. "If you're so clever, why don't you join us?"

"Sounds like fun! I fell asleep reading the paper – if you can believe it. Woke up and there wasn't anybody in the house. Got an extra flashlight?"

"There's one in the glove compartment of the car, Maude," Dad advised. "And you'll need a tin can to put your crawlers in, too."

The four of us were quietly bent over with our cans and flashlights when we heard a voice from the Reilly's backyard, "You lose something over there, Addisons?"

"Gathering night crawlers. Wanta try your hand?" Dad inquired, only half serious.

"Gee! I haven't done that for a long time. I'll get my flashlight and be right over."

"You need a can or something to put them in, Mr. Reilly," I hollered.

In a few minutes, I looked up to see two flashlights, coming across our backyard from the direction of the Reilly house.

"Mrs. Reilly wants to give 'er a try, too."

"Evening, everybody. Beautiful night for crawling!" Mrs. Reilly quipped cheerfully.

The Reillys were truly good neighbors. Whenever I saw them, I thought of the warm and familiar ritual that I often observed from the vantage point of my high-flying backyard swing.

The Reillys kept a flock of eight fat Plymouth Rocks, all hens and apparently good layers. Their coop, a makeshift addition to the garage, consisted of a bank of straw-filled nesting boxes surrounded by a tall cage of chicken wire.

Upon his return from work each afternoon, Mr. Reilly entered the wire enclosure, tiptoeing carefully to avoid stepping on his hens or their freshest droppings. After feeding his hungry flock, he gathered their day's output of eggs. He gently deposited each egg into his gray felt fedora.

Then he closed the coop and hurried toward the back porch to present his prizes to Mrs. Reilly. Dressed in a freshly laundered apron and iron-touched housedress, she sat on the porch glider with patiently folded hands awaiting his arrival. After a dozen approving *clucks*, she pecked Mr. Reilly on the cheek, and arm-in-arm they disappeared through the screen door into their kitchen with the hatful of eggs.

I took pleasure in being the vicarious beneficiary of their daily ritual.

"We heard about little Danny. How's he doing?" Mrs. Reilly inquired.

We updated her on Danny's status. She ensured us that any boy needing stitches twice in the same month was definitely a record-setter. We all snickered at that.

"What are you going to do with all these night crawlers, anyway?" Mrs. Reilly asked after a few minutes of silent hunting.

"We're putting them in Jase's college fund," Mom laughed. "Jase, why don't your tell Mr. and Mrs. Reilly about your new business partnership with Mr. Lyle?"

The Reillys were impressed with our new venture. They would be pleased to contribute their night crawlers. We could water their lawn anytime. Mrs. Reilly suggested that if the five of us hunted every night for the rest of the summer, we could easily pay for my freshman year at Harvard. I respectfully informed her that Harvard didn't meet my standards. I was going to Michigan.

"You lose something out there?"

The voice came from behind the blinding beam of Mr. Shurtleif's official Air-Raid Warden flashlight.

"Come join the party!" invited Mrs. Reilly. "Where's Mrs. Shurtleif? We're helping to send Jase off to the University of Michigan come fall!"

Two more flashlights joined the hunt. After a few minutes, Mrs. Shurtleif asked, "You know what would taste good right now?"

Then she answered her own question, "Some of Mrs. Mikas' sugar cookies."

We all moaned with pleasure at her suggestion.

Like an echo, we heard, "I heer dat. Mrs. Meekas ist komming."

Dad stood up and aimed his broad flashlight beam across the lawn. She was dressed in a rumpled gray bathrobe and pink flannel night-gown. Her open-backed slippers flapped as she scuttled through the wet grass. To our delight, she was carrying a huge serving tray heaped with stacks of Hungarian cookies and glasses of milk.

"Oh, boy!" I yelped.

Mrs. Mikas smiled broadly and admonished us all, "Vat? You den't invites Mrs. Meekas to dah nitz crawlin party. Sheme on you!"

After washing our crawler-coated hands, we settled on our back porch to enjoy our surprise snack. Aunt Maude offered coffee or tea for those who wanted it. But everybody preferred chilled milk with Mrs. Mikas' famous sugar cookies.

I was glad to see Mrs. Mikas smiling. This was the first time I had seen her since the news of Ivan's death. Unfortunately, I still heard her every night.

Our laughter and chatter went on until nearly midnight.

"We've had a complaint about a noisy party in the neighborhood. Hands up! You're all under arrest," Sergeant Jeff declared as he walked into the backyard.

"Jeff!" Dad responded with surprise. "Why're you still in uniform, this time of night?"

"You won't believe what's been going on! I'll fill you in. But, first, I dropped by on official business to tell you the FBI fellows want formal statements from all of us. John, Jase, Danny, and myself – that is."

"What's this mean, Jeff?" Mom asked.

"Well. It's good news – or bad news – depending on your point of view. The FBI got Sheriff Connors' decision overruled – late this after-noon. They've rearrested the Libby girls."

"Oh, my gosh! What have they done with them?"

"By now, they're locked away at the federal women's prison up in Bay City. The FBI guys say they're going to throw the book at them. There's a nasty federal judge up there, so the Libby girls are in deep trouble."

"Where's Louise? How's she taking all this?" Mom asked with concern.

"Last time I saw her she was at the city hall talking to Harry Chambers."

"Harry Chambers!" Dad exclaimed.

"That's right! Somebody talked him into taking the girls' case – on a *pro bono* basis to boot! It won't cost them a penny! They're lucky. He's a very good attorney."

"Boy! He's considered one of the best defense lawyers in the state – even if he is a Riverton native," Dad said. "Who talked him into donating his time? Musta been somebody with a lot of pull. He doesn't come cheap."

"You wouldn't believe me if I told you. But I gave my word that I wouldn't tell anybody," Sergeant Jeff said, crossing his heart.

"That's intriguing. Now, who could it be?" Mom wondered aloud.

We sat silently, trying to absorb Sergeant Jeff's news.

Suddenly, out of the darkness came the sound of a familiar voice, "Any cookies left?"

It was Danny!

16 OPERATION MATLOCK

ACCORDING TO DR. MORAN, TEN DAYS OF "HOME REST" would ensure that "accident prone" Danny stayed off that foot. But, after only five hours, poor Mrs. Tucker had succumbed to Danny's impassioned pleas for early release from the good doctor's sentence.

However, Mrs. Tucker was nobody's fool. She imposed three inviolable conditions that Danny was forced to accept in exchange for his parole.

Condition #1 pertained to protective covering for his wounded foot.

Each day, Danny was required to cover his injured foot with three, loose layers of freshly laundered cotton socks. These would not only keep the foot clean but would "breathe" sufficiently to keep the foot dry. Under protest, Queenie agreed to donate one and a half pairs of her best bobby socks each day.

Mr. Tucker's left horsehide slipper provided the next layer. The rugged slipper offered protection in case Danny accidentally stepped on something. Mrs. Tucker's left, red rubber, knee-high boot served as the outside layer. Around the top of the boot, she snuggly tied Danny's farmer's hanky to secure the entire covering.

Danny had to promise that these layers would remain absolutely intact and unsoiled – or else!

Condition #2 pertained to his behavior, what he was authorized to do and where he was authorized to do it.

Danny was forbidden to deviate from the direct path between his house and mine. And, when at either house, he was forbidden to leave that particular property. He couldn't wade, play in dirt, or climb trees. He couldn't swing. He couldn't water the lawn. He couldn't play in trash, garbage, or any other "nasty stuff." That foot must stay clean – or else!

At this stage of the game, I didn't know Mrs. Tucker very well. But I shuddered involuntarily at the thought of her "or else."

The last condition, Condition #3, pertained to how Danny was authorized to move himself within his narrow roving range. At all times, he must remain ensconced in Sherm's wagon. He could scoot himself along with his right foot, but only when no one else was available to pull him. In any case, that left foot was to remain in that wagon at all times – or else!

Shudder!

Mrs. Tucker required Danny to recite all three conditions from memory each time he left the house. So you can imagine my surprise that next morning when his immediate response to my "Whatta-ya-want-ta-do?" was, "Let's deliver our night crawlers to Homer. Then go to the dump to look for lumber for worm boxes."

His plan was most appealing. After a full second's weighing of the potential "or else" consequences, I threw all caution to the wind and agreed. So off we went. He sat in Sherm's wagon. I pulled. He navigated and corrected my driving. After a few blocks, I began to understand why Mr. Smalley had logged so many sick days since Danny moved to our neighborhood.

For the sake of Danny's comfort and safety, we restricted our travel to streets with sidewalks. This added at least a mile to our journey. But we figured, we had all day, so who cared?

UPON OUR ARRIVAL, AFTER expressing proper condolences over Danny's injury, Homer began processing our first delivery. He was delighted at the prospect of replenishing his night crawler stock. Beaming like King Midas, he counted each wriggling nugget of orange-pink gold before dropping it into its maple leaf bed inside his worm box.

But our cheerfulness was short-lived. Danny and I learned the hard way that storing night crawlers overnight in coffee cans results in extremely high mortality rates, especially for those unfortunate critters at the bottom of the can. Homer was forced to feed a good percentage of our first delivery to the many resident robins that understandably populated his back lawn.

We were demoralized!

"You're lucky you came this mornin'. You kin't keep 'em in coffee cans all night and not lose a good many," Homer scolded. "You gotta build yersefs ah couple ah worm box – er mebbe more."

Homer told us that he still intended to pay us two dollars for our delivery. Owing to the high mortality rate, we actually earned less, but

Homer didn't want us to be discouraged on our very first day. He carefully extracted a pair of dollar bills from his worn black leather snap purse. He handed both bills to me. I tucked them away carefully and thanked Homer, promising to do better next time.

As we departed, we once again assured Homer that we were sold on the need for worm boxes. In fact, we told him, we were just on our way to the dump to find materials to meet that need. We also informed him of the lawn watering "contracts" that we had landed with the Reillys, the Shurtleifs, the Tolnas, and Mrs. Mikas. He was enormously impressed.

We bid Homer adieu and pointed the wagon down Ann Arbor Street toward the dump. As we rolled along, I pulled one of the dollar bills out of my pocket and handed it to Danny.

"Nothing doing!" he insisted, pushing the money back into my hand. "I didn't catch any of those crawlers. You keep it all."

"You mean you don't want to be partners?" I asked, slightly offended by his attitude. "We were partners in the bubble gum-sauerkraut business."

I had him there.

"Of course, I wanta be partners. I just didn't do anything for that money. It's not right."

"Let's get something straight. As far as I'm concerned, we're partners. Partners share the profits. If you don't want to share the profits, then we're not partners. That's just the way it is."

"Okay. Okay. Maybe I'll gather some worms when you're not around – sometimes."

"Right."

Danny pocketed his share with a grin.

As we approached the dump, the familiar bouquet drifted down the access road to greet us. I looked forward to a long, uninterrupted period of scrounging. We uncovered, culled, sorted, and scratched through every pile of trash that had arrived since our last visit.

Despite being wagon-bound, Danny was amazingly productive. However, after nearly five hours of hard work, we had yet to produce lumber suitable for worm box construction. So we agreed to call it a day.

GIVEN THE DEPLETED STATE of our minds and bodies, we decided to take the shortest, most direct route home. We followed the narrow dirt path that led up over the railroad tracks, skirted the canning factory property, and finally popped out on Milford Street.

Frankly, this choice of routes was not the most comfortable or safe for Danny. But the way we figured, what could a few bumps and jostles do to a foot that was wrapped like a mummy?

When we reached the Milford Street sidewalk, I stopped to stomp the dump dust out of my shoes. Danny only stomped his right foot.

"HEY, JASE. WHO'S THAT?" The words hit us like a bomb blast. They were very low, very full, and very **LOUD**. I recognized the familiar Matlock mega-voice behind me.

I turned around. There stood my classmate from Hamilton School. I smiled and introduced Danny, "Hi, Butch. This is Danny Tucker. He just moved here from New Albany. He'll be in our grade at Hamilton this fall. He cut his foot, so I'm haulin' him around in the wagon."

Butch was actually the same age as Danny and me, but he was more than a full head taller. More impressively, at the age of ten, he was built like a modern-day professional wrestler. Muscles stretched his blue-and-white striped tee shirt and khaki shorts.

Butch wiggled his beefy fingers in Danny's direction and bellowed a big bass, but brief, "**HI!**"

Danny was clearly impressed with the boy's woofer and told him so. Butch's face turned red. He knew he had a big voice, but no one had ever acknowledged it with such unvarnished admiration. Based on the amplitude of Danny's *come-out call*, this was indeed high praise.

Butch Matlock was the oldest of five children in his family. And, even though he would only be a sixth-grader, he was acknowledged to be the tallest, strongest, and heaviest student enrolled at Hamilton School. He even beat out all those gigantic eighth grade girls who towered over all the boys in their class. To top it off, he was an unusually handsome boy.

Butch was huge, strong, and handsome. His brothers and sisters were huge, strong, and handsome. Even his mother and father were huge, strong, and handsome. It was a most unusual family in that regard.

I suppose my perception of Mrs. Matlock as a very large woman was a bit biased. Since Butch was born, she had remained in a constant state of expectancy. What's more, Mrs. Matlock possessed a remarkable proficiency for producing huge, strong, and handsome – twins. She was currently expecting her third set. This feat would tie the Michigan record for the number of twin births by a single mother.

To top it off, Mrs. M never produced a baby weighing less than twelve pounds. Dr. Moran predicted that the next set of new Matlocks would enter the world sharing nearly thirty pounds between them!

Everyone knew that Mrs. Matlock loved her children – Butch, Judie and Janie (twin girls), and Jerry and Larry (twin boys). Who, but a deeply loving mother, would regularly undertake the grueling process of bringing more mammoth Matlocks into the world?

In the case of this expectancy, Mrs. Matlock hadn't been seen at street level for months. The unwieldy weight of two potential fifteen-pounders napping in her tummy had contributed to a nasty fall result-ing in multiple fractures of her right leg. A heavy cast from hip to ankle rendered her incapable of standing upright.

Following Dr. Moran's orders, she lay immobile on a sturdy cot strategically positioned just inside the always-open window of her cozy second story bedroom. During her months of indisposition, she tend-ed her flock of children from that little window. Her eyes endlessly patrolled her domain, the entire length of Milford Street from the Grand Trunk tracks to New Albany Avenue.

Reclining on her cot, she smoked a cigarette when she fancied, napped when she tired, and sonic-blasted the neighborhood when any Matlock child failed to toe the mark. From there, she could spot Mr. Matlock returning from one of the two jobs he worked to keep ahead of the growing family grocery bills. Invariably, just as he reached the halfway point between their house and New Albany Avenue, Mrs. Matlock would stop him in his tracks with a booming grocery order that required an about face to Pete's for even more groceries.

On my way home from the dump, if Mrs. Matlock were not nap-ping, I was accustomed to waving and exchanging warm greetings with her. I knew when she was on watch because as I approached I could see her muscular right arm propped on the windowsill.

I didn't see Mrs. Matlock's arm that day, so I assumed she was nap-ping. While we chatted with Butch, I glanced up at her window. I had often seen a curl of tobacco smoke above her cot. But, today, there was more smoke than usual. And it had an eerie orange color. What was I seeing? Oh, no!

"Fire! Fire!" I shouted at the top of my lungs.

I sounded the alarm again and again, jumping up and down under Mrs. Matlock's window. Danny and Butch were frozen. They stared at the window with their mouths open. We had to act fast.

"Danny, quick! Scoot up to Pete's and call the fire department!" I ordered.

He snapped out of his spell and sped off in the wagon, his right leg whirling like an airplane propeller.

"Butch, keep yelling at your mother! You have to wake her up – before it's too late!"

With that, Butch let out a bellow that nearly burst my eardrums, **"MAW, WAKE UP! MAW, WAKE UP!"**

With Butch stuck in REPEAT mode, I ran as fast as I could toward the canning factory. At full speed, I flew around the east end of the building and leaped onto the loading dock near the infamous sauerkraut boxcar.

"Sergeant Rick! Mr. Don! Otto! There's a fire! Where are you?" I shouted as I pounded on the door marked "Retail Storage #2."

Don Paulus opened the door almost immediately. Between gasps, I frantically outlined the situation. I concluded with a desperate plea, "Mr. Don, we gotta get Mrs. Matlock outta that bedroom!"

Don didn't miss a beat. He ran back into the can storage area. I followed him admiring his ability to twist his awkward gait into such a brisk jog. When we rounded the corner, there they were, Otto and his crew of nine.

"Otto! A fire! Bring the men! Quick!" Don ordered.

As we dashed toward the Matlock house, an explosion of fire erupted from the roof, spewing burning debris in all directions. A cloud of angry black smoke billowed skyward.

Neighbors milled round and round in the street, frantically arguing about how best to rescue the imperiled Mrs. Matlock. Three well-intentioned men attempted to quench the fire with garden hoses strung together from the spigot next door. But the angry fire ridiculed their paltry efforts by roaring furiously out of control through the now-gaping hole in the roof, just above and behind the sleeping Mrs. Matlock.

Otto and his crew sped to the scene, arriving well before Don and me. Just as Don and I reached Milford Street, I looked up to see a familiar, now reddened, arm protruding out of the upstairs window. I picked up the pace, leaving Don in my dust.

"MAAAWWWW!!!" Butch bawled at the first sight of his mother's wild-eyed face.

"HELP ME! FOR GOD'S SAKE! PLEASE, HELP ME!" she screamed.

Her eyes quivered with terror. We all felt helpless.

Otto barked a series of short commands to his crew. They responded instantly with what sounded like a football cheer and then, without hesitation, they flew as a unit toward the front door, banged it open and disappeared through the wall of dense black smoke at the foot of the stairs.

Otto followed his crew, in and up, yapping inspirational commands at their heels.

We were mesmerized by what we were witnessing. We stared blankly at the window. Suddenly, POW faces appeared there, around and above the panic-stricken face of Mrs. Matlock. Magically, the form of Mrs. Matlock rose then suddenly disappeared from sight!

Stomp! Stomp! Stomp! Scrapppppe! Stomp! Stomp! Stomp! Bumpideebump! Bumpideebump!

Stomp! Stomp! Stomp! Crasssssssssssssh!

Bang!

The front door burst open. And, out came the POWs carrying the entire cot with Mrs. Matlock, in all her glory, clinging to her mattress. The POWs looked like ten pallbearers transporting a very alive, and very large, corpse.

Whish! Plunk!

Her ten Prussian footmen deposited Lady Matlock and soon-to-be twins, gently at that, right in the middle of Milford Street. Effortlessly. All in a day's work!

I looked up to the window where Mrs. Matlock had lain helpless only seconds before. The ravenous flames now gnawed hungrily at her windowsill. And, within seconds, they fully engulfed her former bedroom.

For once, Mrs. Matlock was speechless, overwhelmed by her emotions. Tears poured from her eyes.

The POWs broke into song. A rollicking German melody in the style of a school fight song filled the air. The smoke-blackened and slightly scorched rescuers bounced up and down, slapping each other wildly on the back.

Suddenly, the crowd of astonished onlookers roared with cheers and applause. They converged on the gleeful Germans, hugging them and pounding their backs. Otto's eyes filled with tears as he and his men garnered the uninhibited outpouring of gratitude and admiration from their American "enemies" from our neighborhood.

Above the din, I heard an anxious plea, "Wait up! Cheese and crackers, Otto! Wait up!" It was Sergeant Rick Prella coming over the tracks, waving one arm and brandishing his tommy gun in the other. I'd almost forgotten who was supposed to be guarding the POWs.

The sight of Sergeant Rick's U.S. Army uniform coming over the horizon incited yet another round of boisterous celebration. He was greeted by a wild flurry of cheers and immediately herded into the winner's circle where Don, Otto, and the grinning Germans stood, basking in genuine affection.

Neighbors who arrived after the rescue were told what they had missed. They shook their heads in honest disbelief at the amazing news.

In the midst of the festivity, Danny wheeled up and tapped me on the leg. He pointed with his thumb toward New Albany Avenue and the trio of Addison adults coming our way. They spotted Danny and me and threaded their way through the crowd toward us.

Before we could speak, the Riverton Fire Department pulled up with sirens screaming and diesels belching, warnings for us to stand aside. The crowd parted allowing the gigantic red fire engines to snuggle up to each other in the Matlock front yard.

Like fleas from a wet skunk, the black rubber-coated firemen leaped to the ground, unreeled their hoses, and rushed for the rusty hydrant at the head of the block. Within seconds, the hoses were fully charged and the firemen began the long process of drowning the Matlock fire and wetting down the nearby houses to prevent wind-blown, still-burning debris from setting them ablaze.

Amid a last round of applause, Otto and his crew allowed Sergeant Rick to reclaim his dignity by insisting that he march them back to the canning factory. A relieved Sergeant Rick appeared grateful for Otto's thoughtfulness.

Butch and his siblings now sat quietly in the street with their backs leaning against their mother's cot. They were a dazed and pitiful lot. Almost as an afterthought, a neighborhood teenager was dispatched to fetch an unsuspecting Mr. Matlock from his second shift job at the Ann Arbor Railroad boiler shop. He was in for a horrible shock!

AS THE SUN DROPPED behind the high walls of the nearby canning factory, neighbors huddled in hushed councils to discuss how best to provide shelter for the Matlock family. Old Mrs. De Stephano thoughtfully provided a light cotton blanket to cover Mrs. Matlock as she slept soundly, surrounded by her loving children in the middle of the street.

The Riverton firefighters had cut off all electric power to the houses on Milford Street. When darkness fell, the sole source of light was a bed of glowing embers, the remains of the once proud Matlock home. In this solemn setting, neighbors began to drift homeward, counting their blessings and silently praying for the poor Matlocks who had just lost all their worldly possessions.

As we headed for home, we knew that we had witnessed one of the finest, yet most tragic, moments in the history of our neighborhood. Danny said it all, "Now, we know what war's really like."

Aunt Maude, Mom, and I strolled along behind the wagon as Dad hauled Danny through the darkness toward Forrest Street.

"Pee-you! Were you boys playing at the dump again, today?" Mom asked, breaking the silence.

"Who? Us?" Danny replied innocently. "I'm not allowed to get my foot dirty."

No one responded except Dad who issued a skeptical, "Harrumpff."

As we got closer, the two dark forms lurking in the black-gray shadows under the box elder tree emerged as cars parked in front of our house. "It's Grandma – and Mrs. Libby!" I announced. "Gee, wonder what they're doing here."

Our two visitors were sitting on the front steps. Grandma looked concerned for Mrs. Libby who appeared to have been crying. When we arrived, she spruced up and stood with Grandma to greet us.

"Hello, Louise. It's good to see you. Hi, Ma. Come on in. We'll make some coffee and have some of Maude's cookies," Mom proposed.

When we were all settled on the back porch, Mrs. Libby put down her coffee cup and looked at us forlornly. She looked as if she might cry again.

"I'm really sorry not to have come sooner. I need to apologize for what my girls did. They endangered you, John – and the boys. They were reckless and foolish. Now, they're in jail for – who knows how long? Since their father –. It's been hard."

She looked down, knotted her hands, and wept softly. Grandma patted her arm. Mom and Aunt Maude rose and wrapped her with hugs. I realized our anger toward the girls had remarkably vanished.

Soon, Mrs. Libby regained her composure.

"You know we've always thought well of them, Louise," Dad assured her. "Basically, they're good girls who – who've gotten a bit off track. It's just an adolescent stage, I'm sure."

Mrs. Libby nodded her head, "I sure hope you're right."

"We hear Harry Chambers's your lawyer. Known him for years. He's the best. He'll convince that judge to see Barb and Anne as – well – two young girls who made a mistake."

Louise Libby nodded her head again and sniffed.

Then she spoke, "Thank you. I've tried to look at the bright side. Mr. Chambers has been wonderful. Do you know he isn't charging us

– me – a cent for what he's doing for Barb and Anne? And you wouldn't believe why. I'd love to tell you, but I'm sworn to secrecy."

We'd heard that line before.

"You're such good neighbors. I'm so grateful for your words of encouragement. Because of the war and the POWs, some people might not be so – forgiving."

"Don't be silly, Louise," Mom said. Then she changed the subject, "Now, what can we do for you? Are you going to be all right alone tonight? Would you like Maude or me to come over and stay with you?"

"Do you have food in the house?" Grandma inquired, focusing on practical matters.

"We could run down to Pete's for you," Aunt Maude offered.

"No, actually, I have plenty of food. Mrs. Zeyer has been very helpful that way. To tell the truth, she's outdone herself. She's come by every day with a dish or two since this all started. I don't know how I'll repay her kindness."

I wondered if those dishes included a quart of chicken soup.

"And I'll be far from lonely tonight – in fact – I have company coming. That's one reason I stopped by. I was wondering if I might borrow some bedding – pillows, sheets, and blankets? And a teakettle for some extra baths tonight?"

We stared at her in amazement. *How could she think of having company at a time like this?* I asked myself.

"Who's coming, Mrs. Libby?" Danny asked, getting right to the point.

Mrs. Libby smiled for the first time all evening. "I've asked the Matlock family to stay with us – with me, I mean – 'til they can get settled somewhere. It was the least I could do for – for neighbors in need. I have extra room – at least for now. And Mrs. Matlock she's – she needs rest. And the children –."

She choked up again. After a minute, she continued, "The Matlocks are over at the Good Mission Church. Edith Squires is fixing them up with clothing and so on – from her rummage sale supply. They don't have a thing left in the world. It's all gone. So I need to get on home and make up some beds before I go back with the car to carry them – and their new things – to my house."

We loaded all our extra bedding into her trunk and offered once again to help her prepare for the Matlocks' arrival. But she politely refused. Obviously, this was something she needed to do all by herself. We understood.

We waved as Mrs. Libby steered her car for home. No one spoke at first. Then Grandma summed it up for all of us, "Doesn't that beat all?"

Once we were settled in on the porch again, Aunt Maude asked, "Ma, what on earth brings you to town so late? Won't Pa be missing you? Or did you trade him for those chickens you brought us?"

After chuckling at that suggestion, Grandma got serious.

"Actually, Pa's the reason I'm here. He heard on the radio weather that we're due to get some heavy rain, day after tomorrow. The hay's all cut and raked in the north field. He wondered if Jase could help him bring it in and put it up – tomorrow and maybe the next day. It's a big job. But, with Jase driving the horses, Pa thinks they could finish before the rain gets here. Sorry for the short notice, but Jase is so good with the horses."

Everyone looked at me. I was embarrassed and proud at the same time.

Under normal circumstances, I would have been thrilled at the prospect of helping Grandpa, especially when it involved driving the horses. That was my favorite job at the farm. But I now had other obligations and concerns.

Thanks to the help of all the neighbors, our first lot of night crawlers for Homer was sizeable. But it would only hold him for a few days. Homer was counting on us to replenish his crawler inventory before the dry days of summer. With Danny restricted to his wagon, the burden of collecting fell on me.

Plus, Danny and I hadn't found lumber to build even one worm box. We'd need three or four to store the crawler harvest after the coming rains. Without worm boxes, we'd risk losing a good number of any crawlers we caught. Since Homer didn't have any spare boxes, he was counting on us to build some.

And who would pull Danny and keep him company while he served out the rest of his modified house arrest? Aside from his uncanny knack for keeping Grandma Compton in stitches, a wagon-bound Danny wouldn't be of much help at the farm. No question about it, Danny had to stay home.

And what about the Libby case? Didn't the FBI want me to make a statement along with Sergeant Jeff, Danny, and Dad? What would they say when they discovered that I skipped town? Besides, how would I keep up with all the news on the fate of the girls in Bay City?

Finally, there was poor Butch Matlock. We were never close buddies, but he was going to need a friend in the coming days. What could be better than having a classmate from Hamilton living just down the street from him?

This was a tough decision.

Evidently, Dad sensed my conflict. Without pressuring me, he cleverly allayed my concerns.

"Danny, you and I will have to hold down the fort on the night crawler front. I think the lawns around here can use another good soaking, even before the coming rains. Whatya think? You can scoot around and get that done tomorrow, can't you?"

Danny nodded his head vigorously, ignoring again the terms of his parole.

"Why don't you do that when I'm at work? Speaking of work, I spotted some good worm box lumber out back of Burkes in that big pile of scrap packing materials. We should be able to put a couple of boxes together after work tomorrow. Okay, Danny?"

Danny nodded again, claiming, "I like building worm boxes."

Dad smiled. He then turned to Mom and Aunt Maude, "You two ladies available for a little night crawling tomorrow night? Probably be about dark when you get home from your teaching out at the camp, Marie. How about it?"

"Boy, that's the best offer I've had in a long time. How 'bout you, Maude?"

"Actually, I enjoyed catching crawlers the other night. Once you get started, you can't stop. It's like eating peanuts."

"Ugh! Let's use another comparison," Grandma said, wrapping her arms around each other and shivering noticeably.

We all laughed.

"I'll call Jeff to make arrangements with the FBI to take our statements after you return from the farm," Dad promised. "Don't forget day after tomorrow is Sunday. So we'll all be at the farm. Assuming Grandpa and you are finished, you can come home, then."

I turned to check all this with Danny. He gave me a big smile and a jaunty thumbs-up. Then he asked, "Would you like me to tell Butch you had to go to the farm?"

I nodded and smiled. *How did he know?* I wondered to myself.

Mom patted Danny's shoulder and complimented him on his thoughtfulness, "That's a good idea, Danny. You go see Butch tomorrow. He'd like that, I bet. Maybe he can help you water those lawns."

After I quickly packed my suitcase, we assembled out front for our goodbyes. I smiled at my partner and gave him a big thumps-up of my own. Then I hopped into Grandma's car.

With Grandma at the stick, the mighty Terraplane roared into the air, came about sharply to a north-by-northeast heading, and streaked toward its hanger at the farm.

Geez! How I loved flying with Grandma Compton!

"LOOK WHO'S UP BEFORE breakfast!" I announced, beating Grandpa to the punch.

"Mornin', Jase. Ready to round up some hay?" Grandpa asked with a smile.

The night before, Mick had celebrated my arrival by jumping into the air about three thousand times. But, this morning, he was unusually reserved. From his box, he squinted at me and halfheartedly flopped an ear in my direction.

"Here's your coffee, Jase. Careful! It's real hot." Grandma warned, setting the huge steaming mug in front of me on the table.

I splashed in fresh cream and two heaping tablespoons of sugar before taking my test sip. Next, I slathered a thick layer of creamery-made butter on a giant wedge of oven-toasted homemade bread and dunked it into my mug. I was in heaven!

Having finished breakfast, Grandpa sat in his rocking chair reading his latest postal-delivered *Riverton Daily Press* with news coverage that lagged current events by nearly two days. He pointed at the picture of the four desperados in front of the sheriff's office just after their arrest at Granville Park.

"Look at the grins on them Libby girls," he said. "Should be ashamed of themselves. But they'll be sorry, soon enough. You'll see!"

I wondered what Grandpa would say this afternoon when the mailman brought yesterday's *Daily Press* with its headlines reporting the Libby girls' unexpected release by Sheriff Connors. And tomorrow, when he'd read about their re-arrest by the FBI.

I decided not to spoil his fun by telling him what I knew of the Libby affair. So I changed the subject, "Grandma told me the north field's all raked."

"Yep, it's all laid in windrows waiting for us ta load 'er. Good crop this year – heavy and delicious. Had a big bite myself just yesterday. Haw! Haw!"

"How long do you think it will take us to get it in and put up?"

"The better part of two days. But we got ta do it – before that rain hits tomorrow night."

"When can we start?"

"Chores're all done. By the time you finish breakfast and we hitch up the horses, the dew will be mostly blowed off. We can start then. Eat a good breakfast. It's gonna to be a long day!"

"You men'll eat your dinner at the house, won't you?"

Grandpa and Grandma always included me in the "men" category.

"That's right, Maw. You needn't bring anything to the field. We can stop to eat back here before – or after – unloading. Why don't you set us up on the picnic table out under the spy apple tree, though? We'll be awful dirty, but we can't afford the time ta wash up."

Recognizing Grandpa's concern about finishing before the rains, Grandma replied, "I'll plan a picnic for us then. And I'll plan to be here when you men unload – so I can retrieve the hauling rope for you."

Rehearsing her role, Grandma gazed out the kitchen window toward the north field. She'd be able to see us when we turned onto Barrington Road with a full load.

"I have to be at church tomorrow morning. I may miss a load – but I guess you can manage one load without me. I still wish you didn't have to work on Sunday, Bill."

It wasn't often that Grandma called Grandpa by his first name. And, when she did, I knew she was serious.

"Now, Maw. Let's not go into that right now."

Except for a scowl, Grandma didn't respond. She knew this was the one issue that Grandpa and she would never agree on.

"Which barn, Grandpa?" I asked, to change the subject again.

"We'll load the near end of the north field first. It's got a lot of timothy in it."

"The horse barn first, then," I said, finishing Grandpa's point.

"That's right," he confirmed. "Horses fare best on timothy hay."

GRANDPA HITCHED JIM AND Fannie to the hay wagon. I took the reins and mounted the front rack as usual. Carefully, I backed the team and wagon toward the tall, giraffe-shaped hay loader designed to lift the hay from the field and deposit it over the back rack onto the wagon bed.

"Whoa!" Grandpa yelled, stopping the team. "Jase, hop down here and help me rassel this loader into place."

By putting his backside against the rear of the loader and pushing with his strong legs, Grandpa inched the bulky machine forward. My job was to align the heavy loader tongue with the hauling hitch that was mounted on the back of the wagon. The instant the two came together, I dropped the steel connecting pin into place. The telltale *ping* signaled a solid hitch.

"That's got her!" Grandpa confirmed. "Let's do some hayin'!"

When we reached the field, I parked the rig at the head of the first windrow, the long brown curl of hay that Grandpa had created with the hay rake after the cutting and drying process the week before. Grandpa hopped off the wagon and engaged the loader's operating gear.

"All set, Jase!"

As I drove the team up and down the windrows, the never-ending stream of hay flowed up and over the back rack of the wagon. Using his pitchfork, Grandpa distributed the hay evenly over the wagon bed, building a growing haystack under his feet and over my head. He worked relentlessly, hour after hour, never seeming to need a break.

My job, as driver, wasn't as physically demanding, but it required hours of exhausting concentration. And standing on the narrow slats of the wagon rack caused my feet to go numb about half way through the day.

When we had our first full load, we unhitched the loader and headed for the horse barn. I pulled the wagon through the huge open doors and stopped between the mows. Grandpa unhitched the team and drove them around to the other side of the barn where he hitched them to the huge hauling rope. I climbed down from the wagon, grabbed their reins, and waited for the next order.

A heavy stainless steel fork, as wide as a man's body, was secured to the other end of the hauling rope. Grandpa scampered to the top of the wagon and lowered the fork from the barn peak. Then he jumped up and down on the fork's top cross member, driving the fork firmly into the hay. When its barbed points had grabbed a ball of hay about the size of Grandma's Terraplane, he jumped off the wagon into the mow and gave me a thumbs-up.

At my command, Jim and Fannie put their shoulders into the load. The hauling rope stretched taut and hummed frighteningly just before the gigantic ball of hay spectacularly broke loose from the wagon and sprang upward toward the pulley carriage. The horses marched in unison outward into the yard lifting the huge hay ball ever upward until the fork met the carriage with a loud *clang.*

At that point, the pulley carriage shot down the steel track. When the giant ball was precisely over its target area, Grandpa yanked the trip line releasing the barbs and dropping the immense wad of hay into the mow with a loud, dusty *thump.*

As I backed the team into position for the next haul, Grandma donned leather gloves and rapidly retrieved the slack hauling rope to avoid entanglement with the horses' hooves.

Even with our team of two good men, two strong horses, and one good Grandma, each wagon of hay took two or more hours to load and unload.

This day was no different.

WHEN WE BROKE FOR dinner, the sun was high in the cloudless blue sky. Hay dust tickled my nose and made my eyes water as Grandpa and I walked from the horse barn toward the house. We had succeeded in loading and unloading two full wagons of hay.

Grandma had spread red-checked oilcloth over the bleached-wood picnic table. My eyes lit up when I saw what awaited us. Tall cold glasses of iced tea sweated in the humid June air. Overflowing dishes of roasted meats, mashed potatoes, and green beans steamed and sizzled before us. Finally, Grandma had outdone herself by baking a luscious apple pie, dearly begging to be eaten.

After we had finished our last helping, Grandma checked our progress, "How goes the haying, men?"

"It's going fairly well – two loads mowed away – that's slower than we'd like. But the good news is that I can't remember a better lookin' crop of hay," Grandpa rationalized.

During the remainder of the day, we loaded and unloaded three more times before the early evening breezes ushered in the dew. At dusk, Grandpa declared the day's end after conducting his time-proven moisture test by twisting a handful of hay to see how much effort it took to snap it in two.

"Too moist to put in the barn, Jase. Better call 'er quits. If you drive the wagon, I'll take a little nap on the way back."

"We're on our way, Grandpa," I gladly assured him.

Grandpa stretched out on the wagon bed for a much-deserved rest while the empty wagon rumbled toward home. I felt exhilarated by the accomplishments of the day. The horse barn was nearly full of fresh, nutritious hay.

After bedding down Jim and Fannie and finishing our nightly chores, we trudged toward the house. The dark western sky was smeared with swaths of red and purple, foretelling a change in weather.

"Grandpa, are we going to use Gene and Teddy tomorrow?"

"We usually use the heavier team for haying. Think the lighter team can cut the mustard?"

"Well, they're young – and smaller – but I'd give them a chance. I bet they'd like to show us what they can do."

"Now, I wonder why you'd think that," Grandpa said, rubbing my head with his hard-callused hand.

"RELEASED WITHOUT CHARGES! WE voted for a sheriff, and we got a jellyfish! Gads!"

Grandpa wasn't happy. He had fallen asleep in his reading chair last night with the *Riverton Daily Press* unopened in his lap. This morning, his first glance at the old news didn't please him.

Should I tell him what I knew? No. That would be like telling the ending of a movie to someone just entering the theater. Besides, his next paper was bound to report the re-arrest. Then he'd be happy.

"Morning, Jase," said Grandma from the kitchen stove. "Did you sleep okay?"

I sensed she wanted to avoid the Libby girl subject, so I helped her. "Boy, did I ever. Don't remember a thing after my head hit the pillow."

Grandpa got the message. "Looks like a nice morning! Still dry, too," he said as he folded his paper and stuffed it unceremoniously under his rocking chair.

Mick was his old self. His greeting was a full-body wiggle. When I sat down at the table, he licked my pants cuff and rubbed his chin on my left shoe.

After breakfast, we hitched Gene and Teddy, the lightweight chestnuts, to the hay wagon and set off to finish the north field. The spirited pair pranced up Barrington Road in anticipation of a good workout.

As we worked, wispy clouds scooted across the sky. The clear blue of yesterday turned to bluish-gray, leaving no doubt about the prediction of rain. We had loaded and unloaded twice, storing the hay in the mow above the cow barn. We were making good time. So we decided to mow away our third load before breaking for dinner.

At nearly one o'clock, a full two hours later than the day before, we finally sat down under the apple tree. It felt good just to sit. We had been working for nearly six hours. The arches of my feet ached from two days on the narrow slats of the wagon rack.

The delayed start had given Grandma plenty of time to prepare our midday meal after church. She had changed from her Sunday dress into her usual housedress and apron before she set out our food.

"Wonder why nobody's here, yet," Grandma pondered, while she sipped her iced tea. "Usually, at least one family is here by now."

"It's probably raining over in Riverton," Grandpa teased. "Nobody's coming this Sunday. We got a fair-weather family, Maw."

"Don't be silly! They'll all be here. You just finish that haying, so you can be sociable. I'll tell those young ones that you'll put on a trapeze show after you're done. How's that?"

"Well, to be honest, it wouldn't be too bad. Being full of new hay, the cow barn mow is extra soft right now. I'd likely fall into a nap the first time I landed on it. You go ahead and line up a show, Maw. I'll do it in my nightshirt."

Grandma chortled. Grandpa and I laughed, too.

As more and more clouds rolled our way, our moods changed. We ate our dinner quickly without further conversation.

Grandma nervously cleared the serving dishes from the table, even before we were entirely finished. She didn't insist on our having second and third helpings this time. Instead, she hurried us back to the field. She was clearly concerned about the foreboding western sky.

As we rehitched the loader, the wind freshened noticeably. "This doesn't look good," Grandpa fretted as he assessed the new wall of thunderheads gathering on the horizon. "We'll have to work fast."

As I turned to take my position on the front rack, I saw Dad's car pull off Barrington Road and into the shade of the tall elm in the corner of the field. He leaped from the car, waved at us, and opened the passenger door. Danny emerged clumsily and hobbled our way on a pair of wooden crutches, his wounded foot dangling limply in the air.

"We got company, Grandpa!"

"How 'bout that! Good! We'll put 'em ta work."

Grandpa walked quickly toward Dad and Danny bringing them within comfortable shouting range. Then he briskly delivered his orders.

"John, it's gonna rain any minute now. We gotta get this last load onto the wagon and into the barn – or we'll lose it. You can help me mow. Go back up ta the horse barn and grab my other pitchfork. Then get on back here in a hurry – please!"

Dad acknowledged Grandpa's orders with a wave of the hand and an about-face. After hurriedly loading Danny back into the car, he sped out of the field and back up the road toward the house.

"Jase, let's you and me finish up this windrow before he gets back."

"Okay, Grandpa," I responded as I quickly mounted the front rack and grabbed the reins. "Ready when you are!"

By the time we had loaded half a windrow, Dad was back with the pitchfork. Danny wasn't with him. Probably helping Grandma in the kitchen, I guessed. I stopped long enough for Dad to hop up on the wagon, then I gave the team an energetic "Giddy up" and away we went.

Gene and Teddy had never had so much fun. I gave them their heads. They soon settled into a moderate trot, much faster than they had ever been allowed to pull the wagon before. I expected Grandpa to slow me down. But, looking behind me, I saw the frenzied blur of coordinated pitchforks skillfully mowing away the hay as it flew off the field, up the hay loader, and over the back rack of the speeding wagon.

Dad grinned at Grandpa as the two men competed for who could mow away the most hay. It was a thrill to watch. I was proud of Dad. Come to think of it, I was proud of all of us.

We collected the last load in record time, about twenty minutes, I'd guess. When we stopped to unhitch the hay loader, the temperature suddenly plunged, and the sky darkened ominously. We were really in for it!

"Let's head for the barn!" Grandpa yelled.

"Hang on!" I cried, while I reined the horses to the right. "Gee on over there, Teddy. Attagirl. Now, gidup!"

I snapped the reins lightly over their haunches. That's all it took! Gene and Teddy surged across the bare hay field, under the elm tree, and out onto Barrington Road. Never had four tons of hay moved so quickly!

I gave out a mighty yowl like a wild Apache! But nobody could hear me. I was well hidden, from sight and sound, up under my scruffy thatch overhang. The chorus of pounding hooves and wheels grinding gravel was deafening.

It was exhilarating!

When we reached the driveway, I pulled back gently on the reins. "Whoa, Teddy. Slow down. Attagirl."

In response, both horses glanced at me over their shoulders as if to say, *Oh, come on, Jase! We're just beginning to have fun!*

As I wheeled into the driveway, the oversized load tipped precariously to the outside of my turn. It righted itself when I straightened out and aimed for the open doorway of the horse barn.

Suddenly, puffs of dust exploded from the rumps of the two horses below me! A spate of huge raindrops dappled their shivering horsehide, signaling the start of the coming deluge. I artfully nosed the gigantic load inside the barn, just in the nick of time. As we came under cover, the wind howled, the skies opened, and the heavy rain descended in blinding sheets.

"Whoa, team. Whoa, Teddy! Whoa, Gene!"

As I wiggled down from my hiding spot under the overhang of hay, I heard a mighty cheer. Grandma and Danny, then Grandpa and Dad, noisily celebrated our safe and dry landing in the barn. Mick yapped loudly and leaped into the air. Gene and Teddy stomped their hooves in self-adulation and whinnied at the top of their lungs.

My blood-curdling Apache war cry flushed a pair of fat pigeons from their dry roosts in the barn rafters. They flapped out the open peak window smack into a solid wall of cool rain. As if in response to my whoop, a blinding flash of lightning coupled with a thunderous explosion answered from the black, menacing skies above.

When I reached Danny, he grinned crazily, slugged me in the left bicep, and yelled, "Wow! That was great!"

"Where'd you – where'd you get the – crutches?" I gushed, attempting to catch my breath.

"They're Homer's extra pair. They're not as fast as Sherm's wagon. But I'll have my stitches out soon."

I nodded my head and caressed the crutches. Danny smiled proudly.

We watched the dark skies for a hint of how long the torrent might last. We weren't enthusiastic about forcing the team, driver, and hauling rope retriever to work in the rain. After a while, the wind subsided and the rain changed to a moderate shower.

"I believe she'll slack off from here," Grandpa predicted optimistically. "Then we can unload her. Whatya think?"

Grandpa looked at me, then at Dad, and finally at Grandma. Nobody objected, so he announced, "Good! Then we'll finish 'er up today and be done with it."

"While we wait, maybe we should go to the house for a little bite of something," Danny suggested. "All the aunts and uncles and cousins are here. They're probably pretty hungry, too. Wouldn't want to keep 'em waiting! Right, Grandma?"

We stared at our favorite tapeworm host in total disbelief. Grandma shook her head and chuckled. She had undoubtedly just fed Danny while we finished the north field. But, in Danny's case, that wouldn't have mattered.

"Chores before eats," I reminded my friend who stared at me as if I were nuts.

When the storm had run its course, we unloaded the hay. Then we all pitched in to help Grandpa with his evening chores. Even the cousins helped.

To our amazement, Danny insisted on a second chance at milking. With Dad and me looking on, Grandpa perched Danny on his lap and gave him a brief refresher on the fine art of hand milking. Confidently, Danny grasped Bessie's soft milk spigot and gave it a mighty squeeze. A long, white stream of warm milk shot straight down – *splat* – right in the bottom of Grandpa's empty milk pail.

No one was more astonished than Danny.

Immediately, he regained his composure, turned to Dad, and declared smugly, "That's how you do it, Mr. Addison."

Dad was too shocked to respond.

"Hole in one!" Grandpa announced. "Can't beat that!"

Danny hopped down from Grandpa's lap and announced that he had milked enough for one day. Apparently, he didn't think he could improve on his first attempt.

IT WAS JUST AFTER sunset when we said our goodbyes and headed for home. Dad and I sat up front while Danny stretched out over Aunt Maude and Mom in the backseat. It didn't look very comfortable for anyone back there, but nobody complained.

After a mile or two, I asked Dad to update me on the Libby case.

"The evidence – including our statements to the FBI – will go to the grand jury in a few days. According to Louise Libby, the grand jury should report its findings in about a week. The U.S. Circuit judge is pushing to hear this case as soon as possible."

"What's a circus judge?" asked a little voice from the backseat.

"*Circuit* Judge! He's a judge that presides over courts in various places around his circuit – his territory," Dad replied patiently. "In any case – by next week – the grand jury should hand down some specific charges. And the girls will be arraigned on Wednesday or so."

"Rained on Wednesday and today, too!" Danny declared with authority from the backseat.

In addition to needing glasses, I thought, Danny might be a little hard of hearing, too.

"Danny, why don't you update Jase on the worm business?" Dad suggested, officially including him in the conversation.

That was all the encouragement Danny needed. A complete report followed.

Last night *we* gathered three full coffee cans of night crawlers. We netted $2.75 from Homer who was delighted with our progress. Homer's worm boxes would soon be full. But that's okay because Dad, with Danny's invaluable assistance, had built three worm boxes for us, out of discarded lumber from Burkes. Dad and Danny (On crutches?) had gathered three burlap bags of maple leaves from the woods across the alley from Mrs. Mikas' garden. The neighborhood lawns had been watered today. Butch Matlock helped but, with today's rains, it may have been unnecessary, once again. In any case, lots of people were scheduled to hunt crawlers tonight, just like last night.

"You mean other people are hunting for us – and we're keeping the money?" I sputtered.

Danny answered with a wide grin.

"That doesn't seem right," I added.

Sensing my discomfort, Dad observed, "I don't think people these past few evenings have the idea that this is a money-making proposition. They've just been having fun – catching crawlers with their neighbors – then, giving their catch to you boys for Homer. I wouldn't count on them to continue forever. But, for now, it's just good, neighborly fun."

I was relieved to hear Dad's point of view.

"Who collected crawlers last night?"

"Help me out here, Danny! Let's see. There was Mom, Aunt Maude, and myself from our house. Mr. and Mrs. Tucker and Chub from Danny's house. Oh – and Danny – of course. Ah, let me think. Oh, yeah. The Reillys came by for a little bit. And – who else, Danny?"

"There was Sherm – and his parents – for a little while. Then there was Mrs. Mikas."

"Mrs. Mikas!" I said with surprise.

Dad started snickering. Mom and Aunt Maude laughed, too.

"What's so funny about Mrs. Mikas?"

Mom filled me in between giggles, "She came in her big pink night gown carrying a lighted candle. She claimed she didn't have a flashlight. She – she – !"

Mom's laughter prevented her from continuing. She was a lot like Grandma in that respect.

Dad rescued her, "Then, when she got down on the ground, she couldn't see. She was too close to earth, she said. Apparently, she's near sighted – or is it far sighted? Anyway, I had to get her spectacles from her bedroom."

Dad began to laugh uncontrollably, so Danny took over for him.

"And she brought a – CHAMBER POT! To put her night crawlers in. Said that she didn't have any tin cans. All squashed for Bohunk Joe," giggled Danny. "Every time she caught one, she'd scream. Didn't like to touch them, she told us. She only caught a dozen or so all night."

Aunt Maude joined in, trying hard not to laugh like the others. "But that wasn't the funny part. When she decided to go home, she couldn't get up. The cool and damp lawn had evidently gotten to her joints."

"So we had to jack her up!" Danny interrupted.

"I used the hand truck from the shed. The one with wheels – that I use for moving heavy sewing cabinet boxes," Dad explained between snorts.

"Yeah! Dad had to slide it under her – her bottom first!" chuckled Mom.

"Once I got her to sit back against it, I was able to wheel her home – to her back porch steps – where she finally got upright – after quite a struggle."

Finally, the four of them broke into hysterical laughter that lasted for at least a mile. I didn't see what was so funny. I guessed you had to be there. Or maybe I was just tired.

"How are the Matlocks doing?" I finally asked, shifting to a less humorous subject.

"Oh, that's right!" Dad said. "We almost forgot."

Dad and Mom described how the neighborhood had poured out their charity in the form of casseroles and clothing. Gentleman Jim and Bohunk Joe came by with a pushcart full of dented cans from the canning factory. A "Matlock Special Order" they called it.

That started a neighborhood movement to donate cans, cartons, and packages of food. Even the Tuckers brought two cases of unwrapped canned goods to add the element of surprise to the meals at the Libby-Matlock home.

Mrs. Libby's house was overflowing with large-sized Matlocks and all the well-meaning gifts. Of course, Mr. Matlock wasn't there most of the time. He still had two jobs to work. Mrs. Matlock had taken up residence in the first downstairs bedroom, Barb's room, so she could follow doctor's orders and stay in bed. And, fortunately, the children played outside most of the time.

The car fell silent for a mile or two. I heard heavy breathing from the backseat. I turned around to see that Aunt Maude and Mom were sound asleep. I wasn't sure about Danny, but his eyes were closed.

I turned my attention back to the Matlocks. Their current situation concerned me. I knew they couldn't stay with Mrs. Libby, forever.

"Where are the Matlocks going to live after the girls come home, Dad?"

"We'll just have to see. I guess they could rebuild their house. But I don't know if that's a realistic option. I don't think Mr. Matlock earns a whole lot, working where he does. And what little he makes goes to feed and care for that large family of his. I suppose they'll have to rent a house someplace. Then sell their lot – for whatever a lot alongside the railroad tracks might bring."

My mind returned to the night of the fire. The children huddled around Mrs. Matlock's cot in the middle of the street. Their home and all their possessions totally destroyed. I felt very sad for them, all over again.

"Dad, how much would it cost to rebuild the Matlock house?"

"Gee! That's a good question."

At that, Dad began talking to himself.

"Let me see. What did our house cost? But they'd need three times the house we have – with that large family. And there's the increased cost of materials, if you can get them at all, because of the war."

I forever marveled at Dad's ability to calculate figures in his head.

"Let's see – that would be – plus that – and that – oh, yeah – that. Okay, I suppose, maybe $3,000 for building materials. That's lumber, blocks, bricks, roofing, plumbing, and electrical supplies. Yeah, that's about it. Then you'd have to add the cost of skilled tradesmen."

Dad nodded his head and gave me his estimate.

"The total would be about $4,000 including tradesmen labor."

"What's tradesmen labor?" asked Danny from the backseat.

So he was awake, after all. I should have known.

"It's the cost of hiring skilled carpenters, bricklayers, plumbers, electricians, and so on," Dad said, speaking softly so not to wake Aunt Maude or Mom.

"Of course, when we built our house, Uncle Van and I did ninety percent of the work ourselves. We provided most of the labor. So, in our case, labor costs didn't amount to much."

Dad contemplated a moment more. Then he added, "I'm not too sure how good Mr. Matlock is with a hammer. I got a feelin' he's not all that handy. He'd probably have to hire more help than we did."

"Are you pretty sure about the $4,000, Dad?"

"Theirs was a modest house. Yes, I'd say so – give or take a few hundred. Of course, that doesn't include furnishings – furniture, dishware, and the like."

After a moment of silence, I heard the tiny voice from the backseat again, "Jase, how much FSG money do we have right now?"

In response to Danny's question, I counted aloud, "$21.00 in bubble gum money. $4.75 in worm money. That's a total of $25.75."

There was no response from the backseat. I turned around, looked him in the eye and asked, "You're not thinking of – ?"

Danny leaned back against his pair of sleeping people pillows, put his hands behind his head, and smiled. Then he declared matter-of-factly, "I think we should help the Matlocks build a new house."

Dad gasped noticeably. I was flabbergasted.

Without missing a beat, Danny added, "$25.75 out of $4,000. Heck! We're almost there!"

17 A NEW CAMPAIGN

THE LOW MURMUR OF HUSHED CONVERSATION WOKE me from a sound sleep. Among the soft voices I heard was Danny's. Could it be?

When I stumbled into the kitchen, Danny was attacking a massive stack of pancakes, dripping with gobs of melted butter and maple syrup. Mom and Aunt Maude were hovering over him, poised to grant his every gastronomical wish. Dad was admiring Danny's marvelous ability to consume hotcakes.

Danny gave me a syrupy smile and waggled his buttery fork in my direction. "Mahn. Wah thum pachs? Ter deshos!" he mumbled incomprehensively.

"What?"

He swallowed hard and repeated, "Good morning. Want some pancakes? They're delicious!"

Ignoring his offer, I asked, "Why are you here so early?"

But he was always here this early. Otherwise, he might miss breakfast, I reminded myself. *Why would today be any different?*

"Well, now that Danny's here, the two of you can tell Aunt Maude and Mom about your Matlock idea. When the idea came up in the car last night, they were both asleep," Dad suggested to change the subject.

"What about the Matlocks?" Mom asked with interest.

Danny pointed his right index finger to the ceiling, wiped his mouth on his shirttail, and centered his corporal stripes. He was ready to answer her question with authority. "People shouldn't have to live in our neighborhood – without a house," he explained.

Content with himself, Danny took an enormous bite of pancakes and gazed smugly at a confused Aunt Maude and Mom. I provided the needed translation, "We think everybody in our neighborhood deserves a house of their own. But the Matlocks don't have a lot of money, so we'd like to ask people in Riverton to contribute to a fund – for rebuilding their house."

"Wow! That's a terrific idea!" Aunt Maude replied enthusiastically. "That would mean a lot more to them than casseroles and cast-offs."

But Mom didn't share Aunt Maude's excitement. She wrinkled her brow and stared into her coffee cup. After a long minute, she said, "I'm real proud of you boys for wanting to help the Matlocks. And I'm happy to hear the details of your plan. But I have to say, I'm concerned."

Danny stopped chewing. *What could possibly be wrong with wanting to help the Matlocks?* I asked myself. Mom answered my question.

"Since the Depression, our neighbors have taken great pride in not being on welfare anymore. Many of them would rather starve than take money from others – regardless of our good intentions or their severe need. The Matlocks may not relish being singled out as a charity case."

Aunt Maude and Dad nodded their heads slowly. Mom had made a good point.

"You may be right, Marie. I didn't think of that angle. I know for a fact that Mr. Matlock is a very proud man. We wouldn't want to insult him," Dad cautioned.

"But Dad! We're only trying to help them."

"Help is defined by the recipient, Jase."

Reluctantly, I had to agree.

"Can you think of a way to convince the Matlocks to accept help from the community, Marie? They sure could use it," Aunt Maude reminded us.

"There has to be a way. I'll talk to Louise Libby. After all, she convinced the Matlocks to accept the charity of her hospitality – seemingly without too much effort. I'll go see her right after breakfast and find out how she did it."

"Good thinking, Marie," Dad said. "Would you like to hear how the boys plan to launch their campaign?"

"Definitely! Tell us how you'll raise the money. By the way, how much money are we talking about?"

"Forthos dahls. Wev ahred ga twafif sevfif!" Danny mumbled between munches.

"Four thousand dollars. We've already got $25.75!" I translated again. "Our bubble gum and our worm money – so far."

"Four thousand dollars!" Aunt Maude cried. "That's a fortune!"

"Tell them your idea, Jase," Dad urged. "You're going to love this, ladies."

I outlined our plan for launching "The Matlock Family Building Fund" campaign. When I finished, "Wow!" was Aunt Maude's only response.

"Boys, it's a terrific plan! Your work's cut out for you. But I'm confident you can do it!" Mom said. "I'll do my best to help you get the Matlocks' permission to proceed."

"Meantime, Aunt Maude and I are off to work," Dad announced, pointing to the kitchen clock. "You boys'll be visiting the canning factory this morning. Am I right?"

We walked Aunt Maude and Dad to the front door.

"Good luck, boys! And Marie, too!" Aunt Maude hollered over her shoulder.

Just then, Sergeant Jeff's police car pulled up in front of our house. He hopped out and walked toward us. "Morning, everybody. John – boys. I've made arrangements for the four of us to give our formal statements to the FBI – and the federal prosecutor – at Sheriff Connors' office after work this afternoon. At five o'clock. I'll pick you up here about four-thirty if that's okay with everybody."

Imagine! I pondered dreamily. *Giving our sworn statements to real G-men.*

"Will J. Edward Hoover be there?" I asked, half in jest.

"He's tied up in Washington and won't be able to make it," Danny stated matter-of-factly.

Everybody laughed. Despite himself, Danny giggled, too. This rare behavior on his part caused the rest of us to laugh even harder.

WHEN WE ARRIVED AT the canning factory, Otto and his crew were busily moving cases of applesauce into a sparkling new boxcar standing on the siding. When they saw us pop up onto the platform, they stopped and waved amiably in our direction.

"Hi, Otto. Is Sergeant Rick here today?" I asked.

"Ya! Inzide," Otto confirmed, pointing toward the nearest door. "You boyz got any big ladies for rezcue todayz?"

We shook our heads and laughed.

Sergeant Rick was right inside the door talking to a tall, friendly-looking man wearing a white shirt with a red and blue striped tie. The man carried a clipboard jammed with papers. "Day Shift Foreman" was painted in white across the top of the board.

"Hello, boys. Haven't seen you since the day of the Matlock fire. Meet Mr. Thacker."

We introduced ourselves to Mr. Thacker who, judging from his comments about the bubble gum-kraut caper, the POW escape, and the Matlock rescue, already knew a lot about us. I liked him immediately. After exchanging pleasantries, Mr. Thacker asked us, "Is there anything we can do for you boys, today?"

"As a matter of fact, there is!" I replied.

We explained how the canning factory could assist us in launching the Matlock Family Building Fund campaign. Both Sergeant Rick and Mr. Thacker were enthralled with our plan. When we finished, they gave us their unqualified support.

"You boys are something else! Wait 'til Otto and his crew hear about this!" Sergeant Rick exclaimed.

"Speaking of that bunch, why don't we use them to put this order together? They're as qualified as anybody in the plant to run the job," Mr. Thacker reasoned. "Besides, they've got a vested interest in the Matlock case. They'd be insulted if we let somebody else do it."

"Good idea!" Danny agreed.

When Otto heard our plan, including his crew's involvement, he whooped his approval. He ordered his men to assemble inside the factory where he explained the details in awe-inspiring, hand-waving German. After Otto's animated crescendo, the POWs cheered and pounded our backs to show their support.

"Okay! Okay! Glad you like it. Okay!" Danny squealed, fighting to maintain his balance under the barrage of back slaps. "Hey! Watch the crutches!"

Otto and his crew headed off to the materials area to assemble what was needed to finish our job for us. Danny and I thanked them and departed for Bohunk Joe's to arrange our transportation.

As we crossed New Albany Avenue, Danny stated what both of us were thinking, "I sure hope your mother gets the Matlocks to give us the go-ahead."

"Oh, she will. She's good at that sort of thing."

Upon our arrival, we found Bohunk Joe cleaning a fat raccoon with his sharp skinning knife on the table next to his knife-sharpening wheel. He explained that occasionally a raccoon gets caught in one of the mink traps "bay mushtak" which means "by mistake" in Bohunk Joean.

After he had finished, he carefully tacked the coonskin to the side of his shack next to a dozen other assorted pelts that were drying there. Then he added the cleaned carcass to his cooking pot along with a fistful of spices from a leather pouch that hung just inside his shack.

As he cleaned his hands on one of his many burlap bags, Bohunk Joe sat down on his front yard chair and gave us his full attention, "Okay! Vat Joe can do for hes boyz?"

We shared our plan with him. He was so moved that two huge tears welled up in his eyes, popped to the hilt of his scimitar nose, and streamed down his cheeks. Between sobs, he pledged his full support and cooperation, "Joe vill halp – in any vay."

Before lending us his pushcart, he insisted we sign him up as Riverton's very first business sponsor for the Matlock campaign. He also offered his services, free of charge, for our planned grand finale.

To be honest, knife sharpening wasn't on our list of necessities for the Matlock campaign. But what did we know? This was our first fundraiser!

We wheeled Bohunk Joe's pushcart back to the loading dock where we waited for Otto and his crew to complete our custom order. After an hour, Mr. Thacker, Sergeant Rick, and Otto emerged from the canning factory. Wearing ear-to-ear grins, the three men approached us with their hands behind their backs.

Otto reached us first. He proudly presented his gift, "Heer ist dah colletshun can!"

It was gorgeous. Otto and his crew had produced the highly polished tin can precisely as we had ordered. It was the size of a large juice can. And it had been machine-sealed at both ends.

Otto pointed out the slot that his men had cleanly punched in the top of each can, "Itz big enuff for da silver dahler. Or cash monez. Or bahnk checzs."

We told Otto and his crew that they had, indeed, done an excellent job. And we meant it! Otto beamed! His crew slapped him on the back.

"Germans sure like slapping each other!" Danny accurately observed.

Sergeant Rick could wait no longer. We gasped our approval when he presented his contribution. It was stunning!

"The can wrapper! Just the way you wanted it."

And so it was!

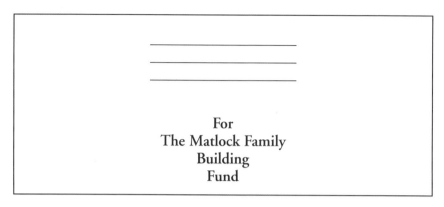

For
The Matlock Family
Building
Fund

"It's great!" I declared. "Boy, the red printing really looks swell!"

"Yeah! And there's plenty of room to write the names of businesses and such – in them blank spaces – right above the fund name," Sergeant Rick boasted.

Those words were apparently Mr. Thacker's cue.

Out from behind his back came a clipboard, just like his. The words "Matlock Building Fund" were inscribed across its top. The clipboard clamp held a pad of lined paper on which someone had boldly printed the numbers from "#1" to "#200." He also held out a bundle of yellow pencils, two marking pens, and a small glue pot with a brush built into its screw cap.

"Credit for these items goes to the ladies in administration. They do all the typesetting for our can wrappers before they go to the print shop. When they heard about your fund-raising plan, they thought you might need some way of tracking your can sponsors. So they also printed these sign-up sheets for you," Mr. Thacker told us.

"Wow! Now, we're really organized," I declared.

"And here's some pencils for writing up the inventory – and glue for attaching the wrapper to the can after you fill it in. These markers are ideal for putting the business name on the wrapper. They're black ink – and make heavy, bold letters. I hope you like the color. I think it will look good with the red printing and the white wrapper."

"Great!" yelled Danny, accepting the clipboard from Mr. Thacker's outstretched hands. "What's this?"

Danny pointed at the pencil writing on the first sign-up sheet.

"Oh, that's the best news! We believed you could use a bit of a head start," Mr. Thacker explained with a smile. "And, besides, we wanted to be the first to sign up for a can – or I should say four cans. Right, Otto? Rick?"

I glanced over Danny's shoulder and read the first four entries on the sign-up sheet:

#1 - **Camp Riverton**
       Prisoners of War

#2 - **Camp Riverton**
       Military Police

#3 - **Chippewa Canning Corporation**
       Hourly Employees

#4 - **Chippewa Canning Corporation**
       Managers and Supervisors

Danny looked at me. Then he asked Mr. Thacker, "Do you need any knives sharpened?"

"Huh?"

Mr. Thacker was stumped by Danny's question, but I wasn't. How would we break the news to Bohunk Joe that he had been summarily demoted from Number One to Number Five?

Otto's men excitedly loaded the cases of Matlock cans into Bohunk Joe's pushcart. When they finished, Sergeant Rick summarized our situation for us, "Well, you're all set. Two hundred cans and two hundred wrappers – minus the four we took out for our cans. Two hundred cans at twenty bucks a can. That's four thousand bucks – right on the button. Wish ya luck, boys. Let us know if ya need any more help from us!"

We thanked Mr. Thacker, Sergeant Rick, and Otto and his crew profusely for their assistance. Then I carefully pushed the fully loaded cart toward the ramp at the west end of the dock. Danny thumped along behind me on his crutches.

"We'll see you on the Fourth for the – Hey! What are you calling the celebration on the Fourth of July?" Mr. Thacker asked.

"The Matlock Can Opener!" Danny answered instantly.

WHEN WE WHEELED INTO his yard, Bohunk Joe was stationed behind his knife-sharpening wheel, dressing the edge of his skinning knife. He tested its sharpness with his thumb, declared it perfect, and returned it to the sheath on his belt.

Then he turned to us and smiled with anticipation. My campaign co-chairman didn't disappoint him.

With Joe looking on, Danny spread a new can wrapper over the table next to Joe's wheel. Using bold black lettering, he printed the name of Joe's business in the blank spaces above the words, "For The Matlock Family Building Fund."

B. Joe's Knife Sharp.
Squawst Tin Cans & Old Newspapers
Used Cooking Fat & Animel Pelts

In a flash, Danny fastened Joe's wrapper around a shiny new collection can with the dripping glue brush. Then, right beside Bohunk Joe's business name, he etched a giant –

#1

With exaggerated ceremony, Danny bestowed the prized can on the sentimental bum. Joe was speechless. He cradled the can tenderly in his arms as if it were the Academy Award. His eyes turned teary, again. He thanked us over and over. Then he turned abruptly and disappeared into his shack.

Danny looked at me and winked. I smiled and nodded my approval.

Danny retrieved the clipboard from the pushcart and entered Bohunk Joe's business name in the fifth slot on the inventory sheet. As we were preparing to leave, Joe appeared at the window and wheezed at us, "Leev me nutter cahn. One for Old Levies. Dee junx mahn."

Danny nodded in a businesslike fashion and prepared another wrapper. This one read simply –

Old Levy
Skins & Scrap Mets.
Southside Junkyard

After affixing the wrapper, he placed the second can on Joe's table. Then we headed for home.

On our way, we perfected our sales pitch and landed three more sponsors. Danny carefully added their names to our inventory.

> **Pete's Grosery-Likker-Hardware Store**
> **Lots - Pop/Candy/Gum**

> **Riverton Ice & Coal Co.**
> **Mr. Stanley - Nice Ice Man**

> **U.S. Post Offise**
> **Neighborhood Male Men**

We parked our pushcart next to the back porch and yelled for Mom. When she opened the kitchen door, we excitedly displayed our fund-raising tools – the shiny cans, the crisply printed wrappers, the clipboard-bound inventory sheets, the marking pens, glue pot, and pencils.

"Look how many we got already!" Danny exclaimed, thrusting the clipboard at her. "And we just started."

Mom was clearly impressed. "This is marvelous. Look at the progress you've made. I can't believe it."

Then she hesitated before saying, "I hope you won't be disappointed. We don't have the Matlocks' approval, yet."

"What did Mrs. Libby say, Mom?"

"First of all, Mrs. Libby thinks your idea is – inspired! Yes, that's how she put it. She's sure Mrs. Matlock will see it that way, too. But she's not the problem. Mr. Matlock's going to be the hard sell."

"Oh, no!"

"Don't get me wrong. He's a very proud man. But it's not impossible," Mom assured us.

Then she smiled. "It seems that Mr. Matlock has a weakness. He loves children. That's where you boys come in."

"I was afraid you'd say that," Danny said softly.

"Mrs. Libby thinks you boys should make your appeal directly to Mr. Matlock – personally and as soon as possible. She's waiting for you to come over – right now. You just have enough time before you're off to New Albany for your FBI statements."

"Holy Crow!" I moaned.

LOUISE LIBBY GREETED US warmly and led us through her kitchen to the living room. When we entered, Mr. Matlock glanced up from the middle of the couch where he sat surrounded by his children. Both sets of twins, the boys and the girls, clung to their father in fear of losing him as they had their home and possessions.

Butch Matlock sat alone in the only other piece of furniture in the small room, a lime-colored overstuffed chair. He looked like an over-sized pink pea, nestled in a green pod.

We couldn't see her, but Mrs. Matlock's strong voice greeted us from the double bed, beyond the open door of the bedroom adjoining the crowded living room.

"HELLO, BOYS! THANK YOU AGAIN FOR YOUR BRAV-ERY AND QUICK THINKING. I WOULDN'T BE HERE IF IT WEREN'T FOR YOU! THANK YOU! WE ALL THANK YOU," she said, her voice charged with emotion.

Her words caught me by surprise. I hadn't thought of our behavior as *bravery!* I was flattered, but embarrassed, by her characterization. In contrast, Danny obviously perceived her warm words as a marvelous introduction. And he wasted no time in taking advantage of the opportunity.

Danny hobbled across Mrs. Libby's braided rug to a spot directly in front of Mr. Matlock. He narrowed his shoulders and leaned forward on his crutches, making himself appear limp and helpless. He looked at Mr. Matlock forlornly while waiting for me to assume my position.

I moved in behind Danny, juggling the assortment of campaign materials that we had brought with us. I felt like a magician's assistant. I cleared my throat to let the Great Dandino know I was in place. Mom and Mrs. Libby peered apprehensively from the kitchen door. A hush fell over the room.

Danny pushed his shoulders back, stood tall in his crutches, and began. His voice was soft but strong.

"Children! Children, Mr. Matlock! We are here today to talk about children. Not just any children, Mr. Matlock. But your children, sir. All children need a home of their own, Mr. Matlock. But your poor children have no home."

Mrs. Libby and Mom stared at Danny in disbelief from the kitchen. We were astounded! Was this passionate speech coming from Danny? Or had the ghost of William Jennings Bryan taken possession of his body?

Danny paused and looked directly into Mr. Matlock's eyes before continuing, "It's not right, Mr. Matlock. But you haven't done anything wrong. You're a good father. You've just had some very bad luck!"

I watched Mr. Matlock carefully. The color of his face changed from the pale pink like Butch's to a deep red-purple. His Adam's apple bobbed up and down like a wren's tail. He choked back his emotions. I feared Danny might have gone too far.

Danny pressed on passionately, "But you are blessed, Mr. Matlock. Fortune has brought good luck. Good luck for you and Mrs. Matlock – but most important – good luck for Butch – and pretty Judie and Janie – and little Jerry and Larry."

Danny paused and smiled at each of the Matlock children as if he were running for office. Then he went on.

"Yes, Mr. Matlock. We – the People of Riverton – want to rebuild your house for you. We want Butch to have a room of his own. And a bedroom for each set of twins. We want Mrs. Matlock to have a brand new kitchen – with an electric refrigerator this time.

"And, when those new twins arrive, we want them to be proud of their new house. Yes, we want them to say, *'Oh! What a pretty house! Let's stay, shall we?'* Children, Mr. Matlock! We are here today for the sake of your children."

With a dramatic sweep of his arm, Danny pointed at his assistant. That was me!

"See these cans, Mr. Matlock. See these wrappers. Look at the businesses that have already signed up to help – just today. All you have to do is give us your okay – and your home is rebuilt. Will you help us do it, Mr. Matlock? Will you say yes? For the sake of your beautiful children?"

Mr. Matlock just sat there, purple as a grape. His Adam's apple danced the jitterbug. I wasn't sure what was going to happen. Danny didn't blink. He continued to stare at Mr. Matlock, waiting for his answer.

After what seemed like an hour, Janie tugged at her father's sleeve and innocently asked, "Daddy, does this mean that Judie and I gonna have our own room?"

That did it!

Poor Mr. Matlock completely lost his composure. Tears gushed from his eyes. He howled! He bawled like a baby. He couldn't catch his breath. Finally, he buried his face in his hands and sobbed mournfully. His body shook with emotion.

"HAROLD! STOP THAT BLUBBERING, RIGHT NOW! AND THANK THOSE BOYS. YOU HEAR?" ordered Mrs. Matlock from her bed.

"Thank you," a broken Mr. Matlock whimpered. "Thank you, boys."

Predictably, Danny attempted to bow, but his feet became entangled in his crutches. I grabbed his arm and marched him off the living room stage and out the kitchen door. I was determined to beat a hasty retreat before Mr. Matlock was overcome by a fit of pride and changed his mind.

Mom and I held hands as we walked toward home. We had just witnessed an astounding feat of persuasion. Danny's phenomenal performance had transcended the sublime.

Reverting to his old personality, Danny declared, "It's always hard to give houses to certain people."

18 POWER OF THE PRESS

WHEN WE ARRIVED HOME FROM DANNY'S MAGIC show, Sergeant Jeff and Dad were sitting on the front steps.

"How'd it go with Mr. Matlock?" Dad asked.

"Fantastic!" Mom said. "Danny gave a fine speech. Mr. Matlock said yes!"

"Wonderful! I knew you could do it!"

We shared all the details with Sergeant Jeff and Dad. After we finished, Dad smiled and shook his head. Then he turned to Sergeant Jeff.

"We're all here. You ready to go, Jeff?"

"Sure am! Can't keep the G-men waiting."

"Let's take some cans and wrappers," Danny suggested. "We can sign up some more can sponsors."

I argued unsuccessfully that our business at the sheriff's office involved matters totally unrelated to the Matlock campaign. But Danny wouldn't budge. So we loaded our supplies into the police car and departed for New Albany.

On the way, Danny enlightened us with a barrage of adages to justify his position. "Be prepared," he advised. "Opportunity only knocks once. Never look a gift horse in the eye. Beggars can't be losers. A penny earned is a penny saved. I never met a man I didn't know. Red sky at night – sailors get tight."

He paused, apparently searching for more sayings. I hoped he'd run dry.

But he started up again, "Early bird gets the word. Strike before closing. Winner takes all. Buy War Bonds."

I had reached my limit. The War Bonds did it. "Okay! Okay! I got it."

"All's swell that ends swell," he added, delivering his coup de grâce.

Unperturbed by my display of impatience, Danny adjusted his army cap and looked around the police car. Then he announced, "Someday, I'm going to be an FBI agent."

Sergeant Jeff looked in the rearview mirror, smiled at Danny, and said, "You'd make a good G-man, Danny. Look how you handled those POW escapees."

Danny nodded his agreement, set his eyes at half-mast, and inspected his fingernails. I'd seen Bob Hope do the same thing in *Road to Morocco.*

"That reminds me, Jeff. What's happened to those two rats?" Dad inquired.

"Colonel Butler was at the sheriff's office yesterday – giving his statement to the FBI. He told me – under the Geneva Convention – prisoners of war can't be punished for attempting to escape. I guess it's kinda their job. They're supposed to get loose and tie up all the police and military forces it takes to track them down."

"I never thought of it that way. Makes sense, though."

"Apparently, German POW escape attempts are rare these days. Most of 'em are on their best behavior. Trying to be model prisoners in hopes of being allowed to stay here after the war. They don't look forward to going home – not with the state of things in Germany. Yep! America's looking darn good to them, now."

"So our two escapees get off Scot free. Is that it?"

"Not quite. Colonel Butler said they'd be assigned to unfavorable camp duties – KP and such. Most important, they won't earn any more chits for the Post Exchange. Outside work for POWs is a privilege, not a right."

"Isn't that something?"

"What's that, John?"

"While the Libby girls face treason charges – with a possible death sentence – their POW accomplices are denied the privilege of buying bubble gum at the camp store. There's something unfair about that."

"Proves the importance of bubble gum," inscrutable Danny offered from the backseat.

When we arrived, the reception clerk escorted us to the small conference room next to Sheriff Connors' office. The room was being used as a temporary office by the two FBI agents assigned to the Libby-POW case.

From next door, we could hear the voices. The FBI agents, the federal prosecutor, and the sheriff were discussing what information they needed from the four of us to wrap up the prosecutor's case against the Libby girls.

After a few minutes, they entered the conference room and introduced themselves. The federal prosecutor told us that we would give our sworn statements, one person at a time.

"Danny, you're on crutches, so why don't you be first? That way we'll save you an extra trip back and forth to the waiting room," Sheriff Connors suggested. "I'll ask the rest of you to wait out front until we call for you."

As we made our way back to the waiting room, the interrogation team closed the door behind us. I heard Danny's voice. Then there was silence. I wondered what was going on.

We settled into our chairs and pawed through the stack of magazines on the impressive, glass-topped coffee table in front of us. I selected a thumb-worn edition of *Saturday Evening Post*. Dad chose a *Life* magazine. Sergeant Jeff opted for *Outdoor Life*.

I was fascinated by a story about a Rhode Island boy who uncovered a ring of lobster thieves that plied the waters of Narragansett Bay. The author called the crooks, "pot rustlers." That was a new one on me.

I had just begun the article when Sheriff Connors entered the waiting room and spoke to Dad, "John, we could use your help in here. Come on back, if you please."

After they had gone, Sergeant Jeff looked at me and shrugged his shoulders. In twenty minutes or so, Dad returned. He was chuckling to himself.

"What's so funny, Dad?"

"Danny refused to make his statement – without his lawyer present!" Dad snorted, struggling to contain his laughter.

"You gotta be kidding!" Sergeant Jeff sputtered.

All I could think to say was, "He doesn't even know a lawyer!"

"Danny wouldn't give the FBI agents or the prosecutor the time of day. Sheriff Connors and I assured him he wasn't accused of any crime. The prosecutor told Danny that the only purpose for his statement was to help the government sort out the facts of the case. He pleaded with Danny to cooperate. Time is of the essence, he told him. Got to get the evidence before the grand jury – by no later than tomorrow. But Danny still refused to cooperate."

Dad burst out laughing.

"Then what happened, Dad?"

Dad snorted again.

At last, Dad calmed down enough to tell us. "Finally, Danny agreed to cooperate – but for a price. His questioners gladly accepted his terms. Now, Danny's in there squawking his head off!"

"What was his price, Dad?"

"He wanted me to show you this," Dad answered, handing Danny's clipboard to me.

I read Danny's new entries.

Chippewa County
Sheriff Offise
Sherf. Connors & Depatees

FBI
Detroit Feeld Offise
All Aggents (G-mens)

Detroit Offise
U.S. Justiss Dept.
Fed. Prosacutters

No denying it. Danny was a born fund-raiser!

When Danny finished his statement, he thumped back to the waiting room and pointed his crutch at me, "You're next!"

As I rose to take my place in the hot seat, Danny added, "I didn't tell them about your bigmouth bass. I saved that for you."

The word "largemouth" leaped to my tongue. But I didn't say it. *Maybe "bigmouth" is more appropriate when it comes to Danny,* I told myself.

I finished my statement in record time. When I returned to the waiting room, I discovered that Danny hadn't wasted his time, either. He had a new can sponsor –

Riverton City Police Department
Sargint J. Tolna
Good Policeman

As Sergeant Jeff rose to take his turn in the interrogation room, he looked at me sheepishly and shrugged his shoulders. "Just couldn't say no," he confessed.

I returned to my article on pot rustlers. Dad picked up another copy of *Life*. This one had a dramatic picture of the D-Day invasion on the cover. Danny chose a *Ladies Home Companion*. "Looking for new recipes," he informed us.

"Good morning, gents!"

The familiar voice belonged to the friendly *Riverton Daily Press* reporter whom I remembered from the press conference at the Riverton High School auditorium.

"Chuck Nichols from the *Daily Press*," he reminded us, shaking Dad's hand. "Howdy, boys. I got a few more questions to ask about the Libby case. Would you mind?"

"No, not at all," Dad replied. "What would you like to know?"

"Just a minute!" Danny asserted abruptly. "Have you heard about the Matlock fire? And about our can campaign to collect money to rebuild the Matlock house?"

"Naturally, I've heard about the fire. Our paper ran a front-page story – with sensational pictures of the burning house – and of the POWs rescuing Mrs. Matlock. But the fund-raising campaign is news to me. Sounds intriguing. Tell me more."

My partner provided all the details. "And we'd be glad to furnish all the information you need on the Libby case – if you agree to two things."

"What two things?" asked the wary newsman.

"First, you have to sign up to sponsor a collection can – for the newspaper office."

"Done! What's the second thing?"

"You need to write a story about the Matlock campaign."

"Piece of cake. I'd ah done that without your asking."

Danny signed him up.

Riverton Daily Press
Reporter Knuckles
Good Guy

After Mr. Nichols got his name spelled correctly, he began his interview.

"Now, let me get this straight – this campaign was your idea, right, boys? How many cans are available? And the Matlock Can Opener will be held on the Fourth of July – at the Good Mission Church?"

He pulled a pencil from behind his ear and made notes in a small pad he carried in the pocket of his sports coat. When he finished asking every question he could think of, he reviewed his notes.

Then he said, "Boy! The Fourth will be here before we know it. Do you boys think there's enough time to collect $4,000?"

"Yep! We'll make it," Danny promised him.

"One last thing – Artie – our photographer is over in the pressroom. Would you mind if he takes a shot or two of you fellas? Only take a second."

When Artie arrived, Danny straightened his army cap and stood high in his crutches. I juggled a can, wrapper, and the clipboard in my arms and stood by his side. I was getting used to being Danny's second.

Having looked at several popping flashbulbs, I could only sit and stare at the green spots on the wall. I never finished the story about Narragansett lobster mobsters.

After Artie and Mr. Nichols left, I remembered, "Hey! He forgot to ask us his questions about the Libby case."

We all laughed.

ON OUR WAY HOME, I realized that I was very hungry and remembered that we were having spaghetti for supper.

"Dad, can Danny eat with us tonight? We want to visit some neighbors this evening – to sign them up for cans," I explained. "Also, we gotta catch some night crawlers."

Dad thought it was a good idea. Danny smiled and tapped me on the left bicep.

After a quick supper, our first stop was the Good Mission Church to ask Reverend and Mrs. Squires to host the Matlock Can Opener. We wanted their commitment before – thanks to Danny – their names were announced in tomorrow's *Daily Press*!

After hearing our plan, Reverend and Mrs. Squires offered their full support. Why hadn't they thought of a Matlock fund-raiser themselves? This idea was nothing short of Divine Intervention, a generous act of God himself. Charity in its purest form.

Knowing the fund-raiser was Danny's idea, I was a bit uncomfortable with the turn the conversation had taken. No telling what Danny might do with unlimited "Divine" authority.

And Danny proved that my concern was justified.

As we were leaving the Good Mission Church, he turned on his crutches and etched a two-finger cross in the air at the startled Squires who clearly hadn't expected to be blessed that evening. They believed they were merely waving good-bye to us from their back porch.

After thanking them again, we started our door-to-door campaign to sign up more can sponsors. I wheeled Bohunk Joe's pushcart behind Danny who bumped along on his crutches. We had wonderful luck.

Using his power as a recently anointed deity, Danny came up with some inspired business names for his wrappers.

> **Riverton Public Works Dept.**
> **Hans Zeyer - Ass. Dirctor.**
> **Good American**

Danny insisted on adding the acknowledgement of Hans' good citizenship to the can wrapper.

> **Burkes Factory**
> **Tool & Dye**
> **Dad - Mr. Addison**

Dad quipped that "Tool & Dye" sounded more like a beauty parlor than a critical defense occupation. Danny said he didn't get the joke.

> **Riverton Central Telephone Co.**
> **Operators - Mrs. Shurtleif**
> **Air-Raid Wife**

> **Grand Trunk Railroad Yard**
> **Mr. Matlock**
> **Father of Thankfull Children**

Danny explained that a little reinforcement of his sales pitch to Mr. Matlock wouldn't hurt.

Homer - Has Worms
Bate Deal.
Good Partner

Chippewa Accounting
Offise Man.
Mr. Reilly & Mrs. - Chickens

I hadn't known that the chicken-loving Mr. Reilly was an accountant.

St. Tom. Catholick Church
For their Son
Mr. & Mrs. Borski

Woolworth Lunch Counter
Waitresses & Aunt Maude
Bad Sprinklers - Good Food

Aunt Maude laughed and told us she wasn't sure what the store manager might think of Danny's wrapper. But it was certainly true. Danny's left foot left no doubt about that.

"I betcha I can talk my business-owner customers into at least a half-dozen more cans at the lunch counter tomorrow," Aunt Maude assured us. We made a date to meet her at Woolworth's the next day.

We had a perfect record. No one had turned us down. We decided to try our luck one last time before calling it a night.

Even though the Graham Market on the corner next to Pete's was officially closed, we noticed that the store manager was working late. We tapped on the window glass and waited for him to open the door.

The manager was a fastidious man who, each day, wore a trim black bow tie plastered against the stubby, stiffly starched collar of his white shirt. His face was drawn back as if someone behind him were pulling his hair. This created the impression that he was looking to both sides, instead of directly at you. In short, he resembled a walleye pike.

From my experience, he was just as likely to bite off your head as look at you, especially if you were a neighborhood boy. I didn't care much for our Graham Market manager, so I seldom went into the store. In fact, I didn't even know the ill-tempered man's name.

"Hello, sir," I said politely, when he cracked open the door.

"We're closed. Go away!"

But we ignored his attitude. We had a perfect record, remember?

"We wanted to give your Graham Market the opportunity to sponsor a collection can to support the Matlock Family Building Fund. We know that –," Danny managed to say before being rudely interrupted.

"Can? No-can-do. It's against company policy. Can't you see I'm busy? Now, go away!" the store manager roared, slamming the door in our faces.

I looked at Danny and repeated the words, "Against company policy!"

Danny glared at the closed door and vowed, "We'll see about that!"

BEFORE GOING TO BED, Dad and I stored the cartons of campaign supplies on top of the new worm boxes stacked against the back of the house. We covered them with a tarpaulin in case of rain.

Next morning, Danny and I borrowed Sherm's wagon, loaded it with supplies, and headed for the bus stop. Danny, trailing behind on his crutches, provided directions.

"A little to the right. That's good. Okay, straight now. Slow down. Watch that root. Don't let that load shift. Pick up the pace!"

He jabbered away. And I humored him by not objecting.

When the bus arrived, Mr. Smalley and I stored the cartons and Sherm's wagon in the luggage compartment. Danny boarded the bus, lowered the window, and offered his theories on optimal storage. Mr. Smalley frowned, but he didn't say a word.

After seating himself behind the huge steering wheel, Mr. Smalley nudged the behemoth bus into traffic and resumed his run toward the downtown station. Danny recognized the opportunity to make another sale.

"Have you heard about our can campaign for the Matlocks, Mr. Smalley? How about the bus company signing up to sponsor a can? Watch that kid on the bicycle! There, on the left, Mr. Smalley. How would you like your business listed on the can, sir? Be careful! Car edging out of Ann Arbor Street. See him? Move over toward the centerline a bit, sir. That's good. Okay! Steady as she goes. What name should I use?"

Danny showed Mr. Smalley no mercy.

Offering to buy the poor driver a *Bromo-Seltzer* from the bus station lunch counter before the next leg of his route came to mind. But I dismissed the idea. "He's a professional bus driver," I rationalized. "Drivers are trained to deal with emergencies – like Danny."

Demonstrating remarkable coolness under fire, Mr. Smalley recommended that we speak to the Chippewa Trails operations manager at the bus station. The manager would surely support the Matlock can campaign. And we could probably convince him to allow us to store our cartons in the luggage checkroom.

What an excellent idea! We needed a downtown distribution center.

Upon hearing Mr. Smalley's suggestion, Danny called off his attack, at least temporarily. The driver looked immensely relieved. He whistled softly and overconfidently as it turned out.

Without warning, Danny struck again. "Mr. Smalley, don't you and Mrs. Smalley sing in the First Methodist Church choir?"

The driver's shoulders slumped noticeably. Then he nodded his head.

"How would you like that written on your can wrapper, sir?"

Mr. Smalley didn't answer, so Danny took it upon himself to inscribe the wrapper in his own special way.

First Methods Church
Mr. Smelly & Mrs.
Bus Driv. & Choir Sing.

As we left the bus, Danny presented the carefully wrapped can to Mr. Smalley. I thought again about treating Mr. Smalley to a *Bromo-Seltzer*. Maybe even a double.

Within minutes after our arrival, Danny had convinced the operations manager to store our cans and wrappers in the checkroom, in exchange for the *privilege* of being one of our can sponsors. What a salesman!

Danny inked the deal.

Chippewa Tails Bus Line
Passingurs & Frate
Safe & Nice Drivers

We stored half our cargo, loaded the other half into Sherm's wagon, and headed out the waiting room door.

"Hey! Wait up!"

We turned to see Chuck Nichols coming our way at a brisk pace. With his pencil behind his ear and his pad in his hand, he was ready for business.

"How's the Matlock campaign going?" he asked as he caught up with us.

"Great!" Danny answered. "Got fifty businesses signed up, already – only a hundred and fifty to go. And it's only our second day!"

"Wow! That's terrific. The whole town's jumping on the Matlock bandwagon, huh?"

"We *did* have one refusal," Danny said with a scowl.

"No! Who's that?"

"We probably shouldn't say, Mr. Nichols," I responded, not wanting to spread gossip.

Apparently, Danny didn't hear me!

"It was Graham Markets! Against company policy – they said," Danny blurted out.

Danny's news apparently touched a nerve.

"Graham Markets! A *company policy* against helping the Matlocks! E.F. Graham's a self-righteous old cheapskate! He's got every nickel he ever made. Did he *personally* tell you about this so-called policy?"

Against my better judgment, Danny and I described our previous evening's run-in with the Graham store manager. Danny also provided our reporter friend with a vivid description of the foul-natured, walleyed man that I – in the name of decency – wouldn't repeat here.

Mr. Nichols gleefully wrote down every word on his official reporter's pad. When he finished, he stuck his pencil back behind his ear and thanked us profusely.

"This is a real scoop! Gotta go back and amend my story. Good luck, fellas. I'll check back, later," he promised, setting off briskly for the *Riverton Daily Press* building.

After he was well beyond earshot, I confronted Danny on his exaggerated estimate of our success, "I may be wrong, but I think we have closer to twenty can sponsors at this point. How come you told Mr. Nichols fifty?"

"I was counting the number we'll have after Mr. Graham reads that article," Danny said, with a sly grin.

When we arrived at the Woolworth Lunch Counter, Aunt Maude had good news. She had tentatively enlisted a number of can sponsors. After reviewing her list, we eagerly departed to close the deals. Over the course of the morning, we signed up all her leads, plus a couple of our own. For example, we thought it only fitting to secure the sponsorship of the Libby girls' attorney.

Chambers & Chambers
Harry Chambers
Good Lawyer

And Aunt Maude's former landlord was an easy sell.

Fazio's Deli
Hot & Smelly
Etailian Foods

After signing up Aunt Maude's last three leads – two women's dress shops and a shoe store – we headed back to Woolworth's to see if she had any additional prospects.

Danny spotted Mayor Simmons from Granville coming our way up the sidewalk. As he neared, the mayor tried to avoid us by hiding behind a copy of yesterday's *Riverton Daily Press*.

"Hi, Mayor! Want a rematch?" Danny taunted, breaching the mayor's paper-thin defense.

The mayor's reaction verged on hysteria, "Oh, no, you don't! You're a ringer. No, sir-ee! No rematch from me – not today. Not ever!"

"Then I don't suppose you'll want to sponsor a Matlock can, either. Every business in town's doing it. Gonna be a big article in today's *Daily Press* about it. All can sponsors will get their names in the paper, too."

The mayor stopped in his tracks. The scrolling neon sign across his politician's forehead read, *Can sponsor. Free publicity! Can sponsor. Free publicity! Can –*

"What's a Matlock can?" he whimpered, helplessly hooked.

Danny inked another deal.

Granville Merchants
Geo. Simmons
Granville Mayor & Walnut

The good mayor insisted that Danny add the words, "Shell Game", after the word, "Walnut." But Danny refused, saying he wouldn't consent to the mayor's censorship. His argument made no sense, but it served his purpose.

The mayor caved again, promising to bring his shell game to the Matlock Can Opener on the Fourth of July and to contribute all his profits to the Matlock campaign. Danny smiled and magnanimously added the two words to the mayor's wrapper.

By now, the mayor was a beaten man. All he wanted was to grab his Matlock can and get out of Riverton.

AUNT MAUDE INVITED US to a late lunch with her at the dime store. We sat in the last booth near the back. Aunt Maude's friend Molly O'Brien took our order. We all chose club sandwiches and lemonade, the best lunch that money could buy, at least at Woolworth's.

A small round man with a huge smile on his face approached our booth. "Are these the heroes of Riverton?"

"Mr. Powell, this is Danny Tucker and my nephew, Jase Addison. Boys, Mr. Powell is our store manager."

"Hello, Mr. Powell. Pleased to meet you," we both replied.

Staring at Danny's crutches, the store manager expressed his condolences, "Hope that foot's better, son. The minute we heard about your accident, we dumped every one of those awful pond lily sprinklers in the trash. When you get better, come on back to the store. You can pick out any other sprinkler you want – at no charge. Yep, this one's on Woolworth's! That fair – or what?"

Danny didn't respond for the longest time.

He slurped his lemonade and sized up Mr. Powell. Finally, he spoke, "Don't need a sprinkler. How about a cap gun?"

"I – ah – sure! We got cap guns – and caps, too." Mr. Powell offered, relieved to reach an apparent settlement.

"And a cap gun for Jase, too?"

"Why – sure! Two cap guns for the heroes of Riverton. Why not?" Mr. Powell agreed.

"And lots of caps. Right?"

"Caps! You want caps, too? Well – I. You bet! A case of caps and two guns! How's that?" Mr. Powell asked, wiping his brow.

Danny didn't respond again.

He took another long slurp. He had Mr. Powell on the ropes. Feeling sorry for the man, I frowned and shook my head at Danny. He accepted my input by smiling at Mr. Powell and offering his hand. They shook on it.

Mr. Powell grinned. His manner turned jolly again.

"Gotta get back to work. But, before I go, there's something I gotta say to you boys. Congratulations on capturing the POWs – and those stupid Libby girls. Ditto for the Matlock campaign. You boys certainly have been busy beavers lately. And good citizens, too. Well done!"

After Mr. Powell's departure, we quietly munched our club sandwiches. Aunt Maude smiled at us and offered her sentiments, "What Mr. Powell said is all true. I'm very proud of you boys, too. I want you to know that."

Danny's face turned bright crimson. I didn't know what color mine was, but it sure felt hot. A compliment from Aunt Maude meant the world to me. And evidently to Danny, too.

"Oh, Jase. With all that's happened, I forgot to tell you. On Saturday, I got a letter from Uncle Van. He asked me to tell you – he's bringing a special gift for you – from Normandy. But he didn't say what it was. I suspect he wants to surprise you."

"It's an SS dagger!" Danny declared.

"What? How do you know that?" I demanded.

"I just do."

And that's all he'd say about it.

Danny couldn't possibly have known what Uncle Van was bringing me. But, despite myself, I asked, "Wonder if I can take my dagger to school to show Miss Sparks – and the students in our class?"

No one answered my question.

"I hoped you'd be here," Mr. Nichols said, slapping an early edition of the *Daily Press* down on our table. "Ink's hardly dry! Whatya think?"

A huge picture of Danny and me, taken at the sheriff's office, covered almost half the front page. Danny looked like a wounded veteran on crutches. With my arms filled with cans and other campaign materials, I looked like Bohunk Joe collecting recyclables for the war effort.

I focused on the blaring headline.

> # POW-TRAPPING YOUTHS LAUNCH REBUILDING CAMPAIGN FOR BURNT-OUT FAMILY
> ## Merchants Show Can-Do Spirit - Graham's Notable Exception

Mr. Nichols' article described our can campaign and announced plans for the Matlock Can Opener on the Fourth of July. He stated that our first day had netted the sponsorship and support of over fifty local businesses including industrial, commercial, and professional establishments.

Then he dropped the bombshell.

According to the article, every business contacted readily agreed to sponsor a collection can – with one exception:

> **Graham Markets has refused to participate in the Matlock rebuilding campaign because to do so would run contrary to a long-standing company policy that forbids support of local charities.**

"That ought to show that old skinflint!" Mr. Nichols said with a grin. We didn't say a word.

"Well! Gotta go. Up to Bay City to cover the grand jury proceedings. It's rumored that the jury will hand down its findings this afternoon. Doesn't look good for the Libby girls. My sources say they'll be charged with treason, after all."

The reporter dashed from the dime store and hopped into his car that was double-parked right out front. The big "PRESS" sign in his window apparently granted him immunity from parking tickets.

Suddenly, his departing words hit me. Treason! Poor Mrs. Libby.

With a sense of urgency, Aunt Maude gave us our instructions, "I can't leave. But you boys get on home as fast as you can. Tell your mother – and Mrs. Libby – what we just heard. The grand jury may report out *this afternoon*. This wasn't supposed to happen until next week. Anyway, Louise will want to get back up to Bay City to be with her daughters. Okay?"

We left our cans and labels behind Aunt Maude's lunch counter and ran-thumped out of the store. We caught the New Albany bus, just as it was about to leave the station.

UPON OUR ARRIVAL HOME, we hurriedly told Mom what we had learned. Tearing off her apron, she said, "Let's go tell Louise. Rumor or not, she needs to know."

Mrs. Libby listened to our news calmly. Then she responded unemotionally, "I'll pack and drive to Bay City right away. Thank you for bringing me this news."

We told her that she was most welcome.

"I'll be all right," she assured us, without our asking.

Wanting to deliver some good news, Danny showed Mrs. Libby the early edition of the newspaper. She smiled, "You boys should be very proud of this article. This will really bring in the can customers, won't it?"

Danny, Mom, and I sat on our front porch waiting to give Mrs. Libby a flurry of good luck waves as she departed for potential bad news in Bay City. Within minutes, she zipped by in her familiar blue Plymouth sedan. We waved wildly, giving her the best send-off we could. She saw us but didn't return our waves. We understood.

As she turned onto New Albany Avenue, it struck me. Mrs. Libby was rushing off to be with her daughters in what, only last week, had been the POW getaway car.

We sat silently, enjoying the brief respite from all the excitement that had flooded our lives lately. It was a while before any of us spoke.

"I wonder what will happen next," said Mom.

Suddenly, a gigantic black Lincoln slammed on its brakes and skidded to a stop in front of our house. Out jumped a tall, gray-haired man dressed in a conservative black business suit. His face was red. He appeared to be very upset.

The man stormed up the sidewalk and introduced himself with a huff, "I'm E.F. Graham!"

"We've been expecting you," Danny replied, without missing a beat.

"What is the meaning of this outrageous article?" he roared, rudely waving a newspaper in Mom's face.

She stared at him without speaking. Her outward calm appeared to disarm him.

He lowered his voice a notch before elaborating, "Beg pardon, madam. But why wasn't this refusal nonsense brought to my attention before it reached the front page of the paper? Why – I'll be the laughing stock of Riverton! Won't I?"

Does he really want Mom to answer that question? I wondered.

"Mr. Frampton – our local store manager – couldn't possibly have told these boys we have a policy against supporting such a wonderful cause, madam. I'm sure the boys – shall we say – *exaggerated* – just a bit. Boys will be boys! Am I not right, madam?"

"That's not true! We –," I began to protest.

But I stopped immediately when Mom put her hand on my shoulder.

Mr. Graham smiled at Mom and winked. "Why, I was once a boy, myself."

With that, Mom rose to her full height. Aided by the fact that she was standing on the first porch step, she looked Mr. Graham straight in the eye. He blinked a few times but managed to stand his ground.

"Mr. Graham! I'm trying my very best to remain a lady. But your bad manners and uncivil behavior toward these boys and me have just exceeded my limits. Forgive me for saying so, sir. But, if you *were* a boy and I *were* your mother, you'd be headed for the woodshed right here and now. Shame on you, sir!"

Mr. Graham's mouth flopped wide open. But no words came out. Mom didn't stop there.

"I was not present during the conversation between your Mr. Frampton and these boys. And neither were you, sir. But, if these boys say Mr. Frampton refused them, I believe them. They are good and honest boys. And they do not lie!"

"But Mr. Frampton is —"

Mom raised her hand. Mr. Graham stopped in mid-sentence.

"Allow me to finish your sentence, sir. Normally, I try not to judge others. So please forgive me. But Mr. Frampton is — by far — the least cordial man in our neighborhood. In addition to his persistent discourteous behavior toward adults, he is particularly ill-tempered with children, which I personally hold to be most offensive. And you of all people should know that having a store manager with his temperament is — if nothing else — just plain bad business."

Never in my life had I heard Mom talk so bluntly about another adult. I wasn't sure I should be there. Of course, she was right. Mr. Frampton, now that I knew his name, was certainly everything she said he was. Grandma Compton called him a "real pill." And, coming from her, that was severe condemnation!

Mr. Graham closed his mouth, put his hand to his chin, and looked at his shoes. Mom continued to stare at him. I wondered what she might say next.

Up to this point, Danny hadn't uttered a word. Suddenly, he looked up at Mr. Graham and asked, "How many stores you got?"

Caught off guard by Danny's remarkable question, Mr. Graham stammered, "I – got – 35. That is, we have 35 markets in our chain. Why do you ask?"

"How much of a starter donation will you be making?"

"Starter donation?"

"When we talk to the newspaper next, we'd like to tell them how much of a starter donation each of your stores will be making."

"Would five dollars per market be acceptable?"

"That's just the figure we had in mind."

Mom sat down. Clearly, her work was done. Danny was now in charge of the proceedings. Mom and I were only there to watch the show.

"Good. I'm glad we got that all straightened out. When do you think you might be talking to that – ah – reporter friend of yours?" Mr. Graham asked in an overly pleasing manner.

Danny informed him that our "reporter friend" was on his way to Bay City to cover the Libby case. That stymied Mr. Graham for an instant.

Then he proposed an alternative approach, "I could call the city editor. I've met him a number of times. Nice fellow. Perhaps, he'd agree to come out tonight and do a follow-up interview with you boys. How's that sound?"

Danny responded quickly, "Shall we tell him about your donation of hot dogs, buns, and potato chips for the Matlock Can Opener on July Fourth, too?"

"Hot dogs? Did I miss something here?"

Danny ignored his question and continued, "Pete's donating all the soft drinks. The canning factory – all the pork and beans, pickles, and ketchup. Fazio's – potato salad, coleslaw, and macaroni salad. And Riverton Dairy is providing the ice cream and cones – and the milk."

He stopped momentarily to let Mr. Graham absorb this new information. Then he added, "The others wanted to donate the hot dogs and buns and potato chips, but we reserved some of the opportunity to participate for you, sir."

Mr. Graham guffawed!

He addressed his next question to Mom, "Is there anything that you need from me, madam? Better take your turn before this *sharpster* cleans me out completely!"

He turned again to Danny, "You'll have your hot dogs, son!"

He shook Danny's hand. Then mine.

As he extended his hand to Mom, he confessed, "You are absolutely right, Mrs. Addison. My mother would have tanned my hide good for the way I acted. Please accept my humble apology. I hope I can make it up to you. I'll start by providing a store manager that your neighborhood deserves. You can count on that!"

"Mr. Graham, I'm very certain of one thing. Your mother would be very proud of your – shall we call it – *quick recovery* here, today."

All the way back to his Lincoln, he chuckled and talked to himself. "I have never in all my life," he muttered over and over.

"Thank you, Mr. Graham!" I yelled.

Danny shouted, too. "Don't forget the buns and potato chips. And please throw in some mustard, sir!"

Mr. Graham raised both of his arms in surrender and nodded his head vigorously. Still laughing, he collapsed into his Lincoln. After regaining his composure, he tromped the accelerator and took off in a swirl of dust, waving at us all the way to New Albany Avenue.

When the dust cleared, I turned to Danny. "I didn't know that we had donations coming from all those others. When did you talk to them?"

"We'll let them know what they're furnishing tomorrow – before they read it in the newspaper."

"You mean you haven't talked to them yet?" Mom asked, incredulously. "How do you know they'll come through?"

"When they hear what everybody else is donating, how can they refuse? Mr. Graham didn't."

"You're probably right," admitted Mom.

Danny grinned impishly.

19 MOMENTUM BUILDS

"HELLO! YOO HOO! WHERE IS EVERYBODY?"

Danny and I were the only ones home. Actually, we were outside filling Sherm's wagon with cartons of cans and wrappers in preparation for another sales trip downtown.

Aunt Maude had promised a new batch of leads by noon. We were torn because this was Thursday, the day we normally devoted to working with our vendor friends at the stockyard.

"Marie? Jase? Where are you?"

"Danny and I are out here, Grandma!" I shouted. "Mom's gone out to Camp Riverton to check on the new POW uniforms."

"You two boys are just who I'm looking for!" exclaimed Grandma Compton as she emerged from the house. "What's happened to those two POWs? How're the Matlocks doing? What about Mrs. Libby? Did the grand jury report out yet? When will the girls go to trial? Has Maude heard from Van lately? Is he all right? How's your foot, Danny? What an attractive red boot! How many cans have you boys distributed? With news at the farm being a day late – and no telephone – a body's got to come to town, just to keep up with things!"

Grandma plunked her substantial backside down on the steps and looked at us expectantly. "Okay! I'm comfortable. Tell me all," she urged, nodding at us to begin her news briefing.

We delivered our update. Grandma listened attentively, asking clarifying questions as we went along. When we finished, she leaned back against the steps and let it all soak in.

"Boys, with all that's happened lately, I'm sure lucky to have you two news sponges to squeeze whenever I come into town."

With that, she opened her arms wide. Danny and I moved in for a real squeeze. It felt good, especially coming from Grandma Compton.

She patted us on the back and said, "Okay! Let's do some can business. I need eight cans. Can you fill my order?"

"Eight cans! You bet!" I shouted.

"On my way in, I stopped by to chat with Reverend Johnson. He agreed to distribute Matlock cans to all six Churches of Christ in the county – the four circuit churches and the two in town. As I drove by the stockyard, I saw the lady who runs the café getting out of her car in the parking lot. She wants a can to set on her counter, right next to the cash register. Then, of course, I need a can for the Barrington Grange Women."

Danny banged out the eight wrappers, affixed them to the cans, and wrote the names of the eight new sponsors on the inventory sheet. Grandma chortled when she saw one of Danny's wrappers:

Barrington Strange Women
Farm Ladies
Good Friends & Food

"Danny, what you have written may be true. But, if you want a full can, this may not be the best time to point it out!" she chuckled.

Danny drew a line through the "St" and wrote a "G" above it.

"Now, that's what I'd call subtle!" Grandma observed, still amused. "What the heck. If they don't have a sense of humor, let 'em grow to grass."

We confidently prepared three wrappers for our favorite stockyard vendors. The first was for the apple vendor who depended on us whenever he suffered from "the after-effects" as he called them. The second was for the generous strawberry man who bought us the best lunches available at the stockyard café. And the last wrapper would go to the melon man who provided pounds of peanuts for us to nibble on while we worked.

Once the new cans were stored in the trunk of Grandma's Terraplane, we piled in. Danny whooped when Grandma soared skyward for our short hop to the Riverton Livestock Yard. We skidded to a slam-stop in the parking lot and let the dust settle before we opened the car doors.

The vendors were already doing a brisk business with those women who habitually arrived early to get the freshest and the best of the available fruits and vegetables. We opened the trunk to retrieve our cans.

When our friends spotted us, the familiar competition for our services began.

They waved and yelled, "Hey! You gonna work for me today? Where you been? Come on over. Who's that? Would she like some fresh strawberries? Nice ones – good for jam! Hey! How about it? Don't work for that cheapskate. I buy you three lunches today – two for you boys – one for Missus, there."

"My goodness! You boys certainly are popular," Grandma said, amazed at the chatter. "Why don't you finish your business here while I take this can up to the café? Can I get you anything?"

"A doughnut would be good," Danny suggested.

Grandma smiled and patted his shoulder, "Doughnuts it is, then. And chocolate milk to wash them down."

Off she went.

Our three favorites were disappointed that we wouldn't be working that day. But they were flattered to be chosen, among all the stockyard vendors, as the only Matlock can sponsors. They told us they'd get the other vendors to urge their customers to participate, too.

Each of them promised to deliver his can to my house at day's end. Danny and I were certain that we could expect three full cans, along with generous parcels of overripe fruit and tomatoes, in the bargain. That's just the way they were.

As Grandma swooped along New Albany Avenue toward Forrest Street, we finished our doughnuts and chocolate milk. She made a perfect four-point landing under the box elder tree. When we disembarked, she wished us luck. Then off she sped to deliver the rest of her cans. We finished loading Sherm's wagon and headed for the bus stop.

From the bus stop bench, we saw Pete come out of his store. He was carrying the wide, red-handled broom that he used to sweep his sidewalk at least four times a day. Because I never saw anything on his sidewalk that needed sweeping, I concluded that Pete's broom break was just an excuse to escape the confines of the store, every now and then.

"Morning, Pete!" we yelled.

He looked up, smiled broadly, and waved. "Gooda morning-ah, boyz! You-sa be gooda today! Okay?"

I wondered if Pete would ever alter his signature greeting to us. As if reading my mind, Pete added, "You-sa boyz do-in gooda ting fora da Matlocksa. Reel gooda ting. Pete-sa prowda you. You-sa gooda boyz!"

In all my days on Forrest Street, I never heard Pete say anything close to what he said that day. After his extraordinary behavior, Pete abruptly terminated his sweeping and hurried back into the store. Suddenly, Danny stood up on his crutches and hopped to the curb.

"Stay there," he ordered.

"Where you going?"

"This would be a good time to let Pete know what he's bringing to the Matlock Can Opener."

With that, the young opportunist thumped across the street, up Pete's immaculate sidewalk, and into the store. As ordered, I sat on the bench, contemplating the complex inner-workings of the mind of Daniel Tucker.

WHEN THE BUS STOPPED, we helped the friendly substitute driver load our cartons and Sherm's wagon. Once aboard, we discovered that we were the only passengers. The substitute driver told us that Mr. Smalley, having been stricken with a severe migraine headache at the bus station last night, was ordered to take the rest of the week off.

We told him we were sorry and hoped Mr. Smalley would soon recover.

After storing our materials in the checkroom, Danny and I called on the generous businessmen who had "volunteered" to cater the Matlock Can Opener. Just as Danny had predicted, each came through with flying colors. Some even suggested additional items of food or beverage that they would be "more than pleased" to provide.

I was satisfied with all the suggested additions except that of Riverton Dairy. I never cared much for buttermilk. Danny claimed that he loved it until he was offered a sample glass. I guess he changed his mind.

The donors thanked us profusely for the opportunity to serve our wonderful cause in their modest way. Danny promised that their generosity would be mentioned in an article in the afternoon paper. All were amazed at our ability to get news of their donations in the newspaper so quickly. Danny told them that we had "connections in the press world."

On that note, each donor signed up to sponsor a can as well.

Having concluded our business with the food and beverage providers, we wheeled Sherm's wagon to Woolworth's to collect Aunt Maude's latest prospects. Molly and she were very busy with the lunch hour crowd, so we didn't stay long. But Aunt Maude did take time enough to urge us to call on Mr. Jules Jones "immediately, if not sooner."

According to her list, Mr. Jones owned the Chippewa Lumber Yard. Following her advice, we made tracks for the lumber company, which was located alongside the river, next to the Chop Suey Diner.

We would have arrived ten minutes sooner, but we were delayed by a long funeral procession creeping down Addison Street, making its way to the cemetery. Along with the other citizens who happened to be on the sidewalk at the time, we stood respectfully, at attention, with our hats over our hearts until the last car had passed.

"Did you notice the American flags on all the bumpers?" Danny asked me as we started walking again.

I nodded my head sadly. I wondered in whose window the new Gold Star would be hanging that night. I thought about all the Riverton husbands, sons, and brothers who had gone off to the war, filled with patriotic zeal, only to return to take their places in graves at the end of processions like this one.

When we arrived at the Chippewa Lumber Yard, our moods were somber. Would this affect our ability to elicit support for the Matlock campaign? I soon found out.

Mr. Jones was a tall, suntanned man who wore a yellow knit shirt, dark gray slacks, and black and white saddle shoes. As he talked to us, he paced back and forth in front of his desk. I wondered if our visit was cutting into his golf time.

"I don't mean to meddle in what you boys have put together. Please don't get me wrong. From all I hear, you've done a crackerjack job. Besides it's a fine cause. And it's bringing our community together. During wartime, we need a strong community. Yes, sir! You've done a real fine job. But I think I can offer some help – help that you may not know you need."

Danny and I sat on the bulky, brown leather sofa across from Mr. Jones' desk. His efficient secretary had just delivered our drink orders, bottles of strawberry pop with twin soda straws. I found it difficult to concentrate on Mr. Jones' words because of the loud rattle generated by Danny's long slurps of cold pop.

"I'm sure we didn't think of everything," I confessed.

Danny stopped slurping, rubbed his shiny red rubber boot, and nodded his agreement.

"Here's what I mean. To build a house you need skilled tradesmen – carpenters, plumbers, electricians, bricklayers, stone masons, painters, and so on. What with the war and all, these trades are in extremely short supply. The younger tradesmen signed up for the Seabees. Or took higher-paying jobs in war plants. The older ones – those already established – well, they've never had it so good. Nope! Today, you just can't hardly get those old boys to work for you – for love, nor money."

Mr. Jones paused to let his message soak in.

"You mean we might raise $4,000 and not be able to find people to build the Matlocks' new house?" I asked.

"Well, these days being what they are, that's exactly what I mean. But that's where I think I can help. These tradesmen need building supplies and materials to do their work. But these kinda materials are hard to come by. Chippewa Lumber is the only supplier in the county. So they gotta come here for what they need to do their jobs. No supplies! No work!"

He shrugged his shoulders and displayed his open palms.

"That's good, then," Danny noted. "They gotta be sure you're happy – or they can't earn a living."

"Hmmmm! Couldn't ah said it better myself," Mr. Jones agreed with a wink.

Danny winked back.

"Now, don't get me wrong. I don't play games with my – my position. When I'm lucky enough to come by lumber and materials from my wholesalers, I sell them on a strict first come, first served basis – without regard for where they'll be used. That's the only way to make it fair for both my tradesmen customers and the citizens of Chippewa County. But – "

"But you might make an exception in the Matlock case." Danny guessed.

"Let's say I might ask my tradesmen customers to – to rearrange their schedules for a good cause," Mr. Jones replied with sly smile.

"Hmmmm! Couldn't ah said it better myself," Danny countered with a sly smile of his own.

"As I understand it, you can start building any time after the Fourth of July. You're gonna need a good foreman for the job. So I'm gonna volunteer the services of my yard manager to be your foreman. He's a former house builder who really knows his stuff. How's that sound?"

Danny held up a finger, "I've got another idea. Why don't we ask all the tradesmen to volunteer their time, too?"

Mr. Jones clearly hadn't anticipated Danny's question, which I considered to be a heck of a good one.

"Well, I don't know – I – I guess we could. Never thought of that. Why not? It never hurts to ask. Maybe you ought to be here when I put the bite on 'em, young man! Ha!"

Danny smiled, winked again, and slurped down the last of his strawberry pop.

"Well, I'll sign them up. You boys raise the money, and we're in good shape. Is there anything else I can do for you, today?" Mr. Jones inquired as he ceased his pacing and moved toward the door.

"We would like you to be a can sponsor, too, Mr. Jones. After all you're doing for the Matlocks, I hate to ask," I said as I stood to leave.

"Oh, most certainly! All along, I assumed that we'd take a can – just like all the other businesses in town. Wouldn't want to miss the opportunity to participate in the giving!"

With his long outstretched arm, Mr. Jones was gently waving us toward the office door. I noticed that Danny hadn't made any effort to prepare for departure. Mr. Jones noticed, too.

He revealed a slight impatience in his voice when he repeated, "Is there anything else I can do for you, today?"

Danny looked up at Mr. Jones from his seat on the couch and observed, "So all the tradesmen who volunteer their time will be buying their lumber and building stuff from Chippewa Lumber Yard, right?"

Danny's question caught Mr. Jones off guard. It took a second for him to respond.

"That's right. Despite shortages brought on by the war, we've got the biggest inventory of building supplies in this part of the state. So they'd probably buy all of their materials from us. Beside we're reasonably close to Milford Street, aren't we?"

Mr. Jones moved away from the door and took up position directly in front of Danny. Danny put his right index finger to his lower lip and ventured, "I'll bet there's a awful big profit in building materials nowadays, isn't there?"

Suddenly, I realized where my friend was heading.

So did Mr. Jones. "You're right there. Must admit, it's been a good business to be in, especially since the war started. What's on your mind?"

"We were thinking you might want to donate some of the lumber and other materials, so the Matlocks have enough money left over to buy furniture," Danny replied.

"Just how much furniture money did you have in your budget?" Mr. Jones quickly countered, thinking Danny wouldn't be prepared for his question. *Foolish man!*

"$1,155," Danny shot back. "Not counting the lawn furniture."

"What? I – ah. Okay! I give up. You gotta deal!" Mr. Jones sputtered.

"Good! Let's have another pop to celebrate!" Danny proposed, raising his empty bottle.

AFTER LEAVING THE CHIPPEWA Lumber Yard, I realized I was suffering from the listless, stuffy feeling of someone who has consumed one too many strawberry pops – or doughnuts – or chocolate milks. I daydreamed about lying down beside the Chippewa and taking a little nap.

But Danny was energized by his recent series of sharp fund-raising deals. His high spirits propelled him along the sidewalk to the exhilarating beat of crutch-tip-on-concrete.

As we rounded the corner on our way to the Chop Suey Diner, we were greeted by the wild honking of a horn. The offending car screeched to a halt at the curb beside us.

And out jumped Aunt Mary!

"I knew it. I knew it. I knew I'd bump into you two! I need a Matlock can. Make up one for me as fast as you can! *Can* – as fast as you – *can*. Ha! That's a hoot!"

Danny stared at her with his mouth stuck on "Wide Open."

"I assure you my piano parents are *going* to contribute! Some of them are rollin' in dough. Oops! Forget I said that."

Suddenly she paused, grabbed us both, and crushed us to her bosom. Then she said, "How are you boys, anyway? Can't talk long – late for a lesson. How about my can?"

While Aunt Mary sputtered, fretted, and picked at her tiny wristwatch, Danny hurriedly inscribed her can wrapper.

**Rich Parents of
Aunt Mary's
Piano Studs.**

He wrapped the can in record time. Aunt Mary glanced at it quickly before underhanding it into her backseat through the open car window. She patted us both on the head, hopped into her car, and peeled off down Addison Street.

"Boy! She doesn't waste any time!" was all Danny could say.

He was right. Her visit had lasted something under two minutes.

Our frenzied encounter with Aunt Mary had drained every last ounce of my energy. I *really* needed that riverbank nap. But it was not to be.

"Wait a minute! Look!" Danny ordered.

He had propped himself against the corner street sign and was pointing upward. I shaded my eyes with my hand and scanned the sky.

Given my depleted energy status, I expected to see a flock of ravenous buzzards circling overhead. But I didn't see a thing.

"No! No! The sign! It says *Addison* Street. That's your name! How come?"

My initial reaction was utter disbelief!

How could Danny be so clever, yet fail to realize that the name of Riverton's main street and my family name were identical? Remembering one of Danny's favorite sayings, *Judge not, 'less you be the judge*, I didn't express my first thought.

Instead, I briefly related the oft-told family history of Dad's ancestors who helped settle Riverton. And how the original city council out of gratitude named the city's main thoroughfare after my great-great grandfather.

Danny was impressed. He immediately personalized the concept and tried it on for size, "Tucker Street. Tucker Avenue. Tucker Boulevard. The Tucker Building. Tuckerville. Tuckerton. Tucker City. Tucker & Tucker. Tucker Railroad. Tucker Bus Lines. Tucker Worms & Bait Corporation. Tuck –"

"Now you got it!" I laughed.

He delivered his capper, "Addison & Tucker, Incorporated."

"Hmmmm! Couldn't ah said it better myself," I quipped with a wink.

We broke into laughter.

When we entered the Chop Suey Diner, it was between shift breaks, so only about a third of the booths were occupied.

"Oooooooo! Wercome, young misters!" squealed Nikki Nakayama. "You come to give us Matrock can – or have runch?"

Suddenly, I felt a pang of hunger. But how could I be hungry? Maybe it wasn't hunger at all, but just an intense desire to spend time in the presence of this attractive waitress. I felt embarrassed and ill at ease. What was happening to me?

But Danny hadn't lost his focus. He marched right up to the cash register and greeted Mrs. Nakayama, "Good morning, ma'am. I 'spect you want one of these here cans. Now, don't you, ma'am?"

Ye gads! It was John Wayne!

Mrs. Nakayama broke into a broad smile and chipped, "You sound rike Jorhn Rayn. Vely funny. Make Missus Nakayama raugh. Hee! Give Matrock can for counter. Good for Matrock – havee you boys herp zem."

Herp zem! What was she saying? I wondered to myself.

"Help them," Nikki whispered in my ear.

I turned around and stared at her. What had happened to her Japanese accent? She winked at me and announced in a loud voice, "Matrocks rucky. Vely rucky!"

Danny focused on closing the can deal. He whipped out a can wrapper, paused, and smiled at Mrs. Nakayama. Then he raised his right eyebrow. Mrs. Nakayama grinned and nodded her head enthusiastically. Danny quickly completed her wrapper.

> **Chop Suey Diner**
> **Good Foods &**
> **Friend. Peeples**

After attaching the wrapper, he held the can above his head for every customer to see. Applause, shouts, and whistles from the small, but enthusiastic, crowd filled the diner. Danny tried to bow, but his crutches foiled him again.

The Nakayama family blocked the door and wouldn't let Danny and me leave until we agreed to accept a "comprementaly runch" on them. We finally gave in. Both of us ordered chop suey and made absolute pigs of ourselves. Especially when Nikki insisted on serving us seconds – and then, thirds.

Amidst another round of applause, we waddled out of the diner and back to work. After delivering another seven cans, we returned to the bus station, loaded Sherm's empty wagon into the luggage compartment, and took our seats on the bus.

After a minute or two, Danny asked, "You going with me?"

"Where?"

"To get my stitches out."

"Want me to?"

"Yep!"

"Okay. How we getting there? Bus?"

"My mom'll take us."

"You scared?"

"Nope. You?"

"Why would I be scared?"

Danny pretended not to hear my question.

WHEN WE ARRIVED AT the Tucker house, Danny's mom was in the kitchen opening some mystery cans for their supper. "Ready to go, Danny?" she asked.

"Yep!"

"You, Jase?"

"Yep!"

Danny insisted on bringing two full sets of materials with us. Anticipating my objection, he recited another string of maxims. They were beauts.

"Be prepared. Judge not, 'less you be the judge. (There it was again!) Strike while the ironing is hot. Two rights don't make a wrong. Early to bed, early to wise. My cup run is over."

I humored him by agreeing to load the campaign materials into the Tucker station wagon – and by not kicking his wounded foot.

Danny didn't settle for Dr. Moran's tongue depressors this time. Instead, he scored another goal for the Matlock team. He emerged from the stitch removal operation wearing one shoe, one slipper, and a big smile. He winked at me, scooped up his can materials, and disappeared again into the inner office.

When we got to the car, he added the new sponsor's name to the inventory.

Dr. Moran
Boys' Friend
No Pain

I gathered from his entry that his stitch removal had gone well.

WHEN DANNY AND HIS mother dropped me off, Danny demonstrated his crutch-free walk for Aunt Maude, Mom, and Dad. They were all duly impressed. Aunt Maude insisted on "settling up" with Mrs. Tucker. After much bickering, they agreed to split Dr. Moran's second bill evenly. Aunt Maude's share was one dollar.

"Oh, my goodness, we almost forgot!" Mom exclaimed as the Tuckers were about to leave. "Look at this!"

Mom spread the *Riverton Daily Press* out on the kitchen table. Mrs. Tucker, Danny, and I hunched over the paper and read the front-page article.

The Matlock Can-Do Spirit

GRAHAM CHANGES STAND; DONATES HEAVILY TO CAUSE

Graham Markets president and founder, E.F. Graham, announced today that his chain of markets is fully behind the efforts of the two local boys who have created the groundswell of support for their campaign to restore the Matlocks to a home of their own.

When asked to explain his change of heart, Mr. Graham replied that he was personally moved by a "Power greater than himself." He refused to comment further. (Editor's Note: Mr. Graham is known as a deeply religious man.)

Graham Markets will offer its customers the convenience of a Matlock donation can in every one of its 35 stores. In a gesture of personal generosity, Mr. Graham seeded each of the 35 cans with a five-dollar bill from his own pocket.

As further evidence of Mr. Graham's generosity, Graham Markets has agreed to furnish the substantial portion of food for the Matlock Can Opener to be held at the Good Mission Church on the Fourth of July. When pressed to comment on this additional gift to the Matlock campaign, Mr. Graham humbly averred, "It's the least we can do."

Other food and beverage donors include Pete's Grocery - Liquor - Hardware Store, Fazio's Deli, Riverton Dairy, and others yet to be named, according to the campaign organizers.

Earlier today, this paper received an anonymous telephone call from a young person purporting to speak for Mayor George Simmons of Granville. The popular mayor has reportedly challenged one and all to beat him at his famous walnut shell game to be performed at the Matlock fund-raising finale on the Fourth. All proceeds will go to the benefit of the Matlock campaign.

Readers will recall that only last week a fire of unknown origin gutted the Matlock home on Milford Street. The neighbors at the scene were amazed by a dramatic rescue of Mrs. Matlock by German prisoners of war working at the nearby canning factory.

The two boys organizing the fund-raising efforts to rebuild the Matlock home are Jase Addison and Danny Tucker who themselves were recently hailed as local heroes because of their roles in capturing the two escaped prisoners of war and the Libby sisters who allegedly assisted in their escape. The Libby girls are currently incarcerated at the Bay City Federal Women's Prison awaiting recommendations on charges from the federal grand jury convened to weigh evidence against them.

The Riverton Chamber of Commerce has urged its members to sign up for the Matlock Can Campaign as soon as possible. The Tucker boy, acting as spokesman for the pair of campaign organizers, warned today that there are only a few donation cans still available. Any business desiring a can should, in the words of Master Tucker, "Get the lead out!"

Danny looked up from the article and declared, "Wait till the *Riverton Daily Press* hears about our Chippewa Lumber Yard deal!"

20 DAY OF RECKONING

LATER THAT EVENING, WE WERE SITTING IN THE LIVING room reviewing the day's events when we heard a faint tapping. Mom went to the door.

"Louise! For heaven's sake, it's you. We barely heard your knock. Please come in. I thought you were in Bay City."

"Sorry to disturb. I've come home for the night. The grand jury has handed down its recommendation and it –."

She stopped abruptly. I had a feeling she might break into tears.

"It's not good news."

"Please sit down, Louise. Could I get you something – a cup of tea – coffee?"

"No, I'm fine. I just need to talk to someone. The Matlocks are asleep, and I feel so – so all alone."

"Tell us what's happened, Louise," Dad urged her gently. "We want to help – any way we can."

"Thank you. I'd like to talk about it."

We settled back in our chairs and waited for her to go on.

"I'm not an attorney, so I may not have all of the details just right."

We nodded our heads.

"Today, the grand jury handed down charges of – of treason against the girls."

I momentarily stopped breathing.

Mrs. Libby paused. Then she said, "I don't want to keep you in suspense. It's a long story. But, mercifully, the girls won't have to face the treason charges."

"Thank God!" exclaimed Aunt Maude.

"Yes. Thank God!" Mrs. Libby agreed. "According to Harry Chambers, when the judge heard the grand jury's treason recommendation, he called a pre-arraignment conference – I think it's called – with the lawyers from both sides. Harry and the federal prosecutor were there with the judge in his chambers. The judge asked the prosecutor to summarize the evidence he had against the girls. Then he asked Harry to tell him about the girls' defense."

Mrs. Libby paused. She turned to Mom and admitted, "You know, Marie, a cup of tea might taste good, after all."

Mom went to the kitchen to make her tea. No one spoke. We just sat on pins and needles. A few minutes later, Mom handed the steaming teacup to Mrs. Libby.

She took two small sips before continuing, "After hearing a summary of the evidence from both sides, the judge told the prosecutor that he couldn't see how the government could possibly prove the – the elements of treason. There had to be some substantial desire on the part of the girls to do damage to our country as I understand it."

Mrs. Libby's face clouded over. I wasn't sure what was coming next.

"The judge told Harry that the girls still deserved a – a stiff penalty – for their misdeeds. But he also told the federal prosecutor that he didn't intend to preside over a kangaroo court in front of a hundred reporters from all over the country. The judge told both of them that he would entertain a proposal to arraign the girls on lesser charges if he could have Harry's promise of – of a guilty plea."

"Lord! This is unbelievable!"

I agreed with Mom. But I honestly didn't know whether their pleading guilty was good news or bad.

Mrs. Libby looked at Mom but she didn't seem to hear Mom's words.

She started again, "At that point, the federal prosecutor objected. Harry told us that it made the judge real mad. The judge told the prosecutor if he insisted on taking the case to trial that he would instruct the jury in such a way that the girls would be turned loose. Then the judge asked the prosecutor if that's what he wanted."

Mrs. Libby paused to look at us. We all shook our heads in amazement.

"Then Harry was excused from the conference to confer with his clients – with us. He told the judge he believed he could get us to agree to plead guilty to a lesser charge. And we did agree."

"Oh, my gosh! What will the charge be now?" Mom asked.

"It's conspiracy. Conspiracy to prevent – or maybe it's obstruct – the U.S. government from its right to imprison prisoners of war. It's a real obscure law, I guess. Harry told us it's seldom used."

"That makes sense," agreed Dad. "I hate to ask this, but what about the sentence? What kind of punishment do people face when they break this law?"

"Well, it's not good news. Harry warned us that the judge could give the girls up to 15 years – plus a $5,000 fine. The judge will decide that after he hears the testimony at the sentencing hearing."

"Oh, my Lord! How could that be?" Mom protested.

"I know. I know. I just feel numb when I think about them pleading guilty," Mrs. Libby admitted. "But the girls were officially arraigned this afternoon. And they did plead guilty to conspiracy. Tomorrow, they're to be sentenced – at ten o'clock in the morning!"

"Holy smokes!" Dad said. "I've never seen a trial – or whatever this is – move so quickly."

Mrs. Libby nodded, and then added, "Harry said the judge wants to move it along, so the government can limit its exposure to any bad publicity. 'Put it to bed fast!' were the judge's words."

"What happens tomorrow?" Dad asked her.

"Harry will call only two character witnesses. I'll be one. My job – in short – is to plead for the mercy of the court. Harry will ask me questions about the difficulty of raising two daughters – without a father – through the Depression and the war years."

Mrs. Libby clouded over again.

"This has to be hard on you, Louise," Mom said softly. "I don't know how you've stood up through all of this."

Mrs. Libby sipped the last of her tea and added, "There'll be another character witness – a non-family member – who has known the girls for some years. Harry doesn't want me to reveal – to tell anyone – who that person is."

"Is it someone we know?" I couldn't resist asking.

Dad looked at me kind of funny. I probably shouldn't have asked my question.

"Yes. You know this witness – you all do," was all that Mrs. Libby would say.

I was dying to know who it was.

"Louise, please forgive me for saying, but I don't think you should drive back to Bay City by yourself. John and I will be happy to take you to the sentencing hearing. Isn't that right, John?"

"You bet!" Dad declared, nodding decisively. "I got some vacation days to use up. This is sure a good purpose."

"I'm so happy you offered. To be honest, I'm a wreck. I don't know whether the girls will be sentenced to a couple of weeks in jail – or fifteen years. And, Lord knows, how I would ever be able to raise enough money to pay a big fine like that.

"I couldn't get it out of my mind – all the way home from Bay City. I hardly remember anything about the trip. Frankly, I'm not quite sure how I got home in one piece."

Dad and Mrs. Libby agreed on the logistics for the Bay City trip. We'd leave at seven o'clock. We'd drive both cars. Then Mrs. Libby delivered a barrage of thanks and left for home.

WE ALL SAT DOWN in the living room to contemplate what we had just heard and to agree on the details for the next day.

Dad had a proposal.

"I think we should invite Danny – and perhaps Mrs. Tucker – to go with us tomorrow. Maude, it's your day off. You'll want to come too, I bet. I'll drive by Burkes on the way out of town. Leave a note with the guard at the gatehouse. Tell them why I'll be missing work. Why don't I drive Louise's car? Jase, you can come with me. Marie, you can drive our car with Maude, Danny, and his mother. Sound okay to everybody?"

We all agreed.

After the lights were off, I lay in bed thinking about the Libby girls. So much had happened. The night their AWOL boy friends drove us off the road. The day they jeered at Otto from the canning factory office window. Their involvement in the sauerkraut theft. The POW escape. Their behavior at Granville Park.

And now, they're going to be sentenced to, who knows? Maybe years in prison. Did they deserve the punishment they were likely to receive? Sometimes it was hard to remember that these were just two girls from our neighborhood. Mrs. Libby seemed so nice. How had her daughters turned out like this?

With these questions spinning in my head, I finally dropped off to sleep.

In my dream, Danny and I were running down Addison Street toward the bus station. Danny was wearing both of his mother's red boots. I asked Danny why we were running. He laughed and pointed behind us. Mr. Graham and Mr. Jones were chasing us, trying to turn in their Matlock cans.

What a weird dream!

MRS. TUCKER AND DANNY appeared at our back door well before departure time. Mercifully, Decibel Daniel refrained from sounding his *come-out call*. Mom invited them in.

When Danny entered the kitchen, I noticed that his gait showed no sign of his recent injury. I also noticed that he was dressed in his church uniform, the one featuring his Tigers baseball cap, not the cowgirl outfit.

"What's for breakfast?" he asked casually, making himself at home.

By now, everyone in the Addison household was quite accustomed to Danny's joining us for breakfast. But, evidently, Mrs. Tucker was not. In fact, she was flabbergasted. She jabbed him sharply with her elbow.

"That's not polite!" she huffed. "Besides, you just *had* your breakfast."

"Yeah," he grinned. "A big bowl of hot ketchup – with cinnamon and crackers!"

Mrs. Tucker's menacing look would have withered a normal boy. But Danny wasn't fazed.

"Ketchup came in a big can. Still a lot left. We thought it was peaches," he chuckled.

Danny was the only Tucker present who found this topic at all amusing.

Dad changed the subject, "Here's how we thought we'd split up the group for the drive to Bay City."

Everybody was content with the plan except – guess who? Danny insisted on riding in Mrs. Libby's car with me. Mrs. Tucker thought that Mrs. Libby should decide. On arriving at the Libby house, Dad checked with her.

"Oh, that's perfectly fine with me. Danny's a very good boy, you know," Mrs. Libby assured him.

In response, Danny bestowed one of his super-angelic smiles on her. Dad and I smiled too – but at each other.

We were well into our trip to Bay City when I realized that Danny hadn't insisted on taking a supply of Matlock can materials with us. I asked him why.

"Don't need to," he explained. "We already got everybody up there."

Could he be right? Let's see. We'd landed the Chambers law firm. The FBI. The Chippewa County Sheriff's Office. The Riverton Police Department. The federal prosecutor's office.

"What about the judge?" I inquired, half joking.

"He said no!" Danny answered with a frown.

At first, I didn't know whether to believe him or not. Had he actually found a way to ask the U.S. Circuit Court judge in Bay City to support the Matlock Family Building Fund? After a quick review of my resourceful friend's recent history, I decided to believe him.

IT WAS JUST AFTER nine when we arrived at the federal courthouse. To our amazement, the courtroom was already jammed with spectators, mostly reporters from their appearance. Mrs. Libby thanked us for driving and for being there for her and her daughters. She called us her "Loyal Contingent of Riverton Supporters."

Harry Chambers had reserved seats for his two character witnesses in the first row, immediately behind the table where he sat with Barb and Anne Libby. The only row containing enough empty seats for our entire Loyal Contingent was the very last one, far in the back of the courtroom. We all sat down and waited for the hearing to begin.

Sitting on the aisle next to Danny, I had an unobstructed view of Mrs. Libby seated next to a large man in a dark suit. I couldn't see his face, but his hair was jet black with flecks of white. And it was cut short, military-style.

We all stood when the judge entered. After he was seated, the judge summarized the situation for those in his courtroom. You could hear a pin drop.

At yesterday's arraignment, he told us, the two defendants had pleaded guilty. And the court had accepted their plea. Today's pre-sentencing hearing would assist the court in deciding on a fair sentence for the defendants. (I soon realized, when the judge used the words "the court", he was referring to himself.)

The court would hear testimony from the People (the federal prosecutor) and from witnesses for the defense. After hearing this testimony, there would be a short recess – a period of deliberation – after which the court would announce the sentence.

"Mr. Prosecutor, please proceed," the judge directed.

The federal prosecutor declared that he had no witnesses. However, "if it pleases the court," he would make a short statement. Obviously, this news did not "please the court." The stern glare from the judge should have warned the prosecutor to keep it short. But the prosecutor didn't get the message. For the next twenty minutes or so, the prosecutor reminded the judge of a number of facts that surely everyone in the courtroom already knew.

We were at war. Prisoners of that war were incarcerated in our country. Our government had the right to imprison former enemy soldiers captured on the field of battle. The Libby girls had conspired to act in a manner that deprived our government of that right. And, not only did they conspire to act, but they had so acted. And so on – and on – and on.

The judge rested his chin on his hand and stared blankly at the prosecutor. The more the prosecutor railed about the criminal acts of the terrible Libby girls, the lower the judge's eyelids sank. By the time the prosecutor finished his tirade, the judge was presiding over his courtroom through thin slits that reminded me of those bone glasses Eskimos wear to prevent snow blindness.

When the prosecutor finally sat down, a hush fell over the courtroom. The judge didn't stir. After what seemed like a lifetime, the deafening silence that permeated the courtroom must have shaken the judge back into consciousness. He recovered nicely.

"Anything else, Mr. Prosecutor?" he inquired cordially as if nothing had happened.

His little nap had obviously improved his disposition.

"No, Your Honor."

"Mr. Chambers. Please call your first witness," the judge ordered as he glanced toward the defendants' table with now, wide-open eyes.

"Defense calls Mrs. Louise Libby," Mr. Chambers announced in a solemn voice.

After she was sworn in and settled in the witness chair, Mrs. Libby answered Mr. Chambers' questions one by one. She explained in unemotional terms how hard she had worked to provide a good home for her girls.

"Yes, it was very difficult to raise two children – alone – during the Depression and the early war years. But it was my duty – and I did it," she testified.

She was composed, calm, and very credible. The judge seemed to concentrate on her every word. He even asked questions about the girls' schooling and about their friends. And some downright candid questions about her financial resources.

When Mrs. Libby stepped down, I thought she'd done a fine job. I looked down our row to see Mom and Dad nodding their heads. They apparently agreed with my assessment.

Danny poked me and whispered, "She was good!"

"Next witness, Mr. Chambers," prompted the judge.

"Defense calls Mr. Charles James Comstock," announced Mr. Chambers with that same solemn tone.

"Who is Charles James Comstock?" Danny asked me in a whisper. I shrugged my shoulders.

Dad whispered something in Mom's ear. His words brought a wide smile to her face. I guessed that they somehow knew this Mr. Comstock.

The mystery witness rose from his seat in the front row and walked toward the witness chair. He still had his back to us.

When the man turned to be sworn in, I saw that he was very tall and handsome. He wore a white shirt with a dark, conservative tie. His tailor-made dark blue suit was slightly small for him. I suspected that it had been borrowed for the occasion.

His clean-shaven face revealed the sun-toughened skin of a man who worked out of doors. And, even from a good distance, I could see that he had warm, clear blue eyes.

Those eyes. There was something about those eyes.

Mr. Chambers rose and approached the witness, "Please state your full name and occupation."

"My name is Charles James Comstock," the witness replied. "I am – I was a high school teacher and coach."

That voice!

I looked at Dad. He had tears in his eyes!

Danny poked me in the ribs and announced in a loud whisper, "It's Gentleman Jim!"

I was astonished.

"Mr. Comstock, please tell the court how you came to know the defendants – Barbara and Anne Libby."

"About a dozen years ago, Mrs. Libby and her two daughters moved in next door. Our two families shared a duplex house in Riverton."

"Tell us about your family."

"There were four of us. But my wife and our twin daughters were killed – an automobile accident – a couple of years after Mrs. Libby and the girls became our neighbors."

"Were you friends with the Libby family?"

"Yes. I'd say we were very good friends. My wife and Mrs. Libby were particularly close. And my wife liked and trusted the Libby girls. They would baby-sit our infant daughters, even when Barb and Anne were very young, just in grade school. They were very responsible and caring. Yes, I have a strong positive opinion of the entire Libby family."

"After the death of your wife and children, was there a specific incident that caused you to increase your regard for Barbara and Anne Libby?"

Gentleman Jim turned and looked at the judge before he answered.

"Yes, sir. They saved my life."

The whole courtroom gasped in response to Gentleman Jim's words.

"After my wife and children were killed, I became despondent. I couldn't eat or sleep. I lost my job at the high school. I began to drink – heavily. I would often pass out on my couch – or at the kitchen table."

Gentleman Jim paused. His face grew somber.

"Please go on," Harry Chambers urged.

"During this period, Mrs. Libby worried about me. She checked on my welfare regularly. Brought me food. Did my laundry. Saw me through some rough days. When she was at work, she often had Barb and Anne look in on me. They came one morning, just as I was about – about to die."

"What do you mean?"

"The oven gas jet was turned on full. It wasn't lighted. I'd been drinking heavily. I was asleep – or maybe passed out on the kitchen floor. I had accidentally – I think – turned on the gas. It filled my entire house. It was winter, so all the windows were closed."

Jim turned to the judge again and confessed, "Nobody knows about this – except the Libby girls, their mother, and me. I've never told anyone about it. And neither have they."

The judge nodded his head and said, "It will be all right. Please go on."

"The Libby girls looked through the window. Saw me lying there on the kitchen floor. They could smell the gas. They were only ten or so, but they had the good sense to know that something was very wrong."

Other than Jim's voice, the only sound you could hear was the *shishing* of reporters' pencils recording his words in small notebooks all over the courtroom. The rest of us sat, dead silent, staring at Jim incredulously.

"Barb smashed the door window and unlocked the door. She sent Anne to call for the doctor while she entered the house. Somehow, Barb managed to turn off the gas. Then she ran around and opened the windows. When Anne returned, the two of them dragged me out of the house into the backyard. That's where I was when Dr. Moran arrived."

Jim paused again. His memories were choking him.

"Please continue," Harry Chambers urged again.

"Dr. Moran told me that, if the girls hadn't acted when they did, I would have died within a few minutes. It was that close. The plain fact is – I owe my life to Barb and Anne Libby."

"Based on this incident – and your long association with the Libby family – what is your assessment of Barbara and Anne Libby?"

"Well, if I learned anything during my time as teacher and coach, it was how to judge the character and potential of teenagers. I judge these girls to be first-rate. They're bright and hard working. They're certainly fun loving – sometimes to the point of being mischievous, I suppose. And I guess they're more naïve than they should be at their ages."

Jim glanced at the Libby girls.

"And I won't deny – in this last case – they made some foolish, adolescent mistakes. But they're not violent, larcenous, or destructive – traits that I normally associate with young criminals. And they're certainly not traitors."

The judge leaned down from his bench and asked, "Wouldn't you consider your opinion of these girls to be somewhat biased by the episode you just related?"

"Yes, sir, I would, Your Honor. I'm afraid I am eternally biased. I will never change my mind about these girls. I'm their loyal friend, and they're stuck with me – for as long as I'm around. I suppose that happens naturally when someone saves your life, sir."

Jim stepped down from the witness box and took his place next to Mrs. Libby who reached over and patted his hand tenderly. He looked down at his new shoes.

"I will now take a short recess. When I return, I will give you my decision regarding the sentencing of Barbara and Anne Libby."

THE COURTROOM WAS ABUZZ with whispers about Jim's incredible testimony. No one left the room. Dad and Mom were huddled together, sharing a very long whispered conversation. I wondered what they were discussing.

Danny looked pensive, so I asked him, "What are you thinking about?"

"Do you think Gentleman Jim is our friend?"

"Sure. Why do you ask?"

"I guess he'll always be our friend then, huh?"

"You bet."

The judge reentered and took his place behind the bench. The courtroom fell silent. The bailiff ordered the Libby girls to stand. Harry Chambers joined them. The judge cleared his throat and looked at some papers in front of him.

Finally, he began.

"We must never forget that our nation is at war – at war with an evil enemy who is bent on overthrowing our splendid democracy and replacing it with an immoral and corrupt alternative. Criminal acts, treated as relatively minor offenses in times of peace, take on much different proportions in times of war – as they should."

The judge paused for a sip of water from his glass.

"There are some in our country who would argue that these defendants deserve the gallows. These people contend that the defendants' criminal acts – regardless of the outcome in this particular instance – might well have added names to the ever-lengthening list of American casualties."

The judge took another sip.

"There are others who would urge this court to be tolerant and merciful. They hold that the acts of these defendants were no more than adolescent high jinks – juvenile delinquency, at the worst. Nothing really bad happened here. The POWs didn't make it back to their units to fight again. They didn't arm themselves. No one was hurt. It was all just a lark."

When he paused to take, yet another, sip of water, I realized I was thirsty, too.

"Acts resulting in additional American deaths. Acts resulting in harmless, overnight escapades. The very same acts, with very different outcomes. How does this court settle on a fair punishment for these defendants when their acts could have produced either of these far-differing consequences?"

He placed his glasses on his nose and read from a paper in his hand.

"The court views the acts committed by the defendants as reckless and irresponsible. Acts that could well have resulted in further death and suffering for American families during wartime. For the commission of such acts, our system of laws requires this court to hold these defendants accountable and to mete out appropriate and sufficient punishment."

The judge looked at Mrs. Libby and Jim.

"On the other hand, this court is not unaffected by the moving testimony of Mrs. Libby and that of Mr. Comstock. Nor is the court insensitive to the financial circumstances of the Libby family."

Then he looked directly at the Libby girls.

"Barbara Libby, you are hereby sentenced to one year and one day to be served in the federal prison for women. Your sentence is to commence immediately."

Mrs. Libby wailed. The courtroom gasped. The girls bent forward as if someone had punched them in the stomach. Harry Chambers didn't move a muscle.

"Anne Libby, you are hereby sentenced to one year and one day to be served in the federal prison for women. Your sentence is to commence immediately."

The judge banged his gavel and rose to leave the courtroom.

Danny spoke for everyone, "Holy Toad!"

The news reporters leaped to their feet and ran from the courtroom. The Libby girls collapsed into their chairs and sobbed deeply. Harry Chambers attempted to console them, with no apparent success. Mrs. Libby collapsed into Jim's arms and sobbed like her daughters.

As the bailiffs led the Libby girls from the courtroom, the Loyal Contingent from Riverton circled Mrs. Libby, Jim, and Harry Chambers. Within a few minutes, we were the only people left in the courtroom.

No one seemed to know what to say, so I took advantage of this opportunity to ask, "Mr. Chambers, why a year and a day?"

Everyone perked up. Apparently, I wasn't the only one who was wondering about the sentence.

"In our country, if you are found guilty of a crime and are sentenced to a prison term exceeding one year, you lose certain privileges of citizenship. For example, the Libby girls will never be able to vote as American citizens."

He paused and then added, "But this was a much lighter sentence than I expected. Mrs. Libby – and Jim – your testimony made all the difference in the world. This judge is a real bear – and an ardent patriot. I didn't want to tell you this earlier, but I was surprised when he chose not to pursue the treason charges."

"Harry, I'm positive your arguments at the pre-arraignment conference had a positive effect on the outcome of this case, too," Dad said, patting Harry Chambers on the back.

"Yes! Yes, I agree. Oh, I'm so sorry. I've forgotten my manners," said Mrs. Libby as she took her lawyer's hand. "Thank you, Mr. Chambers – for all you've done. I don't know what we would have done without your generosity and total dedication to this case. Thank you for Barb and Anne – and for myself."

"You're very welcome, Mrs. Libby, I'm sure," he replied, shaking her hand. "You are indeed a courageous woman and a loyal mother. And I'm certain that your devotion to your daughters will reap many dividends in the future."

"It doesn't feel that way, right now," Mrs. Libby admitted.

"JIM, DO YOU NEED a ride home?" asked Dad.

"No, thanks. I'd better go with Harry. Have to return his fancy duds," Jim said, pinching the lapel of his borrowed suit.

"In high school – as quarterback – you used to be my boss. But I'm no longer your obedient halfback. So, nothing doing!" Harry insisted. "You're going to need that suit for your job interview next week."

"Job interview! What's this all about?" Dad asked Jim whose face had suddenly turned crimson.

"High school needs a new head football coach this fall – and a history and civics teacher, too. Jim's agreed to talk to his old boss about getting his job back. Don't you think it's about time?" asked Harry.

"I do indeed! How about that?" cried Dad, slapping Jim on the back. "Congratulations, Jim! How'd you talk him into it, Harry?"

"Horse trading, pure and simple. In exchange for my taking this case, Jim agreed to get his act together. What he doesn't know is that I would have taken the case without his promise. But I'm not letting him off the hook."

"Barb and Anne's pro bono benefactor! It all makes sense, now."

"Amen!" said Mrs. Libby with a forced smile.

On our way to the parking lot, we congratulated Jim again. He acted embarrassed.

"Don't count your chickens, just yet," he warned. "Everybody in town knows how I've spent my last few years. Maybe people won't want their children coached and taught by a – "

"Quiet with that," Mom snapped. "Of course, they'll want you back. What can we do to help?"

"Say a prayer for me!"

"How many churches do you want us to say it in?" Danny asked.

And so, our agenda for Sunday morning was set.

As we walked across the parking lot, Danny and I smiled at each other when we heard the double-whistled harmony of *Kentucky Home* wafting our way from the direction of Harry Chambers' car.

Our ride home was quiet. None of us wanted to disturb Mrs. Libby's thoughts. When we arrived at her house, Dad got out and opened her door. As he helped her from the car, he asked, "Do need anything from us, Louise?"

"No, I'll be fine. I just need to go in and make sure the Matlocks are okay. Thanks just the same," she assured us. "Boys, we can talk tomorrow about the Matlock Can Opener. I'll want to help, you know."

Then she disappeared inside her house.

We joined the rest of our Loyal Contingent on our back porch. Mom and Aunt Maude served the adults iced tea while Mrs. Tucker was in the kitchen preparing lemonade for us boys.

When she joined us, Dad told everyone about his exchange with Mrs. Libby.

"Thank God for the Matlocks," declared Aunt Maude. "They've given her something to focus on – besides her problems."

"Poor Louise," Mrs. Tucker lamented. "Why do you think things like this happen to nice people like her?"

"You never know!" Mom professed. "It just makes me feel thankful for what we have. Good neighbors. Comfortable home. Loving family."

"Poor Louise!" Aunt Maude repeated.

"There, but for the Grace of God, go I," Mom declared.

We all nodded. You never disagreed with Mom's Grace of God pronouncements.

Then Mom suggested, as an afterthought, "I guess, after today, our neighborhood has three people filling Grace of God jobs."

"Nope! Still just two," Danny asserted, surprising us all.

"How's that, Danny?" Dad asked him.

"Today, Gentleman Jim resigned from his Grace of God job!"

21 ALL'S SWELL

"Jaaaaaaaaaaaaaaaaase. Caaaaaaaaaaaaaaaaaaaaaaaaaaaaan. Youuuuuuuuuuuuuuuuuuuuuuu. Cuuuuuuuuuuuuuum. Oooooooooooooout?"

"Gee, I wonder who that could be?" Aunt Maude sleepily joked. "Hurry out and switch him off before he wakes the whole neighborhood."

Danny was sporting a new uniform. An Uncle Sam ensemble had replaced his normal army garb. His shorts were blue, his tee shirt red and white striped. A flamboyant bow tie of red, white, and blue bunting hung from his neck. It looked suspiciously like the bunting I had seen decorating the old Civil War cannon at the Riverton Armory just the day before.

"Know what day this is, Jase?"

"Halloween, right?" I teased. "Where'd you get the bow tie?"

"Found it."

I decided not to pursue that line of questioning. Instead, I bet on a sure thing, "Want some breakfast?"

"Let's eat at the Good Mission Church. We can help set up afterwards."

The Matlock Family Building Fund campaign had progressed exceedingly well during the days leading up to today – the Fourth of July 1944!

Constant front-page coverage in the *Riverton Daily Press* fanned the fires of competition among businesses and other organizations throughout the county. Everybody wanted to be a Matlock can sponsor. We had exhausted our initial supply of cans and wrappers, but Otto and his crew gladly produced a second batch, the last of which had been distributed just days before.

Confident of achieving our fund-raising target, we shifted our attention to the Can Opener itself. Everything had fallen into place for the ten o'clock kickoff. All that remained was the set up at the Good Mission Church.

By the time Danny and I finished smoking a half-dozen pancake cheroots, the Matlock campaign "accountant" had arrived. Ethel Evans, the Good Reverend's cousin, set up her counting station at the very center of the wide back porch that was to serve as our stage for the festivities. She arranged herself so she could look out on the backyard, which we anticipated would soon be packed with fund-raiser celebrants.

Ethel had brought the giant adding machine from Burke's purchasing office where she worked. She placed the massive counter, with its row upon row of keys, in the middle of a solid wooden table. Next to the machine, she efficiently arranged pencils, pads, and extra rolls of adding machine paper. Finally, she identified the most comfortable among the sundry chairs in the Mission auditorium and positioned it directly behind her adding machine.

Ethel was ready to roll!

Mr. Arthur, president of the Riverton Second National Bank, had agreed to act as the treasurer for the Matlock campaign fund. Sponsors not planning to attend the Can Opener had dropped off their cans at the bank the day before the big event.

"Where you want these cans?" asked the burly bank guard. "I got over a hundret in the van. Supposed to unload 'em, then stay here until after the event finishes. You know, stand guard and such."

Danny and I helped the guard carry the cans to the back porch. We stacked them exactly as Ethel directed. When we finished, her counting station was completely surrounded by a wall of cans.

"Mr. Arthur said he'd be along in a little while. Oh, I almost forgot. I think you'll need these," the guard added.

He handed a bulging shopping bag to Ethel.

"Ooooh, I'm soooo glad you remeeeeembered," she warbled, pawing through the bag. "Let's seeeeeeee. Penny, nickel, dime, quarter, and fifty cent wrappers galore. And money bags, tooooooo. Perrrrrrrrrrfect!"

We set up our can opening operation next to Ethel's counting station. Mrs. Mikas had loaned us her galvanized washtub into which we planned to dump the contents of each can. This would make the job of sorting cash, checks, and coins a lot easier. We centered the tub on the low bench that Buddy Roe Bibs had dragged out onto the back porch from the Mission Church auditorium.

Pete's store had furnished six brand new can openers for the day. Danny, Reverend Squires, and I were designated as primary openers. Aunt Maude, Dad, and Mom were coin counter-wrappers. As the day progressed, Mr. Arthur and Ethel would tally collections and announce the totals. Mrs. Libby had agreed to act as "Supernumerary." Danny and I had no idea what that meant, but we were delighted to have her involved.

We were organized!

"Hey, Jase! Where you want these?" yelled Sergeant Rick. "They're from the First Methodist Church."

Mel Carmody, our congenial usher friend, had made arrangements for Otto and his crew to pick up the First Methodist's entire inventory of folding tables and chairs from the church basement. They would be arranged in the Mission backyard to accommodate the picnics of families in attendance. The shabby tables and chairs from the Mission auditorium would supplement the sleek Methodist furniture, but only if needed.

"Hi, Sergeant Rick! Hi, Otto!" I hollered. "Pull into the alley? Buddy Roe Bib Overalls will show you where Mrs. Squires wants them."

Mrs. Squires had volunteered to supervise, not only the food and beverages, but also tables and chairs. Of course, she also agreed to provide the musical entertainment. "But only after the demands of organizing the backyard subside," she insisted.

I noticed that her piano was positioned on the back porch, up stage right. It was probably the work of her stage manager, a.k.a., Buddy Roe Bibs.

As the trucks of donated food and beverages began to arrive, Mrs. Squires took charge. She organized her forces like a Prussian field marshal. Her troops consisted of the cheerful POWs, drafted deliverymen from donor organizations, and the ragtag Mission trustees.

"Bring those hot dog buns over here. Open a few packages. Put them on the serving table. Not before spreading the tablecloths, for goodness sakes! Put the rest under the table. Take those hot dogs to the kitchen. Tell Keith they'll need to be boiled before people eat them. Line up those condiments – pickles and onions first. Mustard and ketchup last. That's right. Get those bottles of pop on ice. Don't open that Fazio potato salad, yet. Keep it closed and in the shade until people start arriving! Where are those paper plates?"

She was a dynamo!

Grandma and Grandpa Compton came to the fund-raiser, too. Grandma brought the Matlock can from the Barrington Grange Women and fourteen pies of various kinds for dessert. Edith Squires nearly swooned when she saw Grandma's mouth-watering contribution.

One of Grandma's pies was made from sweet wild strawberries that Old Nate had personally picked from the patch behind his outhouse. When he dropped off the berries, he told Grandma that he had wanted to attend the Can Opener, but he didn't have anything to wear. Of course, she was furious over that, but she settled for the strawberries that she counted as a rare gift from the "Old Buzzard."

While the pies were arranged on the serving table, Danny looked forlorn. Grandma took him aside and whispered, "There are two apple pies in the Terraplane's trunk. Just for Jase and you!"

He chuckled and wrinkled his nose. "I knew it!" he said.

We heard the loud, low rumble of the Grand Trunk Railway bulldozer coming down New Albany Avenue toward the Good Mission Church. When the puffing giant turned onto Forrest Street, it became impossible to hear Mrs. Squires' orders. So, like the rest of us, she relaxed for a minute and watched the dozer driver skillfully manipulate his levers to nudge the monster into its parking place under the shade of the giant elm tree near the alley.

This was the same bulldozer that the railroad used to push back the mountains of trash at the dump each fall. Grand Trunk management had donated its services for clearing the debris from the Matlock lot to make way for the new basement and foundation. Danny and I believed the bulldozer symbolized a new beginning for the Matlocks, so we made arrangements for its presence at the Matlock Can Opener.

"The Matlock family lives right alongside our tracks, so we're neighbors," the Grand Trunk operations manager had told the *Daily Press*. "If the Matlocks had asked to borrow a cup of sugar from us, we couldn't have obliged. But, when they asked to borrow a bulldozer, we were happy to be right neighborly."

On the day of the fund-raiser, every child in town – and a good proportion of their parents – examined every inch of the sleeping dozer. The driver laughingly complained that he wasn't sure how he'd get it back to its garage, with his throttle and steering levers completely coated with sticky ice cream.

Families showed up early to claim tables closest to the back porch stage. Immense quantities of food and beverages were consumed even before the first can was opened. But we didn't mind. There was plenty for everyone. Besides, people were having a good time visiting with friends and neighbors and speculating about how much money would be raised that day.

When the Riverton Memorial Hospital ambulance slowly rounded the corner onto Forrest Street, Otto and his crew took it as their cue to depart for the Libby house. When they arrived there, the driver opened the back door of the ambulance and rolled out his heavy-duty stretcher on wheels.

After demonstrating how to operate the clever conveyance, the driver climbed back into the ambulance and drove off to attend to his normal hospital duties. Abreast of the Good Mission Church, the driver waved and briefly touched the siren button to give the neighborhood children a thrill.

Otto and his men wheeled the stretcher through the Libby front door and into Mrs. Matlock's front bedroom. Ignoring Mrs. Matlock's warning that she had gained several additional pounds since they'd last carried her, the POWs effortlessly lifted her out of bed and onto the stretcher.

With great ceremony, they rolled her down Forrest Street toward the Good Mission Church. Just for old times sake, they serenaded her joyfully with their now-famous German school fight song. Mr. Matlock, Mrs. Libby, and the Matlock children, well scrubbed and outfitted in their rummage sale finest, proudly followed Mrs. Matlock and her POW honor guard.

When the guests of honor arrived, a huge roar of welcome erupted spontaneously from the exuberant crowd. Mrs. Squires escorted them to their reserved table right next to the stage. Otto and his men adjusted the stretcher, so Mrs. Matlock could observe the proceedings perfectly.

AFTER A LOUD PIANO flourish from Edith Squires, Mr. Arthur, who had volunteered to be our Master of Ceremonies, called the crowd to order. The first item on the agenda was a surprisingly succinct prayer of welcome and thanks by Reverend Squires. Next, Mr. Arthur introduced the entire Matlock family to another raucous round of cheers and applause.

Then he introduced those of us who had played key roles in the campaign. A rehabilitated Danny predictably responded with his deep bow. Next, he acknowledged all the good citizens who had agreed to sponsor donation cans. Finally, he thanked the merchants who had so generously donated the food and beverages for the celebration. Mr. Graham's awkward imitation of Danny's bow didn't go over that well. Later, Mom assured us that it was "retributive justice" at work.

"But, without further ado, let the show begin!" Mr. Arthur proclaimed with gusto as he delivered a thumbs-up to his counting team.

Our system worked smoothly.

Using our black marker, we placed a big "X" beside each can's number on Danny's master inventory sheets. Then we loudly announced the name of each sponsor. Finally, with great ceremony, we dumped the can's contents into Mrs. Mikas' washtub. The more contents, the more appreciatively the crowd cheered. Danny's clever sponsor names also provided entertainment for everybody, except the sponsor in question, of course.

Mr. Arthur scooped up the checks and currency from the tub and announced their number and denomination to Ethel who quickly tapped them into her huge adding machine, thereby providing an accurate running total. Then he sorted the checks and currency, wrapped them in rubber bands, and deposited them in the moneybags under the watchful eye of the officious bank guard.

Aunt Maude, Dad, and Mom, positioned at a side table close to Ethel, scooped handfuls of coins from the tub, sorted and counted them, and wrapped them tightly in paper rolls. When they finished a roll, they informed Ethel who tapped the appropriate value into her adding machine. The tallied coin rolls were then deposited safely in the moneybags.

As Ethel reached each hundred-dollar milestone, Mr. Arthur loudly announced the new total. At every step, the crowd cheered its approval. We knew our system for processing the cans was efficient, but we hadn't expected the audience to find it as entertaining as they did.

Mr. Arthur's periodic announcement wasn't the only method of tracking progress. Much to the chagrin of the Reverend and Mrs. Squires, Buddy Roe Bibs provided another.

He had fashioned a campaign fund "thermometer" from a life-sized cutout of Betty Grable, attired in a very scanty bathing suit. The cutout had originally been the cardboard centerpiece of an unused cigar display that Bibs had fished out of Pete's trash bin.

Bibs bestowed his thermometer on us just before the ceremony. No one had the heart to tell him he couldn't use it. So, when Ethel's totals were announced, Bibs used a brush and a can of red paint to record Betty's temperature.

Bibs had painted the thousand-dollar milestones on Betty's voluptuous figure before he started. His zero mark fell on the soles of Betty's high-heeled shoes. His $1,000 mark, her kneecaps. His $4,000 mark, the top of her head. But it was his mischievous placement of the $2,000 and $3,000 milestone marks that got him in real hot water with Mrs. Squires. I'll let your imagination tell you why.

As the total mounted, Bibs slowly covered Betty with a swath of red paint. Mrs. Squires appropriately commented that a successful campaign would, not only help the Matlocks, but also provide a degree of much-needed modesty for Miss Grable.

I reached down to open a new can. The wrapper read:

Ann Arbor Bridge
Residents Association
Honor of G. Jim

I hadn't remembered this sponsor, so I asked Danny about it.

He explained that the hobos living under the Ann Arbor Bridge were so moved by Gentleman Jim's ascendance from their ranks that they decided to honor him by sponsoring a Matlock can in his name.

To raise money, they had hopped a freight train down to Detroit where, as a group, they donated eleven pints of blood at the "Pints for Dollars" center located on skid row. Danny explained that the hobos had traditionally referred to the blood center as the "Pints for Dollars for Pints" center. Now, they called it the "Pints for Dollars for Matlocks" center. Riverton hobos were known for their clever mottos.

After things settled into a smooth routine, Mr. Arthur called the crowd to order for some further announcements. His audience groaned when he interrupted, but he continued anyway.

First, he announced the availability of free knife sharpening services provided by Bohunk Joe and his assistant, Mr. Charles James Comstock, better known as Gentleman Jim.

And, of course, the bulldozer was still available for inspection by "kids of all ages."

He drew attention to the terrific ongoing puppet show being performed by Hans and Mrs. Zeyer with the able assistance of Sherman Tolna, whose nose was miraculously dry that day.

And why not give Granville's Mayor Simmons a run for his money in the old shell game? All the proceeds would be donated to the Matlock campaign!

Finally, it was his great pleasure to introduce Edith Squires who would "liven things up" with a selection of boogie-woogie songs on the piano.

What a show!

The impatient audience tepidly agreed with a faint round of applause. At that, Mr. Arthur, who had the good sense to exit the stage at the first sign of approval, tipped his hat and sat down.

The full tub indicated that we openers were outpacing the meticulous currency-check counters and coin counter-wrappers. So we asked Mr. Arthur for permission to take a refreshment break.

While Danny and I were finishing our third hot dog, I spotted Miss Elizabeth Bundy. Our nemesis from the First Methodist Church was carrying her church's Matlock can and a large, brown paper bag.

"Oh, no!" whined Danny as she drew closer and closer.

She was headed straight for Danny. His eyes widened. He looked terrified. She stopped right in front of him and pushed the can into his hands.

Then she said, in a surprisingly warm tone, "You've done a wonderful thing here. I am in your awe. From now on, I hope we'll be friends."

She patted Danny tenderly on the head with her white-gloved hand. He reached up and placed his hand over hers as it rested in his dark hair. They both smiled warmly.

When she finished patting him, she handed him the brown paper bag and advised, "This is for later."

She winked at both of us and disappeared into the crowd. Danny peeked into the bag and smiled broadly. He held the bag open for me to see. Inside was Miss Bundy's Sunday-cowgirl hat – without the white netting.

Danny looked at me and proclaimed, "I've always liked her."

"$3,200!"

As Mr. Arthur announced each new total, the crowd cheered and Buddy Roe Bibs splashed another band of red over Betty's bathing suit. Danny and I basked in the belief that the new Matlock house, slowly but surely, was becoming a reality.

And, in the process, Betty was regaining her dignity.

"$3,300!"

Then it suddenly struck me!

There were only a dozen unopened cans. We couldn't possibly make the $4,000 dollar goal!

I nudged Danny and pointed to the few remaining cans. He responded with a sober stare, indicating that he shared my concern. I looked at Dad who nodded at me. He understood, too.

Dad whispered something in Mr. Arthur's ear. Our Master of Ceremonies put his hand on Ethel's shoulder and announced to the crowd, "We need to take a short break, folks! For a glass of iced tea. We'll reconvene in just a few minutes."

The crowd whined.

"Now, now, folks," he scolded. "It's real hot up here in the sun. Let's give our hardworking counting team a little break."

The counting team met in emergency session on the mission front porch to discuss what appeared to be an impending disaster. With so few cans yet to open, it was unlikely that we would make our $4,000 target. We stared at each other hoping that someone would come up with a way to save the day.

"I don't think this will make a whole lot of difference, but we are missing one can," Reverend Squires reported. "Can #211 is unaccounted for."

"Whose can is it?" asked Mr. Arthur.

Mr. Squires held up Danny's clipboard, "See for yourself."

#211 Unanimous

"Danny, you maintained the inventory sheets. Where is Can #211?" I demanded of my friend. "And whose can is it?"

Danny smiled sheepishly. Then he explained, "I promised not to tell anybody about that can. But I did think it would be here by now."

With that, he nonchalantly folded his arms and stared at the porch ceiling, whistling softly to himself. I was used to Danny's mysterious ways, so I knew we wouldn't learn more until Danny was good and ready to tell us.

From the color of Mr. Arthur's face, however, I sensed that he didn't share my tolerance of Danny's idiosyncrasies. In fact, he looked as if he was about to give Danny a thump to loosen his tongue.

But Dad came to the rescue, "We can't do anything about it now. Let's continue counting and see where we stand without Can #211."

Nobody had a better idea, so we returned to our counting posts. Danny led the way, still whistling.

"Okay! Okay, folks!" Mr. Arthur shouted, bringing the proceedings back to order. "We're ready to recommence the countdown."

We opened the last few cans. Ethel tapped the results into her massive adding machine. Then Mr. Arthur dutifully announced what appeared to be the last, hundred-dollar milestone.

"$3,400!"

As Ethel entered the figures for the last pennies, the final tally became apparent. Mr. Arthur, peered over her shoulder, knitted his brow, and shook his head. After checking her figures one more time, Ethel looked up and nodded firmly.

Mr. Arthur soberly turned to the anxious crowd.

"Folks, we have the final count. The total is – $3,432.53. I'm afraid we have a shortfall of more than $500."

The crowd moaned. The Matlocks were in shock.

Without warning, Mr. Arthur grabbed Reverend Squires by the arm and pushed him to the center of the stage. The Reverend looked at him as if he were crazy.

"I'm asking Reverend Squires to lead us in a prayer – a prayer to God to help you open your hearts and your pocketbooks."

The disappointed crowd growled this time.

"When he's finished, we'll pass the hat to see if we can't reach our goal. Nobody leave, now!"

Reverend Squires had been caught completely off guard. His eyes widened with panic as Mr. Arthur thumped him on the back, shoved him forward, and yelled, "Go get 'em, Rev."

"He'll knock 'em dead!" Danny predicted under his breath.

Having heard a good many of Reverend Squires' fervent and creative pleas for contributions from his down-and-out clientele, I shared Danny's optimism.

And the Good Reverend didn't let us down.

He cleared his throat and began, "Oh Lord, I pray that You may bring charity to the hearts of our neighbors in this time of great need, so that we may send this poor family home again. Home again in Your name – "

As the prayer progressed, I noted that Reverend Squires was doing a particularly masterful job of linking the likely fate of the traitorous German generals – those who had plotted the recent failed assassination attempt on Adolph Hitler – with those of us who failed to open our hearts and wallets for the Matlocks.

The Reverend's chat with the Almighty lasted about fifteen minutes. This was ample time for Mel Carmody, Bibs, and his troop of loyal

Mission trustees, with a bit of enthusiastic supervision from Miss Bundy, to pass their collection plates. After soliciting every last person, the able ushers brought their plates forward and dumped them into the washtub.

WHEN THE LAST PENNY was counted, wrapped, and tapped into the adding machine, Mr. Arthur announced the *adjusted* final total.

"Well, folks, here's the – the bad news. It looks like our final total is $3,516.15."

The crowd moaned again – even louder this time. Some people stood up and shook their heads. I feared people might leave.

An ominous silence descended on the once-joyous crowd.

In the distance, the sound of a lone police siren pierced the air. As it approached, the screaming siren became louder and louder. The crowd stared in the direction of sound. Within seconds, Sergeant Jeff's patrol car skidded to a dusty halt under the elm, next to the sticky bulldozer.

Jeff leaped from the car and ran toward Dad. He was carrying a yellow sheet of paper in his hand. Dad and he huddled next to the porch briefly then they mounted the porch steps and motioned for Mr. Arthur to join them inside the Mission auditorium.

The crowd was absolutely mesmerized by the events that were unfolding before their eyes. I was riveted with curiosity. Danny stood rigidly with fingers crossed on both hands.

The threesome emerged from the auditorium after what seemed an eternity. Once again, Mr. Arthur raised his hands and called for order. When the crowd finally settled down, he stared down on them with a smug smile on his face.

"Now folks! I told you the *bad* news. We didn't have enough in the collection cans to make our goal. But you didn't give me a chance to give you the *good* news. Would you like to hear the good news?"

Buddy Roe Bibs was the only person who answered the question. "No!" he yelled loudly.

Danny shared Bib's opinion of Mr. Arthur's current tactics. He whispered loudly, "Holy Whiskers! He's playing with us!"

Mr. Arthur ignored his critics and continued, "The good news is that the Matlock family has a Guardian Angel. And that Angel just happens to be right here on the stage!"

Our Master of Ceremonies paused for dramatic effect before continuing, "The Matlock Guardian Angel is none other than – Danny Tucker."

The astonished crowd turned and stared at Danny.

"The Riverton Police Department has just received a wire – over the Police Teletype Network," he continued. "The wire directs the police to deliver this message to Danny Tucker. And with his permission, I would like to read this wire for all to hear. Okay, Danny?"

Daddy nodded. And so did everyone else.

"Here goes, folks – "

Police Teletype Network Wire Transmission
#FBI: 440704

Time/Date: 15:55Z / July 4, 1944

From: Headquarters, Federal Bureau of Investigation
        Washington, DC

To: Daniel Tucker, Esq. c/o Riverton Police Department
        Riverton, Michigan

Re: Matlock Can Opener

Dear Danny,

Thank you for your personal invitation to join Jase Addison, you, and the other good citizens of Riverton for the Matlock Can Opener today. Unfortunately, matters relating to our country's war effort necessitate my staying here in Washington, so I am unable to be there with you.

From all you told me, however, I am certain that Jase and you have done a bang-up job in organizing today's celebration. And according to the articles you sent from the *Riverton Daily Press,* you couldn't have found a more worthy cause. I hope you enjoy a large turnout of people with kind hearts and deep pockets.

Please send my personal congratulations to the entire Matlock family on their good fortune as they look forward to having a home of their own once again. I am sure they are extremely grateful to you boys for all the blessings that you have caused to come their way.

When I met with The Boss this morning at the White House, I told him about the latest happenings in Riverton. Here is exactly what he said, "Tell 'em to keep up the good work.

That's the kind of community caring and concern that makes America worth fighting for." I hope you'll pass FDR's message along to those in attendance.

I received the beautiful collection can and put it to good use soliciting my personal staff (including myself) and anyone else who walked into our offices. Because I couldn't get the can back to you in time for the celebration, please accept this wire as my I.O.U. until you receive my check.

And, yes, when it comes time for Jase and you to serve our country, I hope you will honor us by joining the Federal Bureau of Investigation. Based on what I have learned from our Detroit field office about your roles in the apprehension of the two escaped POWs, I can't think of anyone more qualified to become first-rate FBI agents than you two. Well done!

Thank you again for allowing my staff and me to be a part of your wonderful event.

Yours truly,

J. Edgar Hoover
Director

Ref: JEH Personal Check for $500
(Sent by Airmail 7-3-44)

What a showstopper! When Mr. Arthur finished reading, no one spoke. Everyone stared at Danny and me.

Finally, Mr. Arthur managed to croak, "Thanks to Danny and Jase, the final total in the Matlock Family Rebuilding Fund is exactly – $4,016.15! We made it! The Matlocks will have their new home!"

With those words, the crowd exploded with boisterous whoops, whistles, and applause. Mr. Matlock broke into tears. The Matlock children jumped up and down. Mrs. Matlock rose from her mobile stretcher and wrapped her huge arms around her handsome family.

Neighbor danced with neighbor as Edith Squires pounded joyfully on her piano. Her boogie-woogie version of *Under the Double Eagle* was especially enjoyable because I knew she was playing it for Danny and me.

The celebration lasted for the rest of the afternoon. Every person who attended the Can Opener shook the hand of Danny and me – and of Mr. and Mrs. Matlock, of course.

Mrs. Mikas burst into tears as she hugged Danny. When she recovered, she insisted he down two of her huge sugar cookies. For strength to endure the rest of the afternoon, she insisted.

BY SUNDOWN, THE EXHAUSTED crowd had departed, and the Good Mission Church's backyard was restored to its original state. The Matlock funds had been deposited safely in the Riverton Second National Bank. The bulldozer had chugged its way home. The very last walnut shell had been tipped. The POWs had softly deposited a grateful Mrs. Matlock back into her bed.

It was all over.

We exchanged our fond good-byes with the Squires and headed home. We came to rest on our back porch.

Aunt Maude sat on the bottom step with her arm around Danny. Mom and Dad sat with me in the porch chairs above them. We were mesmerized by the shimmering colors of the aurora borealis playing against the blue-black, northern Michigan sky. A merry medley of cricket and tree toad music soothed us as we reflected on the wonderful day.

After a while, Mom broke the silence, "This has been the best Fourth of July I can ever remember."

"Yep! And there weren't even any fireworks," Danny reminded us.

We all chuckled softly.

"But I still don't understand one thing, Danny," Mom admitted. "How did you manage to speak to J. Edgar Hoover – in person?"

Mom had asked the $64 question.

"Simple! When Mr. and Mrs. Shurtleif were catching night crawlers that night – I went to their kitchen and made a unanimous telephone call to the FBI Headquarters – on the neighborhood line. I figured it was a national emergency."

Everyone was aghast – except for Danny and me.

"Another complex mystery, solved by the cunning genius of Special Agent Daniel Tucker and, his partner, Special Agent Jase Addison," I proclaimed smugly. "How's that sound?"

Danny rubbed his chin and declared, "It's got a real nice ring to it."

And so it did!